UNDER MY HAT

UNDER MY HAT

TALES FROM THE CAULDRON

EDITED BY
JONATHAN STRAHAN

RANDOM HOUSE 🏠 NEW YORK

Compilation and introduction copyright © 2012 by Jonathan Strahan

Jacket art copyright © 2012 by Michael Wagner

"Stray Magic" copyright © 2012 by Diana Peterfreund. "Payment Due" copyright © 2012 by Frances Hardinge. "A Handful of Ashes" copyright © 2012 by Garth Nix. "Little Gods" copyright © 2012 by Holly Black. "Barrio Girls" copyright © 2012 by Charles de Lint. "Felidis" copyright © 2012 by Tanith Lee. "Witch Work" copyright © 2012 by Neil Gaiman. "The Education of a Witch" copyright © 2012 by Ellen Klages. "The Threefold World" copyright © 2012 by Ellen Kushner. "The Witch in the Wood" copyright © 2012 by Delia Sherman. "Which Witch" copyright © 2012 by Patricia A. McKillip. "The Carved Forest" copyright © 2012 by Tim Pratt. "Burning Castles" copyright © 2012 by M. Rickert. "The Stone Witch" copyright © 2012 by Isobelle Carmody. "Andersen's Witch" copyright © 2012 by Jane Yolen. "B Is for Bigfoot" copyright © 2012 by Jim Butcher. "Great-Grandmother in the Cellar" copyright © 2012 by the Avicenna Development Corporation. "Crow and Caper, Caper and Crow" copyright © 2012 by Margo Lanagan.

Library of Congress Cataloging-in-Publication Data
Under my hat : tales from the cauldron / edited by Jonathan Strahan. — 1st ed.
v. cm.
Summary: An anthology of short fiction about witches.
Contents: Stray magic / Diana Peterfreund — Payment due / Frances Hardinge — A handful of ashes / Garth Nix — Little gods / Holly Black — Barrio girls / Charles de Lint — Felidis / Tanith Lee — Witch work / Neil Gaiman — The education of a witch / Ellen Klages — The threefold world / Ellen Kushner — The witch in the wood / Delia Sherman — Which witch / Patricia A. McKillip — The carved forest / Tim Pratt — Burning castles / M. Rickert — The stone witch / Isobelle Carmody — Andersen's witch / Jane Yolen — B is for bigfoot / Jim Butcher — Great-grandmother in the cellar / Peter S. Beagle — Crow and caper, caper and crow / Margo Lanagan.
ISBN 978-0-375-86830-6 (trade) — ISBN 978-0-375-96830-3 (lib. bdg.) — ISBN 978-0-375-89881-5 (ebook) — ISBN 978-0-375-86804-7 (pbk.)
1. Witches—Juvenile fiction. 2. Children's stories. [1. Witches—Fiction. 2. Short stories.] I. Strahan, Jonathan.
PZ5.U573 2012 [Fic]—dc23 2011031253

FOR MY TWO FAVORITE WITCHES,
JESSICA AND SOPHIE,
WHO MAKE EVERY ADVENTURE MORE MAGICAL

✳ CONTENTS ✳

INTRODUCTION: LOOKING UNDER THE HAT

JONATHAN STRAHAN

THE STORIES ALL start with a hat, specifically a tall, black, pointy hat. It may all be headology, or it might be something more than that, but we all know that a tall, black, pointy hat is important because of what you find *under* it.[1] Young or old, male or female, good or evil, the person under the hat is always a witch. But what kind of witch?

A witch, my copy of the *Oxford English Dictionary* tells me not very helpfully, is "a woman practicing sorcery." The *OED* doesn't clearly define *sorcery*, either, though it does talk about magic, which it says is the "supposed art of influencing [the] course of events by occult control of nature or of spirits, witchcraft." That's a definition of sorts, I suppose, but it's not the best path to understanding who or what you'll find under a tall, black, pointy hat come Halloween.

Wikipedia is much more helpful—perhaps *too* helpful, in fact. It doesn't define what a witch is, but it does say that "a witch differs from a sorcerer in that they do not use physical tools or actions to curse; their maleficium is perceived as extending from some intangible inner quality, and the person may be unaware that they are a witch, or may have been convinced of their own evil nature by the suggestion of others."[2] So a witch's magic comes from within him or herself, and she may not even know she is a witch!

Now, this will all sound familiar, especially if you've read Terry Pratchett's stories of Tiffany Aching and the Discworld, where most witches are women, sometimes girls, who are more midwives, doctors, psychiatrists, and moral enforcement officers than studiers of spells. Wikipedia goes on at *very* great length about the history of European witchcraft. Witches and witch-craft of some kind are found in almost every culture on earth, and they are usually very different from the witches we find walking the streets in search of candy come All Hallows' Eve. Throughout Asia and Africa, for example, witches are equally likely to be men or women. In Japan they have fox witches: the *kitsune-mochi* and the *tsukimono-suji*. And almost none of them have a hat, never mind a nice black pointy one. Those witches are European, and possibly mostly British.

According to ethnographer Éva Pócs, there are three differ-ent types of witch: the neighborhood witch or social witch, who curses a neighbor after some conflict; the magical or sorcerer witch, who is either a professional healer, sorcerer, seer, or mid-wife, or a person who has through magic increased her fortune to the perceived detriment of a neighboring household; and the supernatural or night witch, portrayed in court narratives as a demon appearing in visions and dreams.

You may also have heard of Wiccans, witches who might

well live somewhere near you. A Wiccan is someone who practices Wicca, a neopagan religion and a form of modern witchcraft. Wicca is often referred to as Witchcraft or the Craft, and its adherents are commonly called Wiccans, Witches, or Crafters. Developed in England in the first half of the twentieth century, Wicca is a duotheistic religion in which a goddess and a god, traditionally viewed as the Triple Goddess and the Horned God, are worshipped. As you can see in Holly Black's story, Wiccans don't wear black hats, but they do practice magic.

And what of the hat? While modern witches don't wear pointy black hats—or any hats in particular, really—there is surprisingly little agreement on the history of witches' hats. One theory, described to me by a friendly witch, is that:

the hat originated in Italy in the thirteenth century, where city fashion included tall, elaborate, pointy hats on women (with veils). There were even some with two horns. This fashion filtered through the European upper classes to Britain, and then from upper class to lower classes. By the time it was so out of fashion that it had become a legal dunce's hat in street punishment, country folk had begun wearing felt pointy hats. In Italy, country people were called *pagani* and many still practiced elements of pre-Christian religion, especially magic and medicine. Eventually, only benign country wisewomen (who practiced magic, medicine, midwifery, etc.) were still wearing the old pointy hats, with a rim to make them more stable. By the time the Church became paranoid about witchcraft, they were likening the point to the devil's horns.[3] Still, as good as the theory is, hats on accused witches in European or British art vary from caps and bonnets to pointy or cut-off Puritan styles, so the truth is elusive. However, we do know that by the time illustrated fairy tales started to be published in the nineteenth century, the pointy hat had been popularized by the Victorians and was firmly attached to the image of the witch.[4]

Stories of witches, though, go back to the Bible and probably earlier. There are references to witches and witchcraft in both the Old and New Testaments, and in Hindu, Jewish, and other religious texts. Countless witches appear prominently in literature, but the earliest "classical witch" is probably Baba Yaga, an old hag from Slavic folklore who flies around on a giant mortar (using a pestle as the rudder), lives in a hut that stands on chicken legs, and sometimes kidnaps small children. She was followed by other weird literary sisters such as Morgan le Fay, the powerful sorceress from Malory's *Le Morte d'Arthur,* and the three witches from *Macbeth,* who spend their time cackling around a cauldron.

The witches we know best date to the rise of children's literature in the nineteenth century, first in the fairy tales of the Brothers Grimm, Hans Christian Andersen, and others, then in novels such as L. Frank Baum's *The Wizard of Oz* and C. S. Lewis's *The Lion, the Witch and the Wardrobe,* and more recently in books such as Jill Murphy's *The Worst Witch* and J. K. Rowling's Harry Potter novels. While Lewis's White Witch Jadis, Murphy's Mildred Hubble, and Rowling's Hermione Granger (who might be a touch more wizard than witch) are among the most popular of modern witches, the most iconic is surely Baum's Wicked Witch of the West. Her appearance in the 1939 film *The Wizard of Oz*, where she is played with panache by Margaret Hamilton, is the definitive evil wearer of black hats, and her cry "I'll get you, my pretty . . . and your little dog, too!" is justifiably famous.

Lovers of witches know, though, that Elphaba, as the Wicked Witch of the West was named by Gregory Maguire in his novel *Wicked,* is not the only witchy option. Whether it be Hayao Miyazaki and Eiko Kadano's delightful Kiki or the studious but bungling Mildred Hubble, the industrious Hermione Granger or Diana Wynne Jones's rather wicked Gwendolyn Chant, the happily suburban Samantha from *Bewitched* or the darkly evil Maleficent from *Sleeping Beauty,* a witch could be anyone.

And so we come to *Under My Hat,* which started life several years ago as a gift for my two daughters, Jessica and Sophie. Some time ago Sophie, my younger daughter, asked if there was one of my books that she could read. As I looked at the book I'd just completed, I realized I didn't have one that was anywhere near suitable for, let alone interesting to, an eight-year-old girl, and so I set out to create a book just for Sophie and her sister. They were raised on *Kiki's Delivery Service, Bewitched,* and the great Disney witches. Each year, when I would travel to the United States at Halloween to attend the annual World Fantasy Convention, I would bring hats, wands, and other paraphernalia home to Australia for them, which were always met with delight. So this book is very much for Jessica and Sophie. I would also be remiss if I didn't acknowledge Terry Pratchett's Tiffany Aching, who inspired the title for this book, and all of the writers who ultimately gave Jessica, Sophie, and I such wonderful stories. I hope you enjoy these stories as much as my daughters and I have, and that we might even get a chance to meet again around another cauldron of tales sometime in the future.

Jonathan Strahan
Perth, Western Australia
April 2011

NOTES

1. Taken from Terry Pratchett's Discworld, headology is a sort of folk psychology that can be summed up as "if people think you're a witch, you might as well be one." For instance, a witch could, if she wished, curse people. However, it is simpler for her to say she has cursed them, and let them assume that she is responsible for the next bit of bad luck that happens to befall them. (Source: Wikipedia)

2. *Maleficium* is a Latin term meaning "wrongdoing" or "mischief" and is used to describe malevolent, dangerous, or harmful magic, evildoing or malevolent sorcery. In general, the term applies to any magical act intended to cause death or harm. (Source: Wikipedia)

3. Witches have often been subject to persecution. Between the fifteenth and eighteenth centuries there was a widespread hysterical belief that malevolent Satanic witches were operating as an organized threat to Christianity. Many people were accused of being witches and put on trial. Witch trials originated in southeastern France during the fourteenth century, before spreading through central Europe and then into other parts of the continent and into European colonies in North America.

4. This theory on the origin of the black hat was provided by Jilli Roberts, a real practicing witch. I have quoted her pretty much verbatim and would like to acknowledge her gracious assistance.

STRAY MAGIC

DIANA PETERFREUND

YOU CAN'T HAVE this job unless you love animals, but if you love animals, it's hard to have this job. We're a no-kill shelter, but all that means is that there are some animals who are stuck here for life, wasting away in their little cages. And sometimes we're too full and we have to turn animals away, knowing they'll be taken to the county shelter, where they'll be put down after seventy-two hours.

Three days. That's how long they give them at county. Three days for their owners to find them if they're lost (which, trust me, they usually aren't), or for them to find a new home. Jeremy, my buddy over there, sends me likely candidates for adoption whenever we have space. Good dogs, adorable puppies that all have the potential to be great companions, if only they get the chance to try.

I don't know what he's thinking with this latest one, though. There has to be some sort of mix-up. Jeremy's voice mail described her as a young golden retriever mix, but when I arrive at the shelter, the crate waiting for me outside the back door does not have a golden inside. What it contains is the most bedraggled, patchy-coated, pathetic creature I've ever seen. The dog's twelve if she's a day. What's left of her fur is a stained and dingy white. Her eyes are bloodshot, her chocolate-and-pink nose is dry and cracked, some kind of mite's been gnawing on her floppy ears, and she's got a big old infected scrape on her belly oozing pus into the remaining mats of her hair.

Adoptable? Not in this state. I wonder what Jeremy was thinking, sending along a hopeless case like her.

I grab a leash and open up the crate door. "So you're the one who they caught out wandering on the highway, huh?"

Highway dogs are the worst. This one was probably dumped by her owner because she was too old, or because she was diagnosed with some terminal illness and they didn't have the heart or the money to watch her get put down. Happens all the time out here. I guess people just delude themselves into thinking their pets are going to live out their days in a nice country farmhouse. People think this is the land of milk and honey for unwanted dogs.

Wrong. It's the land of roadkill and pound euthanasia.

The dog crushes itself against the far corner of the crate. Typical. I see a dozen cases like this a week. Usually they're terrified, and they have a right to be.

"I'm just going to take you inside and get you some nice kibble." I grab her by the scruff of the neck and tug her out into the light.

And darn it if she's not a golden retriever. I'm so shocked, I let go of her, and she shoots off. Or tries to, anyway, as I know that trick well. I snatch up the end of the leash before it disappears, and her flight stops short. She whimpers as I haul her back, and I blink my eyes to clear them, for she's the old white dog again. Strangest thing ever.

She slumps and stops struggling as I lead her inside. The dogs in the cages start up the second I flick on the lights. I lead the newcomer to crate nineteen. "Welcome to Shelter from the Storm. I'm your host, Malou."

She beelines for the blanket in the darkest corner of the kennel and curls up, resting her head on her paws and looking at me dejectedly. Those big brown eyes are just about the saddest I've ever seen—and I work in a pet shelter, so that's saying something. Must be the eyes that got to Jeremy, though he's a pretty tough sell after eight months volunteering at county.

He fits there, though. He wants to be a vet, and they've already taught him how to spay kittens. I just do this to get my dog fix—we can't have pets at home since Carson's allergic. At least, that's what Cynthia, my stepmother, says, but my baby half brother never sneezes when I come home from the kennel covered in fur. I appealed to my dad, but since he's gone most of the time, he lets Cynthia have the final say in all home matters. So if I want to play with puppies, I have to do it at the shelter.

I guess it's better this way. I know if she'd let me I'd bring them all home. "You're going to be fine here," I say to the new dog in that high, soft voice they all like.

No I'm not. I'm doomed.

She might as well have spoken the words aloud. I swear some days I can read their thoughts—not that most of them have thoughts other than "play with me, pet me, feed me." Dogs aren't simple, but their needs are. They don't ask for much, and even then most people let them down.

"I know what will make you feel better."

Doubt it.

"Some kibble." I wonder what brand Libby, the shelter manager, managed to find on sale at the supermarket this week. The food here's not great, but it's better than nothing—which is what a lot of these dogs are used to getting.

I fill a bowl for the newcomer, then start the routine of changing papers and feeding the others. I let the socialized ones out to run around in the yard for a bit while I process our latest arrival. Libby says they adopt better with a cute name, rather than something like "Old white dog" or "Crate #19." I check on the new dog, who hasn't eaten her kibble yet. Sometimes they come in starving and will wolf down whatever they can get, and sometimes they come in too scared or too depressed to eat, especially if they think you're watching.

"What would be a good name for you?" I tap my fingers on my mouth, considering.

My name is Goneril.

The dog doesn't lift her head, but her eyes are glued to me.

"Pearl?" I ask. Something stately, I think. This is not a goofball dog.

Goneril. The thought's more insistent this time. *Goneril Aurelia Boudicca Yseult, to be exact.*

I write "Gaby" on the chart and hang it from the hook at the top of the crate.

The dog lifts her head. *Wait . . . Gaby?*

I swear, sometimes it's like they're really talking to you. "You should have seen some of the names they gave you guys before I came along. Really cheesy stuff. Cuddles. Punkin. You probably would have ended up a Snowball. I guess it helps to get you adopted, but you're too dignified for a name like that, aren't you? No matter what you're looking like now."

Wait, you can see me? The real me? She stands and bats her paw against the bars.

"Are you thirsty, girl?" I kneel to undo the crate door and grab her water dish. Gaby throws herself against it, but I hold it closed. See? I know all their tricks.

You understand me! She sits and her whiplike tail flops once on the concrete floor. I let go of the door. There's something seriously weird going on with this dog.

And you see the real me, too. Gaby stands now and moves into the thin shaft of sunlight that slices across the back corner of the crate.

I fall back on my butt. This can't be real. There's the old white dog, but then, in flickers like a broken filmstrip, I can see bits of golden retriever, hanging in scraps. I watch in shock as the dog noses her golden flank back into place. As soon as she moves, it slips again.

It's the glamour. It's fading. Every spell my master put on me is breaking.

"The glamour?" I whisper, hardly believing the words coming out of my mouth. I am answering the dog. Because . . . she's talking to me.

Gaby bounds back over to the door. Her tail comes out from between her legs, and her eyes aren't quite as filled with despair.

"What are you, Gaby?" I ask.

Goneril.

"Goneril."

I'm a dog.

A talking dog. A talking dog who sometimes looks like a young, well-groomed golden retriever, and sometimes . . . doesn't. "You're not like most dogs I know."

I'm my master's dog. His . . . special dog.

Poor, deluded pooch. They all think they're special, until they're dumped on the side of the road.

And I've lost him.

"You mean you're lost? You wandered off?"

No! One second I was in the car with him . . . and then I wasn't.

A highway dump. I knew it.

I lost him.

And I might just have lost my mind. "How are you doing this?"

The dog—Goneril—snorts. *I told you. It's a glamour. I have all these pieces of magic I got from my master. But now that we're separated, they're falling to pieces.*

I crawl toward the kennel, too flabbergasted to speak. The dogs nearby are transfixed, too. None of the usual barking, whining, scratching, or even snoozing. Whatever's happening here, they're witnesses, too. At least the dogs prove I'm not hallucinating.

And when they're gone, Goneril continues, *I'll die.*

"Mary Louise," Jeremy singsongs into the phone when I call. "What can I do you for?"

"What kind of game are you playing?" I snap.

Goneril paces at my feet, jabbering away. *My master—he's been using his magic to keep me alive for a good fifteen years.*

"What do you mean?" Jeremy asks. "Didn't you pick up the golden?"

"There's no golden." I watch as another shred of the weird golden-retriever filmstrip disintegrates off Goneril's back. "It's . . . something else. And if this is some kind of practical joke, it's cruel."

Without him I'm done for.

Jeremy sighs. "Not another one of your 'No pit bull' speeches. Because first of all, you sound like a broken record, and second, there's no way that's a pit mix. Golden and collie maybe, or golden and spaniel—"

"It's not a golden at all!" I cry. "And it's not my fault that Libby is prejudiced against pits."

Would you believe I'm thirty?

I press the mute button on my phone and look down at Goneril. "Really? That you're two hundred and ten in dog years—*that's* the part you think it's hard for me to believe?"

Good point.

Jeremy's still on mute, so I feel free to talk to the dog. "You're saying all this stuff—the talking, the golden retriever disguise—it's a result of some kind of spell your owner put on you?"

Goneril starts to pant. Her tail flops twice. *My master, yes. He's a witch.*

"I thought witches kept cats."

She snorts. *Not mine! Cats suck.*

"Whatever breed it is," Jeremy is saying, sounding annoyed. I turn back to the phone. "She has a sweet disposition, responds well to voice commands—seems like an excellent adoption candidate."

The talking 210-year-old dog is still going strong. *I need to*

*find my master to mend the spells. The glamour is unimportant—
what I really need is to make sure the spell on my heart is still working. This is why you need to let me out.*

I shake my head at her. I'm not about to let this dog back
on the streets—Jeremy would have my head. "I'm sorry," I say
aloud. "There's no way that can happen."

Goneril sighs.

So does Jeremy. "If you don't think you can place her, I'll
take her back to the pound. . . ."

Is that manipulative or what? Jeremy knows darn well that I
won't give up a dog I can save.

*But I have to get back to my master! At the rate this magic's
failing I'd guess I only have about three days.*

"But you know what that means. She'll only have three days."

"Three days," I say to both of them. "That's a tall order."

That afternoon, I focus on making Goneril look as good as
possible, cutting the mats out of her hair, smearing ointment on
that scrape on her belly, and cleaning up her paws.

She's unimpressed. *This is a waste of time. I can't be adopted
by just anyone. I need my master. My master fixed my leg, he
propped up my heart, he stalled this tumor I've got in my neck.* She
blinked her eyes at me. *See these peepers? No cataracts, thanks to
my master's magic.*

Dogs have the most ridiculously misplaced sense of loyalty.
Libby was on a raid with Animal Services last month and she
brought back horror stories. A bunch of abused animals, starving,
with broken bones and open sores, and they *still* responded to
their master's call.

I want to tell Goneril that her precious master dumped her by the side of the road, but I don't have the heart. If she really is going to die in three days, isn't it better that she dies thinking he loved her?

It's tough to groom her, because I keep catching sight of her glamour. It's hanging in strips all over her body. I wonder if there's some way I can arrange it better. I reach for a strip, but it slides through my fingers like smoke. I try again and just barely manage to catch hold of the end. As gently as I can, I twist it with another strip of glamour, hoping to conceal the gaps and make it look smooth and unbroken again.

Goneril watches me, her eyes narrowed. *You shouldn't be able to do that.*

I mend another shred. This would be better. All the grooming in the world wasn't going to make her real skin look right. "Do what?"

Manipulate my glamour. I wonder if that's what happens when the magic breaks down.

"You don't know?"

Goneril hangs her head. *I never bothered much with anyone who wasn't my master. He was all I ever needed.*

I bite my tongue. What a jerk her master is, throwing her away like garbage. I always suspected that the dogs who came in here depressed or despondent knew they'd been abandoned. I always wondered if every time their ears perked up or their tails started going at the sound of a car on the driveway, it was because they hoped it was their owners coming back for them. Now I know for sure.

I sit back and study my handiwork. She looks a little worse for wear, but at least now she resembles the young golden retriever Jeremy said she was. "This is as good as it's going to get," I say. "Try not to move around too much. I don't want it to slip off again."

Goneril plops down. *Okay, but I'm hungry.*

"Because you didn't eat your kibble."

She cocks her head. *Kibble? Oh, you mean those desiccated little brown pebbles of meat-scented grain? I wasn't aware that was food.*

"What did you think it was?"

She considers this for a moment. *Potpourri?*

I shake my head. "No, it's kibble, and it's all we can afford around here." I wonder what her precious master had been feeding her. T-bones?

Oh. Her head goes back down. *Well, perhaps I can wait to eat until I reunite with my master.*

When pigs fly. Then again, if dogs can talk, who knows what else is out there?

She covers her nose with her paws. *And if that doesn't happen, I won't live long enough to starve.*

Libby's out of town for the weekend, so it's just me holding down the fort. It's fine, though. Gets me out of the house and away from Cynthia's lectures. By the time I return to the kennel the next day, Goneril's nearly frantic. She paws at the cage, her eyes wide with a mix of terror and hope.

Did you find my master? I've been calling for him all night but he won't come.

I rub my temples. Judging from the way the dogs in the

crates nearby are hugging the sides farthest away from Goneril, it's been a tough night for everyone. "Look, Goneril, I think it's possible that you might not ever be reunited with your master."

All four paws hit the floor and she droops her head.

I can't stand it. "What about another witch? What if we found a witch to help you?"

Until my master comes back for me? Her tail starts wagging.

"Sure," I lie.

That would work. Wag, wag. *For a little while at least. You know any witches?*

Not really.

After I do some socialization work with the puppies, give a few unfortunates their baths, check on the stitches of some of our recently spayed inmates, and redistribute the chew toys in the common space, I sit down at our ancient hulk of a computer and try to write up a description for Goneril.

Naturally, I call her Gaby. The name of a murderous Shakespearean princess just doesn't scream "adopt me" to your average pet lover. And then my hands hover over the keyboard. Breed? Should I say golden retriever? I squint at Goneril, trying to guess what lies beneath the age and glamour.

Age? If I put thirty, people will just think it's a typo. Height and weight are easy enough to fill in, and I upload the picture I took right after I arranged her glamour. But then I get to the description, and I pause again.

Finally I type:

A very special dog in need of a good home. Gaby is quite affectionate, and seems to have been much loved by her previous owner. She is well trained, responds amazingly to voice commands, and is in search of a new owner as special and unique as she is. Please contact ASAP as Gaby cannot stay in the kennel much longer.

"Much loved," that is, until he dumped her. I scroll back to *unique*. Should I just lay my cards out on the table and write *magical*?

"Hey, Goneril, is there a word witches use when they mean magical?"

She cocks her head to the side. Her tongue's hanging out a bit. *They just say magical.*

"I mean when they're trying to keep it a secret. That they use in front of nonmagical people."

She scratches at her ear, which just has the effect of messing up her glamour again.

Right, because she never spent much time dealing with anyone who wasn't her master. I feel a fresh wave of rage at her cruel owner as I start over:

Gaby is the most unusual animal we've ever had in this kennel. It's almost like she can communicate with you.

Exactly like it, in fact.

Well trained, with excellent response to all voice commands.

And a few voice commands of her own.

She needs a very special owner who can attend to her unique—

Particular? Peculiar? Extraordinary?

—needs. If you can help Gaby, please respond ASAP.

What are you writing about me? Goneril puts her front paws up on my legs and arches to see the screen.

"Hey!" I say. "Off." She hops back down. "Besides, it's not like you can read."

Her tail stands straight in the air, indignant. *Of course I can! What good would I be to my master if I couldn't read?*

I stare at her, agog. "What do you mean? Were you a service dog? Was he blind or something?"

She cocks her head at me. *Not blind. But yes, I was in service to my master. I explained that part to you.*

"Explain it again."

She stretches her front legs out before her, sticking her butt in the air, then lies down, her head up and alert.

I was my master's special dog. I was his eyes and ears in the outside world. I spied on his neighbors, I gleaned information from his enemies, I walked among his cohorts, unseen and unnoticed, and I observed all. She yawned. *I also fetched his slippers.*

The bell over the door rings and the dogs start barking. I look up to see Jeremy strolling in, his hoodie pulled up underneath his County Animal Shelter jumpsuit. "Hey there, Malou. So where's that golden you say isn't a golden?"

I point at Goneril, who now looks every inch the golden, at least out of the corner of my eye. "Here. Hey, what's the word they use for a witch's cat?"

"Um, 'familiar,' I think?"

I snap my fingers. "Thanks, that was driving me nuts."

He leans down and scratches Goneril behind the ear. Her glamour stays firmly put. She edges away from him and bares her teeth. I can only see it underneath the glamour, though. The golden retriever part of her is still panting happily.

This is the guy that put me in the cage.

I position my fingers over the keyboard again.

Goneril is the most unusual and yet *familiar* animal we've ever had here at our kennel. She's definitely far more than she appears to be at first glance! A retired service dog, she's beautifully trained. It's almost like she can communicate with you. She requires an extraordinary owner who can attend to her unique needs. If you can help Goneril, please respond ASAP. Time is of the essence!

There. That's the best I can do. Maybe any witch who happens upon this listing will take note of the unusual name and the word *familiar* and read between the lines.

But though I'll never tell Goneril, the chance that a witch will come looking for an animal on our website is pretty slim.

"You're a real cutie," Jeremy is saying. "How could someone dump you on the side of the road, huh, girl?"

I wasn't left on the side of the road. Goneril's tail thumps in indignation. *My master would never leave me.*

Jeremy leans on the desk. "So, what're you doing tonight, Malou? Couple kids from school are going into town to see that new spy movie. Any interest?"

I put a checkmark next to "housebroken" and another next to "good with kids" on the Web form. "No thanks," I say. "My dad and I are going to go see that next time he comes home."

Jeremy gives me a skeptical glance. "Think it'll still be out then?"

I raise my eyes to his over the top of the monitor. "What are you getting at, Jeremy?"

He steps back, his hands up in surrender. "Nothing. I just hadn't heard any news about him coming home soon."

"Well, he is," I snap. Lordy, I sound like Goneril, whining about her stupid master. My dad's job takes him away from home a lot. It's not his fault he doesn't get back much, and that when he does, he's always really busy with Carson and Cynthia. After all, Carson's a baby. And a boy. He needs his daddy far more than I do.

"Whatever you say." He sticks his hands in his pockets. "So why you asking about witches?"

"Know where I can find some?"

He grins. "Does your stepmother count?" He does a little drumroll against the desk. "Ba dum bum *ching!*"

Goneril paws at my leg. *Malou, is your stepmother a witch? Is that why you can touch my glamour? Did she teach you?*

I roll my eyes. "No. What she is starts with a *b*."

Jeremy grins wider. If he got rid of that scraggly soul patch, I'd almost think he was cute.

Suddenly Goneril starts hacking away.

"Got a hairball, pup?" Jeremy asks, but I'm horrified. Beneath the glamour, I can see she's in real distress. There's bile and pus trailing from her mouth, and her limbs are shaking and seizing.

I scoop her up and carry her back to her crate as she shudders in my arms, gasping for breath. "Here, have some water."

But when I set her down, her paws buckle beneath her. She lies on her side, panting, her eyes rolling up in her head.

"Is she choking?" Jeremy appears over my shoulder. "She looks okay to me." Why can't he see through the glamour like I can?

"Shh, it's okay," I say softly, stroking her flank.

Master, Goneril sobs. *Master, where are you? I didn't mean to lose you. Please come back. Please, Master.*

I bite my lip and look away.

Jeremy looks at me and back to Goneril. "Do you think she's sick? Is that an infection on her belly? Want me to call the emergency vet?"

No vets. Goneril gives my hand a pathetic little swipe with her tongue. *I need my master.*

Or a witch. How in the world am I going to find this poor dog a witch? I hate her master. If he didn't want her anymore, couldn't he have just taken her spells off while she slept? Let her die in her home?

"She'll be okay," I say to Jeremy. "I put some ointment on that scrape. I think it was just a hairball, like you said."

Jeremy clucks his tongue. "Poor girl." He's quiet for a moment as I stroke Goneril, who's still trembling. "You know, Malou, we don't have to go to the movies."

"Huh?" Of course we don't. I wonder where witches go.

Renaissance Faires? Magic shops? Is there a solstice or something coming up soon?

"We could do something else," he's saying now. "If you wanted."

I look up at him. "A farmers' market."

Jeremy's eyes widen. "Really?"

"Yeah. They have them in town on Sundays, right?" Witches might go to something like that. They need to buy . . . herbs and stuff. For potions.

"Um . . . yeah. You want to go to a farmers' market?" His tone is incredulous.

"I want to hold an adoption event there," I say. "Tomorrow."

"Oh." Why does he sound so down about the idea? Jeremy loves organizing those things. "Okay. I guess I'll see if my boss can get us some space. And the banner. How many dogs you think you want to bring?"

"Three or four." And Goneril will be one of them. "Thanks, Jeremy," I say, returning my attention to the sick dog. "You're the best."

"Yeah." I don't hear him leave, because in my head, Goneril is crying for her master.

By Sunday morning she's a mess. I sit outside the shelter with my four chosen dogs, waiting for Jeremy to swing by with his van. Aside from Goneril, I picked an adorable adolescent beagle, a tan hound with sad eyes and a wiggly butt, and a glossy black spaniel mix I think would be perfect for a young family. Aside from Goneril, they're gorgeous, well socialized, and eminently adoptable. They're all wearing bright yellow vests with ADOPT

ME! printed on them in blue letters. The three normal dogs are straining at their leashes, excited to be part of our outing. Goneril is lying on the ground, getting mud on her vest and occasionally letting out a wheezing gasp.

I'm worried about her. She still hasn't eaten, and this morning her water bowl was filled to the brim. There was blood on the blanket in her kennel, and she limps as she walks. I wonder what Jeremy will see when he looks at her. Even if I can find a witch at the farmers' market, will they be willing to fix her master's broken spells and make her well again?

Jeremy pulls round with the van and we load the dogs into the waiting crates. He's brought along two tortoiseshell kittens, a Rottweiler I just know he's going to try to pawn off on our shelter if any of my charges get adopted, and a terrier puppy I bet gets snatched up first out of all of them.

"This one?" he asks as I lift Goneril gingerly into her crate. "You sure?"

Goneril's glamour is looking raggedy again. "You were the one who said she was such a good adoption candidate." My tone is sharp, and Jeremy just sucks air in between his teeth and finishes fastening the straps to hold the crates in place.

Most of the dogs nap on the way, but Goneril sleeps fitfully, whimpering out loud and calling out for her master in a way that breaks my heart.

"Where did you find that golden again?" I ask Jeremy.

He shrugs. "Out wandering the highway. Another dumped dog. Wonder why—she seems well trained. Came right over to me."

She was probably hoping he'd take her back to her master.

"Bet it was some yuppies who didn't want her after they had kids." Jeremy's voice hisses as he speaks. That's a common excuse, and this is a common game of ours—theorizing about the cavalier actions of our rescue dogs' former owners.

"Maybe it was someone who lost his home and couldn't afford to keep his dog," I suggest. Much as I hate Goneril's old master, I can't help but think he must have been in dire straits to give up on a companion of thirty years.

"Maybe he was sick and couldn't keep her," Jeremy replies.

"Maybe the *dog* is sick," I say. "Maybe she has a terminal illness and he couldn't handle the vet bills."

Jeremy gives me a look. "Maybe you shouldn't take her to an adoption event until we have a vet check her out."

"Too late now," I mumble. He's right, of course. Libby would never allow this—it's completely against shelter policy to put a sick dog up for adoption. But Goneril doesn't need to be adopted— she just needs to find a witch to fix her spells. Like, *now*.

The drive into town is about forty-five minutes, and once we're there we set up shop near the end of a row of vegetable and plant peddlers. Across the aisle from us, someone is selling hand-dyed silk scarves. She's got one wrapped around her head like a fortune-teller. If I'm going to find Goneril a witch, this is the spot. Jeremy sets out the portable dog run and we put a few chew toys and pallets inside. Most of the dogs are happy to stretch their legs and bound around the enclosure, wagging their tails and barking hello at passersby. Goneril slumps, panting hard. Beneath the glamour, I can see that her eyes are clouded over with cataracts. She's frothing at the mouth a bit—it's pink, which makes me think she's coughing up blood again.

I set down a water dish in front of her. "Are you all right?"

She leans hard against my hand for a moment. *This is day three.*

"I know. Don't worry. We'll find someone who can help you." I scratch her behind the ears, and her hair comes off in my hands. She's nearly bald now.

She leans against me even harder. *I wish . . . I just wish I could see my master one more time before I die. I miss him so.*

"You're not going to die," I lie.

I remember when I first became his. She closes her eyes for a moment and her tongue lolls out of the corner of her mouth. *I was just a puppy. Looked a lot more like my glamour, all golden and beautiful.*

She's not white, I realize with a start. She's just older than most dogs ever get a chance to become. I've seen old dogs with white muzzles. Goneril had gone entirely white.

"Just rest," I tell her. "And let me know if you . . . feel any witches nearby."

They'll feel me—they'll notice my glamour. But I can't sense anyone but my master.

If her master dares show his face here after what he did, he'll need all his magic to protect himself from me.

Jeremy and I take our stations. He mans the enclosure, answering questions about the dogs, while I take the beagle for a stroll, distributing brochures and keeping an eye out for anyone who looks particularly witchy.

Problem is, I don't know exactly what I'm looking for. Flowing clothing? A pointed hat? A magic wand? I stop one lady in black with dangly crystal earrings and try to talk her into checking out our dogs, but she insists she's allergic to all animals. I approach a dude trailing a cart piled high with herbs in pots, only to discover he's a horticulture professor at the local college.

Maybe we should have tried a Renaissance Faire after all.

Halfway through the market, I return to the booth to switch places with Jeremy, who's grinning.

"I got the golden to buck up," he says proudly.

I look over at Goneril. She's not exactly bouncy, but she is sitting calmly on a sheepskin pallet near the front of the enclosure, observing the crowd. "How?"

"Picked her up a pig's ear from the butcher three booths down." Jeremy tugs on the string of my jacket. "You can pay me back later."

And then off he goes, armed with a stack of brochures about animal rescue, and the roly-poly terrier. The beagle I was trotting around decides to snooze under my chair.

"Do you feel better?" I ask Goneril.

A little. At least I'll die with a good last meal.

Maybe she was just starving. Maybe all this talk about dying without her master is some kind of doggy hypochondria.

Goneril looks over the other dogs. The poor Rottweiler is standing right at the border of the enclosure, offering a pathetic paw to every person who pauses (and probably freaking a good half of them out). The spaniel is demonstrating her best "roll over" technique.

"Do you know any tricks?"

Like parlor tricks?

"Um, sure."

She yawns. *I can cast a sacred circle, of course. I can go invisible for short periods, especially during the full moon. Let's see. . . . I can read divination bones. My master made me learn to keep me from eating them—*

"I mean, can you shake or catch Frisbees or roll over?"

She crosses her front paws. *Well, of course. But where's the difficulty in that?*

Talking dog or not, sometimes trying to communicate with Goneril is very frustrating. "Wait, can you really go invisible?"

Goneril flickers out of existence for an instant, like the air above a hot road. *I can usually go longer, but . . . I'm not feeling up to it right now.*

"That's okay," I say. "Save your strength."

But even that show of her magic appears to be too much for Goneril, since another coughing fit overtakes her a few minutes later.

A young woman looks up from where she's filling out an application for the beagle. "What's wrong with that dog?" she asks, pointing her pen at Goneril in suspicion. "Is she sick? Are you trying to pawn off sick dogs on us?"

"No!" I cry, rushing to Goneril's side. "I think she just ate something . . ." But it's no use. As I watch, tiny cracks begin to shimmer on the surface of Goneril's glamour. They branch and multiply before my eyes, and within moments the whole thing disintegrates like a dried-up leaf. The pretty golden retriever is gone, and in its place is the balding white dog, rheumy and shuddering.

The woman gasps and drops her clipboard. A few people

look over to see what's causing the commotion in the enclosure. I throw a spare blanket over Goneril's back as the crowd looks on in dismay. Some ask questions, but I'm focused on the sound of Goneril wheezing beneath the blanket. I ignore the people crowding around until Jeremy returns, a look of concern painted across his face.

"What happened?" he asks.

"You're right," I say to him. "She's sick. We've got to get her out of here." I keep her covered up as much as possible, but Jeremy still looks suspicious.

We can't leave, Malou, Goneril is protesting weakly from beneath the blanket. *I need to find a witch. I need one now or I'll die for sure.*

"We should take her to the vet," Jeremy says. "What if it's catching? I can't let the other dogs get sick."

I nod enthusiastically. "Yes, okay. Whatever, let's just get out of here."

Goneril's too weak to walk, so I wrap her securely in the blanket and carry her back to the car. We load up the crates again and I climb into the front seat, resting the sick dog as gently as I can in my lap. As we head toward the highway, Jeremy can't stop casting glances at the bundle in my arms. "She looks . . . weird. What if it's some kind of canine Ebola or something?"

I give him a dirty look. "It's not Ebola. And, might I remind you, *you* were the one who brought her to me."

There's an accident near the on-ramp, so we're forced to detour through town to the next highway entrance. I honestly don't know if Goneril's going to make it back to the shelter. Her breath is shallow and wheezy, and she's trembling all over.

The dogs in the back are awake but quiet. When I look over my shoulder they are staring at Goneril through their cage doors, their eyes glowing with unspoken knowledge. Is this what it's like at the county shelter—all the dogs in their cages, staring at one another in full awareness as the clock ticks down toward their deadlines?

Master, please. I was such a good dog for you. Where did you go?

I bend my head low and whisper comforting words into her ears. Oh, how I wish I was a witch and could fix all her spells. I'd adopt her right now, and my stepmother could just shove it.

At the next stoplight, Jeremy dares to look over again. "Malou, it's okay."

That's when I realize I'm crying. "It's not fair," I say softly. "This poor dog never did anything, and now she's being left alone to die among strangers. . . ." I look away and wipe the tears from my eyes.

Jeremy's hand is warm on my shoulder. His touch slides down my arm, and then he wraps his fingers around mine and squeezes tight. "You did the right thing," he says. "You tried your hardest. It's not your fault if people are jerks." He takes a deep breath. "There's nothing you can do if they don't realize what they have."

I meet his eyes. "You don't understand. This dog is *really* special."

"I understand she's really special to you. And that's enough for me."

I blink the tears out of my eyes and look at Jeremy again. Really look at him, forgetting for a moment the stupid scraggly facial hair and that grin he likes to wear when he's teasing me.

I said once that Jeremy's a tough sell when it comes to saving animals, but he arranged this whole event on a moment's notice because I asked him to. He calls about dogs he thinks will fit at the shelter as soon as he can because he knows I hate how quickly they put them down at county.

"Hey, Jeremy?"

"Yeah?"

"Did you go see that movie last night?"

He tightens his grip on the wheel and looks out over the dash. "No."

"Want to go see it with me next weekend?"

He smiles for real this time—not his teasing grin, but a real smile. "Okay," he says as the light turns green. He starts to put his foot on the accelerator again, and that's when Goneril goes nuts.

Master!

She barks. She jumps out of my lap and throws herself, hard, against the window. *MasterMasterMasterMaster!* She starts scrabbling at it, baying at the top of her lungs.

Jeremy slams on the brakes. "Whoa! What's up with her?"

"Pull over!" I shout. I grab the nearest leash and try to clip it onto Goneril's collar, but she's gone totally wild. Jeremy has hardly had a chance to put the van in park when I open the door and Goneril tumbles out, still barking her head off. She pulls me along, across a parking lot and toward a squat white building. In our hurry, it's all I can do to make out the sign on the sliding front door as we whiz past: MEDICAL CENTER.

Goneril gallops down the corridor. She's panting and limping, but that hardly slows her down. We rush past folks in wheelchairs, doctors and orderlies and nurses. A few of them shout as we pass, but I can hardly hear their protests over the sound of Goneril screaming in my head.

Master! Master! Master! Master! Master! Master! Master!

Finally we reach a door that won't open for us. Goneril begins slamming her body against it. A nurse hurries out from behind the nearby desk.

"Young lady! You can't go back there. That's our critical ward—" She stops short when she catches sight of Goneril. "It can't be," she whispers.

"What?" I ask. I try to hold Goneril back, but she's straining so hard I fear she might break the leash. "What is it?"

"It's like she knows he's in there. . . ." But it's hard to hear the nurse over the barking. Goneril's noise is almost deafening.

Let me in! Let me in! Oh please, oh please, oh please let me in!

I turn to the nurse, eyes wide. "Who's in there?"

The nurse is shaking her head in disbelief. "He was brought in last week. Bad car accident out on the highway. He's not awake often, but every time he is, he asks after his dog. . . ."

Masterrrrrrrrrrrrrrrrrrrr! The leash slips from my hands and Goneril smashes her head into the glass door, butting it over and over.

"I'm glad she got home safe."

I look at the nurse, dumbstruck. "She didn't. I don't know your patient. I'm from an animal shelter."

Goneril was right all along. She hadn't been abandoned by her owner. They'd been in an accident together, and she'd gotten lost.

The nurse worries her bottom lip. "This is *so* against the rules," she says, "but I make exceptions for miracles." She presses the buzzer over the door. Goneril slips through the crack. The nurse and I follow.

But she's already found him. The nurse and I hurry to the bed, where a man covered in bandages and hooked up to tubes and wires is smiling and weakly petting Goneril, who stands over him, licking his face with gusto. Her tail is wagging so fast it's a blur, and I watch in amazement as her glamour knits itself back up. In a few moments, it's so thick on her that I can't see the old white dog at all anymore.

Master! Goneril cries in ecstasy. *Master! I found you! I found you!*

"My sweet Goneril," says the man. He's middle-aged, with soft brown eyes and a gentle smile. "Yes, you found me. Good girl. Good, good girl."

The nurse checks the man's vitals, then departs, muttering something about protocol and pulling a tissue out of the pocket of her scrubs.

The man looks up at me. "Thank you for bringing her back to me, young lady." He has an odd accent. I can't quite place it.

Her name is Malou. Goneril curls up against her master. Her snout is spread into a wide doggy smile, her pink tongue lolling out as she looks at me. *She's been trying to help me find a witch to mend my spells. Of course I told her all I needed was you.*

He raises his eyebrows. "You told her?"

Yes. She didn't believe me, though. She's very stubborn, Master. Oh, and she tried to feed me something called kibble. Goneril grimaces.

"You have a way with dogs, do you?" he asks me.

"Yes, but not usually so much as with yours," I admit.

"So you do understand her." He strokes his dog, and color seems to return to his face as I watch. "That's . . . unusual."

"So's your dog."

He nods, his hands buried deep in Goneril's fur. They both look blissful. Maybe it isn't just about him keeping Goneril healthy. Maybe the magic works both ways.

I should go. After all, I've left Jeremy alone in the parking lot. I'm beginning to back away when Goneril pipes up again.

And she fixed my glamour some, Master. She's really good. Her tail flops on the bedcovers.

"She did?" The man's eyes go wide. Strange lights seem to dance inside them. Must be the painkillers. Or something. "Please, Malou, wait."

I stop.

His stare is unnerving. He doesn't look like a man who belongs in a hospital bed. "You swear you have no . . . experience?"

"With magic?" I laugh. "No, sir."

"Then it's quite extraordinary, what you did. To manipulate another's spells is very advanced magic."

I shrug, sheepish. "I was just trying to help the dog. I'm no witch."

"I'm not so sure about that, my dear." The witch holds tight to his beautiful familiar and studies my face. "Tell me about your family."

PAYMENT DUE

FRANCES HARDINGE

WHEN I GOT home from school, I saw a strange man walking out through our front door, and Gran waving to him as he went.

"Who was that?" I asked as I pulled off my wet coat. Gran needs watching. She picks up strays the way a spike heel gathers dead leaves.

"Oh, don't worry about that. He was sent by a bailiff company, because of that disagreement over the Maitlands and Corn bill. But I explained that it was all a silly misunderstanding."

"He's a bailiff? And you let him in the house?" I dropped my bag and stared at her. "Gran—bailiffs are like vampires! They can't come in unless you invite them, but if you do they can come back whenever they like!" It's the sort of thing you think everybody knows. But Gran didn't, and I realized that there was no reason why she would know.

"It's all right, Caroline," Gran assured me as she carried on grating carrot. "I only let him in to use the toilet. It doesn't count."

Of course the first thing I did was look around, and I soon

found the blue and white official papers he had dropped on the living room table on the way from the bathroom.

"Gran!"

The toilet story had just been a line to get inside the house. I felt a wash of heat pass over my skin as I read through a scrawled list of Gran's best and oldest furniture, her books, her clunky old record player, all "impounded."

It's like a supernatural power. Once a bailiff gets inside the house, he can just walk around, deciding what things cost, and once he has jotted them down he has a right to them. His eye slides over things and they magically become his. DVD collection? His. Hat stand? His. You have five days to pay the debt, and if you don't the bailiffs are allowed to come back to collect "their" possessions, by whatever means necessary.

"Well, I won't have the money in five days," declared Gran, as if that settled everything. "They'll just have to wait three weeks until I can pay them."

They didn't wait. Of course they didn't. About a week later the bailiffs turned up with a van. I was away at school at the time, or things could have gone very differently. As it was, they knocked and demanded to be let in. Gran refused and kept the door on the chain, so they burst it open. When she protested and tried to block their way in the hall, they pushed past her.

They pushed past my Gran.

Gran has thick hair that has flopped over her face her whole life, and still does in a gray bushy way. She knows everything about world politics and organizes letter campaigns about rain forests and herds people into sponsored walks to save the local youth center or whatever. She seems so with it and sharp, and you have conversations that just steam along like she's your own age, right until you hit the great big surprising icebergs of things she doesn't know.

And she's a soft touch. She's the one who gets phoned in the early hours because somebody needs to hide from their boozed-up husband. You know the sort of person I mean? The sort who doesn't flinch when she suddenly gets a teenage bundle of pain and problems beyond imagining unexpectedly dropped on her doorstep, but just starts redecorating and reorganizing her life, and acting like she's been given the best present in the world. That's who they pushed aside.

The worst part was the brave face she tried to put on it when I got back to find the door busted, furniture missing, and lots of Gran's things thrown on the floor. Her sniffle was just a cold, she told me as she carried on making casserole.

"At least they didn't take *this*," she kept saying as she bustled around the kitchen, refusing to make eye contact. "Or *that*. And I'd have been sorry to see the blender go." Past the bushy hair I could see tears making silver snails' trails down her nose. She couldn't keep up the pretense, of course, and finally broke down, admitting the worst of it all.

"They took the photo."

I knew instantly which photo she meant. My mother hated being photographed, but I had managed to snap her once, when her arms were too full of groceries for her to duck away. It was one of the last and best ever taken of her, before illness left too deep a mark. Naturally, Gran had put it in the most expensive frame she owned and placed it in the middle of the mantelpiece, where it had caught the bailiff's eye. The photo had been taken with an old film camera. The negatives had been lost while I was moving in.

"I wish, I just wish I had noticed them taking it," Gran kept saying. "Fancy me not noticing! I know it's stupid, but I keep playing the scene over and over in my head, the way it should have gone. If I had only known, I could have run after them, and said they could keep the frame, but just asked for the photo. . . ."

I'm going into a lot of detail, aren't I? Laying on the misery good and thick. The truth is, I'm making excuses for myself. I want you to know how I felt, so you understand everything that happened later.

Tidying up was horrible. The things left scattered around looked and felt like litter. Somehow I kept seeing our house through *their* eyes. All the dents were just dents, without their humorous or poignant histories. Years had ground our memories and handprints deeply and darkly into the varnish of everything, but suddenly it all just looked grimy.

Two weeks later, when Gran had more money, we phoned the bailiffs and tried to buy back some of her things. They just kept telling us that "things have progressed beyond that point."

A week after that, I confronted the bailiff who had tricked my Gran, in a minimart. He probably should have wondered how I managed to find him. He was middle-aged and balding, with a bland, reasonable sort of face and drizzle-colored eyes. I could see why Gran had trusted him. He didn't look interesting enough to be dangerous.

I wasn't hysterical, even though he kept moving along the aisle and picking up canned vegetables while I was talking. I asked him (really politely by my standards) if he could let us know where my Gran's things had been sold, so that we could try to track them down.

When at last he turned to face me, he wasn't rude. Worse, he had an expression like a shop's "closed" sign, the sort people wear when they walk past beggars.

"I'm sorry," he said, in a tone that snipped the conversation short. "It's too late. They're gone." He turned and walked away. And that was it.

No, that was not it. That was very far from it, as you have probably guessed by now. I didn't try to go after him, but then I didn't have to. I knew that something else would be following him, just half a street behind, something with silver eyes and wings that flickered like old film.

At dusk I was waiting on my bedroom windowsill. It's a good, broad sill that used to hold flowerpots, and it vibrates when the trains roar past behind the house. I love sitting on it after dark with my legs dangling off the edge, when the streetlights are toasting the underbelly of the sky and the air tastes amber. I am on a level with the bats' ballet and the ranks of neatly folded roofs.

Just when sunset had faded to a pale crease behind the tenement buildings, Nab fluttered down to perch beside me, and regarded me with eyes like tiny buttons made of sky.

"Did you follow him?"

Nab looked at me pointedly until I gave him a peanut, then nodded. Or rather, gave the jackdaw shrug-hop motion that means the same as a nod.

Nab is always my first choice for spy jobs. He's smart for a bird. Believe me, if you want a sensible conversation with something winged, pick a corvid—rooks, crows, ravens, daws. I prefer jackdaws myself. Rooks give in to peer pressure, crows try to backstab you, and ravens are a bit obvious, which is a problem if one of them is coming to your window every other evening.

"So—where's his house?"

"Pointy-tree house next to the big roar, just past the great reek. Next to the bongbong tower."

You get used to dawspeak after a while. A house with a spiky tree, next to the railway, beside the clock tower and the other side of the sewage plant, I guessed.

"What does it look like? Any easy way in?"

Nab put his head on its side. If he could, he would have pursed his beak and drawn in his breath through the teeth he didn't have. "Watched it for a long time. Tricky. Doors full of clicks. Windows full of clicks. Garden guarded. Guarded by pet sun. Wakes up when anything goes in the garden. Also guarded by a Teeth."

"A Teeth? What kind of Teeth? Dog? Cat?" I sighed inwardly as Nab hopped and chirped nervously. "Quiet Teeth? Loud barky Teeth? Climbing-trees Teeth?" I never said he was smart. I just said he was smart for a bird.

It turned out that he had been scared half-witted by a quiet, climbing-trees Teeth. A cat, in short. A thought instantly occurred.

"Does it have its own door?"

Yes, apparently it did. But it was a magic door. Other Teeth who tried to enter just banged their heads against it and were turned away. Only the Teeth who belonged there could enter.

"Sounds like a magnetic collar," I muttered. I knew that a

lot of people had cat flaps that locked automatically to keep out strays, and gave their cats special collars that would trigger the opening mechanism.

I had been hoping my bailiff owned a dog. Dogs are easy to fool. If a cat was involved, it looked like I would have to make a deal.

An hour later I was sitting in the courtyard of the clock tower, on a bench covered in plaques to the dead and scrawls of the living. Beyond the nearest fence I could see a holly tree, probably the "pointy tree" Nab had mentioned. Behind the ranks of houses lay the hidden embankment, and from time to time unseen trains bulleted past, ripping sudden, roaring holes in the cloth of night. All that divided me from the bailiff's garden was an inch of wood, but I knew better than to scramble over the fence. The "pet sun" that Nab had mentioned was probably a motion detector that would turn on a light in the garden.

Instead I sat there on the bench, kicking my heels and smelling like mice. Occasionally, just for a change, I smelled of live mackerel asphyxiating on a quay, or wounded chaffinch. Sure enough, after about half an hour of this there was a soft scuffle against the nearest wooden panel, and a shape appeared on the fence.

"Sorry," I said, "but I needed to talk to you."

She didn't believe I had spoken at first, any more than people will usually believe it when a cat speaks to them. For a good few seconds she kept looking to and fro, her eyes moonish, searching for the imaginary mice. She only gave it up when I brought out a tuna sandwich and laid it on the bench next to me, at which point she deigned to come and eat out its innards.

"Well?" Cats don't speak the way we do, so talking with their mouths full isn't a problem. She was a large white creature, covered in black and tan blotches like palm prints. One of them covered the right-hand side of her face and made it look like she was peeping slyly out from under a lopsided cap.

"You want a holiday? I want to switch with you for one day."

She chewed on that thought and a medium slice of Hovis for a few seconds.

"You get to sleep in my bed and eat my food—off the plates on the table," I went on. "You can open doors. Fridges. Cans. All those other cats will be smaller than you for a whole day."

"And . . . ?" She knew there was more to it.

"Three conditions. One: you don't do anything to hurt my gran or her house. Two: you meet me here this time tomorrow night and hand back the body. Three: I get to borrow your magic collar."

"What's in it for you?" She was still suspicious.

"Revenge."

"Oh. How dull. All right, then."

We moved into the shadow of the clock tower. I reached up to my forehead, gripped nothing, and drew a line down from my top to my feet, unzipping as I went. The cat pulled itself up onto its hind legs and did the same, using a delicate claw. We stepped out of ourselves, and our skins tumbled to the floor.

I never like looking down when I do this kind of thing. My discarded self looks so strange and molten lying there, its hands all flabby and flat like rubber gloves, the face saggy and gaping with empty eye sockets. The cat's dropped skin resembled an abandoned glove puppet. And standing over them were . . . well, let's just say that we didn't look like a skinned cat and human. In fact, it was hardly possible to tell the difference between us.

We exchanged some details. I told her a little about myself, where to find my house and school.

"This time tomorrow night, then," I said firmly as we stepped across to each other's skins and put them on. "High moon." I had deliberately left the clothes on my skin, since I know that cats are rubbish with buttons even when they have thumbs.

I watched Fake Me wander away, occasionally dropping to all fours or pausing in wonder to watch its own fingers waggle. I took a moment or two to get a feel for my borrowed body, then took a leap at the fence and only slightly messed it up.

Don't do any of this at home, kids. My mother would have thrown a fit. It was one of the many important rules she hammered into my head when I was younger. *Don't swap bodies with animals you don't know. It's dangerous enough even if you do know them. And don't swap bodies with anything unless there's a grown-up present.* I had left Gran a note in the tea caddy, but that hardly counted.

You're always taking a risk swapping with carnivores. They're killers, and you can't afford to forget that. House pets are usually overfed and out of practice, but you can never be sure. Herbivores bring their own set of problems. They will probably spend their time in your body twitching, terrified and crazy, and they have lousy road sense. And with birds there's always a danger that they'll panic and try to fly away.

With the second try I got over the fence and padded to the back door amid the glow of the automated light. The collar was heavy round my neck, and I could feel the rub where the cat had been trying to lever it off. The grass was thick, close, and full of living scents. My mouth tasted of tuna, and tuna tasted amazing.

The collar was my magic invitation. The cat flap opened when I pushed it with my head, and I entered warmth. I was inside. From the next room I could hear the buzz and warble of the TV. I peered around the corner of the door and saw the bailiff perched on the edge of the sofa, eating what looked like a meat pie with canned carrots. I pulled back and started searching the house.

He was the only one living there, I was sure of that. All the rooms smelled male. Two pairs of boots on the rack, both man-sized. One toothbrush. A little cairn of crushed beer cans in his recycling box. His furniture was a bit of a jumble and I wondered, with a growling sense of resentment in my stomach, if he had bought them cheap from goods seized during his work.

Do you know what a cat is doing when it comes and rubs its head against you, eyes half closed as if in bliss? It isn't overwhelmed with love for you. It has a scent gland just under its jaw, so it's marking you as its property. When you're not looking it does the same to the furniture and everything else that stays still. It really is happy, but with the joy of making things belong to it.

While the bailiff spooned gravy into his mouth, I was running around his house, rubbing my head against this, that, everything, my eyes half closed, my whiskers sleeked back. This bookcase? Mine. This table? Mine. This pretty horrible DVD stand? Mine. Thus I ran around, using a cat's trick to mark things more deeply than any real cat ever could.

Afterward when he was walking about, ready to go to bed, I settled down to meekly playing cat. The food in my bowl was the cheap, dried sort like brown gravel, but I crunched some down to keep him happy. He stroked me heavily, called me Missus, then slopped some water in my bowl and went to bed. He didn't seem to notice that the varnish on his coffee table was starting to pucker and yellow.

Next morning he set off early in his van, giving me a whole day alone in his house. I didn't waste it. Instead I set about twining and snaking around his furniture, my back bristling as my fur shed little flakes of moonlight. I wandered daintily and carefully along his mantelpiece, knocking over nothing, stopping now and then to rub my face against this or that. I licked all his spoons. I rolled slowly over and over across his rug like a fat, furry rolling pin. I tiptoed along the edges of his bookshelves, my tail tip flicking over title after title.

The bailiff got home late, smelling of an unplanned pub stop. He came in, chucking his keys onto his hall table, and halted. Perhaps he noticed even before he put the lights on that there was something wrong with the smell of his house. He sniffed, then drew his hand back from the light switch, turned on his keychain torch, and went to check the gas in the kitchen. It was off, of course, so he risked turning on the light, then took a beer from the fridge and carried it into the lounge.

From my place on the rug by the radiator, I sat and rumbled my purr, watching him all the time through half-closed eyes.

Obviously I couldn't see into his head, but I was pretty sure I could tell what he was thinking. He sat on the sofa, and then shifted a bit uneasily. Were the springs going? The seat seemed lower than usual. He reached for his beer, then paused and rubbed at the surface of the coffee table with his sleeve. There was a flower-shaped yellow discoloration in the very middle of it. He scratched his fingernail against it, looked up at the ceiling for drips or damp patches, and then shrugged and switched on the TV.

The volume was turned up, so it was quite a while before he noticed the creaks. They were stealthy at first, but gradually grew louder, until at last he frowned and turned off the TV to listen.

Silence.

He stood and walked to the window, tweaking the blind, probably worrying that the sound might be somebody trying to break in. Then he heard another creak right behind him, and spun around just fast enough to see the coffee table moving its legs. It had drawn them slightly closer together, its feet rasping against the carpet with a faint *fff* noise.

He stooped. He stared. He tipped the table on its side. He set it on its feet. He rattled it on its legs until its drawer fell out. He put the drawer back in and stood staring at it. Drawer? Since when did it have a drawer?

Then he stiffened as, from all around him, there came a series of small groans and grumbles, as if a wooden orchestra were tuning up. Something on the mantelpiece gave a sound like a sigh. He staggered over and peered, looking for . . . what? Mice? Sighing mice? He paused in front of an old photograph showing two boys on neighboring swings, in floppy old-fashioned haircuts. There was a shadow behind the sunny day in the picture. It looked a bit like a woman's face.

With a clatter, the bookshelf threw off all pretense. It tottered forward, edge after edge, its pinewood blistering and peeling to reveal hand-waxed mahogany. Drawer handles emerged from the unbroken wood with a thunk like silencer rounds. The rug shivered, rolled, and writhed, its tassels withering and molting, its color deepening from marzipan to a rich chocolate. CDs shot gleaming from their boxes, spun together in the air like a Martian landing fleet, then broadened until they became glistening black vinyl. The CD stand itself contorted, blackened, and twisted until it started to look a lot like a wrought iron hat stand.

Then, as one, the rebellious possessions began to glide, totter, and creak their way to the hall. Once there, they rasped and juddered, beating themselves against the wood of the door. Bang, bang, bang. The terrible drum of angry wood and metal, all jumping and stamping at once. *Open the door. Open the door.*

I have to say, the bailiff showed some real guts. He tried to grapple with the coffee table, which by now had a clear chrysanthemum pattern painted on its top face, and held on even when the records started dive-bombing him. The furniture was having none of it, however. The largest and heaviest piece, a walnut sideboard, reared up like a particularly square-cut stallion and dashed the door off its hinges. It galloped out into the yard, overturning bins. The gashes in its woodwork started to heal. The same could not be said for the door.

The bailiff had fallen to all fours and could only watch aghast as the furniture that no longer resembled his danced out into the moonlight. A photo in an ornately carved wooden frame capered past, its front face visible for a moment. The image of the two boys had almost entirely faded. The woman's face was far clearer, pouting in an angry half smile. Did the face look familiar to him? Did it remind him of an old woman he had pushed past not long before, or a scruffy dark fifteen-year-old he had cold-shouldered in a minimart? Who knows.

Leaving his door open to the night, he ran through the empty streets of the midnight town, following the thunder of wooden feet, the tinkle of fugitive spoons. He followed them down the muddy, stinking footpath that stripes across the sewage plant. He barely noticed something white streak past his legs and race down the path ahead of him.

Out of breath, he reached our street just in time to see our door swing wide and the rebel possessions slide politely in, some pausing to wipe their wooden feet on the mat. Something ugly clicked into place behind the bailiff's bland, ordinary eyes. Although he didn't know what was happening, he now had an idea who might be to blame. He crossed the street and approached our door.

"I wouldn't do that if I were you." Seated on a wall beside him was his very own cat, his "Missus," grinning in just the way cats don't outside Wonderland. "You'd wake up Gran and upset her. I wouldn't like that. And what are you going to do, anyway? Beat on an old lady's door in the middle of the night? And say what? That she stole your stuff? The stuff that doesn't even look like yours?"

The bailiff hesitated, and the hand he had raised to knock slowly lowered.

"Go home," I said, in a way that made my pointy cat fangs show. He turned around and sloped off back the way he had come. "I'll send your real cat home to you tomorrow!" I called after him.

Getting my body back turned out to be a bit of a nightmare. The cat had decided to take a longer holiday and probably would have skipped town still wearing me if I hadn't caught up with her first. She was sneaking out of a Tesco's at the time, and when she saw me she tried to run for it. Fortunately I managed to get between her legs and trip her, at which point the fifteen packs of mackerel she was trying to shoplift spilled out from under her coat.

She bit the store detective, and the police were summoned. Eventually Gran was called and picked her up from the station. By that point, several hours of harsh lights, condescension, and bad tea had cured the cat of her enthusiasm for being human. When we got home Gran shut us in a room together, and the cat sullenly unzipped so we could swap back.

My body felt awful. Fake me hadn't bathed or changed her clothes, of course. There was a fluffy taste in my mouth that I thought was probably the result of her grooming clothing with her tongue. I really hoped it wasn't small rodent, anyway. There were lots of bruises and scratches, too. I'm always really careful with a borrowed body, but most creatures just seem to treat them the way a joyrider treats a car.

There was a lot of trouble afterward, and not just because of the shoplifting. Fake Me had bunked off school all morning, and spent it kicking as many of the neighborhood dogs as she could find. She did turn up at school in time for lunch, but didn't exactly get round to attending any lessons. I escaped expulsion only because nobody actually saw her eat the school gerbils.

Oh well. I hadn't put much effort into making friends or pretending to be normal at that school anyway. There didn't seem to be much point, since I never knew when I might have to lend my body to a pine marten or something.

Gran was very angry. Gran was angry while hugging me. Gran was angry while walking around her lounge, touching each of her prodigal possessions with trembling fingers.

Mum was angry with me. I could see that from her photo. That same angry pout over the grocery bags. *Caroline! I told you not to do that! I meant it! Oh . . . but I suppose I'll forgive you. Just this once.*

A few days later the bailiff came by again, without his van, just in time to catch me coming home from school. He looked abashed and uncertain as I strolled to my door and grinned at him in the way that fifteen-year-old girls probably shouldn't, and cats occasionally do. To his credit, he didn't beat around the bush or pretend not to know what he knew.

"Listen. I . . . I think I may have tracked down some of your grandma's possessions, and I might be able to buy them back. If I do that, do you think you could return my things? An exchange? There was . . . there was a photo of mine . . ."

I felt a bit sorry for him, to be honest. But "things had progressed beyond that point" and there was nothing I could do.

"I'm sorry," I said, and kind of meant it. "It's too late. They're gone."

A HANDFUL OF ASHES

GARTH NIX

"THERE'S THE BELL again," groaned Francesca. She reluctantly lifted her eyes from the copy of *An Introduction to Lammas, Night Curses, and Counter-Curses* that she'd been studying, and looked across at the indicator board that dominated an entire wall of the servants' dining room. "Miss Englesham this time. Whose turn is it to go?"

"Mine," answered Mari with a sigh. She had three books open on the table in front of her and was in the middle of making some very precise and careful notes that required great concentration. She balanced her pen back on its stand next to the inkwell, slid off the cuffs that kept the sleeves of her blouse ink-free, and stood up.

"I'll go for you, Mari," said a cheerful young woman who was toasting her feet by the huge kitchen range, without a book in sight.

"Oh no you won't, Tess," instructed a much older and larger woman who was making pie cases on a neighboring bench. "You're finished for the day, and them sizars knows they only study as work allows. Which it don't, right now."

"Yes, Cook," said Tess, subsiding back into her chair.

"Thank you anyway, Tess," said Mari. "Cook is, of course, quite right."

Francesca made a face behind Cook's back and handed Mari an apron. Cook was mistress of the kitchen and a powerful curse cooker, so they could not afford to cross her. Particularly as the two of them were sizars, poor students who were allowed to study at Ermine College in return for menial service. Ermine was one of the seven colleges for witches at the University of Hallows-bridge, the other six colleges being exclusively for wizards. Only Ermine and the wizard college Rolyneaux still continued the tradition of sizars.

Mari tied the apron behind her back as she ran up the kitchen stairs and out across the North Quadrangle, being careful to stay on the path. Walking on the grass was prohibited except for senior members of the college or university, visiting dignitaries such as inspectors of magery, and the head gardener. The lawn was not to be touched by the feet of undergraduates, and certainly not by the ugly worn-out boots of a sizar.

Across the quad, she slowed to take a shortcut along the narrow lane between the ancient, mossy stones of the western wall of Agstood Hall and the smooth brick of the eastern wall of the Oozery. It was the quickest way, though not without its perils, the foremost being that it was off-limits to servants and sizars. But, as it was already dusk, Mari thought it worth the risk in order to save time. The young ladies, as the sizars were supposed to refer to the proper, fee-paying undergraduates, were generally not very patient. Most of them came from homes with numerous domestic staff, and they did not adapt well to the far less available services of the sizars and the limited number of college servants.

The Miriam Oakenwood Quadrangle on the other side was a much smaller version of the North Quadrangle. It was lined on two sides by an L-shaped four-story building officially called Oakenwood Hall but known to everyone as Mo'wood. It housed most of the first-year students. Mari went to the western arm and rapidly ascended to the top floor, where the best rooms were located, and knocked on the door that had a plain white card with "Englesham, Miss C." inserted in its bronze nameplate.

"Enter!"

Mari pushed the door open. Four carefully made-up faces on four elegantly attired young women turned to look at her. The four were sitting on two leather chaise longues that were lined up opposite each other, with a low table in between that currently hosted a very expensive and definitely noncollegiate collection of tea things, including a large enameled bronze samovar that Mari was fairly certain she'd seen in *The Mercury* as being the property of the recently deceased Prince-Wizard Athenanan, sold for a record price at the auction disposing of his worldly goods.

"You rang, Miss Englesham," Mari stated calmly, though inside her heart was racing, and she stood on her toes, ready for flight, all prompted by the sight of her reception committee.

Caita Englesham herself was a typically harmless first-year, if thoughtless. But the other three were third-year students, and a consistent problem for Mari and the other sizars. Aphra Lannisa was a bully of the worst stripe; Susyn Clairmore was a liar and a cheat; and their leader, Helena Diadem, was the worst of the lot, since in Mari's opinion she was well on the way to becoming a bane-witch, though Diadem was too clever to let anyone in authority see that.

"Yes," said Englesham nervously, with a sideways glance at the others. "I had some questions."

Mari stood, waiting for the questions. None were forthcoming for several seconds.

"Ah, I believe . . ." Englesham wet her lips and hesitated again. "I believe that you grew up in the servants' quarters of the college, Mari?"

"Yes, miss," replied Mari woodenly. Lannisa and Clairmore were giggling, but Mari still couldn't see where this was going. Everyone knew that she had been found on the steps of the porter's lodge as a baby and had been taken in by Mrs. Garridge, the porter's wife. She and her husband had died of the Great Ague three years previously, when Mari was sixteen, but not before Old Garridge, as everyone knew him, had managed to call in the many favors owed to him to have Mari made a sizar of the college, so that she might take her degree and thus ensure her future.

"You're smart, my girl," he'd said on his deathbed. "Smarter than three-quarters of them here. You might even be mistress of the college one day. You get your degree and you'll be set for life."

Or so he had thought. But the Great Ague had come again the next year, and the next, and twelve months ago had taken the former mistress of Ermine College. The new one, Lady Aristhenia, did not approve of the tradition of sizars. She liked her servants to be servants, she'd said, and her scholars to be gentlewomen.

Since Lady Aristhenia's installation as mistress, Mari had

been doing a lot more serving and a lot less studying, and with her final exams only a month away, she feared that she would not pass, would not gain her degree, and then would either have to stay on simply as a servant or leave the college that she loved, to find her way in an economically depressed outside world that would not welcome an unqualified witch.

"And you . . . um . . . weaseled . . . your way into becoming a sizar in the Beltane term three years ago," continued Englesham, her eyes darting to the other girls and back again.

I know who's really speaking here, thought Mari. *Helena Diadem.*

"Yes, miss," she replied, trying to stay calm. "Is there anything I can do for you? More coal for your fire, perhaps?"

"No," said Englesham quickly, eager to be done with what she had been told to say. "It's just that . . . we . . . that is I . . . I have found a scrap of the Original Bylaws of the college. . . ."

Mari's eyes narrowed. The Original Bylaws were potent magical artifacts, written in Brythonic and inscribed on stone tablets in the Ogham script to bind everyone in the college to obey their draconian strictures. But fortunately for all concerned, some three hundred years previously the then mistress of the college, the fabled Alicia Wasp, aided by Witch Queen Jesmay I, had nullified the Original Bylaws and buried the stone tablets under the moondial in the Library Garden. Then Mistress Wasp had promulgated the New Bylaws, which were considerably more liberal and, being merely in Latin, much easier to read.

As far as Mari knew, the stone tablets were still under the moondial, and even if they weren't, it was very unlikely that

Englesham could understand Brythonic, or read even a sentence in Ogham.

It was clearly going to develop into some sort of attack upon her, but Mari couldn't work out what the nature of it was going to be, or how the forgotten and nullified Original Bylaws were going to come into it.

"I found a parchment," continued Englesham. She looked over at the wall. "When I moved in, and the wallpaper had to be changed, really it was too awful . . ."

Helena Diadem looked at her. Englesham gulped and continued.

"There was a parchment under the plaster, and the workmen pointed it out to me. It was a rubbing of part of one of the old tablets. I was going to take it to my tutor, but Diadem said—"

"That's enough," said Diadem. "Suffice to say, Mari, that we have found a paragraph of the Original Bylaws, which, curiously enough, concerns sizars in the college. We thought you should be the first to know, before it is invoked."

"That's old magic," said Mari. She tried to look unconcerned, but inside she was scared. "Deep magic. You shouldn't mess with it."

"It's only a sentence or two of the Original Bylaws," sneered Aphra Lannisa. "Most sensible bylaws, *we* think."

Mari took a step back, toward the door. But Diadem pulled a wand out from between the cushions of the chaise longue. It wasn't a weak student wand, a mere stick of wych elm, carved with some simple runes granting minor magics. This wand was very old and very, very dangerous. Carved from a human shinbone, it was covered in minute inscriptions that called upon serious powers: powers of the past, powers of the present, and powers that were yet to be.

"You shouldn't have that," whispered Mari. She felt like someone had just pressed an icicle lengthways against her spine, and her heart faltered in its steady rhythm.

Wands like that weren't just forbidden. They were outlawed. Owning one was a very serious offense. Actually using one put the wielder beyond the law: every witch and wizard who witnessed such activity was then empowered to do whatever was necessary to disarm or even kill the user and keep the wand in place till it could be made safe by the authorities. The only problem being that any sensible witch or wizard would run a mile before tackling the wielder of such a wand.

"Why?" asked Diadem. "It's a family heirloom, and besides, I *don't* have it, as all my friends here will attest if you claim otherwise."

She looked at Englesham.

"Give the fragment to Mari, Caita."

Englesham, anxious to obey, took a small folded piece of parchment out from inside the sleeve of her gown and proffered it to Mari, who locked her hands into fists at her sides.

"That won't do," said Diadem. She made a slight gesture with the bone wand and spoke three words that in passing curdled the milk in the silver jug on the table and frosted the cake with a hideous green mold.

Mari found her hands opening and her right arm lifting up, her joints moving like an old puppet brought out of the attic and forced to answer once more to the strings.

"Read it," said Diadem. "Aloud."

Mari's hands unfolded the parchment, even though she didn't want to. Nor did she want to raise the parchment to eye level, but her arms lifted, answering the gentle string-pulling movements of Diadem's wand.

"I . . . I can't decipher Ogham," muttered Mari through clenched teeth. "Or pronounce Brythonic."

"Liar!" exclaimed Lannisa. "Oh, let me have a turn with the wand, Helena!"

Diadem ignored her friend.

"Really?" she answered Mari. "What was that essay of yours last year? 'The Augmentation of Incantation: Brythonic, Ogham, and A Choir of Seven,' I believe. You certainly convinced our *old* mistress of your familiarity with both language and cipher. She gave you a prize, as I recall."

"Swot," said Clairmore venomously, almost spitting at Mari.

"Read it," commanded Diadem.

Mari tried not to, but she had no choice. Diadem had her in the grip of a geas, which was bane-witch territory for certain, not that any of the others would ever testify against her, and Mari's word alone would not count for anything. She regretted that she had not thought to equip herself with a defensive charm, as she usually did when called to Diadem's rooms. But she had not considered that the inoffensive Miss Englesham would be recruited to Diadem's flock of harpies.

She started to read, roughly translating the Brythonic in her head as she spoke aloud. Most of the words were harmless enough in themselves, but they were joined by words of power in such a way that the totality of the phrase became a very powerful spell.

Scholar-servants of low estate
Brought into learning, of this date
Shall with ashes adorn their face
And must not be adorned with lace
Their coats shall be—

The fragment was torn there, and ended.

"What does that mean?" asked Englesham anxiously. Lannisa and Clairmore did not ask, but looked to Diadem, who was certainly the only other person in the room who had understood the Brythonic original of this small evocation of the Original Bylaws.

"You'll see in a moment," said Diadem. She pointed the wand at Mari. "You will find you cannot speak of this wand. But you are otherwise released."

She slid her wand up her sleeve, and Mari felt the geas lift. Her arms fell, boneless for a second, till she got control.

But even though she was no longer under Diadem's spell, Mari still felt a strong compulsion. It was different, more inside her head than physically controlling, but she could not resist it any more than she had the geas. She ran to the fireplace, knelt down, and, in lieu of immediately available wood ash, ran her finger along the grate and smeared the resulting sticky black coal residue across her face, two messy tiger stripes down each cheek.

A slight smile curled up one corner of Diadem's mouth. Lannisa and Clairmore shrieked with laughter. Englesham bit her lip and looked away.

Mari stood up and returned to the door.

"Will that be all, miss?" she asked calmly. Inwardly she was suppressing a fierce rage. If she had a bone wand like Diadem's, four . . . or perhaps three . . . lady undergraduates would be smoking corpses, and Mari would be a murderer and a bane-witch, to be hunted across the protectorate and all the civilized lands beyond.

So it was probably just as well she didn't have an evil wand, thought Mari as she ran furiously along Agstood-Oozery Lane. She would have to find another way to be revenged upon Diadem, one that did not involve banecraft and outlawry. More pressingly, she needed to find out how to nullify or overcome the Original Bylaw that even now was sharp inside her mind, insisting that the black coal stripes on her face be replaced with fine gray wood ash, in the approved pattern that hadn't even been mentioned in the fragment but that she somehow now knew.

Back in the kitchen, Francesca, her face daubed with coal soot like Mari's, was lighting a fire of hazel sticks in the corner of the vast old range that was now only used once a year to roast the Beltane ox. The other two current sizars in the college, Rellise and Jena, were helping her by breaking sticks. Rellise's face was streaked with what looked like mascara, and Jena's with something gray that defied immediate identification but was possibly a mixture of cigarette ash and toothpaste.

Cook, still working on her pies, was watching the fire-building out of the corner of her eye. When Mari came back in, the huge outside door clanking shut behind her, Cook gestured with a floury thumb at the fire makers.

"I don't suppose you can explain this, Mari?"

"It's in the Original Bylaws," said Mari. "Someone found a rubbing—one paragraph—from the stone, and invoked it. It says we sizars have to daub our faces with wood ash, in a pattern."

"Someone?" asked Francesca. The fire was burning merrily now. There would be a nice pile of ash soon. A handful of ash mixed with olive oil would do nicely to make the lines and swirls that all the sizars now knew, without knowing why they did.

"Diadem and her lot," replied Mari. "As usual."

Cook nodded grimly. Taking up a chopper, she began to split pig trotters. While she did not particularly care for the sizars, whom she considered neither fish nor fowl, Cook was a stern guardian of the other servants, who had often been the target of Diadem's mistreatment.

"I don't suppose it'll do any good going to Lady Aristhenia, then," said Francesca.

The sizars all nodded in mournful agreement. The mistress of the college was some sort of relative of Diadem's, and in any event, she would never take the side of the sizars against the "proper students."

"What about the university proctors?" asked Rellise.

Cook stopped splitting trotters and looked over at the four sizars thoughtfully. They didn't notice. Mari was shaking her head.

"They wouldn't believe us, either. Besides, Diadem hasn't done anything illegal with this, or even gone against the university rules. They've just brought to life an old college regulation. I wish we could get her investigated, since she's definitely a bane-witch. She used a geas on me."

"But surely she's not strong enough!" protested Francesca.

Mari opened her mouth, but couldn't speak of the wand.

"Well, she is," said Mari. "Not that I can prove it, worse luck. How's that ash coming along?"

Francesca stirred the fire with the poker.

"It needs longer. I suppose we should be grateful there isn't a Bylaw to make us wear sackcloth as well."

"It did say we can't wear lace," said Mari. "Not that I've got any."

Rellise and Jena exchanged a look.

"What?" asked Mari.

"I had to change my . . . my unmentionables," said Jena, blushing. "I was wearing some with lace trim . . . it was lucky I was in our room."

"We have to do something," said Mari. She hesitated, not wishing to alarm the others, but then carried on. It was better to have everything out. "It's not just the ash and the lace. . . . Well, it *is* the ash. But it occurred to me that it might stop us sitting examinations."

Three pairs of frightened eyes fixed on her.

"What?"

"You know that to sit the exams we have to present ourselves in 'hat and gown, with wand and athame.'"

The others nodded.

"There's also a bit about being sober and *clean*," said Mari. "I don't know how we'll go with ash-streaked faces."

"But it'll be because of a college bylaw!" protested Jena.

"The university's examination rules came in with the protectorate," said Mari. "*After* our Bylaws were buried, so they were never taken into account. Even in the best case, it will go to the Chancellor's Court, and we'll still miss the examinations this year. And if I . . . if Francesca and I miss them this year, we'll never get another chance!"

"She planned it," said Francesca furiously. Like Mari, she was in her final year, while Jena and Rellise still had a year to go. "Diadem the Arch-Bitch. She's always hated us. Now this, to make us *fail*—"

"No one's going to make us fail," said Mari, summoning up all her reserves of determination. "We will sit the exams and we *will* graduate!"

"How—" Francesca started to say, but the fire fell in on itself, crumbling into ash, and all four sizars were gripped by the Bylaw demanding they clean their faces of their temporary indicators, prepare the ash, and then paint stripes ending in swirly marks on their cheeks.

That took several minutes, some splashing about with cool water and olive oil, and concluded with a depressed silence as the young women looked at each other.

"How?" repeated Francesca.

Mari frowned. She'd been thinking about the problem ever since the Brythonic words had left her mouth.

"I'm not sure," she said slowly. "This is deep magic; there might be all kinds of complications. I shall have to look up the spell the queen and the mistress used, and we'll have to get the parchment as well."

"Who has it now?" asked Francesca.

"Englesham," said Mari. "I don't think Diadem or her cronies would touch it. It's sure to be spelled against bane-witches."

"If it was burned . . . destroyed . . . would that release us from—"

Mari shook her head.

"It can't be destroyed, not now that it's been invoked," she said. "It's not just a parchment. I mean, even Alicia Wasp and Queen Jesmay couldn't destroy the Original Bylaws, only nullify them. But maybe we can do the same, if we can get the parchment. And since Englesham is too frightened of Diadem to hand it over freely, I suppose . . ."

Mari stopped talking and looked at Cook, who was listening intently. The older woman reddened, sniffed, and paced down the other end of the kitchen to noisily rattle through the pots on the shelves there.

"We'll have to steal it from her rooms," whispered Mari.

The other three women drew back. Being caught stealing would mean instant dismissal from the college and probably charges from the civilian authorities as well.

"But we . . . we can't do that," whispered Jena. Rellise nodded vigorously by her side, like a puppet at a village fair.

"*You* won't have to," said Mari. "In fact, it would be best if you and Rellise stay out of this completely. Francesca and I are the ones who won't get a second chance at finals. You still have next year."

"Oh good," said Jena with relief.

"Yes," said Mari. She smiled, though it took some effort. She'd always had a low opinion of Jena and Rellise, who were never to be seen when there was any threat to the sizars, leaving it to Mari and Francesca to sort everything out. But for the sake of civility and kindness she tried not to show her contempt. "If you two stay here and take over our shift, Francesca and I will go and work out what we need to do."

She hesitated, then added, "Whatever we decide, it won't happen for a few days, anyway. So just sit tight and do your work as normal."

"We will," chorused Jena and Rellise.

"Come on," Mari said to Francesca. They got up together and started packing up their books, prompting a sudden inquiry from Cook.

"Hey, where are you girls off to? There's three hours yet—"

"Jena and Rellise are taking over tonight," replied Mari. "If you don't object, Cook."

"Don't suppose it would make any difference if I did," sniffed Cook. She fixed Mari with one of her famously fierce looks and added, "Don't you two do anything foolish. Or if you do, you might want to consider that the mistress is dining out tonight, and will be flying home."

Mari nodded gratefully, and she and Francesca hurried out into the kitchen garden, where they paused to note that the sun had almost set behind the spire of the college tower, and then they continued past the radishes and the rosemary, out through the garden gate into the Old House, and along the back corridor to the room they shared with Jena and Rellise. Unlike the lady undergraduates, who all had their own rooms, the sizars were housed with the servants, but in even more cramped conditions, since there were four of them in a room meant for three, and they also had to keep all of the paraphernalia of student witches: brooms, wands, staves, daggers, books, scrying globes, basic alchemical apparatus, and, most of all, books. Even with daily sorties to and from the library, the room was always overflowing with books.

"So we go and steal the parchment tonight," said Francesca. She kept pacing back and forth as Mari carefully made her way between two piles of books to the window seat.

Mari laughed. "Was I so transparent? Jena won't be as worried if she thinks nothing will happen for a few days, and Rellise only ever echoes Jena. So they'll be happy, and they won't give us away."

"What's the plan?" asked Francesca. "Fly over as soon as it's dark, nip in Englesham's window, and nab the parchment?"

Mari looked out the window. Though they were on the ground floor, it had a good view over the North Quadrangle toward the Oozery. One of the gardeners was doing something to the turf, working in the light of a flaming branch that hung suspended in the air without actually being attached to a tree. A fairly typical illusion for light, but not one she'd ever seen employed by the gardeners, who usually just conjured a simple marsh light or dead man's lantern. Apart from him, there was no one around. In another hour it would be full dark, the tower bell would sound, and the college gates would be locked for the night.

"It's not going to be easy," she said slowly. She looked up at the darkening sky framed by the college buildings, with the bulk of the tower looming above in the distance, a few stars beginning to make their appearance around it. "Diadem's no fool. She'll be expecting us to try to steal the parchment. And as Cook was just kind enough to tell us, the mistress will be flying in at some point. She'll be bound to notice anyone else flying about the place."

"She won't be back till late, not if she's out to dinner," replied Francesca.

"We can't count on that. What if she has a stomachache, or the dinner's awful or even more boring than usual?"

"So what do we do?" asked Francesca impatiently. She was always impatient, her temper matching her red hair. Valiant but foolhardy, in Mari's loving opinion, which she had often expressed to her friend. Francesca for her part thought the dark-haired Mari was too controlled, too thoughtful. Together they made a formidable pair. Both, though they did not know it, were almost beautiful, and would be in time, if they were not worn down in servitude. That was one of the reasons Diadem and her friends were jealous of them, for their incipient beauty and their fierce intelligence, and their potential to transform from down-trodden ducklings into academic swans.

Mari kept staring out the window, arranging and rear-ranging all the salient facts in her head. Every now and then she glanced at the gardener. There was something about him that was prompting a thought, but it wasn't quite rising to the surface.

"What did Cook's nephew end up doing after he took his degree last year?" she asked finally, interrupting Francesca's pacing.

"You mean Bill? What's that got to do with anything?"

"I'm not sure," replied Mari. "Do you know, though?"

"Yes," said Francesca, coloring slightly. "He went away to join the Metropolitan Police. I believe he is already a detective."

"But he hasn't been back?" asked Mari.

"No," said Francesca. She paced over to Mari and looked down, her cheeks red and eyes bright. "Don't be a beast, Mari, you know—"

"Shh," said Mari, taking her by the wrist. "Come here and have a look at this gardener. Remind you of anyone?"

Francesca looked through the window. Suddenly her whole body stiffened and her head lurched forward, like a hunting dog on point.

"Bill!" she exclaimed. "But . . . what's he doing here?"

"Police work, I suppose," said Mari. "I bet it's to do with . . . that . . . well, anyway . . . I'm beginning to get an idea of how we might sort all this out. I'm off to the library to look up how Alicia Wasp and the queen got rid of the Old Bylaws in the first place. You go and say hello to Bill and tell him—"

"I can't talk to him looking like this!" protested Francesca, pointing at her ash-smeared face.

"You'll have to pretend he's just a gardener you don't know, anyway," said Mari. "It's important. Stop and make it look like idle chat, but tell him to be on the lookout for bane-witches flying around outside Mo'wood later tonight. I hope he's got some help. . . ."

"I don't . . . I don't want to get him into danger," said Francesca.

"He's a police officer!" exclaimed Mari. "He's probably been in all sorts of danger already, only you don't know about it."

"It's easier if I don't know," said Francesca. "Not that it's any of my business."

"You could make it your business," suggested Mari. "Starting now. I mean, if this all comes off according to plan, he'll be here for a while. You'll see him again. Without the ash on your face."

"It's not just the ash," said Francesca. She gestured at her rough cotton blouse, sensible but ugly woolen skirt, holed stockings, and clumpy boots.

"He was a sizar, too," said Mari. "He knows to look past the wrapping paper."

"Does he?"

"He's Cook's nephew!" exclaimed Mari. "And he was at Rolyneaux. They spend half their time staring into the dark there. You know what they say: 'What you don't want known, a Rolyneaux knows.' Probably why he joined the police."

"I'm not sure that's any better," said Francesca. "Do you think he can read my thoughts?"

"No," said Mari, carefully not mentioning that mind reading would be unnecessary, Francesca's main thought regarding Bill clearly visible in her face and eyes. "Look, we haven't got much time. After you tell Bill, pick a coven of radishes and start carving faces. Do it here, but don't let Jena and Rellise see if they come in before you're finished."

"Radish girls?" asked Francesca. "Should I gather some yew twigs as well?"

"No, I'll get them on the way back from the library. Oh, we'd both better put on charms. Not that they'll be all that much use against—"

"Against what?" asked Francesca.

Mari groaned through clenched teeth.

"Something you can't talk about," guessed Francesca. "Something Diadem's got—"

Mari clapped her hand over Francesca's mouth and shook

her head violently. The questions were making the geas adopt sterner measures, beginning with her tongue swelling to block her throat.

Francesca raised her eyebrows, acknowledging that she'd worked out that a geas was in effect. Mari took her hand away.

"Lovely night," commented Francesca, careful to make sure it didn't sound like a question. "Full moon later. Lovely. I'd better be off."

"Yes," croaked Mari. "Don't forget your charms."

Both of them put on silver necklaces, the thin, spindly ones that were lent by the college to the sizars, courtesy of some ancient bequest. Francesca added a moonstone ring that was the only thing her debt-ridden father had left her, and Mari put on the turquoise and silver bracelet that had been her foster mother's. Mrs. Garridge had never worn it, because she said it was too old and precious and had been in Garridge's family for centuries. Mari had only worn it once or twice, when she had felt particularly at risk from malevolent magic—which essentially meant the two occasions when she had been unable to avoid responding to a call to Helena Diadem's rooms without a witness.

"I think Diadem and company will be waiting for us to try Englesham's rooms," said Mari as they went out. "But if you do run into them, retreat to the kitchen."

"You do the same," said Francesca. "Or stay in the library. Be careful."

Mari nodded. They turned away from each other and went their separate ways: Francesca out to the North Quadrangle, and Mari through the Old Building, out along the path that ran the length of the Scholar's Garden, around the base of the tower, across the Foreshortened Court, and into the hexagonal, six-turreted library.

The college library was open all hours, though it was not much used at night, since most undergraduates borrowed books and took them away to read in the comfort of their rooms. But there was always at least one Librarian in attendance, sometimes more, though they were usually engrossed in their own tasks and paid little attention to the students, other than to get requested books from the stacks. They did not record what went in and out. All the college's books were ensorcelled. They could not leave the grounds, and would return of their own accord in due course if kept too long out of the library.

Mari was rather surprised to find the Librarian herself strolling between the desks of the reading room, idly flicking a feather duster at every second or third green-shaded lamp. Professor Aiken was not only the Ermine College Librarian, she also held the university chair of bookmaking, lecturing in magical type, paper, and binding. Mari had attended several of her lectures but did not know her, unlike most of the senior members, whom she had waited on as a sizar or known since she was a child in the porter's lodge. Aiken did not live in at the college and was a very infrequent diner there.

Professor Aiken looked across as Mari came in, and then surprised the young woman still more by coming over to join her at the index files, the feather duster still flicking as she zig-zagged between the desks.

"Miss Garridge, I believe?"

"Yes, Professor," replied Mari. Aiken was looking at her face, evidently curious about the ash.

"Keeping up old traditions, I see," remarked the professor. "Tribute to Mistress Wasp, I suppose?"

"I beg your pardon?"

"The sizar ash," said Aiken, pointing with her feather duster, which, now that Mari saw it closely, was not a feather duster at all but a wand with a feather duster end. "You know, you *do* look rather like that first portrait. A fine copy of the bracelet, too. Well done."

"*Mistress Wasp* was a sizar?" asked Mari.

"Didn't you know?" asked Professor Aiken. She wrinkled her nose, then reached into the pocket of her rather horsey tweed coat and pulled out a snuffbox, flicked it open expertly with one hand, and scooped out some snuff on the back of her thumbnail. Inhaling it carefully, she closed the box and stowed it away as Mari stood there gaping at her.

"I suppose they do leave it out of that nasty little college brochure these days," she continued, occasionally taking small, nasal breaths as if she was about to sneeze, but never actually doing so. "But she was a sizar. In her memoirs she wrote it was the greatest advantage she had."

"Advantage? Being a sizar?" spat Mari. "Uh, I beg your pardon, ma'am. About Mistress Wasp's memoirs—in fact, I was hoping to look at them tonight."

"The memoirs are forbidden to undergraduates," said the Librarian. "You can read them next year. But, yes, Mistress Wasp wrote that being a sizar gave her a great advantage. She said, 'I have been forged in a hot furnace, my metal is of the strongest proof. Had I been born higher, I would have not striven to rise so high.'"

"Oh," said Mari. "I didn't know."

"There is a portrait of her as a sizar. Not the big painting in the hall with her in lace ruff and cuffs. There was an earlier one that used to hang in the Mistress's Lodge but was lost a century or so ago. Spring cleaning gone awry. But there is a fine plate of it in *Landsby's Colleges of Hallowsbridge.* I'll fetch it down for you."

"Thank you," said Mari, who was rather stunned by this information. She had never imagined that Alicia Wasp, the most famous mistress of the college ever, had been a sizar.

"What else were you wanting?" asked Professor Aiken. "I could get it on the way."

"Ah," said Mari. "Well, I'm . . . I'm looking into the . . . that is . . . how Mistress Wasp and the queen nullified the Original Bylaws. I was hoping to find a reference. . . ."

Her voice trailed off as Professor Aiken leaned in close and looked at her face again.

"Hmmm," said the Librarian. Her pale gray eyes were very sharp behind her half-moon spectacles. "More to this than meets the eye, I see. The Wasp memoirs would be the best resource, as it happens. Though there is some relevant material in some of the court correspondence of Queen Jesmay, which we don't have here, though there is an *almost* complete collection over at Jukes."

"I see," said Mari despondently. "And the memoirs are forbidden to undergraduates?"

Professor Aiken leaned back and took another thumbnail of snuff. Mari looked at her with a hopeful expression, trusting that it was not too spaniel-like to be effective.

"You sit your finals in three weeks, I believe?" asked Professor Aiken.

Mari nodded.

"I thought so. I read your essay on a choir of seven. You know, your foster father was always very helpful to me when I first came here as a junior fellow. . . ."

"Was he?" asked Mari.

"Very helpful. I'll bring you the relevant volume of the memoirs. Sit down."

Mari slid behind a desk and turned on the green-shaded lamp. When the professor had gone, zooming up the circular stair in the corner to the stacks above, she looked at her bracelet. It was very old, and her foster father's mother had given it to his wife, and the Garridges had been porters at the college for generations . . . but surely it couldn't have once belonged to the fabled Alicia Wasp?

Professor Aiken was back in under ten minutes, which was interesting. The stacks occupied four floors above the reading room, and three beneath it, and a book request, even in the daytime when there might be half a dozen Librarians available, often took an hour or more to be delivered.

"There we are. The portrait is the frontispiece of this one, and here is volume six of the Wasp memoirs. The part you need starts on page one hundred and ten, but I would start at one hundred and six for a little more context."

"Thank you, Professor," said Mari. "Thank you very much."

"I wondered why I needed to come here tonight," mused the Librarian. "Sizar ash-face, and Alicia Wasp's bracelet . . . yes, I'm a little slow, but I now realize it's not a copy. Tell me—is that ash the result of the Original Bylaws being invoked?"

"Yes. A fragment, anyway."

"Oh dear," replied Aiken. "I wonder if whoever did it fully comprehends what it means."

"I don't know," said Mari. "Um, what does it mean?"

"I'm not entirely sure myself," replied Aiken. "But I believe there is a good chance that if even part of the Original Bylaws are released, the New Bylaws might be at risk, and the safety of the college . . . What time is it?"

"Half past eight," said Mari. The library clock was behind Professor Aiken.

"We have until midnight, then," said Aiken briskly. "Do you have the fragment?"

"No," said Mari. "I'm . . . I'm going to try and get it."

"Good. Read the memoirs," said Aiken. "I must go and find the chancellor. Pity he won't talk on the phone. Ridiculous superstition, entirely unfound—"

"The chancellor!" exclaimed Mari. Raised in the college, she regarded the involvement of any of the university authorities as a very last resort, and the chancellor . . . well, the less he had to do with the college the better. "Shouldn't you tell the mistress? I mean, I think she's out, but surely—"

"No, I don't think so," replied Professor Aiken firmly. "I really *don't* think so. I'll be off now. Do whatever you can, Miss Garridge. And good luck."

Before Mari could get another word in, the Librarian was striding off, toward the revolving doors that led outside.

"Professor!" she called. "Couldn't you—"

The doors whisked around. The Librarian was gone.

"Couldn't you just take over?" muttered Mari. Somehow everything had got even more complicated, but she wasn't sure what it all meant. What had seemed to be just a petty act of bastardry against her by Diadem was assuming a new dimension. Where had the bone wand come from? Why were the police secretly watching inside the college? Why did the Librarian not want the mistress to know what was going on?

"One thing at a time, Mari," she whispered to herself, echoing her foster father's advice. "Get the fragment, and get it done with."

She opened *Landsby's Colleges of Hallowsbridge* and looked at the tipped-in, hand-colored plate. It showed a young Alicia Wasp standing against the south wall of the kitchen garden. She was wearing a simple muslin dress and had the ash design on her cheeks and the bracelet on her wrist. The inscription on the painting read simply, "A Sizar of Ermine College."

Mari stared at the painting for a long time. Alicia Wasp did not look at all like her. She had straw-colored hair and freckles. But there was something in her eyes, something Mari recognized in herself. Not the color. Alicia's eyes were green, and Mari's so brown they were almost black. It was something else. Determination. An indomitable will.

At least Mari hoped that's what she saw in both sets of eyes.

She closed the Landsby volume, picked up the memoirs, and turned to page 106.

An hour and a half later, she hurried back to the sizars' room, pausing along the way to break off and collect a bundle of hazel twigs from the branches that overhung the path alongside the Scholar's Garden. Outside the room, she knocked and called out who it was, then entered. Francesca was sitting at the one desk that they all shared, cutting a face in the last of thirteen radishes. Twelve others sat upright around the rim of a silver bowl.

"Almost done," she called out. "Did you bring the twigs?"

"Here," replied Mari, dumping them on the desk. "Did you tell Bill?"

"Yes. I told him. But he didn't want to talk, and he practically ordered me back inside."

"You don't seem to mind," said Mari.

"He cares about me," said Francesca proudly. "He was worried."

"We should all be worried," replied Mari. "There's something bad going on here. I mean, really, really bad, not just Diadem making life miserable for a bunch of sizars."

"What do you mean?"

"I'm not entirely certain," replied Mari. "But I think that because part of the Original Bylaws have been invoked, the New Bylaws will cease to work. At midnight tonight."

"Does that matter?" asked Francesca. "I mean, they're mostly about what time the gates are locked, the lights go on, what time breakfast stops and so forth."

"The Bylaws aren't just about the mundane stuff," said Mari. "They also describe the bounds and wards. Without the full Bylaws, original or new, the college is vulnerable to banecraft and . . . summoning."

Francesca's happy look faded. Summoning wasn't *always* banecraft, but it tended to be, because the things that could be summoned were enormously powerful and dangerous. Summoning was not taught to undergraduates and was used only under strict supervision at Cross-Hatch House, the university's most secure laboratory, where summoned creatures could be properly restrained and, if necessary, banished.

"You think *Diadem's* going to summon something?"

"I don't know!" exclaimed Mari. "All I know is that we have to get that fragment back, and we have to get it in the ground under the shadow of the moondial. At midnight, between the chimes of the tower bell."

"And what exactly is the plan?"

Mari knelt down by the desk, selected a hazel twig, and broke it into small pieces. She plucked one of Francesca's red hairs and, taking a longer stick, used the hair to tie the smaller pieces on the end, making a serviceable miniature broom.

"We make the radish girls and brooms lively at quarter to twelve," she said. "We send them to Mo'wood to fly around outside Englesham's window, drawing out Diadem and her cronies. At the same time, we go into Mo'wood on foot, get into Englesham's room, and get the fragment. Then we dash to the moondial, do the incantation—"

"What incantation?"

"Sorry, the spell to nullify the fragment. I got it from Alicia Wasp's memoirs. I've written it out, here—it's only seven words. She was a sizar—"

"What?"

"Yes . . . look, I'll explain later. It must already be half past ten. We do the incantation, bury the fragment between the bell chimes at midnight, and all will be well."

"All will be well!" snorted Francesca. She finished carving the face of the last radish and picked up some twigs to work on another broom. "I suppose we use your keys to get into Mo'wood?

Even though you swore you wouldn't ever again, after that time we were nearly caught in the Dean's office?"

"Yes, we'll use the keys," said Mari. "It's too important not to this time—even if we do get caught."

The keys were a set that properly belonged to the porter of the college and were imbued with magic that was recognized by college locks, as mere mechanical copies of the keys would not be. Mari's foster father had given the set to her with a heavy wink.

"Not in anyone's inventory, these keys," he'd wheezed out. "Don't use them idly, Mari. Keys can turn into trouble, easily enough."

"Jena and Rellise will be back at half past eleven," said Francesca. She plucked one of Mari's hairs and tied off her first broom. "We'd better clear off before then."

"We can wait in the Library Garden," replied Mari. "I want to look at the moondial anyway. We'll launch the radish girls from there, then run through the New House into Mo'wood."

"Why couldn't my stupid father have just saved his money and stopped gambling?" asked Francesca rhetorically. "Other fathers manage it. Then I wouldn't be a damned sizar."

"Like I said, this isn't just a sizar thing now," said Mari. "But would you really want to be just another rich and self-satisfied undergraduate?"

"Yes," said Francesca. "It would be so much easier."

"Alicia Wasp said being a sizar was the greatest advantage she had."

"I bet she never said that when she actually was one," replied Francesca. She tied off another bundle of twigs. "There, that's my six done."

"And my seven," replied Mari. She picked up a radish girl and speared it through the middle with the stick, to make the little vegetable figure look like it was sitting on the broom. Francesca followed suit, and within a few minutes they had the whole lot done and sitting back in the silver bowl, the brush ends in and the radish faces pointing out.

"You take them," said Mari. "I'll get our wands and the keys."

They only had student wands, green wych elm that would not take on much power. But Mari and Francesca had worked hard to make them as puissant as possible, gradually adding rune after rune in the last three years, and impressing them with cantrips and lesser spells. Mari took out her foster father's keys as well. There were only three of them, huge old iron keys on a bronze ring, but one or the other of them would open every door, gate, hatch, or cupboard in the college.

"We should put on our academic gowns," Francesca said. "It might be the last time we get to wear them. And our hats."

Mari paused to think about this, then slowly nodded.

"Yes. You're right. We will be on college business. I hope."

They put down their various objects and slipped on their black academic gowns over their clothes, topping them with the shorter, student version of a graduate witch's two-foot-high pointy hat. The sizars' hats were mostly cardboard and blacking, unlike the sleek velvet of the lady undergraduates' headgear. But from a distance no one could tell.

It was quiet outside as they carefully made their way around the tower. The air was still and cool, and the moon was rising, big and bright and full. Mari and Francesca tried to stay in the shadows, moving swiftly through the occasional pools of bright light from the gas lanterns that hung over the Old House door, the tower gate, the corners of the Foreshortened Court, and outside the library.

It was darker around the back of the library, the light from the windows falling over their heads as they sneaked along the southern wall. The garden itself was darker still, lit only by the dappled moonlight filtering through the leaves of the guardian rowans, their branches thick with late spring leaves and bunches of berries.

The moondial was in a small clearing in the center of the garden. It was a modest thing, merely a rectangular silver plate hung vertically on a thin stone plinth, so that the moonlight fell on its face and the stubby gnomon cast a moonshadow down to the correct hour, indicated by deeply etched numbers that were gilded with fine lines of gold. In addition to the hours, the plate was also etched with a table for calculating the correct time at phases of the moon other than full, and the college's motto ran around the edges. It was in Brythonic, but written in Anglic letters, not Ogham, and was usually translated as "I make women of girls and witches of women."

"Stay here," said Mari to Francesca as they huddled in the shadow by the trunk of one of the larger rowans. "I need to look at the moondial."

Francesca nodded. She was gazing up at the clear night sky, watching for signs of flying witches, and also keeping an eye on the tower clock. It was already twenty-five minutes to twelve.

Mari crept forward, bending low. At the moondial she lay down on her side and pulled her legs up, spreading her gown across her body so that she might blend in with the ground as much as possible. Then she reached out and thrust her fingers into the turf close to the base of the moondial, pulling back the grass and then the dirt beneath, grubbing away until she'd made a hole some ten inches deep and as wide as her hand.

That done, she crawled back to Francesca, who was still staring up at the sky.

"What's up?"

Francesca pointed at the moon. A thin film of red was beginning to spread across its surface, flowing like spilled blood across a smooth tiled floor.

"Potent banecraft," whispered Mari. "Someone's started a summoning already!"

"Shouldn't we make the radish girls lively now?" asked Francesca anxiously.

"Five minutes," said Mari, looking at the tower clock. It was already becoming indistinct, as a strange fog began to spread horizontally across the college, rather than rising from the ground—another indication of most serious banecraft at work. Chill air rolled in front of the fog, making the two young women shiver. "Too early and the radish girls will get picked off, and then Diadem and her cronies will be after us."

It was a long five minutes. The fog grew so thick that they couldn't see the tower clock, and the air grew so cold that frost began to form on the grass and on the trunks of the rowans.

A single chime, muffled by the fog, sounded high above them. It was the quarter hour before midnight.

"Now!" whispered Mari. She held Francesca's hand, and they both bent down to breathe over the radish girls before quickly stepping back. Brandishing their wands, they recited the spell that would make the vegetables and their brooms lively.

The fog stirred as a breeze wafted through the garden. There was a sound like an ancient gate creaking open, and then instead of thirteen carved radishes speared by hazel-twig brooms, there were thirteen witches sitting astride proper broomsticks. Seven of them looked rather like Mari, and six rather like Francesca, though all of them had redder skin and greenish hair.

"Fly to the Miriam Oakenwood Quadrangle, and there play hide-and-seek," instructed Mari and Francesca together.

The witches nodded, pointed their broomsticks, and rose into the air. Mari and Francesca didn't wait to see them take off. They ran through the garden toward the New House, Mari fumbling with her keys for the one that would open the door. New House had no accommodation, as it was all tutorial rooms, so she hoped no one would be inside.

She and Francesca were barely inside the door when they heard the first scream, immediately followed by a police whistle, both coming from the direction of the Miriam Oakenwood Quadrangle. It was answered almost immediately by more whistles, coming from other parts of the college, and the air above.

"Bill!" exclaimed Francesca. She half turned to go back out the door, but Mari grabbed her sleeve.

"No! The best way to help is to get that fragment!"

Together they ran through the New House to the eastern door that led straight into Mo'wood Hall. Mari fumbled the keys there, uncertain which one was needed. As she tried each key, more screams could be heard, and more whistles, and then a horrible sound that was more a sensation, as if the air some-where nearby had been sucked into a void.

"Implosion," said Francesca. "Hurry up, Mari!"

Mari's hands shook as she tried the third key. It turned eas-ily. With a cry of relief, she swung the door open. Francesca ran ahead of her and raced straight for the stairs, her wand held ready. Mari wrestled the key out and followed as quickly as she could.

First-year students were peering out nervously through par-tially opened doors on the top floor as Mari and Francesca ran past.

"Evacuate!" shouted Mari. "Go to your assembly points! This one, Francesca!"

Francesca had run past Englesham's door. She skidded to a stop and turned back. Mari didn't knock. She thrust in a key, turned it, and pushed the door open.

Englesham must have been close up on the other side of the door, because now she was on her knees, awkwardly crouched on her very nice and expensive carpet, her hand going up toward a bleeding nose. Mari gripped her hard by the shoulders and looked around, ready for an attack.

"Where's the fragment?" she shouted.

Englesham started to cry, tears streaming from her eyes to mingle with the blood from her nose.

"Where is it?" Mari shouted again.

Englesham pointed at the sleeve of her nightgown.

Mari felt inside the elasticized wrist. Her fingers tingled as she felt the familiar magic of the fragment. She gripped it tightly and pulled it out.

There was the sound of glass breaking and timber splintering in Englesham's bedroom. Through the half-open door, Mari saw a shadow on the wall, the shadow of a witch throwing a shattered broomstick on the floor.

Francesca saw it, too, and dashed across to slam the door shut. She began to trace the frame with her wand to seal it closed, but even as she did so, the door itself began to froth and bubble like whisked milk, and a terrible stench of decayed flesh filled the room. One of the bubbles popped, making a hole three inches in diameter. Through it, Mari saw a pallid hand holding the bone wand.

"Leave it!" screamed Mari. She let go of Englesham. "Everyone run!"

The three of them were barely out of the room when the door exploded in a sickening gout of rancid matter, bits of it splattering into the hall beyond.

Mari didn't need to repeat her instruction. Englesham ran one direction and Francesca and Mari the other, back the way they'd come. Terrified undergraduates ran with them, and the two sizars had to fight their way through the crush to reach the connecting door to the New House, rather than out to the quadrangle.

They ran through the New House without any thought for silence, heavy boots clattering on the polished wooden floors. There was still a great deal of screaming going on outside, though fewer whistles.

"Almost there!" called Mari as they burst out the other side, down the steps, and into the Library Garden. "Get ready!"

"Get ready for what?" asked a cold voice that came from a

tall, impeccably dressed witch who was just stepping off her hovering broom a dozen paces in front of the moondial.

It was the mistress of the college. Lady Aristhenia.

"Something that must be done, ma'am," answered Mari carefully as she slid to a halt, Francesca cannoning into her back.

"Indeed?" asked Lady Aristhenia. "I will be the judge of that. Ah, Helena. You have been hasty, I see."

Mari looked behind her. Helena Diadem was coming down the steps of the New House, the bone wand in her hand.

"Let me finish them, Aunt," said Diadem. "Please!"

Lady Aristhenia looked at her niece. It was not the look of a fond aunt, but rather that of someone who has found something displeasing in her morning porridge.

"Where are the others?"

Diadem gestured toward Mo'wood. "Distracting the constabulary and the proctors," she said.

"Who should not be here," replied Aristhenia. "And would not be, save for your foolishness. I told you not to use the wand before I needed it."

"I am the heiress, Aunt," replied Diadem stiffly. "The wand is mine to use."

"But you need me to tell you how to use it *properly*," snapped Aristhenia.

Mari slid one foot forward as the two bickered, hoping they were sufficiently distracted to not notice. Francesca slithered a little to the side, her own wand slipping out of her sleeve into her hand.

"I know how to use it," said Diadem. "It's in my blood. You only married into the family—"

"Don't talk nonsense!" barked Aristhenia. "We haven't got time. The summoning must be made complete. Give me the wand."

"When I've done these two," said Diadem. She turned toward Francesca and raised the bone wand.

In the fog above, the tower clock chimed the first of the twelve strokes of midnight.

Mari screamed a word of power and threw the heavy bunch of keys at Diadem, at the same time diving toward the moondial, while Francesca flung herself behind a rowan.

Diadem's curse struck the tree. Its leaves all fell at once, like a truckload of mulch being dumped, and the bark on its trunk curled and withered. Any lesser tree would have crumbled into dust, but the rowans of the Library Garden were ancient and very strong.

Even as the leaves fell, the bunch of keys hit Diadem on the face. One of them stuck there, the ensorcelled metal suddenly red-hot. The bane-witch screamed, dropped the wand, and tried to pull the burning key from her flesh.

"Idiot!" said Aristhenia. In two quick strides she was at Diadem's side. She snatched up the wand from the ground and gestured with it. The key flew off the younger witch's face, leaving a ghastly brand on her cheek. Diadem fell to the ground, whimpering, little wisps of smoke rising from her ruined face.

Mari reached the hole she'd made. She stuffed the parchment in it and was about to open her mouth to speak the incantation when she was caught in the grip of a geas even more powerful than the one Diadem had used on her before.

"Judicious application of power is to be preferred," said

Aristhenia. She jerked the wand, and Mari found herself standing up as the tower clock struck for the third time. "The wand may prefer the traditional banecraft, with all its gore and foulness. I do not."

Mari couldn't move anything except her eyes. She looked down at her wrist. Surely Alicia Wasp's bracelet would do something now to protect her from this dread magic?

Aristhenia saw her looking, and smiled.

"It's only a silver bracelet. Even if it was once owned by the fabled—"

Whatever she was going to say was lost in the loud report of close gunshots, as Bill suddenly dropped down from the sky behind her, a flying cloak whipping around his shoulders, a service revolver in his hand. He fired three times, the first bullet silver, the second petrified wood, and the third lead reclaimed from the gutter of a house where wizards had lived for more than a hundred years.

None of them had any effect. They went into and through Aristhenia, sure enough, and gaping wounds opened—but no blood came out. Instead a pale fire flickered behind the holes in her clothes.

It was a very unwelcome sign that whatever was being summoned had already mostly arrived and taken up residence . . . inside the mistress of the college.

But the bullets did have one small positive side effect. As the clock struck its ninth, or possibly tenth, chime, Mari turned her head to listen and found she could move again.

Aristhenia turned around toward Bill and raised the dreadful wand.

"Run!" screamed Francesca to Bill. She ran out from behind her tree and dived to the moondial, taking Mari's outstretched hand. Bill's cloak flapped as he leaped up into the air, as Aristhenia's curse flew like an arrow, passing a finger's-breadth beneath the silver hobnails on the soles of his size eleven police boots.

Together, Mari and Francesca said the words. They were in Brythonic. In translation they said something like: "Rest you here, under the moon. If you wake it will be too soon."

The parchment sank into the earth and was gone. A fierce wind suddenly blew across the college, wrapping up the fog and rolling it away. The bloody haze on the face of the moon vanished, wiped clean by an unseen cosmic hand.

"Interfering brats!" shrieked Aristhenia. She swiveled back toward Mari and Francesca, who were crouched by the moondial. In that second, all three of them were caught in the moment of the clock's twelfth and final chime.

The bone wand shivered in the mistress's hand. She spat out a sound, but the word faltered in her mouth, and was never completed. Her fingers came unstrung, and the wand fell to the grass as the last echo of the chime faded into the night.

The Original Bylaws were once again made naught, and the New Bylaws sprang back into force with renewed vigor.

Lady Aristhenia looked down at herself and saw the blood gushing from the wounds in her chest and stomach. She took a step toward the moondial, crumpled forward, and fell facedown in front of the two trembling sizars.

There was a flurry in the air above, and half a dozen proctors in flying cloaks plummeted down, silvered swords in hand. They were followed by a large, bearlike man in a red and gold dressing gown over blue striped pajamas that had the university coat of arms on the pocket. He was sitting in a well-upholstered armchair that landed with a heavy thump on the lawn, to be followed a moment later by Professor Aiken coming to a sliding stop on a broom.

The Chancellor had a saucer and a cup of tea in one hand, with most of the tea slopped in the saucer, and he looked extremely irritated until he saw the body of Lady Aristhenia and the bone wand lying near her lifeless body.

"Hmmm. That old stick up to its tricks again," he muttered. He got out of his chair, handed his teacup to the air, where it stayed, and took a handkerchief out of his dressing gown pocket. He laid this over the bone wand, drew his own, silver-inlaid ebony wand out of his sleeve, and tapped the handkerchief twice. When he picked up the handkerchief and stuffed it back in his pocket, the wand had vanished.

"That'll hold it till morning," he said. He touched the body of Lady Aristhenia with the toe of his dun-colored, fleece-lined slipper and sniffed. "Whom did she invite in, then?"

"One of the dwellers of the most far regions," replied Professor Aiken, peering at the corpse through her half-moon glasses. "I suspect her niece will know which one. Fortunately it couldn't manifest entirely, thanks to Miss Garridge and her friend restoring the New Bylaws."

"Mmm. Yes, well done, you two," said the Chancellor, smiling and nodding at Mari and Francesca. "Grand tradition of Mistress Wasp and all that. Expect nothing less from an Ermine sizar."

"You'd better take over here as temporary mistress, Joan," he said to Professor Aiken. He indicated Diadem, who was curled up in a ball, pallid with shock, and added to the nearest proctor, "Take her to the Infirmary, but keep her under guard. I expect the police will want to talk to her in the morning."

"Yes, sir, we will," said Bill, from the top of one of the rowans. He was untangling himself from his flying cloak. Its trailing edge had been caught by the curse, and the whole garment was being eaten away by a rapidly spreading and highly unpleasant mold.

"Bill!" exclaimed Francesca, letting go of Mari's hand to run to him. He fell from the tree as she reached the trunk, and they embraced tightly before Bill remembered he was on duty and gently pushed her away.

Mari smiled at them and pulled herself upright, using the moondial's pillar as a support. Everyone seemed to have forgotten her. The Chancellor was talking to Professor Aiken; the proctors were picking up Diadem and clustering around in a guarding-the-scene-of-the-crime-long-after-it-was-necessary kind of way; Bill was taking out his notebook to write something while Francesca clung to his arm; several other policemen were dragging in Lannisa and Clairmore, both of them handcuffed; and large numbers of scared-looking undergraduates in a bewildering assortment of sleeping garments were filtering in from the New House and the Mo'wood quadrangle.

Because we swapped duty with Jena and Rellise, I'll be doing breakfast in five hours, thought Mari. She sighed and was about to go and pick up her keys—before anyone in authority wondered exactly whose they were, she hoped—when she felt someone lightly touch her wrist, just next to her bracelet.

She turned and saw Alicia Wasp, the young woman of the sizar portrait, not the older mistress of the college from the portrait in the Great Hall.

"It is quite true that had I been born higher, I would not have striven to rise so high," said Alicia Wasp. "However, I forgot to say that you have to *make* being a sizar an advantage. Never just accept your lot, Mari. And thank you, for my college."

Mari nodded, and then blinked, because Alicia Wasp wasn't there anymore and, as no one else had noticed her, possibly hadn't been there in the first place.

"Never accept your lot," whispered Mari to herself as she briskly walked over and picked up her keys. Then she positioned herself in front of the Chancellor and Professor Aiken and waited for a break in their conversation, which came quite soon as they both turned politely toward her.

"I beg your pardon, Mistress Aiken," said the Sizar Mari Garridge. "But I wondered if, on account of all that's been done tonight, Francesca and I might have a holiday tomorrow . . . that is, today? I believe that Jena and Rellise will most *happily* fulfill our duties."

LITTLE GODS

HOLLY BLACK

WHEN ELLERY WAS little, her grandmother would take her to church on Sundays. Even though Ellery's parents had long ago given up on religion, her grandmother said that was no excuse for raising their child to be a little heathen. It had probably been easier to give in than to argue. Ellery hadn't minded going anyway, even though the sermons could get boring. She liked the songs and the hats; she liked the talk of water turning to wine and fishes turning into more fishes. Most of all she liked to listen to a bunch of grown-ups talk about eternal souls as though souls were real things that people could have and not pretend magic stuff, like rainbow-colored unicorns or webs that shot from your wrists.

Ellery would look at the statues of saints and angels and imagine that they had souls. She imagined so hard that she could almost see them coming to life and stepping down from their pedestals. They would join in one of the songs, their voices soaring higher than human voices could. They would wade into the pews, and their eyes would be golden and their smiles would curl up at the corners. Their wings would spread so wide that every-thing would be shadowed in a canopy of feathers.

Sometimes it seemed so real that she was tensed for it to hap-pen. But it never did.

Ellery looked out the window at the empty street. Then she kicked her duffel bag closer to her with the side of one sandaled foot, so that she could run her hand over the army green fab-ric and reassure herself that everything she needed was inside. Robes. Athame. Clean underwear. Body wash that doubled as shampoo. A couple of t-shirts and a cotton dress. Her Book of Shadows and a couple of gel pens.

"They're late," Mom said. "Don't you think you should call and make sure nothing happened?"

"Bob operates on Pagan Standard Time," Ellery said, telling a joke she'd heard many times at the Unitarian church where her coven met. No one arrived when they were supposed to, and then once they got there, everyone took another ten minutes to bring in cookies or make coffee in the church coffeepot. Then there would be gossip, and before you knew it, an hour had gone by, and then another. Finally, two hours after schedule, they would start to perform the ceremony.

But once they did, they were witches. Real witches.

Mom didn't laugh. The joke probably didn't even make sense to her.

Ellery sighed. Everyone else in her coven was older than she was, so they could be late if they wanted. All their time was their own. They didn't have to deal with parents asking a million questions about the farm they were headed out to, about the girl

Ellery was going to be sharing a tent with, and about whether Ellery was sure she wasn't going to accidentally join a cult.

"I'm not saying Wicca is a cult," her father had informed her as he pushed around his lima beans the night before. "I'm just saying that there are people in every religion eager to take advantage of the disenfranchised and discontented."

Ellery had groaned. "Bob and Cheryl aren't disenfranchised. She's a lawyer and he fixes computers."

"I didn't mean them," her father had said. "I meant strangers."

"They're all people the rest of the coven knows," Ellery had told him. "No strangers."

"Are there going to be any other kids?" her mother had asked. "Anyone your age?"

Ellery had shrugged, trying to hide her nervous eagerness that she was going to be spending a weekend in a magical place, with magical people. "I think so."

Mom and Dad had shared a look. They prided themselves on being liberal parents, identifying with the free-range-kids movement. They allowed Ellery to read whatever books she wanted, to pick the movies she saw based on her own tastes. They trusted her. Or at least they said they trusted her, but she could tell that the only reason they didn't forbid her to go to Beltane at Greenstone Farm was that it would make them look like total hypocrites.

Ellery was tired of being a kid. Underneath her skin, a lot of the time, she felt ancient and mysterious and terrible—but on the outside she was only sixteen. Even at coven meetings, it was hard for her to prove her inner maturity. The other members talked about movies they'd seen and books they'd read, some of which she'd never even heard about. And they talked about people from festivals and workshops and Sabbats—people Ellery had never met. *Silver Raven makes the best mead. Andrew gave such a great talk about chakras. Lorelei is getting so much better with the harp—and wasn't it a beautiful instrument, carved for her by one of her sweeties, using wood from a tree that'd been struck by lightning?*

But this weekend would change all that. Ellery would get to know the same people; the next time they told stories, she'd have been there for the origins of them; she'd be able to laugh at the same jokes.

"Maybe I should take my stuff to the porch," Ellery said. She just wanted to do *something*. She felt restless, itchy with the urge to be in motion, to already be gone from the house and on her way to adventure. Her mother's worrying just made everything worse.

What if they've forgotten me? What if they don't want me to come and they forget me accidentally on purpose? What if they decide not to go? What if the date was changed at the last minute and no one bothered to call?

The dates couldn't be changed, Ellery reminded herself sternly. The Sabbat was tonight. *Tonight.*

"They're here, sweetheart," Mom said. She didn't sound happy, but Ellery didn't care. She looked out the window at the white van idling at the end of her lawn, just to be sure that it really was them. Then she sprang into motion, jumping up with a yelp of joy, throwing her duffel bag over her shoulder, and reaching for her purse.

Her mother grabbed for the duffel, too. "Do you want me to carry anything?"

"Nope. I'm good!" Ellery said it fast, a blur of movement, kissing her mother on the cheek and heading for the door. "Bye!"

As Ellery crossed the lawn, she saw Dawn get out from the open van door, wearing a dress made from patchwork pieces of velvet. Her hair fell down her back in bright blond ribbons, with a couple of small braids bound with fringed leather pieces and a macaw feather.

"Merry meet!" Dawn yelled, and threw her arms around Ellery.

Dawn was twenty and attended community college, studying anthropology. She worked at a bird store part-time and seemed happier than anyone else Ellery knew. Sometimes Ellery wondered if that was because Dawn was also prettier than anyone else Ellery knew. She had bottle-green eyes, enviably long eyelashes, and a tiny mouth.

Dawn hopped into the van and helped Ellery heave her duffel into an unoccupied space. Alastair was already in the back. He was about Dawn's age and Scottish, with a hot accent. He was always dressed in a long leather trench coat—even in summer—and wore fake fangs constantly. Mostly he made snarky jokes, but from the way he looked at Dawn, Ellery could tell that he was thinking about her in the most nonsarcastic way.

Jennifer Shadowdancer was there, too, way in the back, playing with her phone. She was a dental assistant, just out of school. She had a huge collection of Barbies that she'd shown the rest of the coven when they came over for a full-moon ritual. She wore a lot of t-shirts with cats or dolphins on them. Alastair called her

Stepford Pagan under his breath when she was out of earshot. It made Ellery laugh when he did that, even though she was pretty sure he had an equally cruel name for her.

Bob and Cheryl—the priest and priestess of the coven—were sitting in the front seat. Cheryl grinned at Ellery while Bob mumbled hello. Bob was a huge older guy with a big laugh and a bigger red beard. Right then he was wearing a green poet shirt with a piece of antler on a cord around his neck.

The inside of the car smelled like cheese curls and feet. On the dashboard, underneath the GPS, was a Hot Wheels version of the same van they were in, but this one had googly eyes pasted over the headlights and multicolored gems stuck over the wheel hubs. A heavy-looking bag swung from the rearview mirror.

"I'm so glad you could come," Cheryl said, pushing her glasses high on her nose. "But are you sure that you're ready for Beltane?"

"Totally sure." Ellery had never gone on a trip like this—and she had no idea what to expect. But she knew what she wanted. Magic.

Alastair piped up from the backseat. "Afraid her tender eyes will alight on that which will scar her forever? A thing so horrifying that it's practically indescribable? People have been struck blind. That's right, I speak of Bob . . . skyclad."

"You can walk, you know. I leave you here and it's only three hundred miles to the farm," Bob said. Ellery thought he was kidding, but she couldn't be totally sure.

"What's that?" She leaned halfway into the front seat and pointed to the dash, hoping to change the subject.

"Salt." He touched the bag. "Purifies. Keeps away the evil spirits that might want us to break down or get a flat tire."

"I mean the toy van," Ellery said.

"Oh, *Blanche*. That's what I call her. She's the spirit of the vehicle you're in right now—a genius loci. And she's all decked out to please Hermes, the god of the roads. There's your little gods and your big gods, and a wise man pays tribute to both. Like, before I go on any big trip, I always burn a little bit of incense for Blanche."

Ellery nodded.

Bob smiled. "Bonus that it covers up some of Alastair's stink."

Alastair made a rude noise. Jennifer shushed him.

"And I always leave out a bowl of milk for the spirits so they'll look after my house," Bob went on. "The local stray cats probably like it, too, but I don't think that's so bad. And when I get to a hotel room, I light a candle for the spirits that live there. There's spirits in everything."

When Ellery first got into Wicca, she'd discovered the Buckland and Cunningham books. She'd pored over basic dedication and initiation rituals. She'd made an altar in her room with a pewter goblet from a yard sale, two white candles from her mother's candle drawer, some incense, and a piece of quartz. She'd tried to meditate and concentrate and focus. It had reminded her of being in church with her grandmother, of holding her breath, waiting for something to happen. Except this time it had.

There were spells. Spells to open her third eye and to take away her jealousy for girls at school whose clothes always looked perfectly pressed, spells to help her find her cell phone, and spells to bring new friends into her life.

Three days after she cast the one about friends, she saw a sign hanging in the window of the New Age bookshop. A coven was looking for new members. They met on Wednesdays at the Unitarian church across town.

Magic.

The first time she'd gone, Ellery had felt skin-itchingly awkward. Everyone seemed to already know everyone else, except for her and Alastair. Alastair had just sulked near the coffee-pot, so it wasn't as if he made her feel any better. And when Bob finally called the coven to order and got her to introduce herself, he didn't seem to know what to do with an underage member. Ellery wasn't sure they wanted her to stay, but she stayed anyway.

She stayed because sometimes, when they called the corners, she felt as though some power vast enough to ruffle the leaves of all the trees in a forest had for a moment paused to take notice of her. She stayed because on the walk home from Kingston High School she could look at the surface of the stream that ran behind it and remember a story that Jennifer told about seeing an actual water spirit leaping into the air off the coast of Block Island. She stayed because she didn't know what she was doing and they all acted like they did.

"Can we listen to something else? My ears are bleeding," Alastair whined as Bob pulled onto the highway. He wasn't a fan of world music, certainly not the kind currently blasting from the stereo—harp music accompanied by someone singing about faeries dancing.

"It's getting us in the mood to worship the goddess," Jennifer

Shadowdancer said, using her most lecture-y voice. "Beltane is the very middle of spring and sacred to the fey."

Ellery decided it must be Jennifer's iPod they were listening to.

They argued some more as Ellery looked out the window and let her eyes unfocus, so it was all a blur of bright green grass and new leaves. Spring made the air sweet. She let happiness wash over her. She was going to Beltane! *She,* plain old regular Ellery, who once won the spelling bee by knowing the word *taupe.* Who still mailed long letters in purple ink to her best friend, Claire, even though Claire had moved away a year ago and didn't always write back. Whose favorite food was tacos. She was going to Beltane, and she was going to transform into the person she'd always thought she could be. She would come home changed.

They drove for half an hour with Dawn and Cheryl debating which version of the Doctor from *Doctor Who* was the best, before Bob pulled the van into a rest stop.

Ellery climbed out, stretching her arms over her head and yawning. She wanted to ask if they were almost there, but it seemed like something a little kid would ask and she wanted to seem grown-up, so she didn't say anything.

The parking lot was washed in a sea of pink dogwood blossoms.

"It's springtime, motherfuckers," Alastair said, and everyone but Jennifer laughed. She made a face.

As everyone got in line to buy burgers at McDonald's or pizza at Sbarro, Ellery realized she only had twenty-three dollars for the whole weekend and probably couldn't afford to eat. Cheryl had told her there would be food at Greenstone Farm, which she was counting on. But given how overpriced everything was, if she ate now and then had to pay for dinner later, she would be broke. A rest-stop apple cost two bucks. Ellery bought a single cup of coffee, added three creamers, and drank it slowly. She'd read in some teen magazine that coffee would kill hunger—it was on a list of dieting tricks—but she didn't think it was working. She just felt hungry and jumpy.

Then they climbed back into the van.

After a couple of hours, despite the caffeine, Ellery fell asleep listening to a ballad about a witch who lived by a winding mere and rose from a lake half woman and half jet-black mare. Ellery woke when her head knocked against the glass window. They must have hit a pothole.

It was dark outside.

Dawn and Cheryl were asleep in the seats behind her. Alastair was playing on his DS, its glow giving an eerie cast to his face, and Jennifer was knitting in the dark, her needles shining as they clacked together as if she were a fairy-tale witch. The kind who made houses out of candy. The kind who ate you up.

The van pulled onto a dirt road with forest on either side.

"Are we there?" Ellery whispered, leaning forward.

"Yep," Bob said in a low voice. "This is it. Greenstone Farm." He pointed vaguely out into the night. "The place is owned by Thomas Holden, who used to be a big-shot music executive. But after he hooked up with Dragonsong, he let us throw Sabbat parties. Apparently a local coven even comes here for the Esbats."

"Who's Dragonsong?" Ellery asked him. Her stomach growled.

He gave her a crooked smile. "My ex. A real piece of work,

but she's got something." He laughed. "Pheromones. Love spells. I don't know. Men fall head over heels in love with her. Give her whatever she wants."

Ellery had no idea what to say to that, but before she figured it out, they came to a stretch of dirt with a lot of other cars parked there. Everyone started waking up and rummaging around for their stuff. A bonfire burned off in the distance, and she could hear some off-key singing.

"I have to pee so bad," said Dawn, jumping out.

Yawning, Ellery and the rest of them got out more slowly and started unloading the tents and other stuff. There were already a dozen or more tents—a few medieval-looking, most nylon—erected outside an old red barn, light glowing from its windows. The other covens were obviously ahead of them. Ellery's stomach growled.

"We can come back and finish unpacking later," Cheryl said, checking her watch. "Let's go inside and say hello."

"You go ahead," Bob told her, struggling with pushing a spike into the dirt. "Take the kids."

Ellery wanted to go inside so badly that she didn't even mind that he'd called her a kid. She grinned over at Alastair and he smiled back, leaning close enough to whisper to her in accented tones, "You won't *believe* some of the characters you're about to meet."

Which was pretty rich coming from a guy wearing fangs, but right then she was enjoying feeling conspiratorial.

Inside the barn was exactly how Ellery dreamed it would be. There were makeshift tables covered in batik and velvet cloths and piled with cheese, grapes, oranges, olives, bread, traditional

Sabbat oatcakes, and a few supermarket rotisserie chickens. There were cartons of cider, bottles of beer, and a lot of home-made mead. The food was delicious. Ellery stuffed herself.

Everyone was friendly—and fascinating. There was a white-haired crone wearing a silver circlet with a crescent moon on it, a younger man with a long waxed mustache and a brown leather vest, a girl in a belly-dancing costume covered with wide golden beads. There were lots of other people, too, young and old, most of them in the standard pagan uniform of black t-shirt, black jeans, boots, and pewter figural jewelry.

Ellery couldn't stop staring. She had a million questions threatening to come blurting out of her mouth. How had they first discovered magic? How did they know they had power? What spells had they done? Had they seen something that was undeniably proof that there were gods and goddesses and nature spirits? Was it all real?

Ellery wanted it to be real. She wanted to *know* it was real more than she had ever wanted anything in her life.

She was here as a member of her coven, as a practitioner—she couldn't ask if it was real. That would be like saying she didn't believe. And that wasn't true. Not exactly. But there was a difference between believing and knowing. Ellery believed. But she wanted to *know.*

"The ceremony will be at midnight," the white-haired woman said. "If anyone needs to meditate, now would be a good time."

Ellery went to find Dawn. She was near the bathroom, look-ing oddly subdued.

"We should finish pitching our tent," she said. "Before it gets too late."

Dawn nodded. "Yeah, before everyone gets drunk." There was a catch in her voice.

Ellery looked at her, not sure if she'd heard right. Normally Dawn seemed to float along on her own private happy cloud. They walked across the grass in silence.

"Sorry," Dawn said finally, picking up one of the spines of the tent and threading it through the cloth. "I had a bad Ostara here—no, that's not right, I *thought* I had had a *great* Ostara. But now . . . I guess I didn't."

"What happened?"

Dawn smiled at Ellery a little sadly. "I made out with two friends of mine—Chloe and Bill. It was really beautiful and innocent, you know? They invited me back to their tent and we told each other that we respected each other as people and would never let jealousy hurt any of our relationships. But I just saw Chloe on the way to the bathroom and she said that she and Bill broke up. Because of that. Because of me. Now I feel awful and I don't know if I can—" She broke off and started jamming the other spine into the tent cloth.

"I'm sorry," Ellery said. She didn't feel adequate to the task of saying the right thing. She had only made out with three boys. One had even been her boyfriend for a while, but he'd broken up with her because she made a comment about how he always got food stuck in his braces. "It wasn't your fault."

"*Yeah,*" Dawn said, in that sad way that means the opposite. They put up the tent, while Dawn told Ellery about the other people at the gathering. There was Tom, who was very handsome, with a string of beautiful girlfriends, but who made out exclusively with boys when he was drunk. There was a woman about Ellery's mom's age, Regina, who was dating Peter, who was her daughter's age. In fact, they'd met through the daughter, Tanya, who was also at the Sabbat. Then there were Rosie and her two boyfriends, Brandon and Arthur. Ellery tried to remember all the names, but after a while they just rolled over her—stories about people she didn't know and might not ever know. She felt as much of an outsider as ever.

She leaned down to unzip her duffel and realized she'd forgotten to bring a couple of really important things. Like a sleeping bag. Or a pillow. Or even a blanket. She was going to *freeze*. And the worst part was that Dawn was going to think she was a kid after all. An irresponsible kid.

"You okay?" Dawn was looking at her.

"Yeah. I was listening. Are they the people you kissed?" Ellery asked.

Dawn laughed for the first time as she unrolled her sleeping bag. "No, that was Chloe and Bill. Sorry. I guess I'm just blathering on and on. You must be bored to death."

"Nothing about tonight is boring," Ellery said, and meant it.

"Ladies! Stop your dawdling and endless primping!" Alastair's voice floated in from outside the tent. "Opening ceremony's starting."

Dawn rolled her eyes, brushed off her skirt, and swung her hair back from her face. Ellery scrambled for her robe.

They rushed across the tiki-torch-lit meadow to a grove circled in stones. Most everyone was already there, forming a second circle within. Alastair gave Ellery a smirk and waggled his eyebrows.

"What?" she whispered.

"Look who's conducting the ceremony," he said. "Wonder if he still wants to put his maypole in her cauldron."

"Shut *up*," Ellery told him under her breath, but she guessed what he meant.

The white-haired lady with the circlet was standing at the center of the circle, beside Bob. Given Alastair's snickering, she must be Dragonsong. There was a huge stone near them, draped with a white cloth and serving as an altar. It was amazing—like something out of a movie. The few torches burning at the edges of what Ellery could see made everyone look sinister and beautiful in their glow. She felt as though she was outside time, as though they were no longer in the world of van rides and fast food and homework.

Four people Ellery didn't know called the corners, hailing each in turn.

The white-haired woman invoked the goddess, lighting a fat white candle that flickered ominously in the breeze. "Threefold Goddess, Spring Maiden, Lady of Light, come to this Beltane ritual! Roll on our grass and bless our cup!"

Bob lit a second candle. Even though Ellery had seen him be the high priest many times, this time felt different. His deep voice boomed. "Horned God, Sun King, Lord of Light, come to this Beltane ritual! Roll on our grass and bless our wand!"

"Spirits of the trees, of the land, of the rocks, rise up and dance with us," the priestess said. "This Sabbat celebrates life— celebrates the approach of summer and the sweet ripeness of lust, fertility, and love. Let us welcome Beltane into our hearts and welcome the spirits to our table."

The priestess—Dragonsong—took a pitcher from the altar and poured a thin stream of golden fluid into a goblet. Then she poured a little onto the dirt.

"This liquid is the blessing of the goddess. Drink deeply and thirst no more."

"So mote it be," Ellery chorused with the others.

The priestess put the goblet into the hand of the girl who had hailed the guardians of the watchtowers of the east. She took a sip and passed it widdershins.

The priest lifted a plate of what looked like small pancakes. "This food is the blessing of the god. Eat and be hungry no more."

"So mote it be," they said, all together.

Bob crumbled one of the pancakes in his hand and let the pieces fall into the dirt. Then the plate was passed to the person who had called the guardians of the west.

The drink, when it came to Ellery, turned out to be apple juice. And the cakes were basically the same oatcakes she'd eaten inside, only colder and harder. But both, in her mouth, seemed changed from their original state. The wind rose, blowing her hair around her face. The feeling that she was doing something true and real washed over her with a quiet certainty she had never felt before.

"Merry meet, merry part, and merry meet again." At the priestess's words, everyone relaxed into laughter and hugs.

The man with the waxed mustache drank the rest of the contents of the goblet. A boy grabbed one of the torches and people started to follow him into the wood.

Ellery couldn't stop smiling.

Someone lit a bonfire and someone else had blankets to sit on. A few witches said their good-nights and headed back toward the tents. Cheryl signaled for Ellery to come over and share her spot, near several older ladies. The high priestess was one of them.

"So this is your new initiate," the white-haired woman said.

The heady smell of marijuana smoke floated through the grove.

"Ellery," Ellery said, glancing toward a group of young witches passing a joint around the way they'd passed the apple juice. Alastair was with them, laughing.

"I'm Dragonsong," the woman said. "This is my farm."

"It's beautiful," Ellery told her, entirely sincerely. The woman didn't look like a seductress. She looked like someone's grandmother.

Cheryl touched Ellery's hair. "And we're taking good care of her."

"What did you think of the ceremony?" another of the women inquired.

"Beautiful," Ellery said again, before she realized that saying the same word over and over made her seem a little dazed.

The women laughed.

Dragonsong leaned in. "I can tell by your aura—very bright, very clear, lots of turquoise and purple energy—that you're very spiritually advanced. You've had many lives. You're destined to be a very important priestess someday."

Ellery smiled, but something about the words she'd longed to hear didn't feel right. The woman seemed bored, like she'd told a hundred girls the same thing and they'd all been just as flattered. It reminded her of her grandmother's friends coming over to her after church, pinching her cheeks, and telling her how pretty she was going to be when she grew up.

"Come dance!" Ellery looked up to see Dawn spinning around the fire along with the girl in the belly-dancing outfit and a cute shirtless boy with bare feet and loose pants. They were whirling happily. The boy took a long pull from a green bottle and hopped, laughing.

A boy came up out of the shadow, holding a milk crate full of bottles. Dawn stumbled, nearly falling into the fire.

Half rising, Ellery asked Cheryl, "Who is that?"

"He's our resident brewmaster, Bill."

He *was* cute, his brown hair flopping over one eye and the muscles in his arms evident. *Chloe and Bill,* Dawn had said. It must be him.

Ellery jumped up, dancing her way to Dawn to see if she was okay, just as people crowded around Bill to sample whatever he had in the bottles.

"Stay," Dawn said, dragging Ellery closer to the fire and pulling her into the whirling dance. Spinning made Ellery dizzy and the heat of the flames made her skin feel like it was glowing. A few more of the older witches started back to the tents.

A girl took off her top and jumped up to dance, too. She looked like a wood nymph, but it still shocked Ellery.

"She's naked," Ellery gasped, and Dawn slowed down enough to laugh.

"*Skyclad,*" Dawn said, and paused in the dance enough to

pull her own top off, so she was stripped down to her bra and skirt. "Don't be embarrassed. It's natural."

The girl in the belly-dancing outfit took off her spangled top and threw it at a laughing boy. Ellery had seen girls half naked before, changing for gym class. But here it was hard not to look and hard not to feel weird about looking.

After the magnificence of the ceremony, all of this seemed so . . . like a house party. Like no one really cared about the circle—that was just the prelude to a night of getting drunk and hooking up. Like maybe they hadn't felt what she'd felt. Like what she'd felt hadn't been real.

She could just picture Alastair sneering from the shadows, nursing his beer. Or her parents shaking their heads at the sad people in the woods who pretended they had magic powers, who pretended that the indifferent universe stopped to listen to them.

She thought of herself in the church with her grandmother, waiting for the statues to move.

Ellery reeled away from the fire, the mood broken. She felt too warm and thirsty, but all she could find were random half-full bottles, most of them marked as wine or mead. Finally she saw a water bottle abandoned on a batik blanket. She unscrewed the cap and took a sip. It turned out not to be filled with water at all. Strong alcohol filled her mouth and seared all the way down her throat. She started coughing and couldn't seem to stop.

"Are you okay?" a boy said, slapping her between the shoulder blades.

"Water," she gasped.

He scrambled around a bit and came up with a plastic jug of apple juice. She took a swig and finally was able to breathe again.

"I'm Aspen," he said.

"Ellery," she told him, finally seeing him for the first time. By the flickering light of the fire, she couldn't quite tell the color of his eyes. Sometimes they seemed gold and other times they were the color of water. He had a kind face, though. Handsome, too, with short dark hair and a soft, full mouth.

She didn't remember him from the circle or from the kitchen. Maybe he'd gotten to the farm even later than her coven had. She was sure she would have noticed him—he was wearing an open greenish shirt with a necklace of filigreed silver leaves around his throat. He was very noticeable.

"Is this your first time at the farm?" he asked, taking a sip from the bottle of booze and making a face after he swallowed.

"I think that's basically moonshine," Ellery said. "It's probably going to eat through the plastic. Or your stomach."

"A poor offering," he told her, but took another sip anyway. His voice was light and made her think of rustling leaves.

"But yeah, it's my first Beltane here," she said. "My first anything here. I'm part of Bob and Cheryl's coven. A new initiate."

"And how are you finding it?"

She looked around and sighed. "I don't know. It's not what I thought it would be."

"Beltane is the celebration of passion." He glanced over at the people dancing around the fire. "Of yearning and desire. If you want something enough, tonight you might be able to have it."

He probably thought that she was upset that there were naked people. She started to stand.

The boy was still staring at the fire, his expression abstracted. "There are special Beltane rituals—"

"I just bet there are," she said. "*Smooth,* cute witch boy."

He had the good grace to look embarrassed. "Come on, that's not what I meant. Sit back down. I mean rituals—like, well, like you're supposed to wash your face with morning dew for luck, health, and beauty. And if you jump the Beltane fire you can make a wish."

"None of that's real," Ellery said. She took the bottle of moonshine out of his hands and took a drink. It burned down her throat, but this time she expected it and didn't choke. "But it is the holiday of intoxication, so I am observing that."

"What would you wish for?"

"I guess for there to *be* wishes," Ellery said, tilting her head up so that she could look at the stars instead of at his face. It felt shameful to confess. She felt tears prick the back of her eyes. She blinked twice and hoped he wouldn't notice. "I wish something was listening."

"*I'm* listening," Aspen said, his beautiful mouth curving into a smile.

She laughed. The liquor was finally hitting her blood, making her feel warm and liquid. "Other than you."

He took off his necklace. The leaves clinked together lightly. "Since you wouldn't wish for anything I can give you, how about you hold on to this for a while?"

"That's yours," Ellery said. "I can't—"

"Let me make my own offering," he said, clasping it around her throat. The silver leaves felt cool against her skin. "You can give it back to me someday."

She half turned to tell Aspen how nice he was being, even though she suspected that he wasn't being nice so much as hitting on her, when Alastair staggered up to her, one arm around a blond-haired boy.

"You've been over here talking to yourself," he said drunkenly. "Cheryl's worried. She thinks that you've been exposed to impure things and are hiding to protect the tattered remains of your innocence."

"I'm not alone," she said, whirling. But there was no brown-haired witch boy sitting next to her on the blanket. Aspen was gone.

Gone like he was never a boy at all.

She reached up to touch the necklace and felt cool metal. Maybe it was made from moonlight and smoke and would blow away in a moment, but right then it seemed solid under her fingers.

Ellery traced the shape of the individual leaves with awe.

"Well, you're not alone now," Alastair said. "Will you accompany us for a walk, far away from this debauchery? We will escort you, like filthy-minded knights-errant."

Ellery stood up. "I found some very bad booze." She glanced toward the shadowed trees.

"Perfect," the blond boy said. "It can escort you, too. I'm Tom, by the way." He touched his fingers to his brow in a motion that was half salute and half bow. She remembered him from Dawn's stories. He was the one who liked boys when he was drunk.

"Oh! Are you sure you don't want to be by yourselves?" Ellery blurted out. As soon as she said it, she wished she hadn't.

As far as she knew, Alastair liked girls—she'd thought he liked Dawn—and maybe Tom didn't want to admit he liked boys, and maybe they were just hanging on one another because they were too drunk to stay upright otherwise.

Tom laughed, though.

"We are all complicated creatures," Alastair said, pulling her to her feet. He was smiling, too. "With complicated desires."

She wanted to tell them about the boy and the necklace, but she also wanted it to be her secret. They might not believe her. And if they didn't, she might start doubting it as well.

But maybe Alastair was right. Maybe everything was complicated. Maybe it was okay to sometimes believe and sometimes not be sure. Maybe spirits really were everywhere, little gods who'd stop to talk you out of sulks and come to Beltane celebrations, or maybe there were just boys who gave you their necklaces because you looked like you really needed something and that's what they had to give.

Ellery took both their hands and swung them as they walked. Both boys lurched a little and leaned heavily, drunkenly, against her. "I want to tell you about something—something happened. A mystery."

"The answer is the viscount in the library with the candlestick," Alastair drawled. "It's always the viscount."

"Are you *ever* serious?" she asked him. "I don't think there *is* an answer. All I wanted was an answer, but what I have is a mystery."

He stopped, blinking down at her. Tom stopped, too, and staggered back to lean against a tree, seemingly surprised to find they had halted.

"I guess I'm—I don't know," Alastair said. "Was there ever anything you cared about so much that all you could do was make fun of it?"

"No," Ellery said.

Alastair sighed. "I guess it doesn't make much sense. But I am . . . I *am* serious."

"I want to go up to the altar. I want to leave something there." Ellery didn't know what she'd offer. Maybe she'd make a chain of daisies like she'd done when she was a little girl. Or maybe she'd leave the liquor. Aspen had seemed to like it.

"We'll go with you," Tom said, pushing away from the tree and offering his arm gallantly, if unsteadily.

"It might be boring," Ellery warned him.

"You know," Tom said, "one reason for all the rituals we do—the offerings and the ceremonies—is that it's supposed to help us find our divine selves. The part of us that's god and goddess. The magic that's in us." It was drunken philosophy, but he seemed utterly sincere.

"So we become little gods," Ellery said, thinking of Aspen and his necklace, thinking of statues and the tiny toy car glued to Bob's dashboard.

"We're witches, after all," Alastair said, in a hushed way that seemed strangely sincere. Maybe he was acting like that because she'd said that he was never serious, but he meant it, she could tell. "Our gods aren't supposed to be distant. Let's go say hello, one divine being to another."

And so they went to the altar and picked enough dandelions to make a bouquet. They poured out a little of the liquor and drank the rest. They sat in the grass and looked up at the stars, waiting for the sun to rise.

Waiting to wash their faces in morning dew and grow luckier and more beautiful. Waiting for the spirits of the woods to find their gift. And as they sat there, Tom told them how he was trying to sort out whether it was okay to like boys when he was pretty sure he liked girls, too. Alastair told them about moving from Scotland and how much he missed his friends back home. After a while, Dawn found them and stretched out in the grass, complaining that they were having fun without her. And Ellery told them about the necklace and the boy in the woods and they all screamed with joy at the story, whether or not they believed it.

Ellery had wanted so many things from Beltane, but this was better than all of them. It felt like casting a spell, like opening up her heart and letting the universe flood in, like being hungry and thirsty no more.

Her heart was full and it was enough.

BARRIO GIRLS

CHARLES DE LINT

RUBY AND VIDA are best friends. They look so much alike they could be twins but Vida is two days older and Ruby is two inches taller. They live next door to each other in a trailer park where the barrio turns into the desert.

When they were kids, they were in love with fairies and spent a whole summer running around in fairy wings with their hair in ringlets. Nobody had the nerve to make fun of them. Vida's uncle Crusher is a big deal in the 66 Bandas and he put the word out. In North Presidio, you don't get on the wrong side of the 'bangers.

When they turn fifteen, Ruby gets a copy of one of the Shiloh books and now they live, breathe, and dream vampires. They wear black lipstick and black nail polish and black dresses with black combat boots. Vida's family never notices. Ruby's does, but they don't care.

The girls own all the books and can talk for hours about every little detail. Now when they go into the arroyo behind the park, they go at night. They're not scared of snakes or coyotes or pervs, or even the meth-heads that use places like this to shoot up.

Nobody's going to bother a couple of vampire girls. Out here in the night, *they're* the dangerous ones.

Or they would be if they could find the magical pearlstone the way Crystal did in the second book. They search the arroyo every night, walking along the dry riverbed, kicking at trash. The most unusual stone they find has a petrified snail or something in it. Vida throws it away.

"Crystal turned it over and over in her hands," Ruby reads one night before they go out.

They know this passage by heart, but they never tire of it.

"It was no bigger than any of the other river pebbles at her feet," Ruby goes on, "but it glowed with a milky iridescence as though it held a sliver of moonlight deep in its heart. Crystal gave it a closer look. Something seemed to shimmer inside the stone. Her hands took on its glow. Slowly the sparkling gleam rose up her arms.

"That was when she knew.

"The shimmer was her dreams coming true. The shimmer was the first step on her journey to win Rafael's heart, because now she knew she could. This was the pearlstone Auntie Catherine had talked about. The piece of magic that would make her just like him.

"Now they would never have to be apart."

Every night a shadow follows them out of the trailer park. It's cast by a bulky figure that isn't the best at staying unnoticed. The girls pretend they don't see him. They know it's just Pepé Fernandez, one of Tío Crusher's boys, keeping an eye on them. He's built like an engine block and carries a gun, but he dotes on his little Jack Russell terrier, Angelina, so he can't be all badass.

Like a million other girls, they dream about being romanced by Rafael and Jonathan, but when they dream about the vampire twins, they don't picture the actors from the movie. They don't search the Net for gossip and images because they're not happy about the casting. They like the actor who plays Rafael well enough, but Jason Mabe, who plays Jonathan, looks too much like a surfer dude for their taste.

But they love love love Moonstream, who play over the closing credits of the movie. It's the title song from their one and only album, *In Balance with Everything Else.* They share their copies of the books, but they both have their own copy of the CD. The lead singer should have played Jonathan. Anthony Denham has long blond hair, too, but on him it looks refined. Classy. Like the difference between having a beer at the taquería or a chi-chi cocktail at the Model T Lounge—not that the girls are supposed to have sampled either.

They have posters of Anthony Denham on their walls, band T-shirts, a vinyl single that they can't play because neither has a turntable. Ruby even has a Moonstream promo memory stick that she carries wherever she goes, safely stowed under her shirt, where it hangs on a chain. Her older sister found it for her at Bookmans. Sometimes Ruby lets Vida wear it.

Tonight they go out like they always do, dressed in black, Pepé trailing along behind them. They tell each other stories that are like dares.

That owl is the soul of a wicked prince who has to spend one hundred years in flight until he finally learns sympathy.

Those javelinas are magicked bandas boys who need a kiss from a champion roller derby queen to become human again.

That old lady is a *brujá* who tramps up and down the washes looking for—

They stop and look again. She really is there—an old lady out in the desert at this time of night. She probably *is* a witch. She's tall and spooky-looking, dressed all in black just like the girls, but she's wearing a long skirt and a shawl like someone's *abuela.*

"What are you doing in my river?" she asks the girls.

Like the wash isn't the one really convenient path through the desert and only fills with water a few times a year. Like it's really filled with water right now and they're walking underwater.

"Looking for a magic—" Ruby begins, but Vida elbows her as if to say, We don't tell strangers our secrets.

"Magic?" the old woman says. "I can show you magic."

She fixes each of the girls with a sharp look that would have made them nervous if they weren't already vampire girls. Then she smiles. It's not a cheerful smile.

"Do you want to see something funny?" she asks.

When the girls nod, the old woman mutters something under her breath. She takes a pinch of pollen from her pocket, throws it into the air, then points a crooked finger to the line of dark mesquite and paloverde that follows the path the dry wash takes through the desert scrub.

The girls don't think that's particularly funny until Pepé comes walking stiffly from where he was hidden behind the mesquite. He's like a zombie in a late-night horror movie, arms held out in front of him, shuffling down the uneven footing of the wash's bank.

First Vida smiles, then Ruby giggles, then the both of them are holding their hands in front of their mouths. Except it's not at all funny when Pepé loses his footing. The back of his big head hits a rock as he falls and there's this awful sound like the time Chuy threw a squash at a wall and it burst open. The girls' laughter dies when they realize that Pepé isn't getting up. They run to where he lies, dropping to their knees in the dirt on either side of him.

"This is a bad joke," Ruby tells him.

The sand behind his head grows dark with blood. Ruby pushes him with a finger but he doesn't move.

"Get up," Vida says. "Please get up."

"Please," Ruby repeats.

They know he won't. They've seen enough bodies to know when somebody is dead. The victims of drive-bys. Meth-heads who've OD'd.

Vida leans down and kisses his cooling brow. When Ruby follows suit, a tear falls from her cheek onto his. If this were a fairy tale, had those two kisses not brought Pepé back to life, the tear surely would have.

But it isn't a fairy tale.

Pepé is really dead.

Vida glares at the old woman, who only smiles back.

"Why would you do such a thing?" Vida demands of the old woman.

"The night is mine," the *brujá* replies. "It doesn't belong to foolish girls. Go away and don't return."

Ruby and Vida look at each other. Without another word they get up and leave the wash, leave Pepé, leave the old witch woman. They don't go home. They go to the taquería, walk right in the front door. They ignore Juan, who rises up from behind the cash register to stop them, and go to the back, where Vida's uncle sits with his crew at a long table covered with beer bottles and the remains of a late-night meal. The whole place goes quiet as the two vampire girls approach the table.

"Pepé's dead," Vida says.

Ruby nods. "He fell in the wash and cracked his head on a stone."

Tío Crusher stands up. "You're sure about this?"

Now Vida nods.

"You girls go home," Tío Crusher tells them.

The girls leave the taquería, but they still don't go home. Instead they go to the trailer where Pepé lives. Where he lived. They collect Angelina. Taking turns, they carry the little Jack Russell back to Vida's home. They get in bed. Angelina trembles between them, knowing something is wrong.

They were fairy girls once. Now they're vampire girls. In the future they might become something else. Roller derby stars. Famous actors. But that's just a skin they wear over what they really are and always will be: barrio girls. They know what the bandas do when someone kills one of their own. It's the reason they didn't tell Tío Crusher about the old woman in the wash.

"I really really liked Pepé," Ruby says, trying to comfort the dog.

Vida nods. "Me too." She lays a hand on Angelina's shoulders, trying to still the little dog's trembling. "That's why we have to kill the witch."

* * *

The next day Ruby and Vida hear that Pepé's body has been recovered. Tío Crusher and a couple of his boys brought the body to the church. The bandas don't ever call the police. The cops wouldn't come anyway—not for something like this. The thing that has everybody talking is that there was no blood in the body. It should have been pooled around the head wound—Ruby and Vida can remember seeing it soaking into the sand—but by the time Tío Crusher reached the wash, the sand was dry and Pepé's body was pale pale pale.

Ruby and Vida exchange unhappy looks when they hear about this.

Bad enough there was a witch in the wash. A *tlahuelpuchi* makes it even worse.

Vampire witch.

"I don't like vampires anymore," Ruby says.

Vida nods. "Me either. But I still like Anthony Denham."

"Of course we do. He's not a vampire. His band just sings about them."

"We should tell my uncle. He'll shoot her dead."

"We can't do that," Ruby says. "She'll just kill him, too, and then suck away all of his blood. You can't just shoot a *tlahuelpuchi*."

In the end, they don't tell anyone. Instead they put Angelina on a leash and walk with her to the far end of the trailer park where the bottle man lives. He has a shack made of saguaro ribs and cast-off pieces of tin and clapboard. The whole thing has been decorated with spray-painted images of animals and pictographs in bright Oaxacan colors.

It sits on the edge of the desert, across the wash from the trailer park. An old mesquite tree towers above it, its branches festooned with bottles of all shapes, sizes, and colors that tinkle softly when the wind taps them against each other. The ground under the tree and all around the shack is thick with broken glass, but for some reason the pieces have no sharp edges. It's like they've been rolling against each other in a river for years until they're smoothed like pebbles, even though they come from when the monsoons blow hard and the bottles smash against each other in the high winds and rain.

The girls stare out at all the glass. It gleams and glitters in the hot morning sun.

"Magic," Ruby whispers as they climb up out of the wash.

Vida nods.

The glass slides underfoot. It's a little like walking on marbles.

Ruby and Vida have spied on the place many times, but they've never actually been this close before. They've never talked to the bottle man before, either. Everyone in the barrio calls him Abuelo, and he looks older than the oldest grandfather, but he's strong and spry and he doesn't suffer fools. He just likes to be left alone and do whatever it is that he does inside the shack or when he wanders out into the desert. But it's whispered on street corners that he can cure a curse or make a charm, so people come to him. Sometimes he helps, sometimes he doesn't.

The girls used to make up stories about him. They hope he hasn't heard any of them because while in some he's the hero, in others he's a clown who never quite gets things right.

When they slip and slide their way to the door they find the full-length painting of a coyote looking back at them—or rather, the painting of a man with a coyote's head. He's dressed in the colorful garb of the Kikimi, who live in the foothills of the tall range of mountains that can be seen from anywhere on the west side of town.

"You knock," Ruby says to Vida.

Angelina stays close to her, furry body pressed up against her leg.

Ruby touches the Moonstream memory stick hanging from her neck—for luck, for protection—then offers it to Vida.

Vida rubs the stick between her thumb and forefinger before rapping a knuckle on the thin sheet of tin that serves as a door. She's careful not to knock against any part of the coyote painting.

The tin sheet rattles and though they both know it's an illusion, the coyote in the painting seems to shiver as though a breeze is ruffling its fur. They almost change their minds and go, except they hear a footstep in the glass pebbles behind them. When they turn around, the old man is standing there.

He looks older than either of them remember. He also looks more powerful. Maybe it's because of the *brujá* in the wash, because now they know that magic is real. Maybe it's because they've never seen him this close up before.

He's wearing raggedy cotton trousers and an old Grateful Dead T-shirt that must have been black once but has faded to a pale gray. His hair is gray, too, and hangs in dreads on either side of his dark brown face and down his back. He has more wrinkles than cracked mud that's been baking in the sun, and his eyes are so dark they seem black. His mouth is a straight line, neither smiling nor frowning.

Angelina makes a small whine in the back of her throat and hides behind Ruby's legs. Ruby wishes she had a leg to hide behind. But if Vida's anxious, she doesn't show it.

"Good morning, Señor," she says in the voice she reserves for people she respects, like her grandmother. "We're sorry to intrude on your privacy."

The bottle man doesn't say anything.

"We were wondering," she goes on, "if we could ask you for a small favor."

The corner of his lip twitches with the momentary hint of a smile.

"What could a pair of pretty girls like you need from an old man like me?"

His voice is as dry as the dust in the barrio streets.

Vida shrugs. "Do you know how to raise the dead?"

"Raise the dead? What do you think I am?"

Certainly interested, Ruby thinks. The bottle man has straightened up and his dark eyes study Vida carefully. He also seems surprised by the question. She's surprised herself. But having Pepé back would be much much better than having to kill the witch.

"I know you are a wise man," Vida says, "filled with secrets and hidden knowledge."

"That may be, but raising the dead is a black art. I don't dabble in such and neither should you." His dark gaze continues to study her. "Why do you want to raise the dead?"

"A witch killed our friend last night. It doesn't seem fair that he should die just because he was protecting us. She thought it was a joke."

The bottle man shakes his head. "There are ways to bring back the dead, but the one who returns is never the same as the one who died. If you bring Pepé back, you will be more unhappy than you already are."

Neither of the girls is surprised that he knows who they're talking about. The bottle man would know everything that happens in the barrio.

"Then perhaps, if you could," Vida says, "might you tell us how to kill a witch?"

The bottle man nods. "The ways to do so are as many and varied as there are different kinds of witches. The best way is to put some of their hair or nail clippings in a bottle, then put the bottle in a fire. The witch who dies from that little spell never comes back as a ghost."

"Will that even work on a vampire witch?" Vida asks.

He nods again. "I'd heard the body was drained of blood."

"I don't think we can get her nail clippings or hair. Is there any other way?"

"There are many," he says, "but there is only one that's the best to deal with a *tlahuelpuchi*."

"Will you tell us?" Vida asks.

"Do you trust me? Will you do exactly as I say, no matter how odd or wrong it seems?"

The girls exchange glances, then nod.

The bottle man squats on his haunches and puts out a hand toward Angelina. The little dog hesitates. She looks up at Ruby, then slowly moves forward and sniffs at the offered hand. She trembles a little when the bottle man strokes her head, but then she seems to be calmer than she has been since the girls first brought her away from Pepé's trailer.

"I will tell you how to kill your witch," the bottle man says when he stands up once more, "because I like this little dog. And because I liked Pepé Fernandez. And because you have both been so polite. But it will cost you. You must give me something of yours that is precious."

The girls exchange glances again. Ruby nods and takes off the Moonstream memory stick and offers it to the bottle man. He lifts it to his nose and smells it.

"This will be enough," he tells them. "It holds a piece of both of you."

He twirls it by its chain on his finger, then throws it up into the mesquite. The chain wraps around a branch near the top like it's a little snake, and now Ruby's Moonstream memory stick has a new home in the bottle man's bottle tree.

"Listen closely," he says.

He spits in his hand and holds it out to them, palm up. The girls don't know what they're supposed to do. Shake his hand? Take the spit? But then the spit moves on the old man's palm.

"Kill her with kindness," the spit says. "But you must show no fear and you must be sincere."

The old man closes his hand. He walks past them. Opening the tin door to his shack, he goes inside. When the door bangs shut the coyote painted on it almost seems to dance. Ruby thinks it maybe winked at her as well.

She scoops up Angelina, takes Vida's hand, and leads her

slip-sliding across the glass until they reach the firmer footing at the top of the wash. They turn to look at the shack.

"Was that magic, too?" Ruby says. "The spit in his hand talking?"

Vida shakes her head. "That was just ventriloquism. And stupid. How do you kill anything with kindness? We should just go steal one of Tío Crusher's guns."

Vida picks her way down the steep incline into the wash. Ruby puts Angelina on the ground and follows. She catches Vida's arm.

"Remember what he asked us?" she says. "If we trusted him? If we'd do exactly what he said no matter how odd or wrong it seems?"

Vida considers that. "That was pretty strange, spitting into his hand and everything."

Ruby lifts her fingers to her Moonstream memory stick, but it's not there anymore. She looks up into the mesquite tree and imagines she can see it winking there in the bright sunlight.

"I gave up my memory stick," she says.

She'd liked it, too. It had songs from the album on it, along with a couple of live tracks, a video, and lots and lots of pictures of Anthony Denham.

"Okay," Vida says. "We'll give it a try. But we'll bring along a bottle, too, just in case we can get a piece of her hair or a nail clipping."

They hurry home and spend the afternoon getting ready. In the evening they go to the service at the church. They bring Angelina and Ruby holds the dog on her lap. No one says anything about having a dog in the church. They all know she was Pepé's dog and that God and the saints won't mind. In a barrio church anyone who comes with respect is welcome.

After the service Ruby uses some of the money she's been saving for a new skirt from Buffalo Exchange to buy a votive candle for Pepé. She whispers a prayer to the Virgin, then says, "We'll take good care of Angelina. We promise."

Vida nods and adds, "And we'll kill that witch for you."

They don't hate the witch because, now that they're witch girls themselves, it would be like hating themselves. At least they don't hate her for being a witch. Or even a vampire. They hate her for her casual cruelty.

They listen to Moonstream's single "The Night Is My Ally" for luck. After midnight they pack up their knapsacks and sneak out to the wash. They're very careful leaving the trailer because Tío Crusher has now assigned One-Eye Luban as their bodyguard and they don't want the vampire witch to kill him as well. They planned to leave Angelina behind, but the little dog begins to whimper when they're going, so they take her with them.

When they get to where they saw the witch the previous night they build a small fire from dried wood. The flames flicker, casting shadows up and down the wash. The wood crackles. The air fills with the rich smell of the burning mesquite.

"Don't forget," Ruby says. "We can't show we're afraid. And we have to pretend to be truthful."

"That won't be hard," Vida tells her. "We're going to be great actors someday—remember?"

Ruby's not sure Vida will have to act—she's always so fearless. She's more worried about how she herself will do.

But all she says is, "Of course I remember."

And then they wait.

But not for long.

Soon the smell of the mesquite is overwhelmed by another with a sharp bite that's like when the switch burned out in Vida's bedroom last month. They look up to see the *tlahuelpuchi* approach their fire. She doesn't seem to walk so much as glide just above the sand and rock of the wash. Angelina crawls off Ruby's lap and burrows into her empty knapsack.

"Foolish girls," the witch says. "What did I tell you about coming to my river?"

Her eyes flash in the light from the fire. She reaches into a pocket for—the girls aren't sure what. Perhaps more of her magical pollen to start some nasty spell that will turn them into zombies like what happened with Pepé. Perhaps something worse. But before she can take her hand out again, Vida stands up and smiles.

"Oh, we're so happy to see you," she says. "Look, we have a blanket waiting for you by the fire."

The *brujá* frowns.

"Please, have some tea," Ruby adds. "We weren't sure what kind you like, so we made three different flavors."

The mugs are sitting on a stone by the fire, kept warm by its heat.

"I killed your friend," the vampire witch says.

"Yes," Vida agrees. "I'm sure it was an accident. It wasn't like

you would ever *make* anyone fall and crack their head open on
a rock."

"I drank his blood."

Vida nods. "Of course you would. He was already dead, so
there was no point in it going to waste."

"I'm going to kill the both of you."

Ruby works hard at not showing how frightened she is. She'd
rather crawl into the knapsack with Angelina and pretend she's
invisible. But it was her idea to do what the bottle man had told
them, and Vida's being so brave that she knows she has to be
brave, too.

"Before you do," she says, "would you like a cupcake?"

She holds out a plate with a perfect cupcake on it. The pink
and white icing glows in the firelight. The plate only trembles a
little in her hand, and the witch doesn't seem to notice.

"We also have tequila," Vida adds. "We stole it from my
uncle just for you."

Ruby notices a strange thing. She's quite sure the *brujá* was
much taller when she first approached the fire. But each time
they say or do something nice, she seems to shrink a little. And
while the witch makes her threats and says her mean things, so
long as the girls continue to be kind and pleasant, she doesn't
seem to be able to actually cast a spell.

"We also baked you a cake," she says. "You must get hungry
walking around in your river all night."

The witch's eyes are like daggers. If she could throw them,
both girls would already be dead.

"I don't know how you are doing this," the witch says, "but

the moment I am free I will kill you both, and then I will kill all your families. I will bathe in their blood and make a necklace from the teeth of all your little cousins."

"Oh, that will look so pretty," Vida tells her.

Ruby claps her hands. "I wish you'd kill us last so that we could see the necklace before we're dead, too."

They keep it up for hours. The witch curses and threatens them, the girls respond with smiles and cheerful replies, with offers of various drinks and sweets. And bit by bit the witch grows smaller and smaller and smaller.

It's near daylight when the witch has grown so small that she can now fit into the empty glass coffee bottle that Vida took from behind the Starbucks over on Mission Street. Easy as you please, Vida sets the bottle over the witch—the way you might trap an angry hornet that's in your trailer so that you can listen to it buzz against the glass. Vida gives the bottle a quick flip, then snaps on the metal lid and screws it shut.

"Remember the other thing the bottle man told us?" she says.

Ruby shakes her head.

"Oh, you know," Vida tells her. "We just need to put a bit of the witch's hair or a nail clipping in a bottle and put the bottle in a fire."

Ruby nods. She thinks of a horrible thing and doesn't want to say it because she knows what Vida wants to do. But she remembers the awful sound of Pepé falling on the rock, how the witch laughed and drank all his blood. She remembers all the horrible things the witch has been saying to them for hours.

"I bet," she says, "it would work just as well with the whole witch."

Vida smiles. "There's only one way to find out."

She tosses the bottle into the fire. It doesn't take long for the witch inside to begin to roast. They lean forward to watch the entire process with the same morbid curiosity that would have them poke with sticks at the body of a half-eaten dead snake they might find out in the scrub. The tiny witch bangs at the sides of the glass until she finally falls down and dies. They watch her turn black and shrivel away. The bottle suddenly breaks with a sharp crack, but by then there's nothing left of the witch but a smudge of black ashes on broken pieces of glass.

The girls add more wood to the fire. They sit there on the blanket, sipping tea and eating cupcakes as they watch the fire burn. Angelina lies between them, licking crumbs from their fingers.

"We make pretty good witches ourselves," Vida says.

"I think we do," Ruby agrees. "But we must only use our power for good."

"We don't really have much power."

"Maybe the bottle man could teach us how to get more."

Vida nods. "Except do we really want to get lessons from talking spit? Do we even want lessons at all? It sounds too much like school."

"School's not all bad."

"But it's not all good, either."

Ruby grins. "You seem to like Roberto Sanchez well enough."

"I don't *like* like him."

"But still."

Vida gives her a halfhearted slap on the knee and lies back on the blanket. She looks up into the lightening sky. The wash is filled with the cheerful songs of birds. It sounds like there are hundreds of them, but all she can see are a couple of cactus wrens and a phainopepla with his black crest standing at attention.

"I'm going to miss having Pepé skulk around behind us," she finally says.

"Me too. We should tell him that we kept our word."

"Oh, I think he already knows."

Ruby lies down as well. She puts her hands behind her head. She misses having her memory stick, but she doesn't mind having given it to the bottle man. She would have given away a million of them if it could have brought Pepé back. But her neck feels bare now. She'll just have to make herself a necklace out of something else.

Angelina comes up between them and gives them each a lick. Her tongue finds Ruby's cheek, but she gets Vida right on the mouth. Vida quickly wipes her hand across her lips.

"Careful, little dog," she says as she pushes Angelina away. "We're the witch girls now. We could turn you into a toad with just a snap of our fingers."

"But we wouldn't," Ruby says, "because we're good witches." She turns her head to look at Vida.

"We're very good witches," Vida agrees. She waits a moment, then adds in a stage whisper, "Very good at what we do."

Ruby laughs, and the sound of her voice rises up to join the morning bird chorus.

FELIDIS

TANITH LEE

I

"DON'T GO IN those woods—there's a terrifying girl—a *female* there—and she's a *cat*."

"What do you mean?" he asked, the young man standing on the road. "Do you mean she's bitchy—*catty*?"

"Nah," said the other man, the old red fat one on his cart, while the fed-up but poorly fed horse shook its ears. "I *mean*, boy, she's covered in *fur*—and her *hair's* fur. And she's gotten herself two ice-green *cat eyes*. She's bad—she's *evil*. Don't go in those woods. I've warned you."

And with a cluck to the horse, off he trundled in his cart, old red Fatty.

While Radlo still stood on the track in his thin coat, with—he later admitted—his mouth hanging open.

"He's mad," Radlo presently said aloud to reassure himself. In a nearby tree a magpie sounded its rattling scorn. "He didn't agree to give me a lift to anywhere either. So." Radlo looked back at the cloud of late summer woodland rising over the hillsides about two miles off. "So, I might as well go on the way I was going in the first place. I like cats, anyhow," he added, if rather doubtfully. Cats, surely. But *girls covered in fur*? "To hell with it," Radlo finished.

And on he walked.

The second man Radlo met, three hours later, by then deep in the dusk woods, was the opposite of the other. The second man was thin and young, and pallid as egg white, and it seemed he came from the village just smokily visible over a rise.

"Here you," began thin young Eggy. "What you wanting?"

Lots of things, thought Radlo sadly. *A good meal would be nice for a start—or even a friendly word.* "Nothing," he replied.

"You're after *something*," Eggy insisted. "Be off! You're not wanted around here."

Radlo scowled. He hadn't meant to but the scowl had been brewing for thirteen days. "You don't know me," he scowlingly growled. "So how d'you *know* I'm not wanted?"

Idiotic Eggy goggled at him.

"All right," Eggy idiotically said. "Better come with me, then." And led him down through the trees into the village.

There was dull yellowish lamplight starting in some of the cottage windows; the smoke going up from the chimneys had the tang of early cooking. Radlo's stomach gurgled. Near the well a few people lingered, women drawing up a last pail of water, and a woodcutter in conversation with a couple of huntsmen.

"You ought to go have a word with her," said the woodcutter to the hunters. "*She'll* put it right. And if it's a big beast like that you can't be too careful."

This sounded rather odd, but, anyway, having noticed Radlo

and Eggy approaching, one of the huntsmen shook his head and made a gesture plainly meaning *Shut up*. All three men turned and glared at Radlo, while the women with pails stared.

"What's *he* want?" asked the woodcutter. "What you bringing him in for, you blitherer, eh?" This presumably to Eggy.

"Maybe he wants *her*," said the other huntsman. The first hunter shushed him.

"Says he's expected," said Eggy, inaccurately.

"*Who* expects him?"

Radlo, finding all this too tiresome to be funny—hungry and irritated and with nowhere at all to go, and no one at all anymore *to* want or expect him—lost his temper and roared: "*She* expects me. *Her*. The one you keep on about. Who *else*?"

It was impulsive and ridiculous. The moment he had done it he felt a complete fool. The Lord knew who this wretched female was they had mentioned. Probably the local jolly-woman, who charged coins for kisses, or worse—some well-off old nag in whose good books they were all trying to stay.

It wasn't he had forgotten red Fatty's natter of a girl in fur. It was only two and two hadn't yet become four.

"What do you think?" asked the woodcutter of the huntsmen. "Do we believe him?"

"Shall I thrash him?" helpfully inquired the bigger huntsman. "That'll get the truth out."

Radlo was not above fighting, but he and the hunter didn't seem a fair match. Radlo loosened up his muscles, ready to run for his life.

And just then one of the women by the well called out, "Look over there. Better see what *he* thinks."

At which everybody turned, Radlo too, and there sat a black cat with a white triangle, like a little breastplate, on its chest.

"Good eve, Jehankin," chorused the villagers.

The cat gave a flip of its tail—just one. It sprang away into the shadow beyond the houses.

Grumbling now, the men frowned at Radlo. To Eggy, the woodcutter said, "See the way the cat's gone? Better take this fellow up there then. Go on, be quick. She may be waiting, for all we know."

Having not, until the cat appeared, put two and two together, at last Radlo did. And two and two seemed to make ten. The manner in which Fatty had spoken about the girl in fur, the way *this* lot spoke of *her*—they had seemed different females. But Fatty, the outsider, was scared of her. The villagers were in awe?

And there was no method to get out of it now, whatever anyone thought. Eggy was shambling off the way the cat had gone, along a side path that led from the village and up another thickly treed hill. While the big, thrash-threatening hunter gave Radlo a shove, and pushily fell in behind him. Just as a pair of guards might herd a prisoner to his doom.

Well done, Radlo, he congratulated himself sourly.

The woods now were jet black and thick with a night like a horsehair blanket. Somewhere an owl hooted, another bloody joker laughing.

The lamp in the window showed first, dark amber. Then, in the open doorway of the little house up the hill: a young woman, dressed in the ordinary village way.

She *had* gotten herself ice-green eyes. Her hair *was* fur—

short and spiky and furry, in color *tabby.* Her skin—flawless, of course—was covered by a furry velvet nap, like palest pearliest gray velvet.

Radlo's legs gave way.

He landed (prone) at her feet.

Fatty hadn't lied.

2

Did the cats pick him up, and courteously carry him indoors? There were certainly enough to have done it. So far he had counted at least thirty, and some were very alike, and therefore he could have *under*counted, and they could be twice that number.

He'd felt ashamed of fainting. He hadn't eaten anything, it was true, but grass and a withered apple for three days . . . but hunger had happened before. No excuse.

Hers was a rambly cottage, with one upstairs room. Up there she had her bed, behind a curtain most likely, and otherwise did all her work with herbs and potions. Unless invited, who would dare intrude?

The cats *did* go everywhere. Yet Radlo noted from the start none of them relieved themselves indoors or scent-marked walls or furniture. Nor did they spoil the herb and flower beds outside.

She was a witch, obviously. A witch covered in fur. And though he had seen later the green irises of her eyes had each a circle of white around them, as a human eye did, it was a *small* circle of white. And some cats had that too.

She was a cat.

A witch and a cat.

She'd told him her name was Felidis.

And she had been very kind, brought him some strengthening broth, and warm bread baked in her own oven by the hearth, and beer she had apparently brewed as well. Radlo was so hungry he hadn't, right then, had any problem with a cat-woman making and serving up his food.

That evening too, as he sat on the comfortable cushioned bench by the fire, he heard the huntsman, the big one who'd shepherded him there, telling her about a wild cat, a "panther," he called it—no doubt a wood-lynx—that was bothering the village. (This was what they had been talking about when Radlo went into the village with Eggy.) And in her calm cool voice, witchy-catty Felidis had said, "Oh, that's fine. I'll go out tonight and have a word with the panther. I think I did catch sight of him a few evenings back, but I've been that busy. . . ."

Later still, when the moon was well up, splitting the woods into ranks of black pillars and thin white-moonlight spears, out she went. And peering through one of the little windows, Radlo saw her at the edge of the clearing where her cottage stood, moving quietly up and down with a large shadowy cat-thing about the size of a hunting-hound. There wasn't anything dangerous-looking to this interview. If anything it was like a couple of friendly acquaintances taking a short walk after church. (The black and white cat was out there too, the one Radlo had seen in the village. It sat on a tree stump, not seeming concerned about the *other* cat, which was three times its size. It must really trust *her*.)

Eventually she (Felidis) touched the moon-doused shadow-panther's head, and it rubbed once against her hand. Then the animal turned and sprinted from view. Surreal, all this. A dream? But Radlo knew he hadn't dreamed it. Nor the velvet silver of her hair and skin, the luminous green *flash* of her cat's eyes as she walked back to the cottage.

She had said he might sleep the night on the floor of the downstairs room, with a cushion and a blanket and the dying fire for comfort.

"I know how it must be," she had said to him mildly, "to be wandering about on your own in the dark."

When not looking at her, one would never know what she was. She sounded like a human girl. But even in the glow of the last embers—you could *see*.

That first night he'd barely said a word to her. He had gawped at her for hours. She made no remark on this rudeness. Nor had she told the villagers Radlo was quite unknown to her—*not* expected.

He did dream of her, between being disturbed by the bouncing and purring of cats. Of course he dreamed. He was already part-afraid and part-fascinated, and entirely out of his depth.

"What do you want, Puss?" Radlo asked the black and white cat—Jehankin, had they called it?—who was sitting about one-third of an arm's length from Radlo's face when he woke up. Radlo liked animals of all sorts, even snakes, even wolves at a safe distance. But his way of talking to this cat was falsely easy. And the cat gave him a *look*, as if to say, *You don't kid me, young fellow.* He was a young cat himself, strong and glossy and clear-eyed. Even assuming it (he) could take on such a grandfatherly attitude towards Radlo, this cat was a *boy*. (Daft way to think. Daft, all of it. But then, this creature wasn't afraid of a lynx.)

Felidis came in with some red flowers and a basket of apples, and putting these down knelt by the cat and embraced him.

"Jehankin, my prince!" she said, with great happiness and love. And Prince Jehankin purred like a gigantically buzzing bee.

Radlo concentrated on the cat then, not to have to look at Felidis, which with daylight, and feeling better, he decided was almost impossible. (He had a feeling too the witch had patted his forehead as he slept. He wasn't sure he liked the idea.)

However, she was engaged entirely with her cat. Radlo saw that, although she was loving and caring with *all* the cats, she made an incredible fuss of this particular feline.

They rubbed faces for minutes. And she too (oh the Lord!) made a weird purring noise far down in her throat. Then she brought for the cat a dish of meat, and another of curds, and left him to breakfast. When quite done, Jehankin groomed himself, polishing his fur end to end with his spic-and-span pink tongue.

Of course. Jehankin must be the witch's Familiar.

A while after Radlo, to his joy, was given breakfast too. Then he sat on the bench and Felidis inspected him. The cat sat by her and seemed to inspect Radlo as well, with a considering air.

"I must give you a drink of suitable herbs. That seems to be what you must have," Felidis announced finally. "Then you'll be well able to go on with your journey."

At that Radlo was covered by a cloud of depression. He had *nowhere* to go. Besides, a witch would want paying.

"I can't offer you a single coin," he said gracelessly, looking down at the floor now.

"No worry. People pay me or not, when or if they can," said Felidis, turning towards the narrow crooked stair and the workroom above. The cat stalked before her and bounded up the steps.

"You've been generous," said Radlo. "Perhaps—are there any chores I could do to help you out?"

And to himself, *Be quiet, you total madman. Fly while you've gotten a chance!* But, not looking at her, her voice seemed only human, rather musical and pretty.

"That's honorable," said Felidis. "Well, if you will. There's some wood to be cut, if you're up to that. Or the berries in the raspberry vines are ripe to pick."

Outside, swinging the axe, Radlo was aware of endless cats, white patterned black, and black dabbed with white; ginger, and ale-brown, and a few pied like tree bark, and even some pale gray—like Felidis herself. Gold eyes and amber eyes and eyes of jade winked and glittered like jewelry in the bushes.

Radlo found he had begun, almost by accident, to sing. He sang rather well, he had been told. The sun was up and warm on his back. The clearing was attractive, the tall green canopy of woods all around, just lit in places by the first red and copper of fall.

When he had cut and stacked the wood in the shed, he picked two baskets of the lush raspberries. He only ate four—they were irresistible and very sweet.

About a mile off down the slope, and hidden by trees, the village sometimes gave off a homey sound, the tinkle of a sheep bell, the thump of a rug being beaten, or a hammer striking sharp from a forge.

They lunched. He alone, if with several cats. The witch up in her room of spells and medicines. Then she gave him, at his request, other tasks. He said he would move on tomorrow, if she would allow him the pillow and blanket one more night. She answered carelessly that he was welcome.

Radlo thought she wasn't afraid at having a strange man in her house, even now he was well again. After all, she was a witch who could talk to panthers.

3

Am I in love with her?

I can't even look at her half the time, not properly—but am I in love?

Radlo was upset even by thinking this. The one girl he had so far loved had dumped him for the local landowner's son, less than two months before. And after that (or because of that) he'd been in some trouble, and then been thrown out of his own village, and so taken to wandering.

He had no special trade, though he was strong enough to earn his bread—cutting wood, clearing paths, helping with sheep or horses, that sort of thing. Besides, he could read and write. He had been a scholar before the faithless girl ruined his life.

As the year had begun to edge towards fall he grew nervous, wondering what he'd do all winter, holed up the Lord knew where, and that was if any village would make a place for him.

He had been aiming for the big old town that lay along the river, westward. But for a man on foot, and always having to stop to earn some food, the journey so far had taken a while. And in the last thirteen days too, someone had robbed Radlo, someone else had lightly but nastily beaten him up, and last but hardly least, a farmer had cheated him of promised pay.

Now here he was.

Her voice was sweet and tempting as the raspberries and apples he had picked for her. But in evening gloamings that green *flare* of her eyes . . .

No, he couldn't love a being like Felidis.

He had been sleeping on her cottage floor by now for five nights. By day he did work for her in the house or clearing, or went to the village on her errands. He had made friends with some of the cats—those that let him—and was always respectful to Jehankin, the beast that was her Familiar. Jehankin himself stayed with Felidis in her herbarium during a chunk of each day. At night the black and white cat went out on his own business, presumably to hunt or play, like the other cats, in the woods.

On the fifth afternoon (yesterday) a boy had come hurrying up from the village, and dashed past Radlo, who was mending the wall of the second shed. In the cottage, a call, and then the village boy's excited gabble. Somebody was riding directly up here, it seemed, to visit the witch. Somebody important.

Felidis stepped downstairs, swathed in her broad gray apron, wiping her slender furry hands—paws?—on a cloth.

Then they all—she, the boy, Radlo, and some sixteen cats—waited about. Until up the track from the village came an impressive group of callers. There were several mounted soldiers, heavily armed and in the uniform of a moneyed household. Also servants on mules. And in the middle was a rich man in a velvet coat, sitting on a big white horse he looked too sick to ride.

Felidis said nothing. She only looked up at the rich man, calm as cream.

One of the servants broke out haughtily, "Woman, show some politeness to my master—"

But the rich man himself cut the servant off. "She's polite enough. Hello, witch. I see you're as they say you are."

"So," said Felidis gently, "are very many of us."

"Maybe," he answered. "But do you have the skill they rumor too?"

"I have some ability."

"More than that, I hope. I'm not a well man. Can you help me out?"

"Dismount, sir," said Felidis, "and come into my house. We'll see if I can."

The important man was assisted from his horse, and went meekly into the cottage with Felidis, and the last any of the rest of them saw of events, for a while, was Jehankin trotting up and in at the door, before the door was firmly closed.

Then everybody idled about the clearing. The soldiers shared a beer-skin, and the servants muttered, while the other cats sat on stones, on the shed roofs, or up in the trees, and watched. And Radlo himself watched the plaster drying on the mended wall. The village boy who had brought the message idled about too. He began to talk to Radlo, showing off, knowing *everything*.

"Oh, *she'll* get him right as rain."

"Will she. Good. This lot could turn ugly if she can't."

"Did you know, last year the great lady of Tall Trees came here, so sickly she lay on a *litter*—but within two hours she was up and out and pink as a girl. And since then, every month, our village gets a vat of wine and a barrel of grain, on account of the healing Felidis worked for her."

"You don't say," said Radlo. *Little liar,* he thought.

But the boy went chattering on, now about this wealthy patron and now that, or the old monk who was one hundred years old and wanted just one more year to finish painting in the book he was making, and the monk received several more, and Felidis was given a gold jewel from the monastery, which she in turn gave the village for their church, where it hung to this minute.

"She never keeps a thing for herself. Says she never needs it."

Radlo climbed up the ladder to check the shed roof, slightly aggravating the cats now roosting there. But anything to get away from the chatty boy.

It was almost sunset, the sun like a burning house low down in the trees, when the cottage door was undone.

Out walked the rich man. He looked, Radlo noticed, about twenty years younger, and happy as Christ Mass.

"By the stars, she's done it, lads." He had a flask of medicine too, which the servants took charge of.

When they had all ridden off, and even the boy had gone scrambling down the hill to tell the village—no doubt another pack of untruths (the rich man had singled him out, Felidis had confided the secret of her spell)—Radlo left the roof.

He felt angry.

Either it was some trick she'd pulled. Or else she *was* just a jolly-woman after all, and an hour in her cosy arms was what had put Richy to rights.

Inside the cottage he could hear her singing, sweetly too, up in the herb-room. And Jehankin sat half down the stair, washing his paws. His white whiskers seemed to grin at Radlo.

"The hell with it!" Radlo snapped, and flung out for a stamp in the cooling, darkening wood. Here he disturbed a badger set, shocked a big clawed and militant owl, and ultimately stumbled over a tree root, ending in some mud.

I'm jealous. Don't be insane. Of *what*? A *cat-girl* with tabby hair. She probably even had whiskers too, if one went close enough and stared.

When finally he returned, something wonderful-smelling was cooking in a pot on the hearth. (The rich man had brought a present she *had* accepted, it seemed, a roast for dinner.)

And she had laid the table for the three of them: herself, Radlo, and the black and white cat.

His anger melted in the firelight. It was too chilly to storm off. Why not sit down and eat, facing her properly over the candles, and with Prince Jehankin seated couthly between them, sharing everything, having his own bowl exactly like theirs, and a little matching cup of beer?

Oh, in the candle- and firelight, after a little food, she looked— her skin was just . . . pale and velvet smooth. And her hair . . . so she had some gray in it before her time, as you might expect from a woman who worked very hard. And her green eyes? They were beautiful.

She told him a joke and it made him laugh. He told her one,

and she laughed too. The cat sat smiling, and presently lay down on the table, like a nesting pigeon (or a lion), his paws tucked under him.

"Your cat smiles," said Radlo.

"Of course. All things smile. But—apart from humans—animals only when they mean it."

"Humankind. We're *false,* deceivers," said Radlo sadly.

"Maybe we feel we have to be. Poor things, we are."

"Not you," he said.

"I'm the lucky one."

"What did you do to that rich man today?"

"Helped heal him."

"How?"

"Herbs, things I'm lessoned how to use. And . . . a kind wish."

"I thought perhaps—" Radlo faltered. He said, "Were you a bit kinder than just in your wishes?"

She burst out now in a wild young laugh. It was so true and real it made him laugh again too.

"No," she remarked in a moment. "I don't make myself *kind* that way with men. With anyone. That isn't for me. I have no ambition, Radlo, of being any man's lady, let alone his wife. I don't want love or fun of that sort, or marriage, or children." (Radlo stared, astounded. Never in all his days had he ever heard any woman, young *or* old, say such things.) "My path is another one."

"But you've no family," he blurted, astounded now into astounding concern for her loss.

"Don't I? Look about."

Blankly he glanced around. All he saw were fire glimmers

and warm shadows, and here and there a soft gleam of flame on fur, or a glint of a garnet or an emerald or a topaz eye.

"Yes. *They're* my family. All I have and all I want. You've seen what I am. Quarter cat at least."

Radlo sat dumbfounded. Strangely his eyes had filled with tears.

Then she told him quietly how it had been with her. Since she was her own living proof, he believed her.

"I don't remember any mother or father, or anything much until I was—I'd guess from my size then and abilities—about three years old. And how I'd gotten myself into the woods I've no notion. But I have a sort of set of memory *fragments*—things half seen or heard, felt, *hated* . . . these make me think perhaps I escaped from some sort of carnival or fair, where I was shown as a monster, jeered at and starved. But perhaps I'm wrong, and my parents simply abandoned me, having been scared of me from the start and unable to stand me another second.

"The woods are my first certain memory. They were so big and dark, full of night. I think, for me, it must have been how it would feel to be at the bottom of a lake, or under the sea. And it was cold. It was the end of fall, and the leaves raining down and frost shining white.

"But then there he is. Who? Why my rescuer, my prince there, Jehankin. He was younger then but still wise. He was warm and soft to touch, and *good*. He led me away to an old ruined barn, where he and his kind were living. There was a whole tribe of them, two hundred or more, a house full of fur. And they kept me warm and brought me a share of their kills—I won't tell you,

Radlo, what I fed on sometimes. You'd go green. But everything that lives must eat, and they saved me.

"I stayed with them for years. Sometimes some of the cats went away to make new colonies, and sometimes new ones came in and proved themselves of use and stayed. And Jehankin taught me all I needed to know, for he's a clever cat, you can't think how cunning and brainy and brilliant as a star. I even learnt the human language because Jehankin made sure I heard and saw the things I must in order to do so. But the cats were my people. They never despised me that I couldn't copy all their skills. They kept me safe and sane. And in the end, when I was about fourteen, Jehankin found this village, and this cottage, and he and I and some of his sons and daughters and wives came here.

"In the beginning the villagers were afraid of me. But with time they came to understand I could help with healing, and talking to wild panthers and such like—and they could ask for little magics like the lighting of a fire without striking a flint, or the unfreezing of water that seems to come from a single word. Five years have passed. Now the village is quite proud to have a witch, even a furry one. And sometimes, as you saw, persons come great distances for cures, or some spell of good luck. And none of them doubts for one moment—" Here Felidis broke off, she lowered her eyes as if shy— "that I am a genuine witch. Although some more distant villages still fear me, the female who is part girl and part cat."

Radlo found himself speechless. But he also found next minute he said, "Jehankin must have been the tiniest kitten when you first met him. He's only a young cat now—and you've known him, by your own reckoning, nineteen years less three. Yet there isn't a gray whisker in his head."

To which she said nothing, but Jehankin himself sat up and stared straight at Radlo with his eyes of cool yellow clearness. If he was even six years old, never mind sixteen, seemed unlikely. But then, he was Felidis's Familiar, who had woken her true magic gifts.

Just then Felidis rose and Jehankin jumped down and followed her to the door. When she opened it, out he went into the moonless night. It seemed she had known what he wanted, it often did so, without any visible sign.

After that she went upstairs. Radlo put the cups and bowls into water, and made up his bed on the floor.

Something in him, which had been soothed and glad, had grown edgy. And lying watching the fire reflection on the ceiling—above which lay her noiseless room—that question began in his heart and mind:

Am I in love with her? I can't even look at her half the time— can't be in love . . . but am I?

4

How quick the last of summer and then fall fell away, like water through a sieve.

When the first snow came drifting down like flour over the gray-blue afternoon, Radlo was still living in the cottage. He still did the heavier chores, and also he had been teaching Felidis to read and write.

During these lessons Jehankin was nearly always present. He observed everything they did, both tutor and pupil, peering over the witch's shoulder. Though Radlo's writing the cat seemed to prefer to look at upside down.

Radlo grew accustomed to Jehankin, as he had to the other cats. He was used to Felidis saying they were her brothers and sisters, and the youngest ones her nephews and nieces. Once Radlo asked her, if that were the case, how were she and Jehankin related? "Oh, we're not," she said. "Though truly, he's been like the father I never had. But more than that, he's my Liege-lord, my prince. I owe him everything."

Radlo was *not* jealous of Jehankin.

Definitely not. Radlo was not going to be jealous of a *cat*. Even a cat like that one.

But Radlo had gotten used as well to being in love with Felidis, with finding her weirdly beautiful, and despite this, with *never* stepping out of line. He'd no more put an arm around her waist or bend to kiss her than—than what? Than try to bloody well fly.

Love. It was hopeless. But it wouldn't go away. And so, as she still made room for him, neither did he.

Winter wasn't a bad time there. They ate well, the villagers bringing her quite a regular supply of meat, the makings for bread, and other stuff. When the snow became serious they were wedged into a loaf of white ice, but there was plenty for dinner, and at Christ Mass a feast. Radlo fixed the cottage roof, cleared the chimney. He wrote poetry on the last of his store of paper—to her, of course, mentally kicking himself all the while.

Wait till spring. He could get out then. Go away. Make for the damn town on the damn river.

Each night in the firelight, if she wasn't there but working above, he spoke softly to her of her changing her ways, of courting her, of her trying him out.

When she *was* there he talked about the gray foxes he'd seen, the dark pheasant stalking through the snow-glades, or the broken bucket he had patched up.

The thaw began about a month after Christ Mass.

Radlo could have killed it, that warmish, slick wet shiny scent in the outer air, the drip of icicles over the door. The first reddish buds filled him with rage.

"I think I'll be off in a few days, Felidis. Once the slush has cleared a bit. The weather's good. You told that woman who came to ask it would be a forward, lasting spring. Fine traveling weather."

If he had hoped to see her look upset, forlorn, she didn't. She smiled at him. When she smiled, the delicate pearly fur by her lips rippled like a rill along a brook. And her lips looked so smooth, nice . . .

"That's sensible, Radlo. And you've been such a help to me. Only think, with the spring I can send for books on herbal lore, to increase my knowledge. Now I can *read*. I must give you a thank-you gift," she added with—he felt—sudden tenderness. "I wonder, what would you like?"

You.

He stared at her bleakly, biting on the unspoken word.

Then, "What I'd *like* I don't think you'd give. *'Oh shut up, you dumbleskull.'*"

But she turned her cat's eyes on him and he could no longer

look at her. She said, very low, "No, I couldn't. Nor would you truly want it."

"You don't know me. Or that."

"Nor do you know it," she answered crisply. "Or yourself."

"But—" he shouted, getting up, flapping his arms like a crazed goose.

And exactly then, over the afternoon hill began to come a sound of voices and cartwheels, and Radlo knew someone else was about to arrive, needing her in the only way she'd recognize. A man or woman desperate for her sorcerous skills.

He turned and walked out of the cottage, and stood outside in the mud, watching the cart drawn by a big horse, and the escort of several villagers. The woodcutter lay on some straw. He was unconscious, and had been bleeding. But anything like this, and to the witch they came. She had never failed them. And Radlo wanted to bellow with fury at all of them for the interruption; unfair and unforgivable, a spoiled brat. He took himself off into the trees.

Then about a step short of a mile from the cottage he stopped. He turned and went back. But this time moving carefully and stealthily, approaching the house and its out-buildings from the other side, where no one was. He knew every nook and cranny of the place by now, all but her upstairs room where he had never been. Yet, this winter, while roof-fixing, he had discovered there was a little window up there, completely hidden from below. He'd never spied through it. Even had he been so base as to be tempted, the old glass was thick back then with snow. But it was spring now.

"I'll tell you what I want, Felidis, since you asked me," Radlo muttered to the last trees beyond the house. "I want to see what the hell you do with your magic. If I can't have *you*—at least I'll have *that.*"

It was about midnight that Radlo came back the *second* time. There was still a lamp burning in the lower room. When he pushed in through the door no sorcerous spell was spun to keep him out. Nothing seemed changed. The cats that stayed indoors were clustered here and there, sparring, washing, sleeping, as ever. Felidis sat by the fire on the bench, winding a skein of light green wool.

Of Jehankin there wasn't a sign.

But then, he was usually off all night, about his own business in the wood or the world.

His own business—

Radlo slammed the door.

Felidis showed no reaction; her hands never faltered on the wool.

"You're a liar," Radlo rasped in a rough lunatic voice.

It was a fact: anyone who spied on a witch was liable to be smitten mad, or blind, or simply dead. Serve him right, then.

Felidis did not reply.

"I say you're a liar, *cat-girl,* because you're no more a witch than I'm a—than I'm a *cat.*"

At this she raised her face and smiled at him. And he saw, as he never had before, indescribably she smiled just the way Jehankin did.

"Yes," said Felidis. "I thought one day you'd come to find out."

Then Radlo hung his head. He slumped down on the floor and gazed into the fire. But all he could see in the flames was what already he'd seen earlier, through the little window in the roof.

The injured woodcutter, who had been deeply and nearly fatally slashed by a breaking axe-head, lay on a mattress, and he hadn't a flicker of awareness left to him, though he still breathed. Felidis stood mixing a beer-colored fluid in a cup, but every so often she turned her head, and looked attentively at the black cat with the white fur breastplate, her prince, Jehankin. One couldn't miss that by this turning of hers, this pause and then going on with her herbs and the mixture, she seemed to be following a series of instructions. Yet nobody else, aside from the black and white cat and the senseless man, was in the room.

Meanwhile, Jehankin himself, fastidious and spruce from a recent thorough preen, sat about one-third of an arm's length from the woodcutter's face. At regular intervals Jehankin leaned forward and breathed out his healthy meaty cat-breath across the man's closed lids. And then, so subtly, the cat would put out a paw—usually the left one—and place it, claws sheathed, for a split second on the woodcutter's forehead. Radlo watched about five minutes of this until, at one of these touches, the villager opened his eyes. He saw Jehankin, and then he drew in a huge breath and let it go in a vast sigh, as if he'd just eaten a wonderful meal, or woken from a fabulous sleep. After which he blinked and turned and saw Felidis, by which time the cat's paw had been withdrawn. "Ah, lady Felidis," said the woodcutter, "I feel a whole lot better. You're a real wonder, you are." And Felidis had glided to him and held the herbal cup to his mouth.

"Drink deep," she had said. "You'll be right as summer rain by daybreak."

"It's the cat," said Radlo now, as midnight turned to the first hour of morning. "The *cat*. Isn't it? The *cat's* the sorcerer."

"Yes." Felidis's face was abruptly full of delight. She beamed, and threw down the wool, and raised her arms slowly up. "The cat, himself, my teacher and my prince, Jehankin. *He* is the witch. *He* is the genius."

"Then what in the Lord's Name are *you*?" whispered Radlo, weeping now; he couldn't help it.

"I," said Felidis, with the pride and glory of a king, "have the honor to be his *Familiar,* who—while he found me ignorant and all alone—nevertheless woke in him the skill of his true magic."

5

"You didn't tell me what you'd like to say my thank you—"

"I did."

"No, my dear. That *isn't* what you'd really like. Trust me—or trust himself there, for he *knows.*"

"It's a cat," sulked Radlo.

She laughed. He loved her laugh. The cat took no notice.

Of course, naturally, obviously, when dealing with humans—(she had said, "Your *people* need to lose some of their family obsession with their own kind!")—it *had* to seem *she* was the magician. Who would accept the gentle paw of a cat could pass on such miraculous healing, such wonders? (Jehankin had healed Radlo too. Radlo had *not* thanked Jehankin. Jehankin, patently, didn't care.)

"*Listen*," said Felidis. "He told me of a mild spell he'd woven for you, dear Radlo. Please don't scowl. It was kindly done."

"Yeah, yeah," growled Radlo. "Well, I'm off now."

"The Lord bless you," she said. She was so happy and full of compassionate interest in everything—he could have slapped her. But he wasn't that sort of man. Nor such a dolt.

For any dolt who did try that might not like the result, not with Jehankin sitting by the cottage door. Jehankin the witch. The healer. The prince. Her Liege-lord. Oh to hell with it all.

Radlo strode off through the sun-goldening woods, and was as civil as he could be to the villagers who also waved him off on his journey, the woodcutter patting his shoulder and giving him a flask of spiced wine. "You tell them out there, lad. Tell them we have a fine witch here."

"Surely," said Radlo.

Only ten days, nights after did he curse himself for his own foul behavior. But they—she—wouldn't trouble. None of them would care. *He* was irrelevant. And so back came the anger. And full of anger's energy he traveled fast to the west and reached the town by the river in less than thirty days.

That summer in the town, set up by then as a scholar in the university and making a decent living, Radlo met a lovely girl. Her hair was long and the color of sunset bronze. Her eyes were blue as coins minted from the sky.

When once they were friends, she told him she had dreamed, the previous spring, of a cat, black and white and wearing a little silver crown, who called her by name. First the cat, a male, read her a story out of a book—for he could read! Then he told her the love of her life would soon be in the town. And he had been right.

"They're magical, all cats," she said. "Extraordinary creatures descended from the old gods, the *good* gods, who ruled the world before the Lord, and who still sometimes move about here, with His approval."

Radlo kissed her. He loved her and she him, and in another year they would be married, a union that would last the rest of their lives. But Jehankin *hadn't* given Radlo this wedding of love, no more than Radlo had inadvertently taught Jehankin to read. Jehankin was a *cat*. And Felidis. Oh, Felidis . . . she was only a witch in a wood, a female covered in fur, and with hair that was fur, who'd gotten two ice-green cat's eyes. A girl who was a cat. Feline. Felidis.

Felidis.

Felidis . . .

WITCH WORK

NEIL GAIMAN

The witch was as old as the mulberry tree.
She lived in the house of a hundred clocks.
She sold storms and sorrows and calmed the sea
And she kept her life in a box.

The tree was the oldest that I'd ever seen.
Its trunk flowed like liquid. It dripped with age.
But every September its fruit stained the green
As scarlet as harlots, as red as my rage.

The clocks whispered time, which they caught in their gears.
They crept and they chattered, they chimed and they chewed.
She fed them on minutes. The old ones ate years.
She feared and she loved them, her wild clocky brood.

She sold me a storm when my anger was strong
And my hate filled the world with volcanoes and laughter.
I watched as the lightnings and wind sang their song
And my madness was swallowed by what happened after.

She sold me three sorrows all wrapped in a cloth.
The first one I gave to my enemy's child.
The second my woman made into a broth.
The third waits unused, for we reconciled.

She sold calm seas to the mariners' wives
Tied winds with silk cords so the storms could be tied there.
The women at home lived much happier lives
Till their husbands returned, and their patience be tried there.

The witch hid her life in a box made of dirt
As big as a fist and as dark as a heart.
There was nothing but time there and silence and hurt
While the witch watched the waves with her pain and her art.

(But he never came back . . . he never came back.)

The witch was as old as the mulberry tree.
She lived in the house of a hundred clocks.
She sold storms and sorrows and calmed the sea
And she kept her life in a box.

THE EDUCATION OF A WITCH

ELLEN KLAGES

I

LIZZY IS AN untidy, intelligent child. Her dark hair resists combs, framing her face like thistles. Her clothes do not stay clean or tucked in or pressed. Some days, they do not stay on. Her arms and face are nut-brown, her bare legs sturdy and grimy.

She intends to be a good girl, but shrubs and sheds and unlocked cupboards beckon. In photographs, her eyes sparkle with unspent mischief; the corner of her mouth quirks in a grin. She is energy that cannot abide fences. When she sleeps, her mother smooths a hand over her cheek, in affection and relief.

Before she met the witch, Lizzy was an only child.

The world outside her bedroom is an ordinary suburb. But the stories in the books her mother reads to her, and the ones she is learning to read herself, are full of fairies and witches and magic.

She knows they are only stories, but after the lights are out, she lies awake, wondering about the parts that are real. She was named after a princess, Elizabeth, who became the queen of England. Her father has been there, on a plane. He says that a man's house is his castle, and when he brings her mother flowers, she smiles and proclaims, "You're a prince, Jack Breyer." Under the sink—where she is not supposed to look—many of the cans say M-A-G-I-C in big letters. She watches very carefully when her mother sprinkles the powders onto the counter, but has not seen sparkles or a wand. Not yet.

2

Lizzy sits on the grass in the backyard, in the shade of the very big tree. Her arms are all over sweaty and have made damp, soft places on the newsprint page of her coloring book. The burnt umber crayon lies on the asphalt driveway, its point melted to a puddle. It was not her favorite. That is purple, worn down to a little stub, almost too small to hold.

On the patio, a few feet away, her parents sit having drinks. The ice cubes clink like marbles against the glass. Her father has loosened his tie, rolled up the sleeves of his white go-to-the-office shirt. He opens the evening paper with a crackle.

Her mother sighs. "I wish this baby would hurry up. I don't think I can take another month in this heat. It's only the end of June."

"Can't rush Mother Nature." More crackle, more clinks. "But I *can* open the windows upstairs. There's a Rock Hudson movie at the drive-in. Should be cool enough to sleep when we get back."

"Oh, that would be lovely! But, what about—" She drops her voice to a whisper. "Iz-ee-lay? It's too late to call the sitter."

Lizzy pays more attention. She does not know what language that is, but she knows her name in most of the secret ways her parents talk.

"Put her in her jammies, throw the quilt in the back of the station wagon, and we'll take her along."

"I don't know. Dr. Spock says movies can be very frightening at her age. *We* know it's make-believe, but—"

"The first show is just a cartoon, one of those Disney things." He looks back at the paper. *"Sleeping Beauty."*

"Really? Well, in that case . . . She loves fairy tales."

Jammies are for after dark, and always in the house. It is confusing, but exciting. Lizzy sits on the front seat, between her parents, her legs straight out in front of her. She can feel the warm vinyl through thin cotton. They drive down Main Street, past the Shell station—S-H-E-L-L—past the dry cleaners that gives free cardboard with her father's shirts, past the Methodist church where she goes to nursery school.

After that, she does not know where they are. Farther than she has ever been on this street. Behind the car, the sun is setting, and even the light looks strange, glowing on the glass and bricks of buildings that have not been in her world before. They drive so far that it is country, flat fields and woods so thick they are all shadow. On either side of her, the windows are rolled down, and the air that moves across her face is soft and smells like grass and barbecue. When they stop at a light, she hears crickets and sees a rising glimmer in the weeds beside the pavement. Lightning bugs.

At the Sky View Drive-In they turn and join a line of cars that creep toward a lighted hut. The wheels bump and clatter over the gravel with each slow rotation. The sky is a pale blue wash now, streaks of red above the dark broccoli of the trees. Beyond the hut where her father pays is a parking lot full of cars and honking and people talking louder than they do indoors.

Her father pulls into a space and turns the engine off. Lizzy wiggles over, ready to get out. Her mother puts a hand on her arm. "We're going to sit right here in the car and watch the movie." She points out the windshield to an enormous white wall. "It'll be dark in just a few minutes, and that's where they'll show the pictures."

"The sound comes out of this." Her father rolls the window halfway up and hangs a big silver box on the edge of the glass. The box squawks with a sharp, loud sound that makes Lizzy put her hands over her ears. Her father turns a knob, and the squawk turns into a man's voice that says, ". . . concession stand right now!" Then there is cartoon music.

"Look, Lizzy." Her mother points again, and where there had been a white wall a minute before is now the biggest Mickey Mouse she has ever seen. A mouse as big as a house. She giggles.

"Can you see okay?" her father asks.

Lizzy nods, then looks again and shakes her head. "Just his head, not his legs." She smiles. "I could sit on Mommy's lap."

"'Fraid not, honey. No room for you until the baby comes."

It's true. Under her sleeveless plaid smock, her mother's stomach is very big and round and the innie part of her lap is outie. Lizzy doesn't know how the baby got in there, or how it's going to come out, but she hopes that will be soon.

"I thought that might be a problem." He gets out and opens the back door. "Scoot behind the wheel for a second."

Lizzy scoots, and her father puts the little chair from her bedroom right on the seat of the car. Its white painted legs and wicker seat look very wrong there. But he holds it steady, and when she climbs up and sits down, it *feels* right. Her feet touch flat on the vinyl, and she can see *all* of Mickey Mouse.

"Better?" He gets back in and shuts his door.

"Uh-huh." She settles in, then remembers. "Thank you, Daddy."

"What a good girl." Her mother kisses her cheek. That's almost as good as a lap.

Sleeping Beauty is Lizzy's first movie. She is not sure what to expect, but it is a lot like TV, only much bigger, and in color. There is a king and queen and a princess who is going to marry the prince, even though she is just a baby. That happens in fairy tales.

Three fairies come to bring presents for the baby. Not very good ones—just beauty and songs. Lizzy is sure the baby would rather have toys. The fairies are short and fat and wear Easter colors. They have round, smiling faces and look like Mrs. Carmichael, her Sunday School teacher, except with pointy hats.

Suddenly the speaker on the window booms with thunder and roaring winds. Bright lightning makes the color pictures go black-and-white for a minute, and a magnificent figure appears in a whoosh of green flames. She is taller than everyone else, and wears shiny black robes lined with purple.

Lizzy leans forward. "Oooh!"

"Don't be scared." Her mother puts a hand on Lizzy's arm. "It's only a cartoon."

"I'm not." She stares at the screen, her mouth open. "She's *beautiful.*"

"No, honey. She's the witch," her father says.

Lizzy pays no attention. She is enchanted. Witches in books are old and bent over, with ugly warts. The woman on the screen has a smooth, soothing voice, red, red lips, and sparkling eyes, just like Mommy's, with a curving slender figure, no baby inside.

She watches the story unfold, and clenches her hands in outrage for the witch, Maleficent. If the whole kingdom was invited to the party, how could they leave *her* out? That is not fair!

Some of this she says a little too out loud, and gets Shhh! from both her parents. Lizzy does not like being shh'd, and her lower lip juts forward in defense. When Maleficent disappears, with more wind and green flames, she sits back in her chair and watches to see what will happen next.

Not much. It is just the fairies, and if they want the baby princess, they have to give up magic. Lizzy does not think this is a good trade. All they do is have tea, and call each other "dear," and talk about flowers and cooking and cleaning. Lizzy's chin drops, her hands lie limp in her lap, her breathing slows.

"She's out," her father whispers. "I'll tuck her into the back."

"No," Lizzy says. It is a soft, sleepy no, but very clear. A few minutes later, she hears the music change from sugar-sweet to pay-attention-now, and she opens her eyes all the way. Maleficent is back. Her long slender fingers are a pale green, like cream of grass, tipped with bright red nails.

"Her hands are pretty, like yours, Mommy," Lizzy says. It is a nice thing to say, a compliment. She waits for her mother to pat her arm, or kiss her cheek, but hears only a soft *pfft* of surprise.

For the rest of the movie, Lizzy is wide, wide awake, bouncing in her chair. Maleficent has her own castle, her own mountain! She can turn into a dragon, purple and black, breathing green fire! She fights off the prince, who wants to hurt her. She forces him to the edge of a cliff and then she—

A tear rolls down Lizzy's cheek, then another, and a loud sniffle that lets all the tears loose.

"Oh, Lizzy-Lou. That was a little *too* scary, huh?" Her mother wipes her face with a tissue. "But there's a happy ending."

"Not happy," Lizzy says between sobs. "He *killed* her."

"No, no. Look. She's not dead. Just sleeping. Then he kisses her, and they live happily ever after."

"Noooo," Lizzy wails. "Not her. *Mel*ficent!"

They do not stay for Rock Hudson.

3

"Lizzy? Put your shoes back on," her mother says.

Her father looks up over *Field and Stream*. "Where are you two off to?"

"Town and Country. I'm taking Lizzy to the T-O-Y S-T-O-R-E."

"Why? Her birthday's not for months."

"I know. But everyone's going to bring presents for the baby, and Dr. Spock says that it's important for her to have a little something, too. So she doesn't feel left out."

"I suppose." He shrugs and reaches for his pipe.

When her mother stops the car right in front of Kiddie Korner, Lizzy is so excited she can barely sit still. It is where Christmas happens. It is the most special place she knows.

"You can pick out a toy for yourself," her mother says when they are inside. "Whatever tickles your fancy."

Lizzy is not sure what part of her is a fancy, but she nods and looks around. Kiddie Korner smells like cardboard and rubber and dreams. Aisle after aisle of dolls and trucks, balls and blocks, games and guns. The first thing she sees is Play-Doh. It is fun to roll into snakes, and it tastes salty. But it is too ordinary for a fancy.

She looks at stuffed animals, at a doll named Barbie who is not a baby but a grown-up lady, at a puzzle of all the United States. Then she sees a *Sleeping Beauty* coloring book. She opens it to see what pictures it has.

"What fun! Shall we get that one?"

"Maybe."

It is too soon to pick. There is a lot more store. Lizzy puts it back on the rack and turns a corner. *Sleeping Beauty* is everywhere. A Little Golden Book, a packet of View-Master reels, a set of to-cut-out paper dolls, a lunchbox. She stops and considers each one. It is hard to choose. Beside her, she hears an impatient puff from her mother, and knows she is running out of time.

She is about to go back and get the coloring book when she sees a shelf of bright yellow boxes. Each of them says P-U-P-P-E-T in large letters.

"Puppets!" she says, and runs over to them.

"Oh, look at those! Which one shall we get? How about the princess? Isn't she pretty!"

Lizzy does not answer. She is busy looking from one box to the next, at the molded vinyl faces that peer out through cellophane windows. Princess, princess, princess. Prince. King. Fairy, fairy, prince, fairy, princess—and then, at the end of the row, she sees the one that she has not quite known she was looking for. Maleficent!

The green face smiles down at her like a long-lost friend.

"That one!" Lizzy is not tall enough to grab the box; she points as hard as she can, stretching her arm so much it pulls her shoulder.

Her mother's hand reaches out, then stops in mid-air. "Oh." She frowns. "Are you sure? Look, here's Flora, and Fauna and—" She pauses. "Who's the other one?"

"Merryweather," Lizzy says. "But I want *her*!" She points again to Maleficent.

"Hmm. Tell you what. I'll get you all *three* fairies."

That is tempting. But Lizzy knows what she wants now, and she knows how to get it. She does not yell or throw a tantrum. She shakes her head slowly and makes her eyes very sad, then looks up at her mother and says, in a quiet voice, "No thank you, Mommy."

After a moment, her mother sighs. "Oh, *all* right," she says, and reaches for the witch.

Lizzy opens the box as soon as they get in the car. The soft vinyl head of the puppet is perfect—smiling red lips, yellow eyes, curving black horns. Just as she remembers. Beneath the pale green chin is a red ribbon, tied in a bow. She cannot see anything more, because there is cardboard.

It takes her a minute to tug that out, and then the witch is free. Lizzy stares. She expected flowing purple and black robes, but Maleficent's cotton body is a red plaid mitten with a place for a thumb on both sides.

Maybe the black robes are just for dress-up. Maybe this is her bathrobe. Lizzy thinks for a few minutes, then decides that is true. Plaid is what Maleficent wears when she's at home, in her castle, reading the paper and having coffee. It is more comfortable than her work clothes.

4

On Saturday, Lizzy and her mother go to Granny Atkinson's house on the other side of town. The women talk about baby clothes and doctor things, and Lizzy sits on the couch and plays with her sneaker laces. Granny gets out a big brown book, and shows her a picture of a fat baby in a snowsuit. Mommy says *she* was that baby, a long time ago, but Lizzy does not think that could be true. Granny laughs and after lunch teaches Lizzy to play gin rummy and lets her have *two* root beers because it is so hot.

When they pull into their own driveway, late in the afternoon, Lizzy's mother says, "There's a big surprise upstairs!" Her eyes twinkle, like she can hardly wait.

Lizzy can't wait, either. She runs in the front door and up to her room, which has yellow walls and a window that looks out onto the driveway so she can see when Daddy comes home. She has slept there her whole life. When she got up that morning, she made most of her bed and put Maleficent on the pillow to guard while she was at Granny's.

When she reaches the doorway, Lizzy stops and stares. Maleficent is gone. Her *bed* is gone. Her dresser with Bo Peep and her bookcase and her toy chest and her chair. All gone.

"Surprise!" her father says. He is standing in front of another room, across the hall, where people sleep when they are guests. "Come and see."

Lizzy comes and sees blue walls and brown heavy curtains. Her bed is next to a big dark wood dresser with a mirror too high for her to look into. Bo Peep is dwarfed beside it, and looks as lost as her sheep. The toy chest is under a window, Maleficent folded on top.

"Well, what do you think?" Her father mops his face with a bandana and tucks it between his blue jeans and his white t-shirt.

"I *liked* my room," Lizzy says.

"That's where the baby's going to sleep, now." Her mother gives her a one-arm hug around the shoulders. "*You* get a big-girl room." She looks around. "We will have to get new curtains. You can help me pick them out. Won't that be fun?"

"Not really." Lizzy stands very still in the room that is not her room. Nothing is hers anymore.

"Well, I'll let you get settled in," her father says in his glad-to-meet-you voice, "and get the grill started." He ruffles his hand on Lizzy's hair. "Hot dogs tonight, just for you."

Lizzy tries to smile, because they are her favorite food, but only part of her mouth goes along.

At bedtime, her mother hears her prayers and tucks her in and sings the good-night song in her sweet, soft voice. For that few minutes, everything is fine. Everything is just the way it used to be. But the moment the light is off and the door is closed—not all the way—that changes. All the shadows are wrong. A street-light is outside one window now, and the very big tree outside the other, and they make strange shapes on the walls and the floor.

Lizzy clutches Maleficent under the covers. The witch will protect her from what the shapes might become.

5

"When do you get the baby?" Lizzy asks. They are in the yellow bedroom, Lizzy's real room. Her mother is folding diapers on the new changing table.

"Two weeks, give or take. I'll be gone for a couple of days, because babies are born in a hospital."

"I'll go with you!"

"I'd like that. But this hospital is only for grown-ups. You get to stay here with Teck."

Teck is Lizzy's babysitter. She has a last name so long no one can say it. Lizzy likes her. She has white hair and a soft, wrinkled face and makes the *best* grilled cheese sandwiches. And she is the only person who will play Candy Land more than once.

But when the baby starts to come, it is ten days too soon. Teck is away visiting her sister Ethel. Lizzy's father pulls into the driveway at two in the afternoon with Mrs. Sloupe, who watches Timmy Lawton when his parents go out. There is nothing soft about her. She has gray hair in tight little curls, and her lipstick mouth is bigger than her real one.

"I'll take your suitcase upstairs," he tells her. "You can sleep in our room tonight."

Her mother sits in a chair in the living room. Her eyes are closed, and she is breathing funny. Lizzy stands next to her and pats her hand. "There there, Mommy."

"Thank you, sweetie," she whispers.

Daddy picks her up and gives her a hug, tight and scratchy. "When you wake up in the morning, you're going to be a big sister," he says. "So I need you to behave for Mrs. Sloupe."

"I'll be very have," Lizzy says. The words tremble.

He puts her down and Mommy kisses the top of her head. Then they are gone.

Mrs. Sloupe does not want to play a game. It is time for her stories on TV. They can play after dinner. Dinner is something called chicken ala king, which is yellow and has peas in it. Lizzy only eats two bites because it is icky, and her stomach is scared.

Lizzy wins Candy Land. Mrs. Sloupe will not play again. It is bedtime. But she does not know how bedtime works. She says the now-I-lay-me prayer with the wrong words, and tucks the covers too tight.

"Playing fairy tales, were you?" she says, reaching for Maleficent. "I'll put this ugly witch in the toy chest, where you can't see it. Don't want you having bad dreams."

"No!" Lizzy holds on to the puppet with both arms.

"Well, aren't you a queer little girl?" Mrs. Sloupe says. "Suit yourself." She turns off the light and closes the door, all the way, which makes the shadows even more wrong. When Lizzy finally falls asleep, the witch's cloth body is damp and sticky with tears.

Her father comes home the next morning, unshaven and bleary. He picks Lizzy up and hugs her. "You have a baby sister," he says. "Rosemary, after your mother's aunt." Then he puts her down and pats her behind, shooing her into the living room to watch *Captain Kangaroo*.

Lizzy pauses just beyond the hall closet, and before he shuts the kitchen door, she hears him tell Mrs. Sloupe, "She was breech. Touch and go for a while, but they're both resting quietly, so I think we're out of the woods."

He takes Mrs. Sloupe home after dinner, and picks her up the next morning. It is three days before Teck arrives to be the real babysitter, and she is there every day for a week before he brings Mommy and the baby home.

"There's my big girl," her mother says. She is sitting up in bed. Her face looks pale and thinner than Lizzy remembers, and there are dark places under her eyes. The baby is wrapped in a pink blanket beside her. All Lizzy can see is a little face that looks like an old lady.

"Can we go to the playground today?"

"No, sweetie. Mommy needs to rest."

"Tomorrow?"

"Maybe next week. We'll see." She kisses Lizzy's cheek. "I think there's a new box of crayons on the kitchen table. Why don't you go look? I'll be down for dinner."

Dinner is a sack of hamburgers from the Eastmoor Drive-In. At bedtime, Mommy comes in and does all the right things. She sings *two* songs, and Lizzy falls asleep smiling. But she has a bad dream, and when she goes to crawl into bed with Mommy and Daddy, to make it all better, there is no room. The baby is asleep between them.

For days, the house is full of grown-ups. Ladies and aunts come in twos and threes and bring casseroles and only say hi to Lizzy. They want to see the baby. They all make goo-goo sounds and say, "What a little darling!" At night, some men come, too. They look at the baby, but just for a minute, and do not coo. They go out onto the porch and have beers and smoke.

The rest of the summer, all any grown-up wants to do is hold the baby or feed the baby or change the baby. Lizzy doesn't know why; it is *very* stinky. She tries to be more interesting, but no one notices. The baby cannot do a somersault, or say the Pledge of Allegiance or sing "Fairy Jocka Dormy Voo." All she can do is lie there and spit up and cry.

And sleep. The baby sleeps all the time, and every morning and every afternoon, Mommy naps with her. The princess is sleeping, so the whole house has to stay quiet. Lizzy cannot play her records, because it will wake the baby. She can't jump on her bed. She can't even build a tall tower with blocks because if it crashes, it will wake the baby. But when the baby screams, which is a lot, no one even says Shhh!

Lizzy thinks they should give the baby back.

"Will you read to me?" she asks her mother, when nothing else is happening.

"Oh . . . not now, Lizzy-Lou. I've got to sterilize some bottles for Rosie. How 'bout you be a big girl, and read by yourself for a while?"

Lizzy is tired of being a big girl. She goes to her room but does not slam the door, even though she wants to, because she is also tired of being yelled at. She picks up Maleficent. The puppet comes to life around her hand. Maleficent tells Lizzy that she is very smart, very clever, and Lizzy smiles. It is good to hear.

Lizzy puts on her own bathrobe, so they match. "Will you read to me?" she asks. "Up here in our castle?"

Maleficent nods, and says in a smooth voice, "Of course I will. That would be lovely," and reads to her all afternoon. Even though she can change into anything she wants—a dragon, a ball of green fire—her eyes are always kind, and every time Lizzy comes into the room, she is smiling.

On nights when Mommy is too tired, and Daddy puts Lizzy to bed, the witch sings the good-night song in a sweet, soft voice. She knows all the words. She whispers "Good night, Lizzy-Tizzy-Toot," the special, only-at-bedtime, good-dreams name.

Maleficent loves Lizzy best.

6

Lizzy is glad when it is fall and time for nursery school, where they do not allow babies. Every morning Mrs. Breyer and Mrs. Huntington and Mrs. Lawton take turns driving to Wooton Methodist Church. When her mother drives, Lizzy gets to sit in the front seat. Other days she has to share the back with Tripper or Timmy.

She has known Timmy her whole life. The Lawtons live two

doors down. They have a new baby, too, another boy. When they had cocktails to celebrate, Lizzy heard her father joke to Mr. Lawton: "Well, Bob, the future's settled. My two girls will marry your two boys, and we'll unite our kingdoms." Lizzy does not think that is funny.

Timmy is no one's handsome prince. He is a gangly, insubstantial boy who likes to wear sailor suits. His eyes always look as though he'd just finished crying because he is allergic to almost everything, and is prone to nosebleeds. He is not a good pick for Red Rover.

The church is a large stone building with a parking lot and a playground with a fence around it. Nursery school is in a wide, sunny room on the second floor. Lizzy climbs the steps as fast as she can, hangs up her coat on the hook under L-I-Z-Z-Y, and tries to be the first to sit down on the big rug in the middle of the room, near Mrs. Dickens. There are two teachers, but Mrs. Dickens is her favorite. She wears her brown hair in braids wrapped all the way around her head and smells like lemons.

Lizzy knows all the color words and how to count up to twenty. She can write her whole name—without making the Z's backward—so she is impatient when the other kids do not listen to her. Sometimes she has to yell at them so she can have the right color of paint. The second week of school, she has to knock Timmy down to get the red ball at recess.

Mrs. Dickens sends a note home, and the next morning, the next-door neighbor comes over to watch the baby so Lizzy's mother can drive her to school, even though it is not her turn.

"Good morning, Lizzy," Mrs. Dickens says at the door. "Will

you get the music basket ready? I want to talk to your mother for a minute."

Lizzy nods. She likes to be in charge. But she also wants to know what they are saying, so she puts the tambourine and the maracas in the basket very quietly, and listens.

"How are things at home?" Mrs. Dickens asks.

"A little hectic, with the new baby. Why?"

"New baby. Of course." Mrs. Dickens looks over at Lizzy and puts a finger to her lips. "Let's continue this out in the hall," she says, and that's all Lizzy gets to hear.

But when they make Circle, Mrs. Dickens pats the right side of her chair, and says, "Come sit by me, Lizzy." They sing the good-morning song and have Share and march to a record and Lizzy gets to play the cymbals. When it is time for Recess, Mrs. Dickens rings the bell on her desk, and they all put on their coats and hold hands with their buddies and walk down the stairs like ladies and gentlemen. For the first time, Mrs. Dickens is Lizzy's buddy, and no one gets knocked down.

On a late October morning, Lizzy's mother dresses her in the green wool coat, because it is cold outside. It might snow. She runs up the stairs, but the coat is stiff and has a lot of buttons, and by the time she hangs it up, Anna von Stade is sitting in *her* place in the circle. Lizzy has to sit on the other side of Mrs. Dickens, and is not happy. Timmy sits down beside her, which does not help at all.

"Children! Children! Quiet now. Friday is a holiday. Who knows what it is?"

Lizzy's hand shoots straight up. Mrs. Dickens calls on Kevin.

"It's Halloween," he says.

"Very good. And we're going to have our *own* Halloween party."

"I'm going to be Pinocchio!" David says.

"We raise our hand before speaking, David." Mrs. Dickens waggles her finger at him, then waits for silence before she continues. "That will be a good costume for trick-or-treating. But for *our* party, I want each of you to come dressed as who you want to be when you grow up."

"I'm going to be a fireman!"

"I'm going to be a bus driver!"

"I'm going—"

Mrs. Dickens claps her hands twice. "Children! We do not talk out of turn, and we do not talk when others are talking."

The room slowly grows quiet.

"But it is good to see that you're all *so* enthusiastic. Let's go around the circle, and everyone can have a chance to share." She looks down to her right. "Anna, you can start."

"I'm going to be a ballerina," Anna says.

Lizzy does not know the answer, and she does not like that. Besides, she is going to be last, and all the right ones will be gone. She crosses her arms and scowls down at the hem of her plaid skirt.

"I'm going to be a doctor," Herbie says.

Fireman. Doctor. Policeman. Teacher. Mailman. Nurse. Baseball player. Mommy. Lizzy thinks about the lady jobs. Nurses wear silly hats and have to be clean all the time, and she is not good at that. Teacher is better, but two people have already said it. She wonders what else there is.

Tripper takes a long time. Finally he says, "I guess I'll be in sales."

"Like your father? That's nice." Mrs. Dickens nods. "Carol?"

Carol will be a mommy. Bobby will be a fireman.

Timmy takes the longest time of all. Everyone waits and fidgets. Finally he says he wants to drive a steam shovel like Mike Mulligan. "That's fine, Timmy," says Mrs. Dickens.

And then it is her turn.

"What are *you* going to be when you grow up, Lizzy?"

"Can I see the menu, please?" Lizzy says. That is what her father says at the Top Diner when he wants a list of answers.

Mrs. Dickens smiles. "There isn't one. You can be anything you want."

"Anything?"

"That's right. You heard Andrew. He wants to be president someday, and in the United States of America, he can be."

Lizzy doesn't want to be president. Eisenhower is bald and old. Besides, that is a daddy job, like doctor and fireman. What do ladies do besides mommy and nurse and teacher? She thinks very hard, scrunching up her mouth—and then she knows!

"I'm going to be a witch," she says.

She is very proud, because no one has said that yet, no one in the whole circle. She looks up at Mrs. Dickens, waiting to hear, "Very good. Very creative, Lizzy," like she usually does.

Mrs. Dickens does not say that. She shakes her head. "We are not using our imaginations today. We are talking about real-life jobs."

"I'm going to be a witch."

"There is no such thing." Mrs. Dickens is frowning at Lizzy now, her face as wrinkled as her braids.

"Yes there is!" Lizzy says, louder. "In 'Hansel and Gretel,' and 'Snow White,' and 'Sleeping—'"

"Elizabeth? You know better than that. Those are only stories."

"Then stupid Timmy can't drive a steam shovel because Mike Mulligan is only a story!" Lizzy shouts.

"That's *enough*!" Mrs. Dickens leans over and picks Lizzy up under the arms. She is carried over to the chair that faces the corner and plopped down. "You will sit here until you are ready to say you're sorry."

Lizzy stares at the wall. She is sorry she is sitting in the dunce chair, and she is sorry that her arms hurt where Mrs. Dickens grabbed her. But she says nothing.

Mrs. Dickens waits for a minute, then makes a *tsk* noise and goes back to the circle. For almost an hour, Lizzy hears nursery school happening behind her: blocks clatter, cupboards open, Mrs. Dickens gives directions, children giggle and whisper. This chair does not feel right at all, and Lizzy squirms. After a while she closes her eyes and talks to Maleficent without making any sound. Out of long repetition, her thumb and lips move in concert, and the witch responds.

Lizzy is asking when she will learn to cast a spell, how that is different from spelling ordinary W-O-R-D-S, when the Recess bell rings behind her. She makes a disappearing puff with her fingers and opens her eyes. In a moment, she feels Mrs. Dickens's hand on her shoulder.

"Have you thought about what you said?" Mrs. Dickens asks.

"Yes," says Lizzy, because it is true.

"Good. Now, tell Timmy you're sorry, and you may get your coat and go outside."

She turns in the chair and sees Timmy standing behind Mrs. Dickens. His hands are on his hips, and he is grinning like he has won a prize.

Lizzy does not like that. She is not sorry.

She is *mad*.

Mad at Mommy, mad at the baby, mad at all the unfair things. Mad at Timmy Lawton, who is right here.

Lizzy clenches her fists and feels a tingling, all over, like goosebumps, only deeper. She glares at Timmy, so hard that she can feel her forehead tighten, and the anger grows until it surges through her like a ball of green fire.

A thin trickle of blood oozes from Timmy Lawton's nose. Lizzy stares harder and watches blood pour across his pale lips and begin to drip onto his sailor shirt, red dots appearing and spreading across the white stripes.

"Help?" Timmy says.

Mrs. Dickens turns around. "Oh, dear. Not again." She sighs and calls to the other teacher. "Linda? Can you get Timmy a washcloth?"

Lizzy laughs out loud.

In an instant, Lizzy and the chair are off the ground. Mrs. Dickens has grabbed it by the rungs and carries it across the room and out the classroom door. Lizzy is too startled to do anything but hold on. Mrs. Dickens marches down the hall, her shoes like drumbeats.

She deposits Lizzy with a thump in the corner of an empty

Sunday school room, shades drawn, dim and chilly with brown-flecked linoleum and no rug.

"You. Sit. There," Mrs. Dickens says in a voice Lizzy has not heard her use before.

The door shuts and footsteps echo away. Then she is alone and everything is very quiet. The room smells like chalk and furniture polish. She lets go of the chair and looks around. On one side is a blackboard, on the other a picture of Jesus with a hat made of thorns, like the ones Maleficent put around Sleeping Beauty's castle.

Lizzy nods. She kicks her feet against the rungs of the small chair, bouncing the rubber heels of her saddle shoes against the wood. She hears the other children clatter in from Recess. Her stomach gurgles. She will not get Snack.

But she is not sorry.

It is a long time before she hears cars pull into the parking lot, doors slamming and the sounds of many grown-up shoes on the wide stone stairs.

She tilts her head toward the door, listens.

". . . Rosemary? Isn't she adorable!" That is Mrs. Dickens.

And then, a minute later, her mother, louder. "Oh, dear, *now* what?"

Another minute, and she hears the click-clack of her mother's shoes in the hall, coming closer.

Lizzy turns in the chair, forehead taut with concentration. The tingle begins, the green fire rises inside her. She smiles, staring at the doorway, and waits.

THE THREEFOLD WORLD

ELLEN KUSHNER

WHEN HE WAS an old man, honored by his countrymen and foreign scholars alike, Elias Lönnrot was still a humble person. What else would he be, he who had been born in a one-room cottage where people spoke only Finnish, the language of poor peasants? His father was a tailor, who sewed rough clothes for others and taught his son his trade. But young Elias was too hungry to sit still and sew. He wanted knowledge; he wanted the wide world. He wanted it so much that he learned to read, and taught himself Swedish, the language of the ones who had ruled his poor country for hundreds of years. He made his way to school, this boy with the much-darned shirt cuffs and the letters dancing in his eyes, all the way to Turku by the sea, the great capital city.

When he got to Turku Cathedral School, he wasn't the only poor boy, though he may have been the smartest. Elias and his friends, the other hungry ones, slept four to a bed, head to foot—which was all right, as the Finnish winters are bitter cold, even in Turku by the sea. They shared everything: food and heat and their precious books, the Latin and the Greek texts with pages worn and covers battered by the scholars before them.

"There's a world out there," Elias would say, "a world of words and knowledge, and it's ours for the taking, boys!"

He meant "mine for the taking," in those days; for his friends, though good-hearted and intelligent enough, seemed weak to him, lacking in discipline and understanding, slow to grasp what seemed obvious to him in the lectures of the Turku masters. So what if his friends' Swedish ran more smoothly on their tongues sometimes than his? Could his friends recite from memory the Latin poems of Virgil? So what if they knew the tavern gossip about the Frenchman Napoleon's escape from St. Helena before he did? Their tongues stumbled when they read the Greek epics, *The Iliad* and *The Odyssey,* the roots of the civilization that had spawned Western culture, all that a wise man truly needed to know.

And lately they'd even gotten some notion about studying Finnish language and history! But Finnish was useless to Elias Lönnrot. There was nothing to read in Finnish, nothing new for almost three hundred years, and even then just a rendering of a greater work, when the scholar Agricola translated the Bible back in 1548, so that his ignorant people could hear God's word in their own tongue.

Which was, as Elias said, no great surprise. The Finnish tongue was all very well for cowherds and shepherds. Village mothers sang to their children in Finnish—it was the mother tongue, yes, but once one left childhood behind, it was good for no greater purpose. What had their backward nation contributed to the world? If you could even call it an actual nation at all, after centuries of Swedish rule.

"You're wrong," said his friend Johan. "Come to Doctor Becker's lectures with us, and you'll hear differently. Finnish was once the tongue of a people rich in culture, rich in legend, as rich as the Greeks—who were also cowherds and shepherds themselves, by the way."

"I'll have to remember that, Johan," Elias said sarcastically. "Hesiod's *Works and Days* lauds the glories of Greek husbandry, and of course, Virgil went even further in his bucolic *Eclogues*. Excellent point, *Johan*—or should I call you *Jukka,* since that's your Finnish name, isn't it?"

"Shut up," said Johan.

"The one your mother calls you, I mean?"

"I said shut up, Elias."

"Seriously, though; if you're such a champion of the Finnish tongue now, why do you still use a Swedish name?"

"You both shut up," grumbled Fredrik, whose week it was for the middle of the bed, so he was nice and toasty, and wanted to sleep. "Shut up or I'll sing you into the swamp."

"Your voice is ugly enough to sing anyone into a swamp," retorted Elias, just to have the last word.

But he didn't get it. "And where do you think that threat comes from?" Johan persisted. "To 'sing someone into the swamp'? What does it even mean?"

They were all speaking Finnish now, even Elias. "I just said: it's to have a voice as bad as Fredrik's."

"It's spells," said Johan solemnly. "Doctor Becker says that our ancestors sang spells they believed were so powerful they could change the world around them."

"Just by singing?" asked Ludvig, who loved music.

"There were words, too, special words they chanted in a kind of singsong."

"Oh," Ludvig said abruptly, and went quiet.

"How do you sing someone into a swamp?" Fredrik demanded.

Johan shivered. "By making him go where he doesn't want to go, I guess."

Fredrik murmured: "By making the boggy, smelly, muddy waters rise up around him . . ."

"That sounds useful." Elias refused to be drawn into the delicious horror. "There's a few people I'd like to try that out on."

The others chuckled. "If that's an old Finnish spell," Fredrik added, "too bad we've forgotten how it goes."

"Up in Kuhmo," Ludvig said quietly, so quietly Elias could barely hear him, "in my village, there's an old woman from Karelia province who sings when people get sick. She talks to things that aren't there."

"She talks to diseases?"

"Not exactly."

"Do people get better?"

"My brother," Ludvig said. "I'm not saying it worked or anything, but—"

"What happened?"

"He was— Well, it was horrible. I can't say. We thought he would die. And the old woman came in where he lay, and started chanting, sort of singing, sort of like telling a tale, only then it was like she was talking to someone . . . Pain Maiden, she called her; Pain Maiden of Pain Mountain. She asked her to take the pain from my brother and give it to the rocks of the mountain."

"And it worked?"

"My brother married his sweetheart that spring; they have two children now."

"Aww." Fredrik rumpled his friend's hair. "You're Uncle Ludvig!"

"You should tell Doctor Becker," Johan said seriously. "He's always looking for people who know the old songs. He thinks they're clues to our past."

"Our glorious past?" Elias mocked. "You mean the one with magical village witches? That's pathetic, Johan—even at home in backward little Sammatti village, we don't go in for stuff like that."

Johan grabbed Elias's arm and twisted it behind his back. "Are you calling Doctor Becker an idiot?"

"I'm saying this is the modern age." Elias refused to struggle, although it hurt. He would not let them pull him down to their level. If they wanted to act like the Finnish cowherds they so admired, instead of like true scholars, let them. "We fight diseases with learning, not with singing and superstition."

"If you're so modern, Elias, why are you so in love with ancient Greek?"

"Because it is the origin of all that makes us what we are today."

"Tales of long-dead heroes?"

"The glories of the world," Elias growled through clenched teeth. "You could learn a lot from them."

"It's all just singing, Lönnrot—admit it. Even *The Aeneid* starts with 'Arms and the man I sing. . . .' "

"Speaking of singing," said Ludvig, who loved music and peace, and thought it was time for both, "who's for singing with me out in the Square tomorrow?"

They did that, the poor students of Turku: they sang in the street for passersby, hats out collecting money to buy a meal. If singing didn't bring money, the next step was begging, going house to house for scraps from a kindly pot—and nobody wanted to do that unless they really had to.

But that winter they did have to. Even Elias—especially Elias, whose family had used up all they had just to send him to school in Turku to feed his hunger for learning. He went with Ludvig and Johan and Fredrik, and his hollow cheeks and burning eyes often spoke louder than his friends' attempts at charm with the serving maids and the daughters of the house.

They were all glad when spring came. It was a warm spring; the green shoots of the birches budded early, and the birch forests to the east of the city were like slender white women dancing with ribbons in their hair.

Eastward was the way Elias went, the day after he took his final exam on *The Odyssey,* the story of a man's long voyage home. He wasn't going home, though, and he wasn't going to beg; he was going to make his living earning next year's tuition in the way his father had shown him: as a tailor, stitching together what others could not.

The first day was the hardest. He'd grown unused to walking country roads. His feet were sore, his shoulder ached under his satchel, his neck itched under his collar, and he was incredibly bored with nothing to read. He wasn't looking forward to the next few weeks, either: camping in farmsteads and little villages with people who wouldn't know a book if it bit them on the rear, taking their orders and mending their rough old garments, all the while listening to them yattering away in their clickety-clackety rustic Finnish on such fascinating subjects as taxes and sheep. Or maybe barley and sheep. Or, if he was lucky, sheep and taxes and barley and rye. At least they'd have food. Elias sighed, and tugged at his satchel strap.

That's when it began to rain.

Elias looked around him up and down the road, and then from side to side. Nothing but trees, trees, and more trees, with probably a lake beyond them. He turned up his collar, and plodded on.

Suddenly, ahead of him, he heard something: A voice, raised in a song of sorts—but not the sort of song he knew. It was monotonous, repetitive, more of a chant, really; lines promising a story that never quite ended or began.

He couldn't make out the words.

Around the bend he saw a cart, drawn by a tired old horse. Elias lifted his hand. "Hold up!" he called in simple Finnish. "Hold up a moment!"

The cart slowed and stopped in the middle of the road. The driver was an old man, but large and hale, his great hands energetic on the reins. A long white beard covered as much of his chest as you could see above the old-fashioned cloak that enfolded him, and his face was shadowed by a broad-brimmed hat.

"What is it, lad?" He spoke with a heavy Karelian accent. An easterner, then, from the far provinces bordering Russia, a land whose folk sent pine tar and huge pine tree trunks down their sweeping rivers to the shipyards and harbors of the south.

"Where did you just come from?" Elias asked him. "What's up ahead?"

"Nothing you need, lad, nothing you want."

Elias hadn't eaten all day. He was wet and cold, and not in the mood for games. "You don't know what I want. Just tell me, how far is the next village? Or is there an inn or steading where I could take shelter?"

"Young man," the driver said, "I'm just an old peddler. I've come a long way, and I've a long way to go. My cart is full of whatever people want to buy. If you don't want what I've got, my lad, then stand aside and let me pass. For it's raining, if you hadn't noticed, and night comes on whether we like it or not."

"You'll make it to Turku well before nightfall."

"Who said I'm going to Turku?"

"You're on the road to Turku."

The old man drew his cloak around him. "A lot you know."

"I'm telling you, I've just come from there this morning. On foot. With your horse cart, you'll be there in a couple of hours."

"What would I be doing in great Turku, lad?"

"What you do anywhere. Sell things! You're a peddler, aren't you?"

"What I have, in great Turku they don't want."

"Perhaps so. There are, after all, fine shops in Turku," Elias said rudely. "And what's for sale there under your canvas? Pots and pans for farmwives, dried fish from the coast, ribbons and kettles, tobacco and soap. Maybe you're better off turning around and going back the way you came."

"With you up beside me, to spare your tender feet?" The old man laughed. The rain dripped from his hat. And rain dripped down Elias's neck. He was beginning to be sorry he'd been so rude. A ride on a cart, even with this ignorant Karelian, seemed more and more attractive.

"I just meant—I mean, you might find more business if you go down a side road to a smaller town."

"Maybe so." The man leaned out over his horse. "Come closer, lad, and tell me what you do out on the Turku road this day."

Elias held his head up proudly, feeling the weight of his satchel, half of it books in there, well wrapped in oilcloth. "I am a scholar."

"A scholar! That's a fine way to make a living. Are you off to teach your learning somewhere?"

"I know many things," Elias said, unwilling to tell the truth, but strangely unwilling to lie to the bright blue eyes beneath the dripping hat brim. "I'll gladly speak to those who care to listen."

"Well, that's a start. Hop up, then, lad, and let's see where all this is going."

Elias scrambled up onto the cart next to the old man, who shifted his cloak to reveal a dry patch of wood for him to sit on. From his perch on the cart, he saw two narrow roads branching off to the left and right ahead—roads he must have passed without seeing them, for hadn't he just come from there?

"Now, where away?" the man said softly to himself. And, softly, he began to sing. Elias waited. Singing, the man's accent was even heavier, the words incomprehensible.

"If we—" Elias said, and the man stopped singing and nodded.

"Very well, then," the peddler said. He clucked to the horses, and the cart lumbered forward and off to the northward track.

Under the thick pine trees there was even less light, but they barely felt the rain, though it still whispered above them on the uppermost branches.

"So, my young scholar," the old man said, "tell me what you know."

Elias thought. What could interest a rustic Karelian peddler, and pay for his ride to the next town? "Well," he began: "In Turku there are great buildings, some four stories high, as tall as that pine tree."

"Trees grow, and then they fall, and so must your great buildings someday."

"In Turku market square, hundreds of people gather every day to buy and sell."

"In Tuonela of the Dead, the hundreds gather in their hundreds, and there is no end to their days."

"To Turku harbor, great four-masted ships sail from every corner of the world."

"And when they have no one to sing wind into their sails, they are as still as earth."

Elias sighed. "If Turku holds no interest, shall I tell you of the Fall of Troy?"

"Since it fell, what use is it to you or me?"

The old man started singing under his breath again. Elias caught some of the words: *Golden friend . . . dearest brother . . .*

in my mouth the words are melting . . . Northland . . . Sampo . . . Kalevala . . .

"What's that you're singing?"

"Oh, lad . . . Don't you know your own people's stories? I sing the origins of things. Once they were on everyone's lips, the tales of Ilmarinen Blacksmith; of Mielikki, forest goddess, healer, far more lovely than the moonlight; and of wise old Väinämöinen. Sisters sang them at the well, and the water ran sweet. Mothers sang them in the night, and their children slept safe. Uncles sang them by the fire, and the fire burned bright. Wise men sang them at the hearth, and illness fled the house. Now, even children know neither the words nor the tunes. And in this evil age, time is running out."

"Time ran out long ago," said Elias Lönnrot sadly.

"Do you believe that?" the old man asked. "You who are so young and full of a young man's strength?"

"The glories of the world are long, long past," Elias said, staring out at the trees and the rain. "Mighty Hector died at Troy, and Achilles dragged his body round the walls. Aeneas, who carried his noble father Anchises on his back to safe haven from burning Troy, who loved Dido at Carthage and founded Rome—"

"Those names and heroes are not for you, my boy. Not you."

"Oh no?" Elias nearly fell off the cart, so quickly did he turn and face the speaker. "That is where you are wrong. For haven't I spent every minute God sends in reading and study? And don't I know the Greek and the Latin of the ancient heroes, and the stories that go with them? Noble verses, noble lines full of—" He slapped his hand on the cart's side. "Oh, there's not even any word in this miserable Finnish for the beauty, the—the—fineness, the grace—"

"Tell me," the old man said.

"Tell you what? You think I'm just some stupid jumped-up peasant boy with ideas above his station, is that it? You think I'm not fit to know things my fathers didn't know. Not to raise my head above the dirt, not to know what the wise men of the world know—"

"What you know . . ." The man sighed. "What you know are children's tales. What you lack is understanding."

"Are you saying that my scholarship is worth nothing?"

"Can you tell the origins of true things? Can you mend a horse's leg, or a horseshoe, with it? Or a broken bone, or a broken heart?"

"No one can mend a broken heart. But I can mend what I can mend." And Elias took from his bag his sewing kit. "You think me a useless fellow. You may not like my stories. But my hands are not useless. That raveled tear at the hem of your cloak, I can mend that as good as new, with a good, strong patch so you'll never even know it was there. How's that for payment for the ride?"

"Did I ask for any payment, lad?"

"You don't like my stories," Elias said stiffly. "Don't leave me with useless hands."

The old man shrugged. "Very well, then. Show me what you can do."

In the little space on the seat between them, Elias laid out his tools: his bone needle case, his card of threads, his good iron scissors, a parcel of pins, and scraps of cloth still good enough for patches.

"You'll be careful with all that," the man said. "There's ruts in the road."

"I know what I'm doing."

Carefully Elias chose the best patch to match the peddler's cloak (though in the dim light, he could not be perfectly sure of the exact color, for sometimes the cloak seemed green, sometimes gray, and sometimes brown, like the forest itself); he threaded the needle and stuck it in his jacket lapel for safekeeping. Then he took the raveled hem of the peddler's cloak, and folded the scrap around it, and took up the iron scissors to trim it to just the right size.

That's when it happened. Elias felt the horse stumble, felt the iron slip in his hand. He felt the point of the scissors dig deep into his leg, skating down into his thigh. He saw the blood spurt out—and then, in the next moment, he felt it, too.

"*Ptruuu!*" He heard the man call to the horse to stop. Elias had his hand closed over his thigh, but the blood was coming through. It was as if his body was a river that couldn't stop flowing. He saw it pooling on the floor of the cart by his feet. He stared stupidly; he didn't know what to do.

"The iron, boy—give me the iron!"

Elias was still clutching the scissors, holding them in hands slippery with blood. In his right hand, the cold iron was pressed against the wound. He was afraid to let go, afraid to stop holding.

"Open," the man's voice said. "Open once, then close."

The scissors slid from his grasp, like a knife from a wound.

"Now tell me, boy, and tell me if you can, the origin of iron?"

Why was that important? He was feeling dizzy, now, dizzy and sick. But the man's question sounded urgent. "A blacksmith hammers it," Elias managed to say.

"And before that?"

"He melts it. In a fire." He closed his eyes against the dizziness.

"And before that?"

The question rang in his ears, over and over. He couldn't ignore it, though he barely had strength to speak. He had to say something. He searched the darkness for an answer. "Uh . . . mined. Dug. Out of the earth."

"And before that?"

What did the old man want of him? This wasn't a schoolroom. Couldn't he see that Elias was bleeding to death, here on the forest road? Or was it the forest? Where was the cart? He smelled wood smoke, and felt soft bracken beneath him. No rain was falling on him now. He tried to open his eyes, but the darkness swam in front of them.

"And before that?"

There was a gentle pressure on his leg. Something soft was being pressed there, moss, dried lichen, something. It was soaking up his blood like a sponge, but it couldn't hold it all.

"And before that?"

"I—I don't know. . . ." The world was black before his eyes.

"Do you know the origins of things, boy? The deep origins of things eternal?"

"I don't know what you want me to know," Elias whispered.

"Listen, then. For without them is no power."

His mouth was so dry, his hands and feet so cold. But the

old man's singing came clearly into his head, filling him with his words:

"I will sing the birth of iron. I will tell of its creation."

He was in a cave of fire. Iron was cutting his leg. Blood flowed like water.

And the man was singing, his voice strong, his words clear:

"Iron, born of three sky maidens, daughters of the great Creator. Iron lay still in the swamp, silent in the boggy waters. . . ."

The swamp: a vast bog of swirling mists. He seemed to float among them. There was no day and night there, only time and years uncounted.

"Then came noble Ilmarinen, smith he was, who knew the iron, knew its ways and spoke its language."

Elias saw a man—Elias *was* the man, a huge man with muscled arms, his skin pitted with the marks of firesparks from the anvil. His smith's big hands reached into the swamp and brought out a living thing, its spirit glowing with colors no one had ever seen before or since. In his hands he held it, and he knew its purpose.

"From the iron he drew a promise, never to harm any creature, never to draw blood from mortals. Only then would he take iron, turn it from its useless ways and make it into something solid. Iron promised. Iron promised."

Elias heard his own voice repeating the words: *"Iron promised to draw no blood."* And then he was the smith again.

"Ilmarinen raised his hammer, shaped the iron to his purpose."

His right arm hammered, his left arm held, and the iron took shape . . . a hoe, a plow, a kettle, a pot, a pair of scissors . . .

"But the smith lacked one great thing there—lacked the thing to turn the iron from dark matter to bright steel. So he asked the bees for honey, liquid sweet to temper iron. He believed the bees brought honey, and he put it in the water, plunged the red-hot iron after."

Bees swarmed around Elias's head, sweet honey-bearers—or were they hornets? Angry hornets, buzzing, shouting, making it hard for him to hear the singer's words:

"But it was poison tempered steel there, coldest poison in the water. Iron felt the stinging—cooling, yes, but burning, stinging lye that cooled the water."

White steam rose up from the water where the red-hot iron raged.

"So the iron hissed in fury, turning deadly on its maker. Iron broke its vow in anger. Sharp to cut the flesh of mankind, iron turned to blade and ax head, hardened into sword and spear point, sharp and keen and fell and deadly."

Elias felt each of them in his own leg, now, the sharp steel piercing him, attacking him, full of rage, freed from its promise to the smith never to draw blood.

"That's the origin of iron, faithless, cursed, its word all broken."

Elias's leg pulsed in pain to the old man's chant, throbbing the life out of him.

The singing grew louder: "Once it was of little value, having neither form nor beauty. Iron, are you grown so mighty, you, the breaker of your promise? You're like a dog, now, without honor. Weep for shame, you faithless creature, you who have betrayed your maker."

Elias was weeping. He was alone now, alone and old in a room filled with the words of the dead. Pages of Greek and Latin fluttered all around him, impossible to read, impossible to catch, while outside his window forests burned. And he was going to die here, with nothing.

"Come and view your wicked doings! See what your mistakes have cost you. See what your false vows have made you."

There were things he was supposed to do, but he hadn't done them. Promises he'd made, and hopes that he had had. People he should have loved, songs he should have sung. . . . Dreams that he had dreamed, all gone, all come to nothing.

Strong arms were around his shoulders. "Come, amend this flood of damage."

His head was against the old man's chest. "Blood, now cease your furious flowing," the old man murmured in his ear. "If you must course like a river, flow back through this young man's heart, flow forever in a circle through his muscles, bones, and liver, giving strength to this young hero."

He felt it, then, felt the stillness within and without. And his blood beat slow, slow but steady, steady like a heartbeat at the center of the world.

There was a cup at his lips; Elias drank water cool and clear.

"That's the origin of iron. Know my song, my son, and learn it. Learn to hear a million stories; learn to tell a million more such. To conquer something, you must know it, know and name it, all its truths to its beginnings."

Through the fine summer rain, Elias smelled something like ice, like the tang of distant winter. He opened his eyes. The old man's back was to him, bending over a fire, where a pot steamed.

Above him, pine branches made a shelter, with a hole in the roof for the smoke to pass through.

Elias lay exhausted, as though he'd traveled to the end of a very long road. He didn't know if he had strength yet for the journey back. His legs ached, oh, how his legs ached—especially the left one. He was afraid to touch it, afraid to feel a gaping wound. But it hurt so much. . . .

"Hush, now, boy, and still your weeping."

He hadn't known he was weeping. He tried to be still.

The old man dipped a cloth into the pot, and wrung it out, and brought it to where Elias lay. He pulled back the cloak that covered him and pressed the cloth to his leg, where the mark of the iron was still angry and red. Elias hissed in pain.

The old man handed him the cup again, and Elias drank.

The old man said, "I will go now to Pain Mountain. This journey I must make alone. You have traveled far already, long and far for such a young one. Rest now, sleep now, my young scholar."

The cup was taken from his lips, but still he heard the voice, followed it like a thread in the darkness:

"I will ask of the Pain Maiden if she'll do you one good favor: if she'll take your pain and give it back to the grinding rocks and stones there. Rock and stone can better bear it than a man-child of my people. Rocks don't groan about their anguish; stones don't feel the pain that steel wields."

The smell of wild herbs, of yarrow and oak leaves and aspen, filled the shelter. And much as Elias strove to stay awake through the old man's singing, strove to follow him in his strange words and chanting, in the end he slept.

* * *

In the morning of that night, or maybe the next one, Elias woke with his leg healed. The flesh around the dark pink scar was clear, and the ache was dull, not sharp as stone and iron. The old peddler sat by the fire, stirring it to life.

"You've returned," Elias said.

"How, returned? I've been here with you all along, and a weary watch it's been."

"From Pain Mountain," Elias said.

The old man turned around. "You remember that, do you? You're a quick study, my young scholar."

"Can you tell me of the journey? Can you show the path to get there?"

"That is not your journey, scholar. Many years of study you'd need before you dared make that crossing, to cross safely there and back here, traveling the Threefold World."

"The Threefold World? What's that?"

"You live in it, lad."

Elias thought. "I only live in part of it."

"The middle world, aye; the land of the living. But the spirit travels between life and death, between present and past, between truth and told, between knowing and known."

"I'm young," Elias said. "I can learn."

The old man sighed. "I told you, that is not your journey."

"I know the origins of iron. I remember Ilmarinen Smith, and the treachery. . . ."

"Well, you've made a good beginning. Ask me now a different question."

Elias shifted on his bed of moss, feeling alive and feverish and eager. "All right. Can you really sing someone into a swamp?"

The old man's laugh shook the branches of the roof. "If you knew the answer, you would not be so quick to ask the question."

"But tell me," Elias insisted; "what does it *mean,* precisely? How does it work? How do you do it?"

The old man crouched at his side. He smelled of wild herbs, of yarrow and oak leaves and aspen. "There's a story, old in telling, of a brash young man who thought he knew better than everyone around him. He, who was called Joukahainen, met wise old Väinämöinen on the road, Väinämöinen rich in craft and runelore. The young man challenged him to a singing contest, to test his knowledge, not once but many times—until, in great annoyance, old Väinämöinen lost his temper and sang runes of power, runes that brought the young man up to his chin in swamp water."

"And how did the young man get out of it?"

"Did I say he did?"

"Did he?"

"He promised Väinämöinen the thing he wanted most."

Elias felt himself drifting off to a sleep of utter weakness, a sleep of healing. "What do you want?" he managed to say.

"I want you to sleep now," the old man said, and he did.

The next time Elias woke, yellow sunlight poured in the smoke hole and wove its way between the pine fringe of the roof.

The old man was crouched by the door to the little shelter, his cloak wrapped around himself, a bundle at his side. Next to

Elias, on a broad leaf, sat a cup of water and some thick brown bread.

"Well, I'm off," the old man said. "I've got a cartful of things to unload, and no time to waste."

"Wait." Elias propped himself up on his elbows.

The old man said, "I've waited long enough."

"Take me with you," said Elias.

The peddler shook his head. "You're right off the Turku road; you'll find your way."

Elias struggled to rise. "I want to go with you. I want to know what you know."

"What I know? That's many lifetimes of men and women."

"No, wait—"

If he could just keep him talking, delay his departure, ask the right question . . .

"You've your own journey to make, young scholar. And already you've begun it."

And then Elias realized he'd just been given the answer.

"Many lifetimes of men and women." Elias repeated the traveler's words. "We have that knowledge already. Written in books."

"My book has not yet been written."

"Then I shall write it," Elias said.

The old man turned at last and smiled. Even in the shelter's dimness, his eyes were very blue and clear. "There's the Three-fold Path, my young one. There's the way between the worlds: worlds of telling, worlds of hearing, worlds of knowing, worlds of truth."

"But if I do write it down—all the stories, all the singing—will that make it . . . Won't it ruin it somehow?"

"How can writing ruin singing? How can stories ruin truth?" Elias nodded slowly.

"Stitch together what's been lost, young tailor."

"The origins of our people—it's all still out there, isn't it? Like the Greeks, and the Romans, even—it's our story, and we must tell it. That's a different kind of magic." For the first time he used the word, and hardly even noticed he was using it. "But it's all the same, isn't it?"

Outside, a horse snorted and whinnied impatiently. The old man gathered up his bundle.

"Wait," said Elias. The man turned his head to him. "Will I see you again?"

"Head far eastward when you seek me. Ask for tales of Väinämöinen when you go among the old ones. Ask the women by the hearth fires. Ask the healers, ask for runelore. Ask and listen, write and listen . . . Travel far, and travel farther. Stitch together what's been lost."

Elias worked all summer, going from village to village, making and mending for the money he needed to pay for school. And at summer's end, he walked the dusty roads back to Turku. His friends were glad to see him—and they were wise enough to hide their surprise when, in addition to his Greek and Latin studies, Elias began sitting next to them on the benches of Doctor Becker's classes. He listened silently as Becker lectured on the Finnish language. He said nothing as Becker discussed the strange traditions of the Karelian peasants, and what hidden truths might lie buried in the fragments of song that the women sang to soothe their children's fevers, the teasing games the girls played in the fields, and the long stories that bearded men sang to each other by the winter's fires, clasping hands across from one another as they chanted legends of half-remembered heroes.

It took Elias years to earn enough to see himself through university, and his debts were heavy when he left. He went to work for the government up north in the gray town of Kajaani, serving as a physician among poor and ignorant people ravaged by disease and epidemics. But the eastern lands of Karelia were not so far from there. And when summer came, he set out by boat and by horse to find out how far east he could go, and what the people there knew, and remembered.

Year after year he went out seeking, writing and collecting as he went. He learned the songs of these far people, who remembered tales the rest of their country had forgotten. He wrote them down, he sang them himself . . . and when bits were missing, he walked the paths of the Threefold World and found what he needed. Then he wrote down what he heard there, in the places inside himself where the truth of the songs lived, to complete the tales.

And when he felt he had the whole story, the missing pieces of his people, he stitched it all together into a book he called *The Kalevala: Old Karelian Runes from the Finnish People's Ancient Times.*

Now the Finnish people had their story, and stood as a nation among other nations. Soon their language became the language of scholars, and even of judges, banks, and politicians. Great composers took the legends, made them into famous pieces loved by people the world over. Artists painted Väinämöinen, sculpted the young Joukahainen. Children studied Elias Lönnrot's book he called *The Kalevala*.

When he was an old man, honored by his countrymen and foreign scholars alike, Elias Lönnrot was still a humble person.

Everyone knew what he was, though.

But these were modern times, times of steel and iron. Men rode iron engines on steel rails from city to city. They fought their wars with iron guns, bound their ships with iron keels, sent messages by steel wires that sang across the ocean.

But Elias Lönnrot had descended through the world of struggle and the world of loss, to find the meaning at the heart of things, to find the origins of creation, the origins of his own people.

And so everyone called Elias Lönnrot a poet, a writer, a scholar.

And no one ever said: *Elias is a witch.*

THE WITCH IN THE WOOD

DELIA SHERMAN

WHEN I FIRST saw my true love, he was lying by a brook at the foot of a bog oak. One foot trailed in the water, his eyes were closed, his nostrils flared with his panting, and his branching horns tangled among the roots of the oak. An arrow was buried deep in his haunch, fouling his pelt with blood.

The arrow was mine.

I did not know then that he was my true love. I thought he was a winter cloak, a pair of mittens, meat for my larder, fat for my fire, bones for needles and spoons and buttons and combs. I thought he was an eight-point stag.

I'd been chasing him for some time; the sun, which had been above the mountain when I'd shot him, had sunk into the western valley. In my forest, it was already dusk, but I saw him clearly enough, his tawny coat pale against the dark moss. As I crept nearer, my knife ready to slit his throat, the sky flared crimson as the sun set. The air shivered; I blinked. When I opened my eyes, the deer was a man, his long dark hair braided with twigs and small, polished stones, naked and bleeding, with my arrow in his thigh.

Living in the forest, I was used to transformations. Caterpillars become butterflies, blossoms become berries, tadpoles become frogs with the turning of each season. Deer becoming men, however, was beyond my experience. Before I could recover myself, he had seized the shaft of the arrow and pulled it from his leg with a hiss of pain.

It was a brave thing to do, but not a wise one. Blood welled from the wound in a mortal stream that I knew would soon drain him. I crashed through the undergrowth that separated us and dug my knife into the moss, cutting out a handful to pack into the hole my arrow had made. I pressed against the moss to hold it firm, feeling the prickling in my hands that would stem the flow. Only when I knew the blood had clotted did I remove my hands and rip the sleeve from my linen shirt to make a bandage.

Neither of us said a word.

Very conscious of his eyes on me, I dug a fire pit and lined it with rocks and wood, then took up a dry stick and told it to burn. As it bloomed into flame, he gasped—the first sound he'd made since drawing my arrow from his thigh.

"Witch," he said.

"No. Mildryth."

He huffed—a very deerlike noise. "I mean, you are a witch."

I wasn't about to admit I didn't know the word. He was a man, after all, and although I'd never actually spoken to a man before, my mother had always told me men respected only those stronger than they. So, "That's as may be," I said.

"I cannot stay here, witch. You must heal me."

I have never liked the word *must*, even when said in a voice as sweet as birdsong. "I *must* do as I think best. I've stopped the bleeding, but the wound has to heal at its own pace. I'd like it best if I could get you under a roof, but here will do until you're fit to walk."

He nodded. "I see. What would you have done with me had I been a deer in truth?"

"I'd have camped here until I could get you cut up properly and made a litter to drag you home." I thought for a moment. "I can still do that."

"Without the cutting up, I hope," he said, and laughed, which made me so angry I did not speak again until the soup was steaming and fragrant.

"It's venison," I said, giving him a pannikin-full. "I hope you don't mind."

He took the pannikin in a blood-streaked hand. "I don't mind."

He ate in silence, and when he was done, I ate what was left in the pot. As the fire burned low, he spoke again, soft-voiced. "When I am a deer, I have a deer's mind. In the morning, I will run from you and open my wound again."

"No, you won't."

"I will harm myself trying to break free if you bind me."

"You won't." I loosed my hair, which fell to my knees, and cut three hairs with my knife. "Look, here is the rope."

He was silent, his eyes fixed on my hand.

One hair I tied around his ankle, one around his wrist, and one among the narrow braids of his own dark hair. His skin was warm and smooth under my fingers, and his hair smelled salt and a little bitter, like wood smoke. Around his throat I saw a thick braided cord, bright crimson, like fresh blood. As I reached to touch it, he gathered my hair into his hands and, lifting it to his face, inhaled deeply.

I retreated hastily. "It's getting cold," I said. "I should build up the fire. And you must sleep."

He buried his head in his arms and was still. But as I sat listening to the noises of the night, I saw the firelight glitter in his watching eyes.

The birds were singing when I woke, and the mist rose from the brook, pearly in the growing light. The man was still a man, and I watched him sleep, wondering whether I'd dreamed his transformation. The light warmed; the air shivered. Between one breath and the next, the man became a deer lying between the roots of the oak, his legs tucked up under his belly, my shirt-sleeve bound around his haunch, and a crimson cord snugged around his neck.

Long lashes lifted, revealing liquid, nervous eyes. Cautiously I stretched out my hand. Cautiously he sniffed my fingers, licked them for the salt, then began to tear at the moss.

We passed a quiet day. I collected branches, bark, and vines, gathered grass and fresh leaves for the deer, shot a rabbit and put it to roast. While I made the litter, the deer nibbled, slept, lapped water from the pannikin, slept again. I wanted to stroke him, but it seemed unfair, when he could not escape.

Sometime during the long afternoon, a horn's mournful lowing broke the forest calm. The deer started awake, floundered, and tried to rise, blowing and panting with terror. Dodging his flailing horns, I laid my hand on his brow.

"You've nothing to fear," I said. "That's further away than it sounds, and bearing to the west besides."

He fell back onto the moss. For a moment I thought he had understood me. But he only mouthed at the leaves again, and I knew he was just a deer.

At sunset I was cutting up the rabbit when a sweet voice said, "Is that rabbit I smell?" startling me nearly out of my skin.

"It is," I said, and gave him half on a dock leaf. "Eat up. We'll have to leave before moonrise to make it home before dawn."

"Home." He sighed. "I can never go home again."

I chewed rabbit and swallowed. "Why not?"

"Politics. Religion. Wizards." He made a face. "You wouldn't understand."

I did not know those words, either, so I concentrated on finishing my portion of rabbit and thinking about how best to bind my awkward catch to the litter. It was not an easy task, he being alive and hurt besides. He called me a clumsy slut and I threatened to leave him to die. When he doubted, aloud, that a mere slip of a girl was strong enough to move him, I heaved the head of the litter up to my back and dragged it over the uneven ground at a fine pace, with him calling curses down upon my head with every bounce.

Before long, the curses trailed off and he began to moan. Repentant, I went more gently after that, but by the time I reached my home glade and my cottage, the bandage around his thigh was stained with fresh blood, and the man himself had fainted.

I made a nest for him by the hearth, stanched the wound, packed it with cobwebs, and bound it anew before he woke.

"If you were trying to kill me, you failed," he murmured.

"If I'd been trying, I would have succeeded. Drink this." He lifted one brow—I hadn't known that was possible. "It's a sleepy drink—valerian and chamomile and licorice root. It will soothe the deer as well as the man."

"Those hunters hunted me," he said. "Sooner or later they must find this place. And a full-grown deer is hard to hide."

"I have an idea about that," I said. "Drink now, and sleep."

When I was little, my mother taught me many things. She taught me how to coax seedlings to grow by the fire in winter, how to knit flesh and bend living wood into rooted chairs and leafy tables. She taught me to call animals to kneel before me and birds to roost on my shoulders. And she taught me not to use my knowledge unless I must, to survive.

I knew she would not have considered the safety of my deer-man a matter of survival—she had a very low opinion of men, with or without horns. But my mother had lain buried under the holly bush beside the door for three long winters, and I did not want my deer-man to die. So I stood at the edge of the glade and called a true stag to me.

He was an eight-point buck with a tawny coat only a shade darker than my deer-man's. When he knelt before me, I looked into his eyes and cut his throat, catching his blood in a pan. Then I went inside, where my deer-man slept uneasily, and laid hold of the crimson cord around his neck.

It stung me like a nettle.

I glared at the cord, then reached out to test it with that sixth sense that had awoken in me five years ago when first I began to give my blood to the earth. I worked out how the threads were twisted, and when I'd unraveled them, strand by strand, the cord dropped from the stag's neck. He sighed and shifted on his pallet of bracken, then slid deeper into sleep.

While he slept, I skinned the stag I had called, cut him into pieces, and was pinning the heavy hide onto the drying-frame behind the cottage when I heard a commotion of voices and dogs. Hastily I gathered around me an illusion of a woman of middle years, brindle-haired and stern of face, her arms thick with muscle—my mother, in fact, as she'd been before she died—and strode around the house, wiping bloody hands on my deerskin apron.

Twelve men stood in my glade, as alike to my eyes as leaves on a birch tree, tall and supple, their skin darkened by the sun, their hair braided, like my deer-man's, with leaves and feathers and polished stones. Unstrung bows were slung across their shoulders, and long knives thrust through their braided belts. They looked trail-worn and nervous as rabbits.

One of them stepped forward—a pale-haired man, with gold around his arm. "Greetings, good woman. We seek a deer."

I folded my arms to still their shaking. "Then you seek in a good place," I said in my mother's voice. "There are a plenty of deer in these woods. My man killed one yestereve."

The twelve men stiffened, like foxes scenting prey. "Your man, say you?" their spokesman said.

"A hunter, like yourselves. He left me with the butchering. It was a fat buck, with a fine rack of horn. It will serve us well this winter."

"Let us see it."

I shrugged. "The joints are ready for the smokehouse. The hide is pinned to the frame. The head is boiling in the pot."

They exchanged glances. "We will see what is to be seen."

They trailed me to the drying-frame and surveyed the fresh hide with their heads to one side and their mouths screwed to the other. They reeked of fear and confusion, but the spokesman's voice was steady as he asked, "Did you chance to find anything around the stag's neck?"

"I did. A braided crimson cord, as like to that around your waist as one hair is to another. I wondered at such a thing on a wild animal, and told my man, I told him, 'I hope you have not bagged some rich man's pet.'"

The spokesman closed his eyes and sighed. "Bring it to us."

"Wait until I get it."

In his nest, the deer lay white-eyed and quivering. I stroked his soft muzzle and blew into his nostrils, then took up the cord and brought it out to the waiting hunters.

"I hope it will not bring grief to me and mine," I said as the spokesman snatched it from my hand, "seeing as my man killed your deer in ignorance, on common land."

The men muttered and cut their eyes at me, but the spokesman silenced them with a look. "It will bring grief," he told me. "But not to you. The deer escaped his bounds."

I could not read his face, but it seemed to me that his body spoke more of fear than sorrow. Questions crowded my mouth, but I shut my teeth upon them. I wanted the hunters to leave more than I wanted answers.

The spokesman bowed. "Farewell, good woman. I wish you

and your man joy of the stag. He should make a kingly feast." And to my great relief, they ran into the wood with their braids bouncing on their backs.

That night, the deer-man was feverish and restless.

"They'll be back," he said when I told him, with pride, what I had done. "He'll know it's a trick. He'll send them to fetch me. He may even come himself."

I laid a cool cloth on his forehead. "Hush now. Those men believed me. How could someone who wasn't even here know what they did not?"

"Oh, he'll know. He knows everything." He gripped my hand, stared into my eyes with mad intensity. "Heal me that I may fly this place, for your own sake if not for mine."

"I'm doing my best," I said tartly. "It's all your own fault, you know. If you'd left the arrow for me to cut out properly, you wouldn't have done so much damage. As for your fever, that's your body fighting against itself."

He gave a bitter laugh. "It is as he said: those marked for death shall die."

Wounded as he was, I could have shaken him for pure frustration. "Marked for death? I've never heard such foolishness. There's nothing wrong with you that willow bark and cobwebs and time won't mend."

He shook his head wearily. "There is no time. Could I but cross the river back into the Land, if I could lie on her earth, drink of her water, eat of her bounty, my wound would be healed. To die in exile, useless and barren, is no more than my just punishment for trying to escape my destiny."

I knew the river he spoke of. It was only a day's journey

north, wide and rocky, easily fordable. My mother had taken me there after my first blood had come, to show me the boundary of our land. I will never forget how she looked on the flowing waters and on the trees that lay across them, her face as bleak as the rocks we stood on.

"Beyond this river lies the Land that was my home," she said, "until I fled it for my life. There's nothing for me there, nor for any daughter of my body, save grief and death, dark magics and blood."

I had never heard her voice so stern, not even when I had disobeyed her and broken my leg hunting on a moonless night, and did not wish to hear it again. When she required my oath never to cross the river, I gave it to her readily.

And yet, the morning after the huntsmen left my glade found me tramping northward, fully intending to do just what I had sworn not to. My deer-man had grown weaker in the night, his pulse thread-thin in his neck, his skin hot and dry under my hand. I knew I might break my oath to no purpose, to cross the river and come home to find him dead. And yet I knew I must try.

Grief and death; dark magics and blood. I couldn't help thinking that these would be my lot whatever I did.

Once begun, I moved swiftly from the familiar rolling paths of my forest in the foothills to the steeper tracks of the mountain slopes. That night I camped further from my glade than I'd ever imagined being, lying beneath a blanket of stars that were closer and brighter than I'd ever seen them.

I was up and on my way before dawn, and made such speed that I arrived at the river before the sun had reached the zenith. For a time I stood on the bank, staring at the pines and hollies and ash-pale birches on the far shore, caught between past and future, my oath to my mother and my duty to my deer-man, fear of what I might meet in that forbidden wood and a burning desire to know what lay there.

When I stepped into the river at last, the water was cold as winter snow. It ran strong between scattered boulders, but never deeper than my waist. Step by step I waded over small round stones that rolled treacherously underfoot. It was as if the far shore withdrew as I approached, so long did I struggle toward it. But once I passed the halfway point, the footing grew easier, and at last I floundered panting onto the shore of my deer-man's precious Land.

I looked around me. Was the sky bluer, the birdsong clearer and more beautiful, the trees more lush and full than those of my own forest, or was it my stranger's eyes that made them seem so? Above me, I saw a tumble of sparkling water where a stream cascaded down the mountainside. Lacking other guidance, I followed it, scrambling up over boulders and through thickets. As I climbed, I felt the song of the Land rise through my body, filling me until I nearly burst with it.

When I came to my senses, I was kneeling by a rocky pool. At one end, the water churned beneath a wide cascade; at the other, it slipped between two great boulders and out of sight. Great dark hollies stood sentinel around that pool, and its stones were patched with pale, dense humps of moss. Though I'd never seen it before, I knew as surely as I knew my blood flowed through my veins that this moss was what I needed to draw the fever from my deer-man's wound.

As I reached to gather it, a bear's paw, dark-furred and powerfully clawed, reached over my shoulder.

Heart pounding, I plunged into the pool and splashed away, clumsy with panic, glancing over my shoulder to see if the bear followed. The rock where I had knelt was empty. I paddled back, wondering whether perhaps my eyes had been playing tricks on me. Reaching up to the rock to pull myself out of the water, I saw once again the heavy, furred arms of a bear. But this time I knew that they were mine.

With my acceptance of that knowledge came the welcome of the Land. My eyes, my nose, my tongue, the pads of my paws, the wind in my fur, the rustle of the leaves and the song of the water spoke to my blood. They told me that I had lived an exile in a foreign land, starving all that I was and could be, subsisting on crumbs of power when I could have feasted. They told I was home now, and whole.

I do not know how long I stayed in that enchanted place, or entirely what I did there. I know I ate, for when I could think again, I saw fish bones scattered on a rock and my paws were sticky with honey. The sun was low, the wind smelled of evening. All in a panic, I remembered the deer-man waiting in my cottage with his beautiful, hunted eyes and his smell of wood smoke and musk—and his festering wound, which might have killed him, for all I knew, while I frolicked here in enchanted woods.

Gathering the simples that would make my deer-man strong again was easy. I knew what I needed and how to use it as I knew how to walk and breathe. Leaving the pool and the guardian hollies was much harder, but I was not so drunk with power that I'd leave my stag, my deer, my hart to die of the wound I'd given him. And now that I could think again, I found I missed my own forest.

The journey back to my glade was faster than my journey out. Bears can gallop quite fast, I discovered, and do not need to skirt bramble patches. Still, when I crossed the river again, it became harder and harder to keep the bear wrapped about me. Eventually I was forced to go on my two feet, cold and half blind in the dark. Yet, weak as I felt myself, I knew I was stronger than I had been.

By dint of running without rest for a night and a day, I reached my cottage not long after sunset. My deer-man was alive, but only just, his hands twitching feebly in fever dreams, his face ashen, his eyes sunk deep in bruised hollows. When I tore the bandage from his thigh, his wound ran with pus and stank of foulness.

I made up the fire, drew water, and heated herbs in it, along with a pinch of soil from the handful I'd dug from the Land. As the posset steeped, I drained my deer-man's wound, washed it with herb-scented, earth-tinted water, packed it with the white moss, and bandaged it afresh. Finally I held a cup of the same earthy brew to his lips, and when he had drunk it, I crept into his fur-lined nest, took his head on my shoulder, and slept the sleep of exhaustion.

Some time later, I felt something tickling my cheek and opened my eyes to find myself nose to velvety nose with my stag. Seeing me awake, he snorted, as though in greeting.

I put a hand on his bandaged haunch; his hide shivered, but he did not startle away. Gently I unbound the cloth and unpeeled the moss.

The wound was closed and almost fully healed, a pink scar amid his tawny hair. Why this should have made me weep when his suffering had not, I do not know, but weep I did, my forehead against his haunch. Finally he nudged me ungently with his nose, telling me as clearly as speech that he would be up and out of the cramped, dark cottage and out in the wide forest.

Little as I wanted to, I let him go.

I have never feared solitude. All my life, I have lived content with the forest and my mother for company, nor wanted any other. After she died, I missed her, oh, most terribly. But I was not afraid until the day my hart left me to run in the forest. Every sound made me jump in case it was my deer returning, or the hunters, or some danger I could not foresee. I lost hope of seeing him and found it again, over and over, in a frustrating cycle that was more exhausting than a day's hunting. And when I was not fretting over him, I was staring at my thin, brown, naked hands and wondering if my mother had ever had the power to turn into a bear, and why she had given it up if she had, and why she had been at such pains to keep that power from me. In late afternoon I came to the conclusion that my unhappy state was all my mother's fault, and that my deer was gone for good. Then I wept and dried my eyes and went to fetch water for dinner.

As I reached the stream in the gathering dusk, my hart stepped out of the trees, lowered his head, and drank.

I stood as though I'd been turned to stone, my bucket on my hip. The deer raised his dripping muzzle from the water. The sun set, and the man rose from his crouch and tossed back his tawny hair.

Next moment, I was across the stream with my arms around him. Under my hands, his back was warm and smooth and hard, his unshaven cheek rough against my face. A pounding shook my body—his heart or mine, or both—and my breath came fast and shallow, as though I'd been running. For a moment, he stood like a tree in my embrace, and then his arms lifted to encircle me, and he was mouthing my ear, my cheek, my lips, and I was mouthing his and we were both breathless and so unsteady that our legs would not hold us upright. We fell to the moss, and what happened there transformed me as utterly as crossing the river to the forbidden Land.

Later that night, we warmed our cold feet by the fire and ate toasted chestnuts and hearth cakes with honey. My deer-man's hand was never far from my body, nor my body from his hand. We smiled when our eyes met. And haltingly, shyly, we talked. I told him as much of my history as I knew. It was little enough—that I was born not long after my mother had fled the north, that we had lived together peacefully, that she had died in my fourteenth year, that I had lived now three years alone, that I had never met or spoken to any man or woman apart from her until the day my arrow had felled him and brought twelve hunters to my door.

"So now you know what there is to know about me," I said. "I would know as much about you. What is your name? Who are your parents? Are you a shape-shifter by nature, or is it a curse?"

This made him laugh. "You might call it a curse. *He* called it an honor, a glory, a test of my spirit and my strength."

"He?"

"Arnulf. My wizard." That deerlike huff again. "Not so much mine as I was his, though. *His* candidate. *His* pupil. His Little King."

I had had enough of pretending to understand. "I don't know what you're talking about, my hart."

Something of the deer's blind panic widened his eyes. "I can't tell you any more. It's forbidden."

"Who forbids it?" I was losing patience. "Your precious wizard Arnulf? Whom you fear and flee as from a wolf?"

He turned away from me, head bent. "It's no use, Mildryth. I cannot be to you what I want to be. I am a fugitive, an outcast, disgraced. The best thing—the only thing—I can do now is run and never look back."

I seized the skin draped over his naked shoulders in my fists, brought his fine, high-bridged nose up to mine. "The best thing for whom?" I growled. "Not for me, and not for you, either, whatever you say." I gave him a shake. "Begin at the beginning."

At first he would not tell me. The bear in me wanted to growl and threaten, but deer run from bears. Remembering how my mother would coax me with games to some task I loathed, I kissed him and tumbled with him until I thought he'd forgotten such a person as Arnulf existed. And then, when we lay curled together by the dying fire, I asked him again for his story.

His name, I learned, was Erdwyn. He was one of a cohort of royal half-brothers begotten by the last king on one of his regular progresses through the Land. It was one of a king's chief functions, to breed armies for future kings. Another was to lead the sons of past kings into battle, if the need arose. Another was to die, returning his blood and his magic to the Land, that it might be rich and strong. The real rulers of the Land were the wizards, whose council oversaw trade and commerce, cast spells of plenty and healing, and kept the complicated lists of bloodlines that determined which women should come to the king's tent when a progress brought him to a town.

Erdwyn had been one of these princelings, born in the foot-hills of the mountains between his Land and mine. When he was five years old, he'd been sent north, as the law dictated, to the Royal Holt of Karleigh.

"And what did your mother say to that?" I asked.

"I don't remember my mother at all," he said, and his sweet voice was full of sadness. "All my memories are of training and learning and fighting with my brothers. Until last year."

"What happened then?"

"I was chosen by a wizard to be a Little King."

"By Arnulf?"

"By Arnulf."

"And what does it mean, to be a Little King?"

"There are—were—twelve of us." The words came halt-ingly. "I suppose the rest are dead by now—all but one. We lived in the Wizard's Holt, learning the magics of war and increase, of the hunt and of the field. It was very wonderful: sacred and terrible." He shrugged. "I cannot speak of it—I have no words. Anyway, that lasted until a month or so ago, when the old king, Anselm, gave his blood to the Land."

He fell silent. I stroked his hair, my hand catching on the twigs tied into it. "And Arnulf turned you into a deer?"

"It is the ordeal of kingship. The wizards work transforma-tion on the Little Kings, turning us into deer and releasing us into the forest." He moved restlessly in my arms. "What happens then, I cannot say. Deer do not think as men think, and I was half crazed with magic besides. But I was told that he who is able, by strength of will and the Land's magic, to return to the Holt as a man is the true king."

I lay in the dark, listening to his breathing, knowing the story was not yet done. "What becomes of the other Little Kings?" I asked gently.

"Their blood and magic return to the Land," he said. "Only the true king can be allowed to live."

"And you?"

"I ran away. Whether as king or as deer, I knew I must die before my time, and I did not want to die. And Arnulf—well, I hated him." It was on the tip of my tongue to ask him why, but there was that in his voice that made me tighten my arms around him and hold my peace.

He sighed. "I don't remember how or when I crossed the river, but I will never forget how I felt when I found myself a man again. I thought I was free—free of Arnulf's spells, the sacrifices and duties of kingship, the threat of death. Then morning came, and I was a deer again. That night was worst of all, for I knew then how far I was from freedom." He wound his hands in my hair and kissed my mouth. "Until I met you, and found how sweet it was to be bound to one who loves you."

That night I dreamed of a strange bear running through the forest. I knew, as one knows things in dreams, that this bear was searching for me, and when he found me, he would kill me if he could. He was bigger than I, and older, but not so fast. He stumbled as he ran, as though he were wounded, though I saw no blood on his fur. Closer and closer he came, until I could smell the spoiled-meat stench of his breath. Roaring with fury at his trespass, I reared up on my back legs and charged.

And woke. It was dawn; my head was pillowed on warm, living hide, and a deer's frightened heart thuttered under my ear.

As I lifted my head, my hart sprang to his feet, forelegs braced, nostrils and eyes wide.

"I know," I said. "But he is not in his Land. He is in mine, fed with my monthly blood, obedient to my magic. This is a fight I can win."

My deer huffed and tossed his horns, bringing bundles of drying herbs down from the rafters. Rising, I put on tunic and leggings, opened the door, and stepped outside just as twelve familiar huntsmen entered my glade.

Between one breath and the next, they had unslung their bows, whisked arrows from their quivers, and drawn their bowstrings to their ears. My stag belled a challenge; the bear within me stirred and growled.

A man pushed through the wall of hunters, a tall man, barrelchested and bearded, a bearskin draped around his shoulders.

"Go away out of this, you fools!" he cried. "This is wizard's business!"

The hunters melted into the forest.

It was Arnulf, of course. I knew the scent of him from my dream, as he must have known mine. Even as a man, he was more than half bear. He glared at my stag from under his bristling brows. "I am ashamed," he growled in a voice like summer thunder, "to find any Little King of mine hiding behind the skirts of a Southron hedge-witch."

My deer tossed his head, lifted his forefoot, and pawed the ground angrily.

Arnulf laughed. "You know it's futile to challenge me, Erdwyn. You learned that even before you learned that witches are an abomination and must be killed. But come, let us not threaten and bluster at one another. Today is a day of great rejoicing. Your brother the Little King Gertwyn returned two days ago to the Wizard's Holt. He'll be crowned at the full of the moon. In honor of our new king, I am willing to be generous. Return to the Land with me, give up your blood as you are bound to do, and I will spare the witch's life."

I listened to this speech with rising anger. "He doesn't want to come with you," I said. "He's not ready to die, and I don't see why he should have to, just because you say so."

Arnulf's beard writhed. "Silence, witch!" he snarled, his eyes fixed steadily on my deer. "Do not meddle with magics you do not understand."

The bear within me stirred angrily. "I understand, *wizard,* that this is *my* land, by right of my blood and my mother's blood, spilled on it at each full moon. If it comes to a fight, I think I will win."

Arnulf's eyes flicked toward me and away again. I had no skill to read his face, but body and smell told me he was afraid. "Witches have no land. You are nothing but an exile, lingering on the borders of power, untrained and half savage."

"I am not without power and I am not untrained. I healed your Little King, after all."

"Healed?" Arnulf roared. "You've done much more than that, witch. You've bound him to you, blood and body, as the witch Hild bound King Detlef five hundred years past."

"And what's wrong with that?" I asked.

Arnulf's face twisted. "A witch is an abomination. That is

enough. The wizards give their blood to the Land. As they give the blood of any girl-child born with unnatural powers." Arnulf drew a knife from his belt, the honed bronze bright and glittering as a sunbeam in his hand. "As your mother's should have been given. As I will give yours."

For the first time he looked full at me, his gaze an almost physical pressure.

I pulled the bear around me, roaring from a mouth grown wide and full of teeth.

Arnulf startled, his eyes and mouth rounding. I smelled shock on him and confusion.

"Stop!" he shouted. "I did not know! I will not harm you, I swear it! See, I throw down my knife!"

But it was too late. The bear possessed me. I lumbered toward my enemy, grunting my challenge. My stag followed me.

The hunters Arnulf dismissed had not gone far. In a heartbeat, my deer and I were in a ring of arrows, nocked and ready to fly.

My bear instincts told me to claw and rend; my human mind told me to surrender. Frustrated beyond endurance, I roared to shake the forest.

"For the Land's sake, stay your hands!" Arnulf shouted. "The man who harms her forfeits his life."

Then he backed slowly away, his head turned aside, whuffing submissively, acknowledging defeat.

This abrupt surrender so astonished me that the bear fell from me. My legs buckled; I threw my arms around my deer to hold myself upright.

"Put down your bows, you fools!" Arnulf cried, and the

hunters hesitated, eyeing him as foxes eye a wolf. "Well, what are you waiting for? Make a fire and fetch water and unpack my bag. If I must bargain with a witch, I'd as soon do it over a cup of tea."

And so it was, some little time later, that I sat across an open fire from the wizard with my deer at my side, sipping a hot amber brew that made my heart race.

Very much at his ease Arnulf seemed, for a man sharing a hearth with an abomination. Yet I could smell eagerness on him, like a bear within paw's reach of a honeycomb, and was afraid. For among the many things my mother had told me was no hint of how to bargain with a wizard.

Now that he had decided to speak to me, Arnulf was very full of questions. What was my mother's name, he wanted to know, and where did she come from? Who was her father? Who was mine? Where had she learned her craft and what had become of her? I did not know the answers to these questions, nor would I have answered them if I could. So I only stared at his wagging beard and his bright, deep-set eyes until he fell silent.

"I see you do not trust me," he said. "I do not blame you. You are a power in your land as I am in mine, and yet I came to you with threats and arrows and brazen knives. Forgive me, if you can, and hear me, for I offer you a bargain that will benefit both you and me."

"I will not forgive you," I said, "but I will hear you. Hearing is not agreeing, after all."

His thick beard bunched over his cheeks. "It is not. Well, then. I promise to take my huntsmen and depart from here in return for this: one thing of my choosing, to be collected by me, in person, from you, at the end of a year and a day."

He offered this speech with the air of one bearing an armful of flowers. But even I, untutored as I was, could see the nettle hidden among them. "And what if you should choose the deer, or my life, or perhaps enough blood to satisfy the hunger of your Land?"

He grinned, and I saw his teeth had been filed into points. "Half savage, perhaps, but not stupid. Will it content you if I swear by the Land that I will not take the deer, or, if you succeed in breaking the enchantment, the man, nor any part of you or him that would threaten your life or your safety?"

My stag gave an oddly undeerlike snort. I glanced down at him, surprised, to see his leaf-shaped ears pricked and his gaze fixed on Arnulf.

"He is bound to us by blood." Arnulf sounded amused. "Of course he understands us. You may ask his advice, if you wish. Though I should warn you that even when he walks on two legs, he is a better fighter than a strategist."

Since I did not know what a strategist was, and since it did not seem fair to take such a decision alone, I stroked my deer's wiry back and said, "What do you say, my hart? Shall we take this bargain?"

"Think carefully, Erdwyn," Arnulf said, "understanding that, if you refuse, there is nothing left for either of you but an early death and scorched land where once a cottage stood. Considering what the Land loses—what *I* lose—in losing you, I think my offer more than fair."

It was not fair by my reckoning, but I thought it was the best we could hope for. My deer must have come to the same conclusion, for he dipped his head twice.

"We accept your offer," I said. "Now take your tea and your hunters and go."

The moon has grown round and shrunk again six times since that day. I have spent the time in learning to tame and use the magic awakened in me when I crossed the border into my mother's Land. By my will, my true love is a man again by day as well as by night, and takes his bow to hunt mountain sheep, deer, and rabbits. I do not hunt, for like the moon, I am round and heavy with my growing child. How Arnulf could have seen within me a seed so newly planted, I cannot tell, but we have no doubt, my love and I, that he knew what I carried. It was our child he bargained for, and it is our child he will claim in six months' time.

Therefore, we will leave this forest I have bound with my monthly blood and journey to the plains to the south, where men live in cities built of stone and magic is as rare as berries in January. We will find some patch of land there to build our house and raise this child—and the children that follow him— far from the dark magics of the north. I will give my blood to that land as I have given it to my forest, binding it to me and to my sons and daughters after me, passing on my mother's wisdom and my mother's stories, teaching them what I learned when I was the witch in the wood.

WHICH WITCH

PATRICIA A. McKILLIP

LIESL, THAT GRINCH, stole my G string. "Borrowed," she said. Ha! So I had to limp along on a Spinreel G so old it was liable to snap at any moment with a twang in pure country, while she wailed along like she was summoning the devil to dance, with her long black hair tangling in her bow until it seemed she was pulling the song out of her hair instead of her fiddle.

Maybe she did. Summon up the devil, I mean, since that night was when Trouble joined the band.

I know Cawley warned me. I know that. But it had to have been while I was on the floor slithering like the snake in the Garden into my tightest black jeans, or trying to bend over after that to buckle the Mary Jane strap on a seven-inch lollipop-red heel and then zip a black ankle boot on the other foot, or surrounding myself with puddles of sequins, satin, leather, and lace, trying to find just the right top for my mood. Pirate Queen, or Good Fairy/ Bad Fairy, or maybe I'd just wear my glasses and my crazy-quilt jacket and Cawley on my shoulder and be Scholar Gypsy.

Cawley hates being used as an accessory, unless I'm in dire need. Which I wasn't then. Or at least I didn't know it. Though I would have if I'd listened to him. But I was on the floor, et cetera, while he was fluttering on his wooden perch trying to take my attention off my clothes. Translating crow requires concentration. I thought he was asking me to open the window so that he could fly out, and I finally did give it a shove up, in the middle of putting on a shirt covered with roses and skulls.

"There," I said. "Bye. You know where I'll be."

But he didn't leave, just kept squawking. Since he had hopped from his perch to the sill, I thought he was talking to his clan, which had covered the tree outside like very dead leaves. They were all chattering, too. Where to go to dinner, or the sun about to go down, or somebody spilled a ginormous order of french fries in the middle of B Street. Something like that.

So you can't say I wasn't warned. I pulled off the shirt, which wasn't right, then limped in one-shoe-on, one-boot-on mode to the window and pushed it shut behind Cawley. I nearly caught his tail feathers. He whirled in a black blur and could have cracked glass with the word that ripped out of his open beak.

I yelled back, "Sorry!"

But what I thought he squawked wasn't what he said at all.

I hadn't really had him that long. Some witches find their familiars; some familiars find their witches. Liesl's smoke-colored cat with golden eyes had been put in an animal shelter along with her seven siblings. Liesl had a dream about her and went searching. They recognized each other instantly. Liesl smiled; the cat started a coffee grinder purr that rattled her tiny body. Of course Liesl named her Graymalkin. Why not? Who'd guess that names among familiars are remembered through vast webs of families and histories, way back into antiquity? Naming a cat Graymalkin is like adding yet another Josh or Elizabeth to the human list.

As for Cawley, yes, that too is pretty much obvious. At the time, I thought it was clever of me. To name a crow Cawley. Duh.

Cawley found me.

Liesl had it easy in the sense that she didn't have to learn to understand cat. They just read each other's minds. If Graymalkin presents herself with her back arched and every hair standing up on end, that pretty much says it all. But Cawley doesn't have a stance for *Be afraid, very afraid.* When I first saw him, he was pacing on a rain gutter next door and imitating the endless barking of an obnoxious dog in a neighboring yard. The noise had crept into the background of a dream I was having, and finally woke me up way too soon after a long night. I stumbled to the window and pushed it open to find out what exactly was the dog's problem. Then I saw the crow waddling to and fro on the gutter and barking back at it. I laughed, and the crow flew over to me like he'd just been waiting for me to get up.

I didn't understand a word he said. But I felt as though somebody—something—had slipped a fine gold chain onto my wrist and said, *Mine.* I didn't argue. I liked that feeling of having been chosen, of belonging to a dark, mythical bird that had my best interests at heart. Also, Cawley gave me status. I was True Witch now, not Apprentice or Journeyperson Witch. Familiars don't stay with witches who are not yet True.

I had gotten into the habit of watching crows. I never guessed they were watching me back. Who does? City crows mingle so easily with people that people hardly notice them. Crows know the habits of cars. They don't even bother to stop pecking at roadkill or bugs or a spilled bag of chips in the middle of a street until a car is almost on top of them. They move aside grudgingly for the monster outweighing them by several tons, but with no real sense of urgency. They have the same hysterics teaching their fledglings to fly that human parents have teaching their kids how to drive. They imitate noises that catch their interest; that's what Cawley was doing when we met. They get bored; they play tricks. And, at sundown, they all fly the same direction to some mysterious place, a coven of crows gathering at dusk for reasons Cawley can't yet explain in ways I can understand.

A murder of crows. That's what they were called in medieval times. Maybe for their habit of chowing down on the dead. Maybe for something more sinister. But the city crows I see seem basically civilized. True, when they're nesting they might peck at people, or they might chase a pet across the yard for fun. But mostly they act like they're beneath our notice.

I notice. Maybe that's why Cawley came to me.

The others in Which Witch, except for Rune, have their familiars, of course. Madrona, the skinny, white-haired whippet on percussion, has a parakeet named Hibiscus. Pyx, our lead singer, has a white rat named Archibald. Makes sense: Pyx is bald. They have squeak-fests together. Sometimes Pyx wears Archibald on her clothes along with a lot of ugly old brooches her mother left her, made of gold and diamonds and sapphires.

So that's us, Which Witch: Liesl, Madrona, Pyx, Pyx's boyfriend Rune on bass, and me, Hazel. I know. Just like the witch hazel bush. Like Graymalkin and Cawley: with a name like that, what else could I be?

Where was I?

* * *

French fries, indeed. Granted, we crows like a snack now and then, and are not above a discarded bit of burger, preferably with pickle, or a salty, lightly tailpipe-smoked fry. But what I tried and failed so miserably to get my witch Hazel to understand was exactly why we had chosen the tree outside her window for our Twilight Coven. The monster creeping toward her as her attention flitted like a magpie to this red shoe, that purple sequin was ancient, powerful, and thoroughly nasty.

And we were not just any tree full of gabbling city crows. We were a gathering from all over the land, most of us experienced, some of us with powers, and a few of us scandalously older than we had any right to be. My great-grandmother on my father's side was still with us. She spotted the peril first. She had recently retired to live on warm southern beaches where plump briny critters and picnic leftovers were readily available. Having no human to guard, she watched everything else.

"It broke out of the sea on a wave, crawled up to dry sand on a roll of froth and foam in the moonlight," she said excitedly. She was looking pretty good for an old crow, though her tail feathers were a bit scraggly. "In the wee hours of the morning it gathered itself up and chose its human form. Cutest lifeguard you ever saw. Great abs. Spent the day sunning on its high chair, watching behind its dark glasses and flirting back at the girls who came up. I searched everywhere, couldn't find what it had done to the real lifeguard. It was gone after sunset. I lost track of it while I watched the sun go down.

"So I took to the air. I never spotted it again, but I followed rumors of it in the night roosts and covens between ocean and here.

"Here, it stopped."

"I saw it last night," I said, clutching the branch in my claws so tightly that the tree gave a little, irritated twitch. "Last night, where my witch Hazel plays music."

"Did you warn her?" my uncle Rakl asked sharply. What did he think? That I'd recognized it and gone on preening my feathers and picking at fleas?

"I tried." Uncle Rakl was watching me out of one eye, a bleak, annoying gaze, as though he expected nothing more or less from me.

"You tried."

"We haven't been joined long. I forget what human words I've learned when I'm agitated, and she is still struggling with crow."

He made the noise like his name, causing a half dozen youngsters on a bough beneath us to explode into raucous mimicry. They were screeched into silence by various parents; the fledglings subsided, perching sedately and pretending they didn't know each other.

"What shape was it?" my great-grandmother asked practically.

"I felt it long before I saw it. The club was shadowy and very crowded. My witch's band is extremely popular," I added proudly and unnecessarily, then got back down to business before Uncle Rakl could open his beak. "I found the source of the dark emanation in an aging biker's body, with stylishly frayed jeans, black leather boots, and a long, gray-brown braid down its back. Earrings, thumb rings, tattoo of a skull with roses in the eye sockets. No other visible piercings. Wealthily scruffy."

There were mutterings and soft rattles throughout the tree:

that dead body shouldn't be hard to spot if it was still in any recognizable form. A couple of messengers left immediately to spread the word to the night roost in the city park, a couple of miles away as we crows fly.

"I smelled the death and the power in it. And it smelled me, so I had to leave."

"You left your witch?" Uncle Rakl again, ever ready to believe the worst of me.

"Only," I rasped back, "to get it to follow me. Which it didn't. But when I flew back inside the club it was gone. I stayed with my witch, but she roosted with a friend that night; I had to sleep outside. They gave me no chance to try to warn her until this evening. She didn't understand. As you saw."

I glanced over to my witch's window. She had finally chosen her costume for the evening, a process I will never understand, and was giving herself a wide-eyed glare in a mirror, brushing the small hairs in her eyelids with a mixture of glitter and blue paint.

"Perhaps," Uncle Rakl said heavily, "it went its way already. Whatever it wants or seeks isn't in this city at all."

"Maybe," my great-grandmother said. "And maybe not. What kinds of powers does your witch have?"

"I wonder," my young cousin Ska mused, "how that glitter would look on my tail feathers."

There was another rackety outburst of hilarity from the fledglings, during which my great-grandmother forgot her question. Just as well, since I had no idea. All I really knew of my witch Hazel's powers is that she had drawn me to her side. And the ooze that had shaped itself into a semblance of the dead to watch her in the shadows of the bar, she might have drawn to herself as well. It was my fate and my duty to make such distasteful assumptions, and to go where few self-respecting crows should ever go.

"Anybody up for some music? I can get us in as stage props."

Uncle Rakl rackled. My cousin Ska preened. The fledgling chorus erupted, along with most of the coven, until my witch turned her stare to the window, and, across the way from her, somebody threw a beer bottle at the tree.

"Pipe down, birds!"

We all fluttered up, with a great deal of noise and confused energy. A window slammed. As was our habit, we came to our decision suddenly, reading each other's thoughts, including the image of where to go in mine, before we settled back down again in leisurely fashion, all of us talking at once.

"That's it, then," Great-Grandmother said briskly. "We'll all go. But you go with her. Cling to her, do what you must to make her understand. Peck her head if you have to, Whatever-it-is-she-calls-you. Cawley."

I had to listen to the derisive echo of that—*Cawley, Cawley, Cawley*—as the black cloud flowed out of the tree and swarmed away into the twilight sky over the city. I flew to my witch's window, stood on the sill, and pecked at the glass until she let me in.

Cawley was still trying to give me a language lesson when I left for the club. It was only a few blocks away and Quin would meet me there. Quin was Quinton Matthew Tarleton III. He had wandered with some friends into a place we were playing a couple of weeks before, looking earnest and geeky and too sweet for words. He had taken me out for ice cream on our first date. For breakfast. Later, after our first kiss, he had bought me a gecko pin for my hair. So it was a little hard for me to concentrate on what Cawley was saying, what with the slight weight of the gecko sparkling just above my ear and making me think of Quin.

Finally one word penetrated, making me stop dead in my tracks, or rather, wobble to a halt in my high-heeled lace-up boots.

"What? Wait. Did you say danger?"

I was so proud of myself for picking that out of all his noises that I forgot for a moment what it meant. He flew around my head three times, squawking so excitedly that people ducked away from us, alarmed.

"Cawley." My voice did something strange then: it got sharp and slow and focused all at the same time. "Please. Stop. Sit. Start over."

He shut up abruptly and fluttered onto my shoulder. Luckily, I was wearing a retro 1940s-style jacket with some major shoulder pads in it; even so, I could feel his claws, loosening and tightening nervously. "Danger," he said again, then another word I actually recognized. "You."

"Me? I'm a danger?" I looked at my outfit bewilderedly. "Why? Because I'm showing four inches of skin and a fake garnet in my navel between my shirt and my skirt, or I would be except I've got my jacket buttoned now and nobody can—Cawley, why are you suddenly sounding like my mother?"

He pecked my head. Not hard, just a fingernail thump, but I couldn't believe he had done that.

"Cawley!" I yelped, seriously irritated. I wanted to smack him with my fiddle case. I shrugged my shoulder hard instead, shaking him off. "Go," I told him in that voice again. "Just go. Leave me alone until you can talk to me like a normal familiar. You're pretty much useless to me like this."

He hovered a moment in midair in front of my face. Then he made a sound, a sort of crow rattle of total frustration that I understood completely. He sailed off in the direction of the club. I stomped off after him, still smoldering, and wishing I had a familiar that was easier to talk to, like maybe an iguana.

When I walked into the club it was like walking into some weird power field. I could feel the hair lift on my head, and I prickled everywhere, like a cat coming nose to nose with the Hound of the Baskervilles. I knew immediately: this was what Cawley had meant, what he had been trying to say. I could feel it creeping under my skin and dragging at my bones like a cold, bleak fog or the nasty breath of some animal that's been eating roadkill. It weighed me down, fogged my brain, so that when I glanced around the club to see what caused it, the candles on the tables dimmed to a yellowy brown, and the shadows looked like solid blocks of black.

I recognized Quin through the haze in my brain. He stood at the bar sipping at his usual undrinkable mix of sparkling water, tomato juice, and lime he called a Toothless Vampire. He lightened the air a bit, inside me and out. I took a step toward him. Then I saw what stood beside him, holding a mug and gazing at the ceiling.

I glanced up, too, and saw every single fake ax-split rafter in the place crowded with crows, silent and motionless in the shadows, as though they were all waiting for someone to die.

I wanted to shrink down into something very small and skitter my way out between the incoming feet. The thing beside Quin poked him in the shoulder and made some comment, laughing. It looked like the dark-haired, blue-eyed fry cook from the club's kitchen, idling at the bar before her shift began. But she—it—had forgotten to change its shadow. What clung to her cowboy boots and slanted away underfoot across the floor didn't look like anything remotely human.

People were crowding into the place behind me, paying the cover and getting their hands stamped. I forced myself to move, wave at Quin until I caught his eye. I didn't dare glance at the shape beside him. It would have looked through my eyes and into my brain and seen everything I was thinking. When Quin saw me, I slapped a smile on my face and tapped my wrist: late for work. He waved a kiss at me, then tapped his head where, on my head, the little, glittery gecko was pinned. He made a circle with his thumb and forefinger. I grinned like a pumpkin and nodded so hard the gecko nearly fell off.

I felt its attention then, as though a new moon had looked at me, enormous, invisible, full of black light.

I turned away fast and headed for the stage.

Walking into the tension there was like trying to hurry underwater. Everyone seemed normal enough, dressed by a passing tornado and wearing the usual assortment of animals except for Rune, who was still Journeyperson status. He was tuning his bass, looking like a hairy Viking who had forgotten to do his laundry. He thumbed a note as I picked my way through cords and equipment, and said, without looking up, "Which witch are you, I wonder?"

It was our code for *Man, have we got Trouble. Anybody know what that is?*

Even the familiars looked spooked. Pyx was wearing every brooch she owned. Gold and diamonds, dirty silver and hunky jewels of every color flared on her orange silk vest. Usually she wore Archibald in the middle of them, the white rat with the garnet-red eyes, clinging with his strong little paws to her threads among the treasures. But he was on her shoulder, snuggled as close to her ear as he could get and probably wishing she had left some hair on that side of her head for him to crawl under. Madrona's yellow parakeet was half hidden in her wild white curls. Hibiscus's feathers were completely puffed out, as though she tried to convince Trouble she was two or three times her tiny size. Graymalkin was in her usual spot inside Liesl's open violin case. But she wasn't curled up and napping. She was crouched, motionless, staring into the crowd like she was watching a ghost. I had a feeling that if I put a hand on her fur I'd get a shock that would untie my bootlaces.

"I'm the Wicked Witch," I answered, which meant: *I know. I'm armed and dangerous.*

Well, I could hope.

"You look more like the Good Witch," Liesl murmured, stroking her strings with her bow. I puzzled over that for a moment until I realized it wasn't code, it was a comment.

"Sorry," I said meekly. "I couldn't figure out who I am tonight."

Madrona, who lived, slept, and possibly showered in black, said sweetly, "You look nice," which of course is code for *Your grandmother would love what you're wearing.* She sat down and picked up her drumsticks, which usually caused Hibiscus to take cover in the violin case with Graymalkin. But the parakeet only deflated a bit and shifted farther back into Madrona's hair. She bopped a cymbal lightly and asked, "Do we have a set list?"

Of course we did; we always had a set list. That was code for *Does anyone have the slightest idea what to do?*

Liesl shrugged speechlessly. She was the Gypsy that night, from the rings on her bare feet to the gold loops in her ears and the ribbons in her long black hair. I opened my case and took out the bow, tightened the strings, then picked up the violin, which, freed from years of lessons, turned promptly into a fiddle.

"Wing it?" I suggested, and above my head a crow—maybe Cawley—rustled feathers noisily. I hoped they might know what to do, not that any of them could tell me. I listened to Liesl's tunings, tightened my A, then my G, which promptly snapped and curled with a little mournful wail. I said something I hoped the mikes didn't pick up and scrabbled among the strings in the case. "Where is that . . . Liesl, did you take my G string?"

"Borrowed," she said unrepentantly. "In rehearsal yesterday—you were in the bathroom. You have another one."

"You took the good one. Do you know how expensive those are?"

"Sure I do. Why do you think I grabbed it?"

Madrona gave us a drumroll and a bling on the cymbal. "Pick it up, ladies. We've got a heavy night ahead of us."

That was pretty much code for *If we get out of this alive, I'm calling my mom every week, I promise, and if I ever think of buying another pair of frivolous shoes, I'll donate the money to the food bank instead.* I clamped my teeth, changed the string, and wished with all my heart that Cawley would fly out of the shadows and come and sit on my shoulder.

"Where is Cawley?" asked Liesl, who sometimes read my mind. I shrugged, and her eyes narrowed incredulously. "Did you guys have a quarrel?"

"How would I know?" I muttered. That thing at the bar had one hand on Quin's shoulder and he wasn't smiling anymore. "We can't understand a word we say."

Madrona raised her sticks, woke the Thunder Gods with them, and announced to us and the cheering crowd, the coven of crows above us, and whatever familiars and aliens were among us, "Which Witch Can Dance."

They all took off without me.

I was still tightening the new string. Worry makes Liesl edgy and feisty. She was all over the notes I needed to tune; I half expected to see smoke rising off her strings, the way her bow danced. Pyx was blasting away at the song with her eerie voice, which could slide deep, then shoot freakily high on the same word. She sparked as she moved, colors from all those cut jewels flinging out spangles of red, green, yellow, and ice white. Archibald must have decided that her bare neck was too slippery. He had crawled down among the pins, hanging on to a diamond with one hind claw, a chunk of topaz with another, his foremost claws on a coil of tarnished silver and garnets. I finally finished tuning and positioned my bow to jump in.

I saw Cawley then, perched on the beam where the bar glasses hung, right above Quin's head.

He might have been carved out of wood himself, he was that motionless. The monster fry cook beneath him still had its hand on Quin's shoulder, and it was staring across the room at us. I forced myself to look away from the weird little group of Quin and crow and creepy thing. As I started playing, something flashed across my brain, glittery and green, that caught the light like Pyx's pins. It flew in and out of my thoughts a second time; I saw a golden eye. I hit a sour note, recognizing it. The gecko pin. It was on my hair; what was it doing in my head? Liesl caught my eye and grinned maniacally; she loves it when I screw up. The gecko skittered across my thoughts again. This time it made a sound. I had no idea geckos sound so much like crows.

My fingers froze. Gecko. Gecko pin. That was what Cawley said to me. The thing at the bar let go of Quin. He swayed a little, blinking confusedly. It was staring at me now, grabbing at me with its eyes. I felt my skin crawl; insects skittered all over me. My bow was still stuck in place. Liesl lost her smile and covered for me. *What about the gecko?* I cried silently at Cawley. *What about the pin?*

The monster took a step toward us, and Quin upended his Toothless Vampire onto its head.

Then he jumped all over the fry cook, which caused the startled bartender to shoot him with the tonic water hose. The fry cook melted away. A black shape, familiar but bigger than I'd ever seen, streaked over the crowd, aiming not at me and my worthless-but-of-sentimental-value gecko, I realized then, but at Pyx's pins.

Cawley came to life, flying off the rafter after it.

A note came out of Pyx that I'd never heard before. But I recognized its power and so did one of the pins on her vest. The spiral of blackened silver and garnets started spinning, covering the open-mouthed crowd with gyrating red stars. Everybody applauded wildly. I felt the colorful force shoot past me and added something of my own: a shriek of bowed string and a word my mother taught me early on to yell in emergencies. Of course it was the Spinreel G string, and it promptly broke. Liesl added her version to mine, and Madrona walloped a cymbal so hard the reverberations scudded like fast flying golden ripples across the air at the incoming magic. Rune hit the lowest note on the bass while a deep demonic sound came out of his mouth, making the crowd go crazy again. Through it all, Archibald hung on to that pin with one claw, whirling around and refusing to budge, and Graymalkin yowled like the walking dead out for your brains.

All that didn't stop the thing flying at us, but it did slow a bit, bouncing over Madrona's waves and splashing into the wall of power we raised against it. I heard a strange, muffled squawk in my head, which was the only way I could have heard anything in all that uproar. It sounded like Cawley, only sort of squashed, like something was sitting on him.

Then I saw him, fluttering furiously against the grip of a claw bigger than my head.

Several things, all of them incoherent, flooded into my head at once. Cawley might be a disaster of a familiar, but he was my disaster, and nothing could break that bond without losing teeth. Or in this case, feathers. I felt myself fill like a balloon with outrage; in the same moment I glimpsed Hibiscus, who was puffed up like a yellow cloud on top of Madrona's head, facing off something nineteen hundred times her size. A good idea, it looked like, so I puffed, and I puffed, staring that looming monster smack in its moon-black eye, until it seemed that feathers were breaking out all over me. My fiddle wailed a couple of times; more strings broke. I dropped it. A black cloud came down out of the rafters all over the club and covered the gigantic crow-thing from beak to tail feathers, and I discovered, as we started pulling and shredding, that I was one of them.

A murder of crows.

The crowd went totally bonkers, especially when Pyx hit the note she did and caused a sizzling short in the stage lights overhead. I hung upside down on the humongous claw, pecking and biting at it, while some gigantic feathers drifted into me from the rumpus on the monster's back. Cawley got his head free and grabbed a beak full of claw. I couldn't tell if we were winning or losing. But judging from the things flying around us—high heels, baseball caps, lit keychain flashlights, even a T-shirt or two—the crowd was loving our act.

Then a wave of garnet came at us like an exploding red star, and all the lights in the club went out.

I hit the floor and realized that my bones were back where I was used to them being. "Cawley!" I yelled in the dark. I felt claws tangle in my hair. I scrambled to get up, managed an undignified wobble onto my heels, and started off toward where I thought I had left the stage, worried about Pyx and her exploding pin. Cawley squawked in my ear. I said, "Oh," and turned the opposite direction. His claws left me abruptly. I stepped on someone's feet, and we grabbed each other for balance. Then a few of the lights went back on, and I found my hands full of Quin.

He stared at me. His mouth opened, worked noiselessly a

couple of times in goldfish mode. Then he got words out. "That was . . . ," he breathed. "That was . . . that was . . . truly awesome."

I straightened the gecko pin and smiled, still feeling a bit wobbly. "You were great. The way you tackled the fry cook?"

Behind him the crowd, dead quiet now and standing in a litter of fallen flying objects, including various drink garnishes, lipsticks, and an order of fried onion rings, still faced the stage, waiting for more.

"She was evil," Quin said flatly, and I felt him shudder. "Bad, wicked evil."

"I know." I glanced around. It was gone, whatever it was, and so were all the crows, including Cawley. I wondered if they had finished the brawl or just taken it outside. I listened. But there was no Cawley in my head. I looked for him, saw the bartender, the waiters, the kitchen staff, all motionless, gazing speechlessly at each other, at the band.

I counted heads onstage, found four humans, to my relief, and four familiars. Four? I counted again. Rune had one, I realized suddenly. He was grinning crookedly at the garter snake wound around his wrist like a cuff. Archibald still clung to the garnet pin; it smoldered, flaring red now and then, like fire dying down. Graymalkin had quit her caterwauling and Hibiscus had dwindled to her usual size, but they still looked alert, tense.

Pyx cleared her throat but even she was speechless. Madrona brought her sticks very lightly down on the snare and said shakily, "We'll slow things down a bit for our next number, shall we? Hazel? Are you out there?"

Cawley! I called again, this time silently, wanting to know what had happened to him, where he had gone, and was he coming back? Every other witch in the band, even Rune now, had a familiar; where was mine? *Cawley!*

An eerie image formed in my head: a monster crow under a tree, surrounded by a wide ring of hundreds and hundreds of crows, all watching it while only one spoke. Now and then the huge bird twitched a wing or a tail feather, but it didn't seem able to fly.

". . . for the terrible deeds upon which all crows should look with abhorrence and which deeds no crow deserving of the name shall commit and still remain crow . . ."

Cawley! I cried again into that dark, still place in my head, and the crow voice I heard interrupted itself petulantly.

"Your witch Hazel seems to be listening in to private coven matters."

"Uncle Rakl, she became crow and helped us fight." I realized, with surprise, that I recognized Cawley's voice. "My witch Hazel earned the right, by the powers that she possesses."

"I think he's right, Rakl," said an unfamiliar voice, higher and more rattly than the first. "Private coven matters weren't so private in that place, and she fought well and fearlessly for my great-grandson. And for her friends, who seem to be in possession of ancient jewels of extraordinary power. Now, can we get on with this? My tail feathers are a mess and my claws are killing me."

I went back to the stage. The crowd sent up a cheer when I reappeared, maybe just because I made it up the stage steps without toppling over. Madrona clanged the cymbal for me. Liesl handed me my fiddle; she had already replaced a couple of broken strings. I'd have to play around the missing G, but that seemed a piffling matter by then. Rune's snake flicked its tongue in friendly fashion at me as I passed. It was a sleek, sturdy, pretty thing with a fine golden stripe down its back. Rune grinned proudly. He was True Witch now, and he had earned it with the subhuman growl that had come out of him. Pyx still seemed a little stunned by the ugly old brooches she'd been wearing without a second thought.

"Sorry," she said softly to us. "My mother never had time to teach me about them before she died. I just wore them to remember her."

Liesl nodded, looking very curious. "Soon," she promised, "we'll help you find out if they can do more than summon evil monster-crow-god thingies."

Madrona hit the cymbal again, this time a thorough whap to bring the crowd back to life. People were still crowding the floor, wanting more, even while they picked up their stuff and dodged brooms sweeping up the squashed onions. The sweepers watched us mindlessly, running into people as they waited to see what we could follow that act with.

"Gentle people of every persuasion," Madrona said into the mike, " 'Which Witch Are You?' "

Midway through that song, Cawley fluttered onto my shoulder, where he belonged.

"Thank you, Witch Hazel. Very impressive work indeed."

I wasn't sure anymore which language he was speaking, human or crow, or if I heard it with my brain or my heart, but I understood exactly what he said.

THE CARVED FOREST

TIM PRATT

CARLOS DIDN'T BELIEVE in witches, of course, but he did believe in crazy old women with shotguns who menaced anyone who wandered onto their property, so he parked his mother's car some distance away and approached the witch's house on foot, avoiding the long driveway and cutting through the piney woods that surrounded her property. If he could find Maria and bring her home before his parents realized she'd run away, things might be all right and the holiday might be salvaged—assuming Maria would come quietly. Assuming she wouldn't denounce their parents as monstrous dictators or whatever over Thanksgiving dinner tomorrow. A lot of assumptions. But finding her was the important thing.

The witch's house was old, a weathered gray two-story farmhouse with a wraparound porch. The walls crawled with kudzu, the creeping vine that devoured old tobacco barns and rusting grain silos all over North Carolina. The witch was locally famous, though in a secondhand way, as almost no one had seen her in a generation. The stories lived on, though: The post office had stopped delivering her mail thirty years ago when she shot up the mail carrier's car. She'd once been married to the richest man in town, but when he died and their baby died, she'd gone mad, and her vast inherited holdings of land had been gradually taken by the county in lieu of unpaid taxes—not that she'd ever noticed, as she never ventured beyond the end of her driveway. She was a million years old; she could call the moon on the phone; she could turn into a possum and stare with gleaming eyes through your bedroom windows if you did something inappropriate all alone in the dark; she wasn't a witch at all, just a poor misunderstood old woman with a touch of dementia; her hobby was digging tiny graves for her hundred thousand cats. Some people said she'd been dead for years, her house still crammed with the detritus of a life gone cancerous and wild and wrong, no living relatives or else no relatives who could be bothered to sort through the external manifestation of a mad life.

But she was alive. At least Maria said so. Maria had secretly visited her six months ago with the idea of interviewing her for a school project about "living history," an attempt to get fourteen-year-olds to interview their elderly neighbors and relatives to get a sense of the arc of progress over generations. And when Maria had run away from home, leaving a note saying she was never coming back (a note that, fortunately, Carlos found before his parents did), it occurred to him that she might have come here, to the witch's house. Maria had refused to tell him in detail about her conversation with the woman, saying only that "she isn't the way people think she is." Maria certainly hadn't managed to get a paper out of whatever they'd talked about, instead hastily interviewing their *abuela* about her childhood in Baja

California, in a long visit that had bored everyone, their *abuela* included.

Carlos crept toward the house from the side, passing a rust-covered natural-gas tank and stepping over a flower bed full of dead leaves. He felt faintly ridiculous, even a little criminal, skulking around like this. He was sure Maria had just marched up to the front steps and knocked. No reason he shouldn't do the same. Except plain elemental fear of the witch, instilled over all seventeen years of his life.

He tried to peer in the windows, but they were curtained. He followed the wall of the house toward the back—

And found a grove of human figures filling the backyard, tended by the witch.

There must have been a grove of trees there at some point, long ago, but the tops of the trees and any lower branches had been lopped off, leaving stumps that stood five or six feet high, dozens of them dotted irregularly around the yard like oversized fence posts. Almost all the wooden pillars had been intricately carved into the shapes of people, slightly less than life-sized, and about two-thirds of those were fully painted, right down to the irises of the eyes and the buttons on the shirts. The carvings were amazingly lifelike, but the figures were carved only from the waist up: where the legs should have been there was only smooth wood running down to the roots in the ground. They had no hands, either, none of them—the arms were all carved close to the bodies, and the wrists disappeared into the stumps.

All the stories about this old woman, and none of them had mentioned a forest of statues? How was that possible? Now that he really looked, the stumps seemed to stretch off behind the house forever, more than mere dozens, easily hundreds, maybe even more, and beyond the carved ones there were even more stumps, plain and untouched by knife or paint, waiting their turn to be cut into existence.

The witch—she could hardly be anyone else, with her wild torrents of tangled gray hair, complete with autumnal dead leaves stuck in the locks, and her faded blue housecoat decorated with hand-painted golden stars and silver moons—walked slowly through the forest of people, touching them on the tops of their carved heads, occasionally taking off a sliver of wood here and there with the knife in her hand. In her other hand she held a paint-spattered tin can with a paintbrush sticking out. She had her back to Carlos, so he stayed still, watching, as she folded the knife and put it in her pocket, then drew the paintbrush from the can. The witch daubed a bit of flesh tone onto the cheeks of one of the unfinished statues, then dipped the brush into the can again and painted in red lips, then dipped again and painted on brown eyebrows—how did she get three different colors from one little can of paint, without even rinsing the brush in between?

He began to feel he was being watched, and glanced around, hoping to see Maria—but instead he saw himself, or a carving of himself, right at the edge of the forest of figures, dressed in the same sweatshirt he was wearing right now, staring at him with a carved expression of comical surprise.

"Hello, Carlos," the witch said, not looking around. Her voice wasn't raspy or high-pitched; it was a voice made for singing lullabies, full of soothing resonances. "Maria is in the kitchen having tea and toast. Why don't you join her? I think she has some news for you. The back door is open."

He looked at her, but she didn't turn around. When he glanced back at the carving of him, it was different, mouth no longer gaping open; now it looked merely confused. Carlos backed away, considered running . . . but Maria. He'd have to grab her first, take her away, get back home, then he could think about this, figure things out.

The back porch was screened in, and he did his best to back up the steps so he didn't have to take his eyes off the witch, who was painting liver spots on the head of a statue that looked exactly like Principal McNeill. Eventually he had to turn around, though, to push open the door and step inside the house.

The kitchen was rather dim, with an abundance of white tile that made him think of hospital hallways, and counters so spotless it seemed likely the witch never cooked. Maria sat at a square wooden table in the center of the room, a delicate porcelain teacup on a saucer before her, munching a piece of dry toast. She saw him, swallowed, and gave a little wave. "Hey, Carlos. Nice of you to come looking for me. You didn't have to do that."

"Maria, we have to get out of here, before that old woman . . ."

Maria waited a moment, then said, "Before she what?"

"I don't know. Does something awful."

His sister shook her head. "She's not like that. She doesn't hurt people. She takes care of them." Another bite of toast, another swallow. "And she's going to teach me to be like her. I'm going to be her apprentice."

Carlos gaped at her, which Maria—never hesitant to talk—took as an invitation to explain. "She asked if I wanted to when I visited her last spring. She told me some of the things she could do, but I didn't believe her. Who would? But you know how I've been fighting with Mom and Dad, how bad the summer was, I was grounded all July . . . I started sneaking back up here, and she *showed* me what she can do." She shrugged. "I'm sick of living with Mom and Dad. They treat me like a baby. Nedra—her name, it's Nedra, I think it might be short for something, I don't know—she treats me like a *person*."

"Adolescence is a social construct," Nedra said from behind Carlos, and he hunched his shoulders, feeling vulnerable, but hesitant to turn and face her. "Once upon a time, a girl Maria's age would be considered an adult—and treated like one. Look at me, Carlos."

Carlos turned slowly, and the witch smiled. She didn't look a million years old. More than forty, certainly, but less than sixty, which didn't make sense, because she'd been an old woman even in the stories his parents had heard when they were children in this town. She had streaks of paint on her chin, but her eyes were kind. Not that you could necessarily trust a witch's eyes.

"Are you going to make trouble for us, Carlos?" she said. "Try to take Maria away, when she's chosen of her own free will to stay here?"

"She's a kid," Carlos said, forcing himself to stand straight. The witch was a foot shorter than him, but try as he might, he couldn't manage to loom over her. "She can't make a decision like that."

The witch made a noise in her throat, a sort of clicking hiss, something that didn't sound human—an entomologist had brought a glass tank full of giant hissing cockroaches to his biology class one year, and the noise she made was almost exactly like that. "Maria, those changes we talked about making in your parents, I think . . . we'll have to make them in Carlos, too."

"No," Maria said, and her voice was solid as a house foundation. "Carlos has always been good to me. I won't let you mess with him like that. If you do, I'll leave, I won't stay with you."

Nedra smiled, just slightly, but her eyes weren't kind anymore. "I could make some changes in *you,* too, Maria. . . ." She sighed. "But you wouldn't be any good to me as a student then. Your mind needs to be your own. All right, I suppose it won't matter. I'll let you say your goodbyes, and finish up my work on your parents and your teachers and so on." She took the knife from her robe, and Carlos grabbed her wrist, which was bony and felt fragile. But feelings could be deceiving.

"Our parents? What is she talking about, Maria?"

The witch pulled her wrist away effortlessly and left the kitchen, slipping out the back door.

"She won't hurt them," Maria said. "She'll just make them forget me, and really, they'll be happier. They don't seem to like having me around much."

Carlos started to speak but changed his mind. His mother and Maria had been very close until Maria turned twelve, when Maria became "possessed by the demon hormones," as their father put it. She'd been something of a terror since, with lots of door slamming, shouted curses, shrieks of "I hate you!" and general dramatic disobedience . . . but she was still Maria. Carlos remembered his own sullen early teen years well enough to think the storm would pass.

Maria was still talking. "She says she'll just make a few cuts in the heads of their statues, little things, and that will take care of everything—"

"What statues?" He pulled out a chair and sat down, suddenly exhausted. "What are you talking about?"

"The carvings. Of Mom and Dad, and everyone else who knows me, except you. Back *there*." Maria gestured toward the backyard.

"She has carvings of our parents?"

She nodded. "Of Mom, Dad, you, me, Abuela—everyone in town. They're magic. That's how she keeps us safe. As long as our carving is safe, *we're* safe. I'm not sure how she does it—something to do with mixing a little bit of our blood into the paint."

"This is crazy, Maria. She's not magic, she's just a crazy old woman. And where would she get our blood, anyway?"

"She can turn into a possum, or an owl, or a dump truck, or the reflection of light on the water," Maria said. "You think she can't make herself look like a *nurse*? Whenever a baby is born in town, she goes to the hospital or the house and gets a little bit of blood, and starts a new carving for them."

He shook his head. She was old enough to know better than to believe nonsense like this. "If you don't leave with me right now, I'll come back here, with Mom and Dad, and the sheriff if we have to, and bring you home. She can't keep you here. It's kidnapping."

"You come visit whenever you want." Maria reached across the table and touched his hand. "But Mom and Dad . . . well. You'll see."

This was stupid. He came around the table, grabbing her arm—and suddenly flew across the room, thumping painfully on the kitchen floor. "No!" Maria shouted. "Don't hurt him, he's my brother!"

The witch, Nedra, was standing by the table now, and as Carlos got to his feet, groaning from the hit he'd taken, she bared her teeth. "Fine. Can I at least . . . escort him to his car?"

"Gently," Maria said, and Nedra rolled her eyes.

"You can't," Carlos began, but when he finished the sentence, saying, "do this," he was staring out the windshield of his mother's car, parked in the driveway of his house. There wasn't even a moment of blankness in his mind, no discontinuity of memory: one moment he was aching and bruised in the kitchen, and now he was here, with no pain at all. He got out of the car and rushed to the front door. "Mom, Dad!" he shouted. "You have to help me. Maria is in trouble!"

His mother was in the kitchen, making pies for Thanksgiving dinner, and his father stepped in from the living room, a paperback book—true crime, probably—in his hand. "Maria," his mother said thoughtfully. "Is that the girl from your English class?"

He frowned. Had she misheard him and thought he said Alicia? "No, Maria, my *sister*."

His father grinned. "Ah, you love her like a *sister* now, is that it?"

Carlos stared at them. Were they joking? They couldn't be. . . .

"Now, what kind of trouble is this girl in?" his mother said. "Nothing to do with *you*, I hope."

Carlos thought furiously. "Ah, no, her car just broke down, she wanted me to pick her up—could I borrow your car?"

"You *already* borrowed my car, two hours ago, to go to the store to get me condensed milk," his mother said. "Which I see you've forgotten. Go, go, just remember the milk when you come back, okay?"

"You're a good-hearted boy, son," his father said, wandering back to the living room. "But don't let this *sister* take advantage of you."

"I just . . . let me get my jacket," he muttered, and rushed through the house. He went past his own door and pushed into Maria's bedroom.

Her canopy bed was gone, as were her dresser, her posters, and her bookshelves. The room was now a neat and anonymous spare bedroom, with a layer of dust on the bedside table, as if no one had stayed here in some time.

Carlos backed out of the room. *She'll just make a few cuts in the heads of their statues,* Maria had said. Cutting out their *memories*? Making it so Maria had never existed?

The old woman was a witch. Really a witch. How did you fight a witch? Not with silver bullets, or crosses, or garlic. There was some precedent for throwing a bucket of water at her, but Carlos didn't think that would work. Except holy water, maybe? Good luck getting any of that out of Father Norris, not with a story like this. Burning and hanging were traditional, but he couldn't imagine doing that; he didn't want to kill anyone, just free his sister . . . who didn't want to be free. Their parents could be a pain sometimes—but was living with a witch better? Maybe the promise of power was.

He settled for stopping by the garage and getting the ax his father used to split wood. Maybe if he threatened to cut down her grove of statues, the witch would let him take Maria. It wasn't much of a plan, but what else could he do?

"Go ahead," the witch said, leaning casually on a carving of Mr. Jennings, manager of the grocery store. "Chop away. Which of your fellow citizens are you planning to murder?"

Carlos frowned, lowering the ax. "What?"

The witch thumped the statue's head. "That just gave Mr. Jennings a little headache. The carvings and their subjects are linked, Carlos. It's basic sympathetic magic. Chop one down, and you'll kill them, or at least wound them. It might look like they were in a car accident or they got caught in farm machinery, but *you'll* be the real cause." She sighed. "This would be much simpler if I could just slice your memories of Maria out of your head, but she's adamant. Not ready to give up *all* her old life yet. She's stubborn to a fault, which is actually no fault at all in this line of work. What do I have to say to convince you that Maria is better off with me?"

"Nothing. There's nothing you *can* say."

She snorted. "Let me try anyway. You'd prefer she got pregnant by some high school boy at seventeen like half your cousins do? Live in a trailer park, get fat, see all her dreams dissolve, watch TV? With me, she can have a meaningful life."

"It won't be like that." Carlos tightened his grip on the ax and took a step forward. "Maria is smart, way smarter than me, she'll get out of this town and make a life for herself—"

"No. She won't," the witch said. "No one gets out of this

town. Oh, people might take vacations, maybe even go away for two or four years of college. I'm not a monster, but no one really leaves, no one puts roots down anywhere else. Haven't you noticed?"

"That's not true, I know lots of people who've left and—" *And all come back.* He racked his brain for an exception, but the only ones he could think of didn't live in *this* town, they lived in one of the next towns over, or in an unincorporated township, and just attended the high school in town. "I . . . I'm leaving, though. Going to college in California. I'm going to stay there."

"Ha," she said, but without any humor. "I don't think so. Haven't you noticed all these carvings are rooted in the ground? That's to make you *stay.* How can I keep you people safe if you're scattered all over the world?"

"That's not keeping us safe, it's keeping us in a *cage.* Who appointed you the warden of this town anyway?"

She sighed. "Come with me." She turned her back and walked deeper into the forest of carvings, and it occurred to Carlos that he could bury the ax between her shoulder blades . . . but he couldn't even quite visualize himself doing it, let alone actually take the action. He wasn't a murderer, apparently. He wished he could take pride in that, instead of feeling vaguely disappointed in himself.

The witch gestured at a pair of unpainted stumps standing some distance apart from the rest of the grove. They were crudely hacked things, recognizable as human figures but only just, nothing like the eerily lifelike statues all around them. It was almost like there were things trapped in the wood, trying to claw themselves out, but unable to make it more than halfway.

They were far more unsettling than the more perfect effigies elsewhere in the grove. "What are these, your first attempts?" Carlos said.

"They were meant to be my husband and daughter," she said. "My attempt to bring them back from the dead. I had their blood, I had hair, I had—I had *pieces* of them—but nothing worked. The carvings wouldn't take. There are some things beyond my reach, things I couldn't unlock even in my madness and grief just after they died, when the shadows and the moon and the stars and the stones all poured their secrets into my ears and gave me powers. Do you know, they died before your parents were even born, but I still see them both perfectly the moment I close my eyes. They whisper to me from the shadows every day and night, and the pain of losing them, it's still *here*." She tapped her chest. "Like an open wound inside me, infected, forever. They say time heals everything . . . but there are some things time can't touch. The way I feel, they may as well have died just this morning. There is no bridging the gap from here to death, not really, and if I can't resurrect anyone . . ." She shrugged. "Then I must preserve. I couldn't save them, but I can save all of *you*. My husband used to say people in our position, wealthy, influential people, we have a *responsibility* to the community, and I honor his memory. And now I have Maria to help me. It's not like having my daughter back—not really—but it's better than this loneliness."

"You're a monster," Carlos said. "You have to let people live their own lives."

"I do," she said, rounding on him, eyebrows drawn down. "They have wonderful lives, safe lives. No one has been murdered in this town in decades. There aren't even burglaries.

There are barely even *accidents,* not within the town limits, anyway. So what if you can't leave? What's so wonderful about the rest of the world? The rest of the world is *worse* than our town, I know, believe me, the rest of the world is what took my family from me."

"And now you've taken my family from me," Carlos said. "My sister."

She made a sharp, dismissive gesture with her hand, like she was chopping the head off an imaginary chicken. "Nonsense. She's here, and you're welcome to visit anytime. Most people can't even find my house—they start down the driveway and walk a while and end up back where they began. But you need to be *nice,* Carlos. Don't make trouble for me, or I'll . . ."

"Now come the threats," he said, with a certain amount of satisfaction. "Or what?"

"I can't threaten you or your parents. Maria would never forgive me. But . . . this is the girl you like, isn't it?" She put her hand on a carving, and yes, it was Alicia, the girl from English class, the one he'd had a crush on since junior high, and she'd *finally* broken up with her boyfriend—

"You wouldn't hurt her," he said.

"I never hurt *any* of my people," she said, and then the knife was in her hand, and the little paintbrush. He lifted his ax—just to threaten her—but she gestured at him, and the wooden handle writhed in his hands, sprouting small branches that stabbed at his palms. He gasped and dropped the weapon, and the handle put down roots, transformed into a living sapling with an ax head dangling from one branch like strange fruit.

"There," the witch said, and Carlos stared at the carving of

Alicia. Her eyes were different, now, with long slit pupils like a cat's, and her lips were far redder, her face far paler, and she had fangs, bone white and needle sharp—

"She looks like a vampire," he said.

"Mmm-hmm," the witch said. "Don't worry, she won't bite my people—there are plenty of folks who just work in town, or go to high school here, but they're not *mine*. She can feed on them. But I'm afraid you might not like Alicia much anymore— there are going to be some inevitable changes in her personality."

"This is crazy!" he shouted. "You can't do this!"

"There are very few things I can't do."

He backed away. "What do I have to do to make you change Alicia back?"

"Just be a good brother. Support your sister's decision. Is that so much to ask?"

He shook his head. "No. No, it's fine."

"Good. Now go away. I need to teach your sister how to conjure and conceal."

He called Alicia, doing his best to make casual small talk, and she said she was fine, that she'd gotten a terrible migraine earlier and had to lay down in a dark room for a while because the light hurt like crazy, but she was feeling better now. Carlos lay in his own dark room long after night fell, staring up at the ceiling, thinking. Mostly he was thinking about living the rest of his life as the only person in his family who knew Maria even existed. It would be like being haunted by a ghost, but the ghost of someone no one else even realized had died. He didn't know anything about magic, but he had to do *something*.

A few hours before dawn, he went to the garage for a few tools, then took the car, putting it in neutral and pushing it out to the street so his parents wouldn't hear him start it up in the driveway, and driving out of the subdivision before turning the headlights on. He would have walked—it was only a couple of miles—but he didn't want to carry all the blades and things on foot that far.

The witch's house was dark, which was good, since he'd worried Nedra would be awake, perhaps incapable of sleep. But if she was up and around, there was no sign of it. Navigating the grove in the dark with nothing but moonlight to guide him was difficult, but he did his best, creeping low to the ground, pulling the canvas bag of tools after him. Sometimes it seemed the carvings were moving slightly, or even breathing, and once his eyes adjusted to the dimness he realized almost all their eyes were closed, as if sleeping. That was better, somehow—no sense that they were watching him.

He'd wondered if he might find the witch's own likeness somewhere in the grove, but it was too vast, too full of familiar faces and strangers, so he went with his original plan. The wood was surprisingly easy to cut through—either because of magic or dry rot—and the handsaw his dad used to hack off dogwood branches sliced through them easily, showering sawdust around his hands. He even didn't need the hand ax or the mallet or the wedge. He got a cramp from trying to saw while lying on his belly, and the angle was awkward, and dust got in his eyes, and there were squirming bugs in the wood, but he gritted his teeth and persevered, cutting through both stumps in less than an hour. He would have liked to destroy the roots, but absent a tractor or explosives that wasn't going to happen. He'd have to hope this was enough.

Carrying his tool bag slung over his shoulder and one rotting log under each arm was an ordeal, but he crept through the grove and back to his car successfully, placing the carvings in the trunk. He drove a few miles until he reached the desolate field where the county fair had been set up a couple of months earlier. In the first glimmerings of dawn, he set fire to the two stumps he'd cut: one of the witch's dead husband, one of her dead daughter. They burned quickly and hot, as if soaked in gasoline. The smoke writhed strangely, making human shapes in the air, and it didn't smell much at all like burning wood—more like burning hair, a stink he'd smelled once as a kid and never forgotten—and he thought he heard a long, low sigh escape as the wood turned to ash.

After the carvings had burned out, he poked through the ashes with a stick. There were a few bits of white that might have been bone fragments or baby teeth, but nothing else recognizable. He yawned hugely, went back to his car, and drove home before his parents could miss him.

Carlos crawled into bed, wondering if he'd accomplished anything at all.

His cell phone rang, and he stared at it blearily, still half asleep. Maria. "Are you okay?"

"Carlos, can you come? The wi—Nedra, she's acting really weird."

He clamped the phone to his ear with his shoulder and

pulled on a clean pair of jeans. "Are you in trouble? Is she threatening you?"

"No, she's . . . she's *crying.*"

His mother was in the kitchen, of course, working on Thanksgiving dinner, and she called to him as he ran through the room, but he didn't answer. He jumped into the car, driving off while his father yelled at him from the front yard, where he stood holding a rake. Moments later his cell phone started to ring, but a glance showed him it was his mother, so he turned it off and raced through back streets and up the seemingly endless driveway to the witch's house.

Carlos didn't bother knocking, just burst through the front door, and Maria was there in the living room—which was like a time capsule, if someone inexplicably decided to fill a time capsule with hideous country furniture from the 1940s—staring in worry and bewilderment at the witch, who was curled on the floor, sobbing.

"What's wrong with her?" He sat beside Maria on the couch and put his arm around her shoulders.

The witch looked up, cheeks streaked with tears. "I can't remember their *faces*," she said. "My husband, my daughter, for the first time today, I closed my eyes, and they're gone. I reach for them with my mind, I probe for them, I listen, but I can't feel anything, I can't hear them whispering . . . they're just *gone.*"

Carlos let out a long, relieved breath. "But . . . that's good. I think you had them trapped, or some part of them, their spirits, I don't know, in those carvings you tried to make. That's why the memories never faded for you, why the pain never stopped.

Your magic worked, just not the way you meant. You kept them here, but only partway, stuck between life and death, between this world and . . . whatever comes after."

Her eyes widened. "Trapped? Their spirits? You're sure?"

"I *wasn't* sure. But I thought maybe—you said you could still see them, still hear them, and that sounded like a sort of haunting to me, and so . . ." He took a deep breath. "I set them free. Cut the wood down, and burned the carvings, and released them. I think I saw their spirits rise into the sky, heard their last breaths." Carlos braced himself for an attack, but the witch just rose unsteadily and sat on a stiff-backed wooden chair.

"I never realized," she murmured. "I never *meant* . . . I just wanted them back. I didn't want to keep them from . . . moving on." She looked from Carlos to Maria and winced. "I may have been . . . misguided, carving the forest, trying to protect everyone from everything. It's easier to think straight now, without that ache of grief in my chest, that howling emptiness under my ribs, distorting everything, making the world seem ugly and danger-ous . . . but it's strange. I miss the pain now that it's gone. I'm not sure I want it back . . . but I do miss it, in a way. It was reliable. Familiar." She wiped the tears from her cheeks matter-of-factly. "Maria," she said in an oddly formal voice, "I will not be able to continue training you. You must go back home to your parents."

Maria shot to her feet. "What? That's not *fair*—"

"What wasn't fair was me taking a daughter away from her mother," Nedra said. She raised her hand before Maria could protest further. "Listen. When you're older, when you're ready to leave home, if you want to come here, I will teach you then. All right?"

"What, like when I'm eighteen? That's forever!"

"Go wait in the car," Nedra said. "Your brother will be along shortly."

Maria shot a venomous glare at Carlos, then stomped out of the room. For someone who barely weighed ninety pounds, she was a magnificent stomper.

"Go, have your Thanksgiving dinner," Nedra said. "I'll restore the memory of your sister to your parents and the rest of your family."

"I was wondering about that," Carlos said. "A lot of relatives from out of town are coming, and surely *they* would remember Maria, you don't have carvings of them—"

"The town is mine," Nedra said simply. "Things work out the way I want them to here, and as long as they *were* here, or even calling someone here, they'd forget Maria, and later simply forget they'd forgotten. Listen, though. Come back tomorrow. All right? I could use your help with something."

Carlos stood up. "I . . . all right. Listen, Nedra. I'm sorry. About your husband, and your daughter—"

She shook her head. "Don't be sorry. It was a very long time ago. *Finally,* it was a very long time ago."

Carlos took Maria home. His parents were annoyed that she'd left the house that morning without telling them where she was going, but they were too busy getting ready for their visitors to make much of it. Maria sulked in her room until noon, but she came out when the cousins started arriving, and devoured their mother's apple pie after dinner, as always, and Carlos allowed himself to believe that things might be okay.

* * *

His parents wouldn't let him borrow the car the next morning, and anyway it was blocked in by the cars of the various relatives who'd stayed the night, so he said he needed to take a walk, and hiked for Nedra's house. The driveway seemed shorter, somehow, this time. He knocked on the front door, and Nedra stepped out onto the porch. "Come to the back," she said, and led the way around the house to the grove.

For a moment they stood by the back steps, surveying the vastness of the carved forest. Then Nedra sighed and handed him a folding knife identical to her own. "Let's get started. We have a lot of work to do."

He looked at the blade in his hand. "Started? Doing what?"

"Carving legs for all these people. And uprooting them from the earth, so they can go where they will. Do you want to start with your own carving?"

"No," he said, opening the knife. "Show me Maria's."

"You're a good brother," she said, a bit grudgingly.

He grinned. "I try. But then, yeah—I'll do mine next."

BURNING CASTLES

M. RICKERT

ONLY RECENTLY HAVE I come to suspect she lies about everything. Ever since I was a little kid she has told me not to feel bad about the genes I carry. "They say it skips a generation," she says. "It doesn't mean you can't have a magical life."

She even likes to dress her lie, wearing long skirts and flowing scarves; she paints Goodwill boots with acrylic scenes of butterflies, sunsets, black trees, autumn leaves, and snow; she wears her hair long, she smells like fire, her jewelry cackles.

"Is your mother a hippie?" Shelly Vogle asks me, her eyes wide.

"No," I say, watching my mother sweep through the school hallway, scarf, skirt, and sleeves floating as though she is on the edge of flight. "My mother's not a hippie," I say. "She's a witch." Shelly's eyes glint with the small flame I ignited, her mouth closes, her lips tight. I like to watch it happen. I like to watch people turn, slowly, to assess my mother with a combination of fear and awe. She thinks she is the one who creates this reaction, but I learned early that in spite of my poor, unmagical nature, I still have power. "Careful," I whisper to Shelly. "Don't let her catch you watching." She turns away, refusing to look at my mother even when she says hello.

"I don't know why your friends are so afraid of me," my mother says, loud enough for anyone to hear. She says it as though it is an upsetting matter, but anyone can see she is pleased. "Are you ready?" she asks. "It's important not to be late."

I slam my locker shut. I pretend that I can't look at her, as though she has some power over me that I am not equal to.

"Where are we going?" I say.

"Marissa, you can't be serious." I'm not, but I don't let her know. She doesn't know anything, it turns out. All those times when I was a little kid and she said she could read my mind, she did nothing of the sort.

"You know we're meeting Duke's mother today. You know he doesn't want us to be late. Don't do this to me, Marissa, not today."

We walk down the long blue hallway together. In spite of my mother's floating way, she is a noisy walker. Her boots click across the linoleum, her bracelets clank. In the otherworldly silence of the mostly empty school, my mother announces our passage; beneath all her other noise I think I hear the bell-like sound of her earrings, which are long and shaped like Christmas trees. When we emerge from the school into the light, I squint and lower my head; my mother groans. That's something we share; neither of us likes the sun very much.

When I was a little kid, I thought she was perfect, better than any fairy-tale queen, my mother and only mine, with her beautiful long hair, her layers of silk that brushed my skin when she leaned down to kiss me with her cinnamon lips. I misunderstood the way strangers looked at her, thinking they were seeing what I saw: the most amazing woman in the world, my mother, who could make birds sing, flowers open, stars fall. Though, strangely, none of this magic helped our circumstances; we frequently moved from rental to rental, dingy house with poor plumbing to even dingier house with better plumbing. Once we had a bathtub, and twice we had a porch. Currently we live in an apartment with neither, but we're moving after the wedding.

"Just be nice," my mother says as she backs out of the parking space in the school parking lot. I sink down into the seat, not wanting to be seen in this car that looks like something put together in pieces. My mother says it was a blessing that Duke found it for us when he did, but I have reason to suspect this is another of her lies. She is careful to keep mud smeared across the license plate and she slows down considerably around police cars. "I know you have doubts, Marissa, but don't blow this for me, all right? You can have your little teenage breakdown in a few weeks. That's all I'm asking. Just pretend for a while longer."

I nod solemnly, having learned from the master that it means nothing at all to say yes, to say no, to lie.

"What you're feeling is perfectly normal," she says, tapping the steering wheel with her long fingernails, painted a subdued pink. "It makes perfect sense that you would be jealous."

"I'm not jealous," I say. I can't stand the way she talks lately, as though everything I say has a reason beyond the reason I say it does.

"Well, whatever it is you are. It's normal. I mean, look at us, kiddo. It's just been you and me all these years, and now I bring this man into our lives. Of course you'd feel . . . whatever it is you're feeling." She grabs my knee with her pink manicured hand and smiles down at me, revealing, in this bright light, never-before-seen dimensions of her face. "What?" she says, concern making everything worse.

"Nothing. I hate it when you do this when you're driving. Just keep your eyes on the road, Mom," I say.

She knows I'm lying, I'm sure, but isn't it easier to go along with it? When she looked at me in that bright afternoon light, her face was lined with tiny cracks as though she'd broken it and glued it back together again without me even noticing.

Maybe it's a past-life thing. Maybe for a moment time broke open and I saw her from a life before, when she was an old lady and I was someone else, like her dog, maybe. Maybe, in some past life, I was my mother's pet. My eyes slide sideways as I consider the other option: maybe she was mine. It is obvious she doesn't know what I'm thinking. She looks happy.

I have had much reason lately to think of past lives, ever since my mother brought him home and the dreams returned, the ones I'd forgotten for years.

"Night terrors," my mother said. "You used to have them all the time. They don't mean anything real. The doctor told me it was just your way of dealing with your father leaving us to join the circus."

"But I never knew him," I said to her, sitting at the kitchen table, staring at the candle there, lit against the gray morning light. It had taken all my courage to tell her what I remembered.

She shook her long hair, then rubbed her fingers over her head in this weird gesture she had of both tousling and tidying as though she never could make up her mind. "These are dreams," she said, barely opening her mouth to let out the words.

"But it really happened."

We sat there in silence. The gray light changed to a lighter gray, but we were trapped in the fog that always seemed to reside in the dingy rooms of our apartment. I didn't say anything for a long time. What else could I tell her? Even so, after sitting in silence, watching the candle burn low, my mother blew out the flame, pushed her chair back, stood up, and said, "Not another word. Not another word of your lies." She left me alone there, with my memories of being murdered and the acrid scent of smoke.

"This looks like the place," my mother says, turning into the driveway marked with a sign: Senior Glow Retirement Living. "Senior Glow," she snorts, and I almost laugh with her before I remember what she is doing to me. She parks the car in the first open space. In spite of myself I do laugh, a short, quick bark. "What?" she says.

"You don't want her to see the car?"

My mother shrugs, even as she smirks. "Come on, let's get this over with."

We walk up the driveway, our heads bowed against the light.

"Is he going to be here?" I ask.

"Well, of course he is." She rolls her eyes but, when she sees me watching, tries to cover it with a hair toss, rubbing her fingers through the long strands.

She's made every attempt to look normal—her fingernails painted a virginal pink, her hair brushed tame—but my mother has been a witch for so long she's lost perspective. She still looks wild. Realizing this, I feel the pain in my chest. I want to protect her. I hate her. How could she do this to me? I consider stopping right there, refusing to go in. She hops over the curb, in that way she has, for a moment all jangled and afloat. I cannot make myself abandon her the way she's abandoned me.

She holds the glass door open to let me pass. She's right about one thing. For so long it was just the two of us. I was her dancing partner, the one who made her laugh, her valentine, her darling, her date.

We click past the receptionist, who peers over her dark glasses at us. My mother wiggles her fingers and the woman offers a tight smile.

"Have you been here before?" I ask.

Even before my mother speaks I know I have given her this opening. "Isn't that what you've been saying? Haven't we all been here before?" She smiles at her own joke as we click down the long hallway and I try not to remember.

I was raised on a policy of no rules. I learned early to put myself to bed when I was tired rather than collapse in strange locations: the couch, which was comfortable enough, the floor, which was not. My mother thought it was funny that I chose the bed. "I'm afraid you're going to be ordinary," she said. "You take after your father."

We celebrated the seasons with fire and wine, though I was instructed to lie about both. "You don't want the government to take you away from me," she said. "Do you?"

I did not. She fed me cake for breakfast, laughed at my jokes, decorated all year with Christmas lights, danced like something tossed by the wind, and told me that we had more than one chance to get it right.

"We live many lives," she said. "This is not our only shot."

"Here we are," she says, and we turn into a room, immediately too warm, with a strange odor, a room where the windows have never been opened, a room where people come to die. She clicks and jangles her way over to him, where he stands in front of the window. "Duke," she says, brushing his arm with her strange nails, turning to swoop down on the old woman sitting in the chair, planting a kiss on her cheek. "Mrs. Lavish," my mother shouts, "how are you? You look like you're feeling better."

"Who are you?" the old woman says.

My mother extends her jangled arm and flaps her fingers at me, a signal to step closer. "This is my daughter. Come here, Marissa. She's a little shy."

I do not move. I am sure my mother thinks this is a defiant act, an attempt to destroy her, but the stifling room, all of us together again, the way he watches me, it's just too much. I spin on my heels and run.

"What on earth?" I hear the old woman say.

"She hasn't been feeling well," my mother says smoothly, so comfortable with her lies.

I wait for her in the parking lot, too hot to sit in the car, which she's left unlocked, of course. I sit on the curb, wiping my nose with my sleeve. This, I think, is the nightmare, not those terrible memories that are in my dreams. This is the reality I cannot escape.

"You're not listening," I told my mother at our kitchen table.

"I remember him. He's a murderer. He murdered me. You can't marry him. He's not the way he seems."

We sat in silence for a long time, watching the candle burn lower, until she blew out the flame, pushed her chair back, stood up. "Not another word," she said. "Not another word of your lies."

Sitting on the hard curb has made my butt sore and I am sweating a sour scent. My nose keeps running and I have to wipe it on my sleeve. *How can she do this to me?* I ask myself over and over again, even as I accept that nothing I've said has worked. It's time to try something else.

I hear her before I see her. She is clicking and jangling and I remember how I used to love the sound of her; next comes the scent, the smell of sweet smoke and burned flowers, the way the kitchen smells after one of her ceremonies. When I see her, my heart opens like one of those flowers before it turns to ash. She doesn't understand; all this time she pretended to have the power when I'm the one who does.

She sees me, and for a moment I think I've been wrong about her. She looks like she knows what is about to happen. "Marissa."

"He touches me," I say.

"Marissa, don't do this to me."

"He comes into my room in the dark."

She is just a woman, after all. Not old, exactly, but certainly not young. The sun is low in the sky behind her. She looks so insubstantial that she could be made out of paper. We look at each other for a while, then she walks over to the car, opens the door, and gets inside. After a moment I join her. We drive home in silence.

THE STONE WITCH

ISOBELLE CARMODY

HERE'S THE THING. I hate kids. Always have.

I mean, I know the job of the race, biologically speaking, is to achieve immortality through reproduction, but the idea of getting impregnated and blowing up like a balloon as I serve as a carrier and service unit for this other person who will eventually burst out of me in the most terrifying way imaginable, then carry on using me one way or another for the rest of my life, is right up there with throwing myself off the top of a twenty-story building. If I have a biological clock, it is digital and does not tick. Moreover, I am fine with being solo. I mean manless as well as kidless. Not everyone needs someone, no matter what the greeting cards say.

So it seemed like the height of unfairness that I should have a kid seated beside me for the trip. I mean, this was business class and I thought they banned children. Or was it just that adults with kids never got upgraded? Anyway, what was with spending all that money on a kid, given this one was easily small enough to curl up and sleep in an economy-class-size seat?

Seating the child next to me, the flight attendant gave me

one of those hundred-watt beaming smiles that makes you want to squint or confess something, and asked me to keep an eye out. *For what?* I would have said, but I was speechless with indignation to have booked business class and find myself a designated child watcher. No doubt some of what was going through my mind showed because for a moment the honey-pie smile froze, but flight attendants are trained to cope with anything, and before I could marshal my objections, she looked at the kid and said reassuringly that she would come back after takeoff.

I watched her walk away twitching her ass in a perky way, wondering, *Why me?* I mean, I am not old enough to have a grandmumsy look, and I don't have that flowerlike eagerness that beautiful young women have precisely in order to entice a man to want to make them a mother. I am not curvy. I am skinny in some places and I have actual fat in other places, and the end result is not the sort of woman men gaze at in magazines with thunderstruck longing. I don't do vacuous smiles or friendly aimless chat. Especially I don't do it with a kid. Come to think of it, I have probably not spoken to a kid since I was one, and even then I didn't much like them.

I looked at the kid. I could not tell if it was male or female because it was a skinny, malnourished waif with jeans, a hooded jacket, and a choppy, chin-length bob that might have been a designer do but also could have been the result of someone having at it with the nail scissors in a dark room. The kid looked back at me. The disconcerting thing about this was that it did not smile. It just looked in that steady, slightly creepy unsmiling way little kids have. I wondered how old it was. Ten? Eleven? Seven?

I mean, how do you tell? I knew it wasn't a teen yet because it didn't sneer.

I could have asked but decided I didn't want to know badly enough to break my rule about never making conversation with anyone on a plane at the start of a long journey. No matter how interesting the stranger next to you is, you will not want to spend thirteen hours talking to them. Ergo, no conversation or eye contact until the last fifteen minutes of the flight, and then only the sort of fleeting friendliness you feel toward other survivors of a flight. The eye contact thing was already blown, of course, but the kid would not speak unless I spoke to it, I was sure, and I had no intention of doing that.

I fumed silently about having a kid next to me until the plane started taxiing down the runway, then I gave up fuming for imagining all the terrible things that could happen if the plane tilted and caught its wing on the ground, an engine burst into flames, or a terrorist leaped out brandishing a glass knife. I have always had a terrific imagination, and this was one of the occasions—like when you wake in the middle of the night and wonder in the pitch dark what woke you—when an imagination is not a good thing.

"You don't need to be scared," the kid said in this slightly raspy voice.

I glared at it. "I'm not scared," I said frostily, consciously loosening my white-knuckled grip on the armrests.

"You *look* scared," said the kid.

"I am *not* scared. I am *concentrating*," I said, enunciating carefully through clenched teeth.

The kid said nothing, and I looked at the back of the seat in front of me and concentrated on not looking scared or show-ing by any outward sign of how much I hate takeoffs, which is only a little less than how much I loathe landings and a little more than how much I hate flying. My irritation at the kid was swallowed up in a spurt of fear at the slight judder in the plane carriage as we took off. I wanted to ring for the flight attendant and point it out except she would be buckled in her seat, and if she came, everyone in the plane would know who had risked her life by selfishly summoning her while the seat belt sign was illuminated.

I listened to the clunk of the wheel carriage retracting and told myself that if there were anything wrong, the pilot would notice and land the plane. I looked out the window, but as far as I could tell we were not turning back. We were, however, tilted heavily to one side.

What if they had forgotten to put petrol in one of the tanks? But again, the pilot, or copilot, would notice and turn us around. If we were not turning around, nothing was wrong. The mantra had just started to calm the hysterical dialogue I always had with myself after takeoff when I noticed a faint knocking sound. I have extremely good hearing. It is a curse because I can always hear things no one else hears.

I said my mantra again: *Nothing is wrong if we are not turn-ing around.* Even if the captain couldn't hear the things I could, he had all those instruments. They would tell him if something was wrong.

By this time, the plane had stopped climbing and banking and we had leveled out. The belt sign went off with a loud ping, and a smooth voice announced that we could get up and move around if we wanted but if we stayed sitting, we should keep our seat belts on. This seemed to me to be a barely disguised warning from the captain that leaving the seat was risking your life, in case we hit an air pocket or an unexpected hurricane, so I remained seated and buckled.

I closed my eyes and breathed slowly.

"Are you still concentrating?" asked the kid.

I stayed as I was and hoped it would think I had gone to sleep. I stayed that way for a long time, but when I opened my eyes a slit and looked sideways without turning my head, I encountered the kid's rapt dissective gaze, which clearly had been on me the whole time.

"Are you meditating?" the kid asked solemnly.

"I am minding my own business," I said coldly, and leaned forward to dig my book out of the pocket of the seat in front of me. I unlatched my tray table so I could rest the tome on it, and opened it up. It was a book on birds. The kid said nothing, and although reducing it to repressed silence had been my desire it was not long before I began to find its silence distracting. Surely it was unnatural for a child to be that quiet. I wanted to look at it but feared it was still staring at me. Indeed, the more I thought about it, the more I could feel its eyes boring into me. I licked my lips and pretended absorption. I read the same paragraph several times without taking it in, with growing irritation, knowing that if I did not soon turn the page, the kid would want to know why. I tried again to concentrate on the book, but to no avail. I closed the book and set it squarely on the tray table, just as the flight attendant bent over to pass the child a yellow plastic purse.

I turned to watch the kid accept it gravely. It did not smile, and it cheered me slightly that this seemed to disconcert the attendant. Her peachy pink smile dimmed, and she asked the kid if it was okay. She did not look at me, but I sensed that she suspected me of doing something to the kid. I felt the guilty heat glow in my cheeks. It was intolerable because I blush easily and noticeably, and when her eyes flickered over me, they seemed to harden slightly.

I did not know what to do. To say I was innocent would be like the man saying he no longer beat his wife. Silence would be the wiser course, given that the child had made no complaint. Even so, I noticed another flight attendant passing by a minute later giving me a hostile look, and imagined the first one telling the others to keep an eye on me. That infuriated me, but there was not a thing I could do about it.

I closed my eyes, reclined my seat as far as it would go, and willed myself to sleep.

The plane gave a frisky little buck, and my eyes flew open. The plane gave another buck and then a sideways lurch that had a hostess staggering hard sideways. The captain came on with a ping and told everyone to sit down, including the cabin crew, because we were flying into unexpected turbulence. I didn't like the word *unexpected*. Turbulence was seldom unexpected. What had probably happened was that some turbulence had gone where it was not expected to go. A hurricane sheered off from a coast at the last minute, sparing the people there the destruction they were battening down for, or rain somewhere fell unusually hard and long, causing a flood, which resulted in some sort of shift of air that pushed a fog bank inland. And the displaced turbulence had wound up in our flight path.

The plane lurched hard sideways and then dropped before rising again. I swallowed and found my throat unpleasantly dry.

"Is the plane going to crash?" asked the kid. My head creaked around and I looked at it. It did not appear to be scared, and I was still trying to find some words to say when it added, "I've never been on a plane before."

My brain scrambled to do something with these two statements, but the plane now gave a series of playful little jumps and then suddenly banked viciously left. I heard a few gasps and a cry, and was amazed none of it had come from me. Then the plane reared up and my stomach did a slow queasy roll.

But then we leveled out and were flying smoothly, and it seemed the worst must be over. The only reason I didn't relax was because the flight attendants were still seated. I could see one of them a few rows forward, sitting on one of those seats that come from nowhere and blocks the aisle, facing back along the plane so he could watch over the herd. I could see that he was not smiling, but did he look scared? I noticed his lips were moving very, very slightly.

Is he praying? I thought incredulously. I wondered if the captain had told him and the others more than he had told us. Or maybe he was just running through the chores he would have to do when he was allowed to get up.

We flew for some time, everyone belted in and the plane giving the odd skittish lurch or tremble, but more or less moving smoothly, which made me wonder why I was so totally wound up.

But the body cannot sustain fear at a high level for very long, so after a while I relaxed and glanced at the kid, who was staring out the window. I felt a small twinge of conscience then.

"Are you okay?" I asked.

It turned and looked at me, the same grave, considering look in dark eyes too big for its face. Its mouth was a nice curly shape and it had very long lashes, like little black brushes. The chin was delicate and slightly pointed, the neck a thin white stalk. A girl, I thought.

"I think the plane is going to crash," she said.

My conscience shriveled. "The plane's fine. If it wasn't, the captain would have turned us round and headed back to the airport."

"Not if it was too late," said the kid.

The plane jerked sideways and a shudder went through it that had people muttering curses and prayers. Then the plane began inexorably to tilt forward and speed up. There was a ping and the oxygen masks came snaking and bouncing down. People grabbed at them. I couldn't lift my hands. The speed of the plane was pressing me back into my seat. I felt heavy and weak. My body relaxed completely without my telling it to do anything. It had its own ideas. I stared at the oxygen mask tilting away from me. I saw that the kid's was swinging forward as well. I remembered the demonstration and the cartoon hostess telling me to fit my own mask before I helped anyone else.

I looked at the kid. "Do you need me to help you put on your mask?" My voice sounded as if I had my head underwater. The air was thrumming. Dimly I heard a woman sobbing. I looked forward and saw the flight attendant had his hands over his face. Somewhere outside the plane there was a terrific noise.

"You want to hold hands?" asked the kid solemnly.

I let go of the armrest and turned my hand up. The kid put

hers in it, and I closed my hand loosely around it. The hand inside mine was small and warm and slightly damp, like a little hairless mouse.

I closed my eyes.

I must have fainted because all at once I was dreaming a dream I had had so many times in my life that I immediately knew I was dreaming.

I was walking over a flat, dark plain. I could not see far because a mist or a brownish murky-looking fog was billowing around me. A blighted light revealed pitted boulders here and there but no grass or trees. Not even dead ones. I had the feeling nothing had ever grown in that place. Nearby was the bed of what had once been a river, now bone dry and dusty. The air tasted dry, too.

It's the air in the plane, I thought. *I'm dehydrated. I can wake up and make that snotty smiling flight attendant bring me some water. I could even ask her for a cup of tea and she would have to make it for me.*

Usually, thinking about waking woke me, but not this time. It seemed to me that I heard something where I had never heard anything before, and when I looked around I was startled to see the kid from the plane walking alongside me.

"Hey," I said.

She looked at me. Now that she was walking I was certain she was a she. Something in the delicacy of the way she put her feet down. Bare feet.

"Where are your shoes?" I asked.

"I took them off on the plane," she answered. "Are we dead?"

I looked at her. Maybe it was an accusing look because she

shrugged apologetically. "This is a dream," I said firmly. "I am willing myself to wake."

"Is it your dream or mine?" asked the girl after a moment, when nothing happened.

I said nothing, feeling baffled and uneasy. And thirsty. Somehow anxiety always manifested as thirst for me.

"I'm thirsty," said the kid.

"It's just a dream," I said.

"How do you know?" she asked.

"Because I've dreamed this dream before," I said.

"Was I in it before?" asked the kid, sounding interested.

I stared at her. "No."

I don't know if she would have said anything to that, but we both heard the sound of footsteps approaching. That had never happened before, either. The kid was right beside me, and her hand crept into mine again as we waited. It seemed a long time before the fog stirred and a woman emerged. She was about sixty with iron-gray hair plaited and hanging over one shoulder to her waist. She wore a gray shift and cardigan and black gumboots, and she was carrying a broom of the sort you get from a craft market, made from a lot of little trimmed branch ends bound around the end of a pole. Padding along at her side was an enormous, ferocious-looking Doberman. It was big enough to have put its jaws around the kid's whole head. Its ears had not been cropped but otherwise it looked like the dogs that the young cloned Hitler in *Boys from Brazil* ordered to eat his interrogator.

The old woman and the Doberman stopped in front of us. I noticed that the dog's sleek, brutal head was level with the kid's.

"Don't be uneasy about Jasper," said the woman in a brisk, no-nonsense voice. "He doesn't bite unless he has to. I'm Rose."

"Did you dream of *her* before?" asked the kid.

The old woman's gaze switched from my face to the kid's. "Who in the blazes is this? No one said anything about a child."

"The hostess seated her next to me on the—" I began, then stopped.

"Why is she *here*?" the woman demanded with asperity. "How did she get here?"

"Where is here?" I asked, deciding I needed to take charge of my dream, which seemed to be getting out of hand. *Wake up,* I willed myself.

"Stop that," said the woman crossly, lifting her gaze from the kid to glare at me. "The point is that she is not supposed to be here. You ought not to have brought her with you, and she will have to be put back."

"Put back?" I echoed faintly.

"Back where she belongs," Rose snapped. "In the plane."

"The plane was going to crash," said the kid.

"Of course it was," snapped the old woman. She looked at me again and added severely, "No one authorized you to bring a child."

"I didn't," I said. "I mean, I don't know what you are talking about."

"She thinks she's dreaming," said the kid.

Rose rolled her eyes and muttered, "God, just once give me a little originality."

"No," I said. "I have dreamed this dream before. Lots of times, and I always wake up."

"Not this time," said Rose impatiently. "Can we skip this part? It is unbelievably tedious how difficult adults find it to believe in anything but death and income tax. How about you pretend to believe this is not a dream for a bit, so I can get on with the introductory lecture. But before that, the child has to be returned to the plane."

"I want to stay with her," said the kid.

"You might survive," Rose told her. "Not everyone will die."

"I don't care," said the kid mutinously. "I don't want to go back."

"I'm afraid it is not up to you," said the old woman repressively. She held out a hand to the dog. "Jasper?" He padded closer and she laid a hand on the back of his head. Then she let out a *tch* and looked annoyed. "Land sakes, I am so rattled by all of this that I am forgetting myself." She held out her hand to me. "Take my hand. Since you brought her here, I need to be in contact to send her back."

"No," I said. The kid and the woman and the dog stared at me. I would have stared at myself if I could have. I had not meant to speak the word aloud. But now that it was spoken, I felt stubborn. "No," I said again.

"You cannot proceed with this child," said Rose.

"Proceed where?" I asked.

"With the testing," Rose snapped. She gave a huffy sigh. "Look, you have been brought here to be tested because you have a certain untapped potential and your life is about to end. A quest has been assigned you, which will reveal if you are able to make use of your abilities. If you are, you will become one of us.

If you fail, you will be returned to the plane. There is no place in any of this for a child."

"If this is real, then sending her back means she will die," I said, more for the sake of argument than because I was able to believe what I was saying.

"People die every day. Children die every day. Now, if you'd had the sense to bring an animal with you, it would have been a whole different thing. You could have taken it as your familiar. But there is no place for a child here."

"A familiar?" I said.

"As in a witch's familiar," said Rose brusquely. "A cat is traditional, but owls, snakes, and dogs are also common choices. Even a goat or the odd frog has been used. Your choice."

"All right, I choose the kid as my familiar," I said, thinking, *Did she say* witch?

For the first time Rose looked taken aback. "You cannot take a *child* as a familiar!" She sounded shocked. "A familiar is a resource to be drawn on to increase and focus power, and sometimes to be sacrificed. Would you use a child so?"

"Better than putting her back in a plane that is about to crash," I said.

"I want to stay with her," said the kid.

I looked at her and felt a moment of unease, but then sanity reasserted itself. This whole thing was a dream, and soon I would wake up from it. Insisting on not putting the kid back in the plane was just pigheadedness because I hated being told what to do.

"It is wrong," Rose insisted, an edge of worry creeping into her voice. "If you take this child as your familiar, there is a very high chance that you will fail your test, and if you do so, you will face a horrible death in the plane."

"Don't hold back," I said.

"This is no time for jokes," Rose told me severely.

"I'll take my chances," I said flippantly. I was getting thirsty again.

"You leave me no choice," Rose said very coldly. "I am afraid you will regret this. Both of you will regret it. The Desolation is no place for a child."

"The Desolation?" I echoed.

She spread her free hand in a gesture that made the mist swirl, and I noticed the tips of her fingers were stained green. "*This* is the Desolation, where you will undergo your test."

Rose drew herself up and again rested a hand on Jasper's head. The Doberman fixed me with its hot brown ravenous eyes as she announced in sepulchral tones, "Your quest is to wrest the amethyst egg from the demon king, Chagrin."

"You have to be kidding me!" I said. It sounded like the description of a bad role-playing game.

Rose gave me a reproving look. "Your levity is inappropriate. The amethyst egg was stolen from one of us long ago by the demon king. It has great power, and Chagrin will not easily give it up. Take the child's hands if you are truly resolved to bind her to you as your familiar."

Despite the gumboots and ink-stained fingers, the look on her face was so solemn that it gave me pause. I had to remind myself that Rose the witch and her familiar, Jasper the Doberman, had been jerry-built by my subconscious.

"Go for it," I told Rose, holding my other hand out to the kid. She took it, looking nervous but determined.

The witch pursed her lips and lifted her free hand. I was about to make some crack about a wand and a puff of purple smoke, but to my astonishment I saw that greenish gas was seeping from the green tips of her fingers. *Maybe not ink-stained after all,* I thought, trying for inward humor. I reminded myself that this was a dream, and in dreams all manner of weird stuff could happen. The trouble was, the longer the dream went on, the less it felt like a dream.

I watched the green gas detach itself from Rose's fingers and wind together in a sort of gauzy cord that snaked down to weave the sign of infinity around our clasped hands. I felt it as a cold wind around my wrist, and the kid, whose pointy little face was lit by a greenish glow that made her look sick, had her eyes fixed on the luminous bond.

"Will you bind this child to you?" Rose asked.

I could barely hear her over the sudden howling of a wind impossibly blowing up from the ground through the circle formed by our bodies and clasped hands, but I said I would and just like that the wind died. The fog about us billowed slowly, untouched by the freakish wind from the earth. The silence that followed felt hollow and portentous. I released the kid's hands and looked at the old woman.

"Until death do you part," she said grimly. Beside her, Jasper suddenly yawned hugely, giving me a gruesome view of his ivory fangs and red throat. Rose went on. "You had better get moving. The demon's keep is not far, but it will take you time to find the amethyst egg and deal with him. Here, you will need this." She held something out to me, and automatically I stretched out my hand. She put an eyeball into it. The eyeball stared at me. "It will enable us to keep an eye on your progress, excuse the pun. You have until the Dreadful Dawn. If you have not got the amethyst egg by then, you will be deemed to have failed."

"What's so dreadful about the dawn?" I asked, still staring down at the eyeball. It felt warm in my palm, and the thought of putting it into my pocket made me feel nauseous.

"I imagine it is because those who fail know they have done so when the sun rises over the Desolation. Or maybe it's because of the harpies that will come seeking meat when day dawns. *You* can't die here, of course, though you can suffer excruciating pain. Your familiar, however, can suffer pain and die, in which event you may request another. Now get moving."

Rose added brusquely, "My advice is not to waste time trying to decide if this is real or not. If you must do that, do it and walk at the same time. Try to learn how to draw on the energy of your familiar as you go."

"How do I know where to go?" I asked.

"Use your familiar," Rose said. "I linked her to the amethyst egg when I bound her to you." With that, Rose turned and marched away, Jasper at her heel.

"Hey!" I protested, but she neither turned nor responded. "Wonderful," I muttered after the murk had swallowed her and the dog up. "Welcome to the Twilight Zone."

"The amethyst egg is that way," said the kid, pointing with one hand and lifting the other to her heart as if she was making an oath. She set off eagerly, veering left from the direction taken by Rose and Jasper, and I followed her lead, trying to decide if

I was really starting to believe in what was happening and what this might mean in terms of my mental health. The only other alternative was that there had been a plane crash and I was in a coma, trapped in a new variation of a recurring dream, in which case it probably didn't matter much what I did. Just the same, I wished I had asked a few more questions about how I was to find the amethyst egg in the Demon's Keep, whatever a keep was, and steal it. Rose hadn't mentioned stealing, but they never call it that in those dumb fat fantasies geeks read, either, where a kitchen boy is sent to get a magic cup or sword from some wizard.

"I'm thirsty," said the kid. "Can you magic me an orange juice?"

I stared at her. "Are you nuts? I'm not a witch, and this is a dream."

"You could do what she did with the dog," the kid went on. "It must have been her familiar." She touched her shoulder.

I sighed. "I could try," I said, to shut her up. I rested a hand on her shoulder and visualized an orange juice. Nothing happened. I felt like an idiot.

"Maybe you have to chant what you want," suggested the kid after a minute. "Say some Words of Power." I swear there were capitals in her tone.

"I don't know any words of power, unless you mean swear words, and I don't say those aloud," I said through gritted teeth. I took a deep breath and intoned, "We want some fresh-squeezed cold orange juice!" Just for good measure, I visualized the last glass of orange juice I had got from the juice bar in the food court near my apartment.

A tray appeared on the ground at the kid's feet, exactly as

I had imagined, with a glass jug of orange juice cold enough to cause beads of water to form on the outside of the jug, and two glasses with the little curly crest of Juice Bar.

"Oh boy," said the kid.

I drew a long breath and then bent down and poured until both glasses were full to the brim. I stood up and handed one to the kid, my mouth watering in anticipation of my own juice. Then I saw she was white to the lips, her eyes wide and dark.

"What's the matter?" I asked.

"I . . . it hurt," she whispered in a thready voice. I noticed she was pressing her free hand to her heart again.

I set my own glass down and guided the glass of juice the kid held to her lips. I made her drink the lot and then I poured the contents of my glass into hers and handed it back to her. I watched her drink and was relieved to see that some of the color had come back into her cheeks.

"You didn't have any," she said, pointing to the empty jug.

"I don't like orange juice," I lied. I was not sure what to do with the tray and the jug and glasses. It felt wrong just leaving them there, but it would be idiotic to carry them with us. I might have tried wishing them away, but I was uneasy at the thought of what that might do to the kid. Clearly summoning the juice had drained her, and it made me remember uneasily what Rose had said about her not being a good choice as a familiar. I had insisted because I had not liked the thought of consigning her to a crashing plane, even if it was just a dream, but now it struck me that Rose might have been telling the truth when she said the Desolation was no place for a kid.

"That way," she said, pointing. It seemed to me she was

pointing in a different direction than before, and I said so. "I can feel it," she said wanly, and again her hand went to her chest.

"Okay," I said uneasily.

She set off and I followed, the feeling of unease beginning to edge into actual fear. What the hell had I got myself into? Was this really real?

The kid looked over her shoulder at me. "I can feel it when you have doubts," she said. "It makes it hard for me to feel where to go. It's like the buzzing on a radio when you can't get the station." She went on without waiting for me to respond.

That was downright creepy, I thought, but I forced myself to follow and tried not to think about anything, to avoid sending her white noise. We had walked maybe half an hour across a stony, broken terrain when the kid stopped, her eyes widening. The look on her face scared me, but I could see nothing in the thick murky fog.

Then the kid slipped her hand into mine.

Little by little the mist thinned, and I saw a grotesque edifice, part medieval dun, part oil refinery, surrounded by what looked for all the world like a moat. The tower had turrets and kill holes and a cupola and arched doors but also rows of round windows with metal rims and rivets and great wide metal chimneys banded in white, freckled with rust, and belching steam or blue-tinged flame. Several pipes ran flaccidly from the base of one of the towers to disgorge green sludge into the moat that surrounded the tower. The water was as black and greasy-looking as crankcase oil. There was a stone staircase that rose and arched high over the moat, but instead of going to the ground on the other side, the steps wove around and around in a coy spiral that ended in a little lookout above the castle like a crow's nest on a pirate ship. I could not see anything holding the thing up except spars of smaller steps, which arched like flying buttresses from the main stair to doors at different levels of the keep.

I drew my hand from the kid's grasp. "You'd better wait here," I said.

"But the witch said—"

"She said a lot of things," I agreed. "The question is, was she telling the truth about any of them? I mean, how many stories did you ever read where the witch is the good guy? Not too many, right? And maybe there's a reason for that. Maybe witches don't come in good."

"In stories, something bad always happens when people separate," she countered. "Besides, you need me to find the egg." I had forgotten that. As we set off again, the kid gave me the same sympathetic look she had given me when she had asked on the plane if I was afraid. Then she added, "I can feel it, but there is something with it, too. Something slimy and full of hate. Maybe it is the demon Chagrin."

"Maybe," I said, wondering why ordinary names were never good enough for the bad guys. They couldn't be Harold or Mr. Jones, though at least Chagrin was better than Bloodsucker or Ripper. If its name defined it, then bad temper I could deal with. "So where is the egg?" I asked. "Up in the belfry or down in the dungeon?"

The kid knitted her smooth brow and then shrugged apologetically, saying she couldn't feel how the passages went inside the castle. "We need to get closer."

We went to the bottom of the steps. They were stone, solidly mortared together hundreds of years ago, but they were ancient and crumbling now and they would be on a condemned list if there were any sort of sensible authority here. They would probably crack and fall the first time anyone set foot on them. In fact, what if they had been designed to do exactly that? That would be a clever way for a demon to deal with unwanted visitors.

"We have to go in," said the kid.

"Fine," I snapped, humiliated that a perfectly reasonable response to this madness should feel like cowardice. I began to mount the steps, and the kid followed in my wake. When we passed over the moat, I saw that the gelid black liquid below was quivering and sending up hungry little wavelets. Bubbles broke the surface, and when one floated free and burst close by I heard the distinct sound of a belch.

"I think it's alive," the kid said.

I pretended not to hear, but I did not breathe again until we had cleared the moat.

"How are we supposed to steal this thing without the demon king stopping us?" I muttered.

"He might be asleep," said the kid, which made me think of Jack the giant-killer creeping around the sleeping giant until the smell of an Englishman woke him. *Fee-fi-fo-fum,* I thought cheerlessly, wishing I were American because then I would have a .44 Magnum or a Colt or even some sort of baby pistol in a clutch bag. Instead I didn't even have the can of pepper spray I usually had in my purse because you were not allowed to carry any sort of aerosol onto a plane. I didn't even have nail scissors. What I did have was a sudden wild desire to laugh hysterically.

By the time we reached the first spar of steps leading to the keep, I was panting hard and seeing little bursts of light before my eyes. *I have to get more exercise when this is over,* I thought, and then winced at my idiocy. I looked back at the kid, who was not even breathing hard, and asked if she could feel where the amethyst egg was now. I had no idea what we were going to do when we found it. I kept hoping a brilliant plan would occur to me, but so far all I could imagine was racing in, grabbing the thing, and running out.

"I think something is watching us," the kid said. "Out of those windows." She nodded toward a row of portholes on the level of the steps. The first spar of narrow steps ran down to a heavy-looking door of dark wood just above them. I took a quick look at the windows but saw only darkness behind dusty glass. I told myself the kid had got spooked and had imagined eyes the way kids do.

As we approached the hinged wooden door at the end of the spar of steps, it swung open to reveal darkness so complete it looked like a solid wall. *Maybe it is,* I thought. I licked my lips and stepped into the darkness.

I found myself in my own kitchen, only the furnishings and crockery sitting on the benches and in the dish drainer were those my mother had used when I had been a child. I heard a footfall and turned to find her coming toward me. It startled me how obese she was. She had a baking tray loaded with freshly baked muffins.

"Yummy muffins for my baby," she sang in her wheedling little-girl voice.

"I'm not hungry," I said. The words were out before I could stop myself, because all of a sudden I was remembering this day.

Tears filled her eyes, and the smile, painted in shiny coral-pink lipstick to match her coral-pink fingernails, wobbled. "So Mama made these all for nothing, did she? She might as well throw them in the rubbish, then. Doesn't matter that the ingredients cost money, does it? Mama's little girl doesn't have to eat them if she doesn't want."

"Please, Mama, I just meant I have to go to the library now," I said. "I can have one later."

"Maybe they won't be here then!" she snarled, and she slammed down the tray and began stuffing muffins in her mouth. Her cheeks and her eyes bulged as she tried to chew. Then she started choking, spraying chocolate crumbs all over the spotless floor, dribbling chocolate drool down her apron front. Her face was purple and terror shot through me. I pounded her on her back, terrified she might die. But she gave some explosive coughs and then collapsed heavily into a chair, burying her face in her hands.

"I'm sorry! I'm sorry!" she wailed. "I try so hard but it's never enough and never the right thing. It was the same with your father. You can't wait to grow up and get away, and then I'll be all alone. I could die and no one would know or care."

"Mama, I won't leave you! I won't ever," I promised hysterically. I grabbed a muffin and shoved it into my own mouth, chewing frantically, tasting the sticky, rich sweetness.

"Did you keep your promise?" asked the kid, and I realized she was holding my hand again. My mother and the kitchen had disappeared, and we were standing in a little round room with dusty black and white paving stones laid out in an eye-watering geometric configuration on the floor.

"I . . . you saw that?" I said, reeling from the vividness of the memory or vision. She nodded. "Was I a kid again?" I asked. She nodded again. I blew out a breath of air, the fright and emotions sinking into a strange heavy feeling of sadness that I always felt whenever I thought about my mother and her life. Slowly I said, "It was real. I mean, it happened. But why did I remember it? What was the point?"

"Maybe it was to make you forget about finding the egg," the kid said. "It's not here."

We went back out and mounted some more steps. "I did," I said. She looked back at me. "I kept my promise, and I'm still keeping it, even though my mother died years ago. I never left home. I lived there until she died, and I still live in the same house. I never moved out." I said the words, wondering if it could really be true, that this incident in the kitchen had been the moment I had decided never to leave home.

The kid said nothing, the way kids can and adults can't, and I was grateful. We went on till we came to another spar of steps that brought us to the next door. This one was lacquered red and shiny like a Chinese puzzle box. I hesitated, wondering if there was another memory behind it waiting to ambush me. The door swung open with a whisper, and this time there was a muddle of light and noise coming through it. I entered and found myself at a party. People were standing around talking and laughing. There were servants with little trays of canapés and others with trays of half-filled champagne glasses.

"Hey there!" said a voice, and I turned to find myself looking at Emily, the wife of my first employer. She was a small, rounded, very pretty woman with a soft voice and straw-pale straight hair, cut with a perfectly straight fringe à la Alice in Wonderland. She was wearing a neat blue apron over a blue dress, and her pale glossed lips were curved into a smile, but her eyes were anxious, urgent. "Is Mike with you?"

"He's . . . he is coming along later in his own car. He got caught up in a meeting," I said. I didn't say he had gone off to play golf, sending me in his place to his eldest daughter's thirteenth-birthday party.

The anxiety in his wife's eyes turned to weary disappointment and for a moment the smile faltered, but she sucked it up and asked me brightly if I would like a drink.

"I'll just put Mr. Willot's gift in with the rest, shall I? He didn't want it not to be here if the present opening happened before he got here, so he asked me to bring it with me." I was gabbling because I could see she knew her husband had ordered me to get something appropriate and had sent me, knowing that he would not arrive before the party was over. She knew that she and his kids were window dressing for his life as a banker. I wished I'd had the courage to refuse him so that I could have avoided seeing the pain and humiliation in her eyes as she turned away.

"My father isn't coming, is he?" asked a familiar voice in a clear grammar school accent. I turned from the gift table to face Amanda Willot. She was tall and slender like her father, pretty like her mother, but with a sharp cleverness that showed in her eyes and manner and that made her more striking than them both.

"Hello, Amanda," I said. "Happy birthday. You father got caught up, but he says he'll try to be here before it ends."

She gave me a look of cool dislike. "Does he pay you to tell lies for him?"

I swallowed and thought, *I will never let this happen to me. I will never be that wife being lied to or the mother who has to watch her daughter learning to hate her father. Better to be alone. Better never to trust anyone.*

"Is it?" the kid asked, and we were standing in a vast empty ballroom with two cobweb-draped chandeliers. The kid had laid her hand on my arm, and it struck me that her touch had ended both visions.

"Is it what?" I asked.

"Better to be alone? Better not to trust anyone?"

I looked at her. "You can hear what I am thinking?"

"Only when you're remembering," she said.

I shifted away from the kid, unsettled at the thought of her having access to my inner monologue, unsettled by the visions I had experienced, both of which seemed to show me making decisions I had not realized at the time I was making. I had always felt as if I had been sidelined by life, cheated out of the things other people seemed to get as a matter of course. Was it possible I had chosen the course of my life? And what did any of this have to do with the demon and an amethyst egg? Unless the kid was right and the whole point was to get me caught up in analyzing the past.

"Let's go," I said. Outside there was a red blush on the horizon; if that was east, and if this place obeyed at least some of the laws of the known universe, it meant the Dreadful Dawn was approaching. I looked at the kid. "Can you feel yet where the egg is?"

"Up," she said.

We got almost the whole way to the top before she pointed to a glass door at the end of a short set of steps running down from the main stair. Once again the door swung open as we approached, but this time when we stepped inside, I reached out to take the kid's hand. I thought I had figured out that it would stop me having a vision, but instead I found myself in a kitchen I didn't recognize. There was a small child with a shaggy mop of hair playing with a rag doll under the table. I realized I was under the table with the kid. Suddenly two sets of legs came in, one after the other. Both wore suit trousers and shiny black shoes.

"What about the kid?" one man said.

"Welfare will take charge until they sort it out with the relatives. They're not keen on getting involved. Can't hardly blame them for thinking twice about taking on the kid of two drug addicts."

"Some kids got no luck."

"You never know," the other said. "Maybe the parents taking off and leaving it is the best thing that could have happened. Sounds cold, but who knows what would have happened if they'd stayed around. I mean, parents that would leave a kid like a sack of clothes they didn't want."

"Pity the relatives won't step up," said the other man.

The kid sitting beside me looked at me with eyes that were a pale honey yellow at the center, running to butterscotch at the edges. It was the kid from the plane. Her eyes were so sad it made my chest ache. I reached out to rest a hand on her shoulder, and the kitchen vanished, leaving me standing in a cramped sitting room with two dusty mismatched sofas pushed against the walls to form an L.

"I was under the table playing with Rosa when the men came in," the kid said. "They were from the government. One of them took me to the home and I stayed there for a long time because I was too old for anyone to want. Then one day the man came back. He told me my mother's sister had decided to take me after all. He said she and her husband felt it was their duty to take me. I said I didn't want to go, but the man said I was a kid and kids have to do what adults decide is for the best. Then he put me on the plane."

"What a prince," I muttered.

"It's close," she said in a voice so soft it was almost a whisper. She went back outside, and we both stopped dead to see what we had been too intent on our purpose to see before. We had finally climbed high enough to rise above the roiling murk. It lay below like a blanket of dark clouds seen from a plane window. All around were high mountain peaks, and above them the sky was a very clear and dark blue on one side, running to red and purple on the other side.

"The Dreadful Dawn," said the kid.

"Not quite," I said. I turned to her. "Where now?"

The kid pressed a skinny hand to her heart again, and then she pointed down. Only then did I see there were metal rungs set into the side of the building, going down to a gaping hole of the kind you see in bombed-out buildings. There was fear in her eyes, but it was not fear of harpies and the Dreadful Dawn. It was the greater fear of abandonment; of being left behind. I knew I ought to leave her because whatever lay in the hole below was nothing good, and every bone in my body said you didn't take a kid with you into a thing like that. Nor did I subscribe to her view that staying together was safer than being alone. Hadn't I built a life out of being alone because that was better than being eaten alive by someone else's needs? And wasn't it the kid's need that was sucking at me now like quicksand?

But somehow I found myself saying, "I'll go first."

The gratitude in the kid's face was so intense it pained me. I forced myself to concentrate on climbing because it was a lot of years since I had done it and the rungs were coated in a greasy slick that made me afraid of slipping. There were fifteen rungs down to the level of the hole blasted in the side of the wall. I stepped into the rubble gingerly. A second later the kid swung in like a monkey and beamed at me. I turned to squint into the murky darkness, all too conscious that if the witch had meant it about the harpies coming at dawn, we would be sitting ducks.

"I'll show you," said the kid eagerly, and before I could stop her, she had darted ahead. Cursing, I followed, stumbling over the broken stone underfoot and wrenching an ankle painfully. Limping on, I opened my mouth to hiss at her to slow down but then saw that she had entered a cavern rather than a room. There was a great hole in the floor, and rising from the near edge was a plinth of white marble cradling an oval of amethyst as small as a regular egg but faceted. The kid reached out to take the egg, and immediately the facets began to pulse delicate flashes of violet and lavender. The color was so beautiful it ravished my senses, and I felt a jealous hunger for the egg take hold of me.

I looked into the kid's face expecting to see my own possessiveness reflected there, but there was a different sort of hunger in her face. Her eyes were bright with pride as she came toward me, holding the egg out to me reverently.

"I am sorry to interrupt this touching little scene, but I am afraid that belongs to me, ladies, and I suggest you put it back where you got it," said an urbane masculine voice with just a hint of laughter.

We both turned to see a form rising from a brown armchair with the stuffing boiling from a slash in one arm. The demon king, I thought, and my heart gave a great salmon leap of fear. But when the form stepped into the light cast by the amethyst, it was a tall and extremely handsome man clad in a charcoal sports jacket, a Neo Tokyo T-shirt with a Japanese motif, gray jeans, and loafers. His hair was very short and he was clean-shaven, but when he smiled again I saw the flash of a black stud on his tongue.

"You are the demon king," I said.

He smiled. "I am, and you are yet another thief sent by the hags."

"I have come to take back something you stole," I said evenly.

His brows lifted and his smile widened. "Just like that?"

I drew a shaky breath and reached out to scoop the egg from the kid's hands. I looked down at it and that was a mistake, because when I managed to look up again the demon had the kid, and although he was still handsome, there was an ugly look in his eyes.

"Let her go," I said.

"The hags lied to you. They will never turn you into one of them. That is witchkind for you. They are all about themselves."

"The witch said—" I began.

"Yes, yes, that you were chosen because you had special abilities, yada yada. You didn't fall for that, did you? I mean, no offense, but look at you. They offered power to a weak, powerless woman, and they backed it up with a threat. A terrible death versus magic powers. Hmmm, tough choice."

"You are lying," I said.

"I lie often and well, but I can also tell the truth if it suits me. Did the hags tell you the witch I took the stone from had originally stolen it from me?"

"You'd say anything to get your hands on this."

He laughed, revealing perfect white teeth. "My dear woman, do you really imagine I can't simply take it from you, even using this weak human form? You are middle-aged and fat, and you were never fit. And this form you see is only the form your mind has cloaked me in, because it is too weak to see the truth. But you are correct, of course. I would lie and cheat and murder to possess the egg. Indeed, I have done all of those things for far lesser prizes. But in this case, the truth should do nicely. The witches are using you, and when you bring this to them, you will be returned to the plane crash. End of story. Literally."

"In the movies, the bad guys always talk too much," the kid said suddenly.

The demon king smiled down at her, but I saw her wince and realized he was digging his fingers into her shoulders. Only for a moment his fingertips looked like claws. The egg pulsed in my fingers, but I managed not to look down. I looked instead at the plinth on the edge of the hole and wondered why the demon had asked me to set the egg back on the plinth. Surely he should desire to have it safe in his hands.

"Do as I have said, while there is time," the demon said, and this time there was the hint of a snarl in his pleasant voice. I looked up to see that his brown eyes had gone red, and his smooth hair had lost its sleekness. He smiled, and my blood ran cold to see that his white teeth were now pointed and the dark stud on his tongue looked bigger.

"Okay. Maybe you are telling the truth. Let the kid go and let us get to the ground on the other side of the moat, and I'll give it to you," I said. "But you have to promise to return us to the airport before the plane takes off."

The demon's eyes flared. "I will return you, but first replace the egg on the plinth. Do it now, or forfeit the child." He nodded to the hole. "That goes directly into the void."

I saw acceptance on the kid's face and knew she was thinking, as I was, that Rose had said a familiar could be sacrificed. As I looked back at the demon it suddenly struck me that I didn't like kids because their vulnerability scared the crap out of me.

"What makes you think I would exchange a kid whose name I don't even know for this?" I held up the egg in one hand. "I hate kids. And what makes you think I will give it to the witches, either? That is what I told them, but once I can figure out what to do with this, I will deal with the witchfolk."

I had been moving closer to the demon as I spoke, and now, without warning, I tossed the egg at his face. He threw up his hands, gave a guttural scream that had more bird than human in it, and reeled back, only to stumble into the hole. The kid over-balanced and fell backward, too, but I was already diving forward. I caught one of her flailing hands in mine. She was slight, but there was enough weight in her to bring me thumping painfully to my knees at the edge of the hole.

"Take my wrist with your other hand," I cried, for her small hand was slipping from my grasp.

She shook her head, and I saw that she was holding the amethyst egg in her free hand. "Take it," she said, holding it up, eyes shining with triumph.

"I can't. If I let go of one hand, you'll fall. Throw it up and take my hands, quickly!"

"What if it breaks!" she said.

"Better it than you. Now come on!" I screamed.

She threw it, and it gave a great blinding pulse of light as she caught hold of my hands. Immediately I adjusted my grip and hauled her up laboriously until she could scramble the rest of the way. We both lay on the edge of the void for a second, panting and gasping. Then the kid's expression changed, and I knew from her stricken face what I would see when I turned.

The amethyst egg lay in small pieces, all of them dull.

"That's that, then," I said as red light speared into the grotto.

Rose was waiting for us at the foot of the steps. On the other side of the moat, Jasper stretched out on the ground with his massive head resting on his paws. The fog had long gone, and the plain stretched out dead and black in all directions, the early morning light giving it a reddish brown tinge that reminded me unpleasantly of congealed blood.

"I failed," I said.

"No," said Rose. "You got the amethyst egg from Chagrin before the Dreadful Dawn."

"But I broke it," I said.

"The child broke it," Rose said mildly. "We saw what happened because of the eye you carried."

"How could it see anything in my pocket?" I asked.

"It is a metaphorical eye," the witch said impatiently, as if I ought to have known that. "You were clever to work out that the demon could not bear to touch the egg. Chagrin defeated those who came before because they did not reach the egg. But instead of walking away when you had it, you chose the child over it."

I glared at her and asked, "So what happens now?"

She chuckled.

"Now you go back to the real world and learn to see it through the eyes of a witch. Then the real work will begin." Rose dropped her hand to Jasper's head, and just like that, we were all standing on the little path leading to my front door. The cottage, bathed in golden morning light with its little garden full of roses and lavender and the twisted lilac bush, humming with bees and glistening with spider threads, had never looked lovelier.

"It's perfect," said the kid, looking past me at the house wistfully.

"The bond of witch and familiar cannot be broken unless the familiar dies," Rose said, looking at me. "However, she can be taken to her original destination, if you prefer."

I glanced at the kid, who was carefully not looking at me. "Maybe we'll stick together for the time being," I said gruffly.

"Very well," said Rose. A black crow appeared and landed on

the edge of the verandah roof. It uttered a drab croak, and the witch sighed. "I am summoned, but I will return in due course. In the meantime, see what you can figure out for yourself. Just one tip: when you summon an orange juice, try not to be so specific. Calling up anything from a specific moment in the past consumes a lot of energy."

She set her hand on Jasper's head, and they both vanished. The crow uttered a croak and launched itself into the air, too. I watched it until it had flown out of sight, then I looked down at the kid and said brusquely, "I am Hester Hallow."

She gave me a glimmering smile and said shyly, "My name is Katya, but you can call me Kat."

ANDERSEN'S WITCH

JANE YOLEN

THE BOY LAY in his too-small settle bed, his feet dangling over the end. Papa had promised and promised a new bed for months now. "Because of your stork legs," as Papa called them. But the green wood brought out of the forest by Grandfather still lay outside the front door, curing on the ground.

"Rotting, you mean," Mama said. She talked like that when she'd had a lot of schnapps, but once she'd been kind and loving. The boy wanted to remember her that way, but she made it very hard to do.

In his long-enough bed, Papa coughed all day and night, his shoemaker's lasts gathering dust and cobwebs on the other side of the one-room house. For weeks he'd been too ill to fix the boy's bed, or work on shoes, or do much of anything at all.

Luckily for the family, Mama had managed to take in more washing this month. Odense, Denmark's second-largest city, was growing rapidly, nearly five thousand people at the last census.

"If I could do *all* their laundry, we would be wealthy," Mama said. "And then we could have an elegant house, in a fashionable street. Not this pig hole." Then she added, "And perhaps get invited to the prince's castle dinner."

Papa had roused between coughs. "Get your head out of the clouds, woman. It gives the boy ideas above his station. Don't count chickens before they hatch." He took a breath. "You live in fairy tales. We have to live in the real world."

She turned away from the onslaught of his words, but Papa was not deterred. "Woman, we will live and die on Munkemolle Street. I am, by the devil's wish, a craftsman, though I wanted to be a teacher. And you are a washerwoman, which is all you are capable of doing. And all the laundry in the world will not buy us an elegant house. If you had such a house, someone else would do the laundry and then how would we eat?" But the speech had exhausted him and he fell back against the pillow.

The boy thought this made a certain amount of sense. But perhaps his stepsister, Karen Marie, could just get more money from her gentlemen friends, enough to keep the family for a while. Of course, he knew better than to say this out loud. Karen Marie was not well thought of by Papa or Grandmother. Or even Mama.

"At least for now I can still put food on the table," grumbled Mama, sitting at that very table, another glass of schnapps in front of her. "You lie abed with nothing more than a winter catarrh, while the leather waits in the corner over there, and no shoes are resoled. Men—you are all such babies. If you don't get up soon, husband, I shall be forced to call the Greyfriars to come and take you into the hospital. At least it will be one less mouth to feed."

Papa's lips thinned, and he gave his wife a look that should have frozen her to the spot. But Mama looked away.

When he got no response from her, Papa threw the covers back and sat up—still coughing—his nightshirt well above his bony knees. "At least help me to the pot."

"Help yourself, old man." Though she was years older than her husband, the words stung.

The boy turned his face to the wall, understanding that any old affection between them had soured with the hardships of life on Munkemolle Street, the way children too often chastened out of love turn stubborn. He felt a sudden restlessness in his soul. But he did not weep. It was too cold in the little one-room house for weeping.

And what about my bed? he whined, but only to himself. They all hated it when he whined, or complained aloud about his stomach cramps or about the constant bullying at school. It was bad enough that Mama and Papa seemed to hate each other. The boy knew he could not bear it if they hated him as well. No, it was best to simply fade away while they argued. Closing his eyes, he practiced fading, just like a swamp plant, which is what he sometimes called himself. Feet in the water, the same color as his surroundings. *You cannot see me. I am not here.*

Before he knew it, he'd managed to fade so completely that his parents' argument became a mere mumble that couldn't be heard above the wuthering winter wind or the waves constantly warring against the shore. In fact, he faded himself right into sleep and didn't hear when they went to bed still arguing, that argument ending, as always, in frantic, deep kisses.

* * *

Later, with everyone safely snoring, the boy sat up, then stood on the settle so he could stare out of the little window above it. The sky was without stars, for a low cloud cover, like a well-made bed, kept everything neat and tidy. There were few lights in the town except far, far away at Prince Christian Frederick's castle. It was lit up till it sparkled as if the stone walls themselves had been carved out of ice.

The perfect time for prayers, the boy thought, and he climbed off the settle bed, slipping on his wooden shoes for warmth. Sinking down on his knees, he began to pray—not to God, who Mama said had done little enough for the family, but to the Ice Maiden. Mama had told him all about the Ice Maiden, with her white hair and snowy skin and eyes the faded blue of the sky in winter. Mama might not be able to read like Papa, but she knew all about these things.

"The Ice Maiden can grant wishes," Mama had said just that morning. "Three of them." She'd held up three fingers. "But be careful what you wish for. If she thinks the wishes are foolish, she can also carry you away to her cold ice palace, where there are only polar bears and seals."

"Is it colder than here in Odense?" the boy had asked.

"Much colder," Mama answered. "So cold, your nose turns black with the bite of the frost and tears freeze upon your cheeks till they are hard as jewels."

The boy liked seals. And polar bears. Though he wasn't so sure about the cold. Odense was cold enough in the winter for him. He couldn't imagine colder. But how the Ice Maiden could get him to her palace was a puzzle. Would they walk? Or fly? Perhaps she had a sledge pulled by reindeer. He liked reindeer.

"Is she a witch, then?" The boy was wary of witches, knowing that they promised to feed you but shoved you in an oven instead.

"Ice maidens are not witches," Mama said. "It's a very different thing." Then she smiled and patted him on the head. He could smell the schnapps on her breath. She was always happier after her glass of schnapps. "But they do expect payment. Just like witches do."

"I have no money," the boy said. Though not usually so sensible, he did have some sense, especially where money was concerned. Or the lack of it.

"She has all the money she needs already," his mother answered. "After all, she has a castle."

"But don't castles need a lot of money to maintain them? For the chairs and the jewels and the big beds?" the boy asked. "And the wars?"

"The icicles are her jewels, she has all the chairs and beds she needs, and she makes no wars." His mother's smile was broad. The schnapps were making her very happy.

"Then how shall I pay her?" The boy had really needed to know this.

But Mama had gone from his side, back to the schnapps bottle waiting on the table even though it was not yet lunch and Papa said drinking was for nighttime and for fools.

The boy knew he couldn't ask Papa about the Ice Maiden. After all, Papa didn't believe in Mama's stories, not about the Ice Maiden or the trolls or the mermaids or any of the other fairy creatures she talked about. Often Papa read books aloud to him, books with hard words in them and no pictures.

The boy couldn't ask Grandfather, either, for Grandfather was off again, into the snowy woods, to sing and dance under the trees and wear beech leaves in his hair till the policeman brought him back: "Keep old Crazy Anders at home, please."

His half sister, Karen Marie, would be no help, either, for she was away with her gentlemen callers.

And while Grandmother often took care of him, she didn't like to talk about what she called wicked things, which meant—as far as the boy could ascertain—anything even slightly interesting or amusing.

And surely, the boy thought, *there is something wicked about the Ice Maiden if she takes people away.* Which was something witches did as well. So he was still confused on that point.

But the Ice Maiden granted wishes. Both the boy and his mother believed that. And if there was one thing the boy knew the family needed, it was for wishes to come true. Which is why—even without knowing what payment would be exacted—he got down on his knees and prayed. He was five years old. Perhaps old enough to know better.

"Ice Maiden," he called, hoping she would come to him. Three wishes was all he would get. This was so in every story he'd ever heard. He unlaced his fingers from their prayer grip and counted the three. A new, bigger bed, to begin with. And for Papa to feel better and be able to make more money. And then the other thing. The most important thing. The thing he could hardly admit to wanting, even to himself. Three wishes. What payment was to be exacted, he would discuss with the Ice Maiden only if she first promised to grant him all three.

* * *

Slipping back into the settle bed and pulling the covers up to his nose, the boy waited to warm up, but instead he only got colder. He glanced up at the little window and finally saw a single star in the sky. At first the star was quite distant, which was proper for a star.

"Star bright," he whispered, and watched as it suddenly fell precipitously in a downward arc. The longer he looked at the star, the closer it seemed to get, until it came right through his window and settled, icy and shimmering, by his bedside.

"Oh," he said. He hadn't any other words for it. Pulling his long legs in, knees to chin, and shivering in the cold, he stared at the star as it slowly resolved into the figure of a tall, beautiful woman with long white hair and eyes the color of a winter sky. Oddly, he could see her clearly through the darkness of the room.

"Are you . . . are you the Ice Maiden?" the boy asked.

She smiled, though the smile did not reach her eyes. "Of course, Hans. Didn't you just ask me to come?"

He nodded and pulled the covers closer, all the while wondering how she knew his name. But, of course, a witch would know.

"Are you afraid of me?" That strange smile again.

He shrugged. What good would it do to be afraid now? Heroes were not afraid. They were . . . heroes. He would be a hero.

"You knew enough to call me." She ran a hand through her hair, and little sparkles of cold fire winked on and off, like stars.

"Mama told me."

"Mamas always do."

Hans was so cold now, he could no longer feel his toes, his fingers, his ears. Even his teeth were cold. It was as if he were already in the Ice Maiden's palace, his nose turning black and the tears freezing like ice jewels on his cheeks. He wished he had some matches to strike to help him keep warm, but they were on the other side of the room by the fireplace and he was afraid to get off his bed, because that would mean he'd have to go past the Ice Maiden, go too close to her. Not perhaps how a hero would think, but he was really only a little boy.

"I will grant your wishes, but you will have to tell them to me aloud." She folded her hands together, lacing the fingers, as if she herself were praying.

"Why?" asked Hans.

"Because," she said, just as all grown-ups do when they are waiting for you to do what they say or give a proper answer.

Hans was never good at giving proper answers. He always had different answers in his head, odd answers, answers that his teachers and his parents and his grandmother and even his crazy grandfather seemed to think were wrong. But they weren't *wrong* answers, they were just *his* answers. He wondered suddenly what the Ice Maiden would do if he gave *her* a wrong answer. And, thinking this, he found he couldn't open his mouth at all.

"I'm waiting," the Ice Maiden said. And then again, "I'm waiting, Hans. I do not like to wait."

Hans took a deep breath. He could feel the cold air rush down into his throat, down into his chest, almost stopping his heart. And then he said all in a rush, "I want a new bed long enough for my stork legs, I want Papa to get well enough to make lots of money, and I want to be a *digter,* a poet, and make even more money for the family." There, it was done. Three wishes spoken aloud.

The Snow Queen's hands unlaced and she sketched a little sign in the air before her. As if etched in ice, a picture appeared. It was of a tall, thin, ungainly man, with a big nose and squinty eyes. His clothes looked quite fine. Hans had never seen a tail-coat up close before, or such a high hat. The man seemed to be writing in a notebook.

"This could be you," the Ice Maiden said.

"He is not very handsome," said Hans, wondering if that was the payment due.

"A *digter* needs to *write* beautifully," the Ice Maiden said, "not *be* beautiful."

Hans nodded. It was true. He looked again at the icy picture. The man did not look happy, just hard at work. "Is he sad?"

"Did you wish for happiness?"

Hans shook his head.

Suddenly he worried that he'd have to have much more schooling to become a *digter,* and he hated school, where everybody bullied him, even the masters. It occurred to him that being a *digter* might not be a good way of earning a living, not even as good as being a shoemaker like Papa or a washerwoman like Mama.

"You worry about the payment," the Ice Maiden said as, with a single movement of her hand, she erased the picture in the air.

How did she know what was in his mind? A witch! He was sure of it now. Afraid to speak further, afraid to get more cold air down inside him, he became silent. He started to fade. But mostly he was afraid that this was just a dream and so there would be no wishes fulfilled.

"Of course there will be a payment. I do not give wishes for nothing." The Ice Maiden's voice was suddenly as cranky as Mama's. "But you do not have to make the payment until much, much later. We will discuss it when you are earning your way, the greatest poet and storyteller Denmark will ever have."

"The greatest in *Denmark*?" Hans breathed. All of a sudden it was like breathing fire and smoke, not ice. He began to cough a deep chesty cough, sounding like Papa. Then without giving it further thought, he burst out with, "Why not the greatest in the *world*?"

To his astonishment, the Ice Maiden laughed, short, sharp sounds, like glass breaking.

"That's okay, then," he said, relieved. Everything would be all right. Wishes would be granted. He would be the hero. Like a fairy tale. Happily ever after. "I will pay. Gladly."

"Lie back down, then, little swamp plant," the Ice Maiden told him, and as he did so she placed her ice-cold hand over the blanket covering his chest.

Hans felt something like a little sliver of ice pierce his heart, and he fell into a sleep that was so deep, his mama found him in the morning and thought he had died in the night. After all, in Odense, such a thing was not unheard of. She was sobbing uncontrollably.

He sat up. "Mama, Mama, why are you crying?"

His mother looked at him. "I thought you were gone, little one, and so who would take care of me in my old age?"

If he thought that an odd thing to say, he didn't mention it. He was only five years old, after all. Instead he said, "I have gone nowhere, Mama. I am right here in Odense. I will take care of you." All thoughts of becoming a *digter* disappeared, and he was only a little boy with his weeping mama, whom he would care for, and that was enough.

It would be another fifty years, when Hans was writing his memoirs, before he remembered clearly what had happened that night with the Ice Maiden, but already the payments had begun. Yes, he'd gotten a new bed within a fortnight, long enough for his stork legs, made for him as soon as Papa was no longer ill. But then Papa chose to go off into the army because he could make more money fighting a war than fixing shoes. He came home from Holstein a broken man and was dead before Hans was eleven. His mother took religiously to the bottle and, no longer having her husband to abuse, turned her flaying tongue on Hans.

To escape this hard life, Hans would walk about with his eyes closed so as not to see all the sadness around him. But of course he could still hear it. So he took himself more and more often to Monk Mill, watching the great splash of water over the mill wheel, happy that it drowned out the sound of everything else. Except . . . except he could still hear stories in his head, and so he lived more and more in them. In his mind's eye he could see the lovely curling turrets of the Empire of China, which he was certain lay beneath the millrace. He believed it was an empire whose prince would someday take Hans to his palace.

And so Hans's childhood passed by in a farrago of dreams, though eventually he understood that Odense could not offer him the Ice Maiden's last promise, not even with the magic of the mill wheel. Just as Papa had to do the actual building of the bigger bed, just as Papa had given his life to make more money for the family, now it was Hans's turn to grab up the final wish with both hands. After all, Odense was too small a place for a boy who'd been promised that he would become Denmark's most famous *digter.*

So he ran off to Copenhagen with his mother's drunken blessing, to do the actual work of writing his books.

Years went by, lonely, hard, amazing years. Everyone from his old life was dead—father, mother, grandparents, half sister. But as the Ice Maiden had promised, Hans prospered.

Did he remember the childhood bargain? Hardly. It was only a fairy story he'd told himself as a child when everyone around him was failing. He knew how hard he'd worked to write, how hard it was to do readings at town halls and great houses. Hard work—not a child's wishes—had made him a great man.

However, sixty-five years after his bargain with the Ice Maiden, lying on his deathbed at a friend's house just outside Copenhagen, Hans sat up after a fright-filled dream. It had been about the ice witch, whom he hadn't thought of in half a century or more. His hands and face were ice cold with fear of the dream, though the cancer in his liver seemed white hot. He was sweating and shivering at the same time.

Surely a price will be demanded, he thought feverishly. *Witches promise you sweets and then shove you in the oven.*

"Sir, shall I call the doctor back again?" asked the man-servant his friends had loaned him.

"A doctor for the *digter*?" He laughed at his own play on words. Even in a fevered state, he could not stop himself from making word jokes.

"Sir," the servant said, his face stern. His entire body radiated concern far beyond what Hans's friends were paying him.

"No, no. No doctor. Just help me change out of these wet clothes." Hans did not feel shame in asking. After all, that's what a manservant was for.

When the man came back with a dry nightshirt, Hans shook his head. "No, no, not the nightshirt. I am afraid I have not been clear. I have to dress in my formal clothes. I am expecting a most important visitor."

The manservant looked momentarily confused. "There is nothing written in the diary, sir, about a visitor." In fact, Mrs. Melchior, the mistress of the house where old Hans lay dying, had given the servant specific instructions: *No visitors. Wake me if there is a change. Do not be afraid to send for the doctor. And for the Lord's sake, do not stint on the pain medication.*

"Nevertheless, my visitor is coming today," Hans told him.

"Do you want a dose of morphia, sir, to ease the pain?"

Hans shook his head. "I need to be sharp for *this* visitor. Pain keeps me sharp."

"Pain keeps you . . . in pain," the serving man said.

"Please . . . do as I say."

Once dressed, even down to his leather shoes—shoes that Papa never would have had the skill to produce—Hans dismissed the man. "Wait in the kitchen till I ring," he said.

"But sir—"

"Do it."

The servant went out, for he had to follow orders.

But as soon as the man left and the red-hot flare in his belly subsided once again, Hans remembered the story of his promise to the Ice Maiden as if it were one of his own tales. He spoke the tale aloud, as if telling it in the royal court, as he had often done in Denmark and in Germany. The tale of an old *digter* and his bargain with a powerful witch.

And when he got to the end, he whispered, "Aha, so it is only my death that is the payment. A good bargain after all."

But the story did not sit well in his mouth. Death as a payment for a good life lived was not enough of an ending. Everyone dies: the good people and the bad people, the good storytellers and the bad ones. And people who were not storytellers, well, they died, too. Hans knew that his story demanded a different ending. Something stronger. It needed to be revised. Hadn't his own little mermaid found a way into heaven after her awful bargain with another kind of witch?

He forced himself to tell the story again, this time his voice as slight and light as a child's. He didn't push the story where he willed it, but let it go to its natural end. *Inevitable but surprising,* he reminded himself.

"Ha!" he said when he'd finished. Now all would be right. He settled back to wait for his visitor.

The warm summer's day closed around him. He let go of his vanity and opened the top button of his shirt, loosened the collar. She would have to take him as she found him. He closed his eyes and, like the swamp plant of old, began to fade.

A sound like wings called him back to himself. He opened his eyes to a shift in the room, like a curtain blowing. Something white and shimmering floated into his sight, cold and distant as any star.

"Hello, Ice Maiden," he said. "You look a great deal older." It really wasn't the way to address a woman of a certain age, but Hans was beyond such niceties now.

"So do you, Hans," she answered, shaking her hair till it was like falling snow. "A *great* deal older. As you can see, I am no longer an Ice Maiden but the Snow Queen, thanks to you. My castle, though, is still the same—seals and polar bears."

"Ah," said Hans, "I remember. And the cold."

"Yes, of course," said the Snow Queen, "always the cold. Are you ready to come away with me now?"

He smiled, maybe more of a grimace, for a sharp pain caught him right before he spoke again. He let it pass through, then said, "Oh, I doubt you'll want me for your palace, you old witch, for I have beaten you at your game."

"No one beats me," the Snow Queen said, smiling, though still the smile did not reach her eyes. "And *no one* calls me a witch." There was a strange tic beating beneath the skin of her right cheek.

"Well, *I* have," said Hans. "It all has to do with storying."

"*Storying?*" She came a step closer, her breath pluming out before her. He could smell the coldness of it.

"As I was lying here," Hans said, "thinking over my long life— for that is something humans do, you know, when we reach the end—I realized that I have stood alone almost continually since I was a child of five. However kindly people behaved toward me, I still remained cut off from them. And this, I believe, was the bargain we made."

"Ah," she said, but nothing more.

"You told me when I made my wishes that I would under-stand the payment much, much later. It does not come any later than this."

She nodded, saying nothing, for indeed, what need was there for her to speak? Hans had told the truth.

"You gave me poetry and stories, even a story about you," Hans said, sitting up in the bed despite the pain of the cancer. He ground his fist against his belly to quiet the ache.

She gazed at him without pity, even though she understood how much the talking cost him.

"You knew my soul longed for true recognition as a thirsty man for water, and had so even as a child."

This time when she smiled, it radiated from her eyes. They were greedy eyes, hungry eyes, a witch's eyes.

He leaned toward her despite the pain. "But I realized today that you kept as payment any love that I would have ever gotten. Not from a woman, not from a man. So I never had a single grown person in the entire world who loved me just for myself." Hans shifted his position, trying to find somewhere comfort-able, but his body would not obey him. Finally he stopped trying and, with that, the pain seemed for a moment to cease. "I never married, never had a home of my own, always lived in someone else's house." He made a small gesture with his head, indicating the very room they were in. "I am even going to die in someone else's house."

"A fair trade," the Snow Queen said, her voice satisfied. "I have made the same barter with poets and writers and musi-cians and—"

"Ah, yes, you do not think yourself a witch, but did it ever occur to you that you are a fairy godmother?"

"Never!" she cried, and he realized he had scored a point. Something like a smile passed across his plain face and made him seem almost handsome.

He took a moment more, covering the intense pain with another smile, before saying, "Your mistake was thinking there is only one kind of love." The pain in his gut was sharp again, and he had to stop, take a shallow breath, before going on. But the years of storytelling helped him here, and he made the moment of silence work for him.

"I make no mistakes." Now the Snow Queen stood very still, arms folded, like a woman who knew how to wait. He had met very few of them in his long life.

Then the pain ebbed a bit, like a receding tide on an Odense beach, and he told her the rest. "You see, my dear ice witch, I have had the love of *children* from all over the world because of my stories. A child's love is the perfect love, for it is given with a whole heart. That love will outlast me a hundredfold. And it will outlast you as well."

"Never," the Snow Queen said, but her voice was way too high, and her face contorted in anger. The tic he'd noticed earlier was beating again under her right eye, but this time it was more pronounced.

"Oh, I am sure of it," said Hans. "The children will know you from my story, and in that story you lose to little Gerda because of her perfect child's love for Kay. And here, in this room, you lose again." He held out his hands, but not to her. She began to tremble, then collapse, and at the last dissipated into water vapor.

Hans no longer saw her. His gaze was focused past the vapor and beyond, his hands held out to the other figures gathering in the room, a group of small children from all over the world, wearing crowns of roses.

One of them, whose crown was made of just the briars and thorns, tiptoed over to Hans's bedside. Now holding the dying man's hands, he said, "We are here to bring you home, Papa Hans, but first you must tell us a story."

"With all my heart," Hans said. "It is about a beautiful witch who was outwitted by an ugly old *digter*."

So saying, he sat up straight on the bed as if he were as young as they, and told them that one final story about his life as a fairy tale. When he finished, the children all clapped their hands and laughed delightedly, and his old worn-out body fell back against the waiting pillow, no longer in pain. But his spirit, set loose of the body's gravity, rose to go hand in hand with the children through the stone walls of Mrs. Melchior's great house, into the soft Danish air, and home.

—*For Hans Christian Andersen; this is his story, sort of*

B IS FOR BIGFOOT

JIM BUTCHER

WHEN PEOPLE COME to the only professional wizard in the Chicago phone book for help, they're one of two things: desperate or smart. Very rarely are they both.

The smart ones come to me because they know I can help—the desperate because they don't know anyone else who can. With a smart client, the meeting is brief and pleasant. Someone has lost the engagement ring that was a family heirloom, and has been told I'm a man who can find lost things. Such people engage my services (preferably in cash), I do the job, and everyone's happy.

Desperate clients, on the other hand, can pull all sorts of ridiculous nonsense. They lie to me about what kind of trouble they've gotten themselves into, or try to pass me a check I'm sure will bounce like a basketball. Occasionally they demand that I prove my powers by telling them what their problem is before they even shake my hand—in which case, the problem is that they're idiots.

My newest client wanted something different, though. He wanted me to meet him in the woods.

This did not make me feel optimistic that he would be one of the smart ones.

Woods being in short supply in Chicago, I had to drive all the way up to the northern half of Wisconsin to get to decent timber. That took me about six hours, given that my car, while valiant and bold, is also a Volkswagen Beetle made around the same time flower children were big. By the time I got there and had hiked a mile or two out into the woods, to the appointed location, dark was coming on.

I'm not a moron, usually. I've made enemies during my stint as a professional wizard. So when I settled down to wait for the client, I did so with my staff in one hand, my blasting rod in the other, and a .38 revolver in the pocket of my black leather duster. I blew out a small crater in the earth with an effort of will, using my staff to direct the energy, and built a modest campfire in it.

Then I stepped out of the light of the campfire, found a comfortable, shadowy spot, and waited to see who was going to show up.

The whole PI gig is mostly about patience. You have to talk to a lot of people who don't know anything to find the one who does. You have to sit around waiting a lot, watching for someone to do something before you catch them doing it. You have to do a lot of searching through useless information to get to one piece of really good information. Impatient PIs rarely conclude an investigation successfully, and never remain in the business for long. So when an hour went by without anything happening, I wasn't too worried.

By two hours, though, my legs were cramping and I had

a little bit of a headache, and apparently the mosquitoes had decided to hold a convention about ten feet away because I was covered with bites. Given that I hadn't been paid a dime yet, this client was getting annoying, fast.

The fire had died down to almost nothing, so I almost didn't see the creature emerge from the forest and crouch down beside the embers.

The thing was huge. I mean, just saying that it was nine feet tall wasn't enough. It was mostly human-shaped, but it was built more heavily than any human, covered in layers and layers of ropy muscle that were visible even through a layer of long, dark brown hair or fur that covered its whole body. It had a brow ridge like a mountain crag, with dark, glittering eyes that reflected the red-orange light of the fire.

I did not move. Not even a little. If that thing wanted to hurt me, I would have one hell of a time stopping it from doing so, even with magic, and unless I got lucky, something with that much mass would find my .38 about as deadly as a pricing gun.

Then it turned its head and part of its upper body toward me and said, in a rich, mellifluous Native American accent, "You done over there? Don't mean to be rude, and I didn't want to interrupt you, wizard, but there's business to be done."

My jaw dropped open. I mean it literally dropped open.

I stood up slowly, and my muscles twitched and ached. It's hard to stretch out a cramp while you remain in a stance, prepared to run away at an instant's notice, but I tried.

"You're . . . ," I said. "You're a . . ."

"Bigfoot," he said. "Sasquatch. Yowie. Yeti. Buncha names. Yep."

"And you . . . you called me?" I felt a little stunned. "Um . . . did you use a pay phone?"

I instantly imagined him trying to punch little phone buttons with those huge fingers. No, of course he hadn't done that.

"Nah," he said, and waved a huge, hairy arm to the north. "Fellas at the reservation help us make calls sometimes. They're a good bunch."

I shook myself and took a deep breath. For Pete's sake, I was a wizard. I dealt with the supernatural all the time. I shouldn't be this rattled by one little unexpected encounter. I shoved my nerves and my discomfort down and replaced them with iron professionalism—or at least the semblance of calm.

I emerged from my hidey-hole and went over to the fire. I settled down across from the Bigfoot, noting as I did that I was uncomfortably close to being within reach of his long arms. "Um . . . welcome. I'm Harry Dresden."

The Bigfoot nodded and looked at me expectantly. After a moment of that, he said, as if prompting a child, "This is your fire."

I blinked. Honoring the obligations of hospitality is a huge factor in the supernatural communities around the world—and as it was my campfire, I was the de facto host, and the Bigfoot my guest. I said, "Yes. I'll be right back."

I hurried back to my car and came back to the campfire with two cans of warm Coke and half a tin of salt-and-vinegar Pringles chips. I opened both cans and offered the Bigfoot one of them.

Then I opened the Pringles and divided them into two stacks, offering him his choice of either.

The Bigfoot accepted them and sipped almost delicately at the Coke, handling the comparatively tiny can with far more grace than I would have believed. The chips didn't get the careful treatment. He popped them all into his mouth and chomped down on them enthusiastically. I emulated him. I got a lot of crumbs on the front of my coat.

The Bigfoot nodded at me. "Hey, got any smokes?"

"No," I said. "Sorry. It's not a habit."

"Maybe next time," he said. "Now. You have given me your name, but I have not given you mine. I am called Strength of a River in His Shoulders, of the Three Stars Forest People. And there is a problem with my son."

"What kind of problem?" I asked.

"His mother can tell you in greater detail than I can," River Shoulders said.

"His mother?" I rubbernecked. "Is she around?"

"No," he said. "She lives in Chicago."

I blinked. "His mother . . ."

"Human," River Shoulders said. "The heart wants what the heart wants, yeah?"

Then I got it. "Oh. He's a scion."

That made more sense. A lot of supernatural folk can and do interbreed with humanity. The resulting children, half mortal, half supernatural, are called scions. Being a scion means different things to different children, depending on their parentage, but they rarely have an easy time of it in life.

River Shoulders nodded. "Forgive my ignorance of the issues. Your society is . . . not one of my areas of expertise."

I know, right? A Bigfoot saying "expertise."

I shook my head a little. "If you can't tell me anything, why did you call me here? You could have told me all of this on the phone."

"Because I wanted you to know that I thought the problem supernatural in origin, and that I would have good reason to recognize it. And because I brought your retainer." He rummaged in a buckskin pouch that he wore slung across the front of his body. It had been all but invisible amid his thick pelt. He reached a hand in and tossed something at me.

I caught it on reflex and nearly yelped as it hit my hand. It was the size of a golf ball and extraordinarily heavy. I held it closer to the fire and then whistled in surprise.

Gold. I was holding a nugget of pure gold. It must have been worth . . . uh . . . well, a *lot*.

"We knew all the good spots a long time before the Europeans came across the sea," River Shoulders said calmly. "There's another, just as large, when the work is done."

"What if I don't take your case?" I asked him.

He shrugged. "I try to find someone else. But word is that you can be trusted. I would prefer you."

I regarded River Shoulders for a moment. He wasn't trying to intimidate me. It was a mark in his favor, because it wouldn't have been difficult. In fact, I realized, he was going out of his way to avoid that very thing.

"He's your son," I asked. "Why don't you help him?"

He gestured at himself and smiled slightly. "Maybe I would stand out a little in Chicago."

I snorted and nodded. "Maybe you would."

"So, wizard," River Shoulders asked. "Will you help my son?"

I pocketed the gold nugget and said, "One of these is enough. And yes. I will."

The next day I went to see the boy's mother at a coffee shop on the north side of town.

Dr. Helena Pounder was an impressive woman. She stood maybe six-four, and looked as though she might be able to bench-press more than I could. She wasn't really pretty, but her square, open face looked honest, and her eyes were a sparkling shade of springtime green.

When I came in, she rose to greet me and shook my hand. Her hands were an odd mix of soft skin and calluses—whatever she did for a living, she did it with tools in her hand.

"River told me he'd hired you," Dr. Pounder said. She gestured for me to sit, and we did.

"Yeah," I said. "He's a persuasive guy."

Pounder let out a rueful chuckle and her eyes gleamed. "I suppose he is."

"Look," I said. "I don't want to get too personal, but . . ."

"But how did I hook up with a Bigfoot?" she asked.

I shrugged and tried to look pleasant.

"I was at a dig site in Ontario—I'm an archaeologist—and I stayed a little too long in the autumn. The snows caught me there, a series of storms that lasted for more than a month. No one could get in to rescue me, and I couldn't even call out on the radio to let them know I was still at the site." She shook her head. "I fell sick and had no food. I might have died if someone hadn't started leaving rabbits and fish in the night."

I smiled. "River Shoulders?"

She nodded. "I started watching, every night. One night the storm cleared up at just the right moment, and I saw him there." She shrugged. "We started talking. Things sort of went from there."

"So the two of you aren't actually married, or . . . ?"

"Why does that matter?" she asked.

I spread my hands in an apologetic gesture. "He paid me. You didn't. It might have an effect on my decision process."

"Honest enough, aren't you?" Pounder said. She eyed me for a moment and then nodded in something like approval. "We aren't married. But suitors aren't exactly knocking down my door—and I never saw much use for a husband anyway. River and I are comfortable with things as they are."

"Good for you," I said. "Tell me about your son."

She reached into a messenger bag that hung on the back of her diner chair and passed me a five-by-seven photograph of a kid, maybe eight or nine years old. He wasn't pretty, either, but his features had a kind of juvenile appeal, and his grin was as real and warm as sunlight.

"His name is Irwin," Pounder said, smiling down at the picture. "My angel."

Even tough, bouncer-looking supermoms have a soft spot for their kids, I guess. I nodded. "What seems to be the problem?"

"Earlier this year," she said, "he started coming home with injuries. Nothing serious—abrasions and bruises and scratches. But I suspect that the injuries were likely worse before the boy came home. Irwin heals very rapidly, and he's never been sick: literally never, not a day in his life."

"You think someone is abusing him," I said. "What did he say about it?"

"He made excuses," Pounder said. "They were obviously fictions, but that boy is at least as stubborn as his father, and he wouldn't tell me where or how he'd been hurt."

"Ah," I said.

She frowned. "Ah?"

"It's another kid."

Pounder blinked. "How . . ."

"I have the advantage over you and your husband, inasmuch as I have actually been a grade-school boy before," I said. "If he snitches about it to the teachers or to you, he'll probably have to deal with retributive friction from his classmates. He won't be cool. He'll be a snitching, tattling pariah."

Pounder sat back in her seat, frowning. "I'm . . . hardly a master of social skills. I hadn't thought of it that way."

I shrugged. "On the other hand, you clearly aren't the sort to sit around wringing her hands, either."

Pounder snorted and gave me a brief, real smile.

"So," I went on, "when he started coming home hurt, what did you do about it?"

"I started escorting him to school and picking him up the moment class let out. That's been for the past two months—he hasn't had any more injuries. But I have to go to a conference tomorrow morning and—"

"You want someone to keep an eye on him."

"That, yes," she said. "But I also want you to find out who has been trying to hurt him."

I arched an eyebrow. "How am I supposed to do that?"

"I used River's financial advisor to pull some strings. You're expected to arrive at the school tomorrow morning to begin work as the school janitor."

I blinked. "Wait. Bigfoot has a financial advisor? *Who?* Like, Nessie?"

"Don't be a child," she said. "The human tribes assist the Forest People by providing an interface. River's folk give financial, medical, and educational aid in return. It works."

My imagination provided me with an image of River Shoulders standing in front of a children's music class, his huge fingers waving a baton that had been reduced to a matchstick by his enormity.

Sometimes my head is like an Etch A Sketch. I shook it a little, and the image went away.

"Right," I said. "It might be difficult to get you something actionable."

Pounder's eyes almost seemed to turn a green-tinged shade of gold, and her voice became quiet and hard. "I am not interested in courts," she said. "I only care about my son."

Yikes.

Bigfoot Irwin had himself one formidable mama bear. If it turned out that I was right and he was having issues with another child, that could cause problems. People can overreact to things when their kids get involved. I might have to be careful with how much truth got doled out to Dr. Pounder.

Nothing's ever simple, is it?

* * *

The school was called the Madison Academy, and it was a private elementary and middle school on the north side of town. Whatever strings River Shoulders had pulled, they were good ones. I ambled in the next morning, went into the administrative office, and was greeted with the enthusiasm of a cloister of diabetics meeting their insulin delivery truck. Their sanitation engineer had abruptly departed for a Hawaiian vacation, and they needed a temporary replacement.

So I wound up wearing a pair of coveralls that were too short in the arms, too short in the legs, and too short in the crotch, with the name "Norm" stenciled on the left breast. I was shown to my office, which was a closet with a tiny desk and several shelves stacked with cleaning supplies of the usual sort.

It could have been worse. The stencil could have read "Freddie."

So I started engineering sanitation. One kid threw up, and another started a paint fight with his friend in the art room. The office paged me on an old intercom system that ran throughout the halls and had an outlet in the closet when they needed something in particular, but by ten I was clear of the child-created havoc and dealing with the standard human havoc, emptying trash cans, sweeping floors and halls, and generally cleaning up. As I did, going from classroom to classroom to take care of any full trash cans, I kept an eye out for Bigfoot Irwin.

I spotted him by lunchtime, and I took my meal at a table set aside for faculty and staff in one corner of the cafeteria as the kids ate.

Bigfoot Irwin was one of the tallest boys in sight, and he

hadn't even hit puberty yet. He was all skin and bones—and I recognized something else about him at once. He was a loner.

He didn't look like an unpleasant kid or anything, but he carried himself in a fashion that suggested that he was apart from the other children; not aloof, simply separate. His expression was distracted, and his mind was clearly a million miles away. He had a double-sized lunch and a paperback book crowding his tray, and he headed for one end of a lunch table. He sat down, opened the book with one hand, and started eating with the other, reading as he went.

The trouble seemed obvious. A group of five or six boys occupied the other end of his lunch table, and they leaned their heads closer together and started muttering to one another and casting covert glances at Irwin.

I winced. I knew where this was going. I'd seen it before, when it had been me with the book and the lunch tray.

Two of the boys stood up, and they looked enough alike to make me think that they either had been born very close together or else were fraternal twins. They both had messy, sandy brown hair, long, narrow faces, and pointed chins. They looked like they might have been a year or two ahead of Irwin, though they were both shorter than the lanky boy.

They split, moving down either side of the table toward Irwin, their footsteps silent. I hunched my shoulders and watched them out of the corner of my eye. Whatever they were up to, it wouldn't be lethal, not right here in front of half the school, and it might be possible to learn something about the pair by watching them in action.

They moved together, though not perfectly in synch. It

reminded me of a movie I'd seen in high school about juvenile lions learning to hunt together. One of the kids, wearing a black baseball cap, leaned over the table and casually swatted the book out of Irwin's hands. Irwin started and turned toward him, lifting his hands into a vague, confused-looking defensive posture.

As he did, the second kid, in a red sweatshirt, casually drove a finger down onto the edge of Irwin's dining tray. It flipped up, spilling food and drink all over Irwin.

A bowl broke, silverware rattled, and the whole tray clattered down. Irwin sat there looking stunned while the two bullies cruised right on by, as casual as can be. They were already fifteen feet away when the other children in the dining hall had zeroed in on the sound and reacted to the mess with a round of applause and catcalls.

"Pounder!" snarled a voice, and I looked up to see a man in a white visor, sweatpants, and a T-shirt come marching in from the hallway outside the cafeteria. "Pounder, what is this mess?"

Irwin blinked owlishly at the barrel-chested man and shook his head. "I . . ." He glanced after the two retreating bullies and then around the cafeteria. "I guess . . . I accidentally knocked my tray over, Coach Pete."

Coach Pete scowled and folded his arms. "If this was the first time this had happened, I wouldn't think anything of it. But how many times has your tray ended up on the floor, Pounder?"

Irwin looked down. "This would be five, sir."

"Yes it would," said Coach Pete. He picked up the paperback Irwin had been reading. "If your head wasn't in these trashy science fiction books all the time, maybe you'd be able to feed yourself without making a mess."

"Yes, sir," Irwin said.

"*Hitchhiker's Guide to the Galaxy,*" Coach Pete said, looking at the book. "That's stupid. You can't hitchhike onto a space-ship."

"No, sir," Irwin said.

"Detention," Coach Pete said. "Report to me after school."

"Yes, sir."

Coach Pete slapped the paperback against his leg, scowled at Irwin—and then abruptly looked up at me. "What?" he demanded.

"I was just wondering. You don't, by any chance, have a Vogon in your family tree?"

Coach Pete eyed me, his chest swelling in what an anthro-pologist might call a threat display. It might have been impres-sive if I hadn't been talking to River Shoulders the night before. "That a joke?"

"That depends on how much poetry you write," I said.

At this Coach Pete looked confused. He clearly didn't like feeling that way, which seemed a shame, since I suspected he spent a lot of time doing it. Irwin's eyes widened and he darted a quick look at me. His mouth twitched, but the kid kept himself from smiling or laughing—which was fairly impressive in a boy his age.

Coach Pete glowered at me, pointed a finger as if it might have been a gun, and said, "You tend to your own business."

I held up both hands in a gesture of mild acceptance. I rolled my eyes as soon as Coach Pete turned his back, drawing another quiver of restraint from Irwin.

"Pick this up," Coach Pete said to Irwin, and gestured at the spilled lunch on the floor. Then he turned and stomped away, taking Irwin's paperback with him. The two kids who had been giving Irwin grief had made their way back to their original seats, meanwhile, and were at the far end of the table, looking smug.

I pushed my lunch away and got up from the table. I went over to Irwin's side and knelt down to help him clean up his mess. I picked up the tray, slid it to a point between us, and said, "Just stack it up here."

Irwin gave me a quick, shy glance from beneath his mussed hair, and started plucking up fallen bits of lunch. His hands were almost comically large compared to the rest of him, but his fingers were quick and dexterous. After a few seconds he asked, "You've read the *Hitchhiker's Guide*?"

"Forty-two times," I said.

He smiled and then ducked his head again. "No one else here likes it."

"Well, it's not for everyone, is it?" I asked. "Personally, I've always wondered if Adams might not be a front man for a particularly talented dolphin. Which I think would make the book loads funnier."

Irwin let out a quick bark of laughter and then hunched his shoulders and kept cleaning up. His shoulders shook.

"Those two boys give you trouble a lot?" I asked.

Irwin's hands stopped moving for a second. Then he started up again. "What do you mean?"

"I mean I've been you before," I said. "The kid who liked reading books about aliens and goblins and knights and explorers at lunch, and in class, and during recess. I didn't care much about sports. And I got picked on a lot."

"They don't pick on me," Irwin said quickly. "It's just . . . just what guys do. They give me a hard time. It's in fun."

"And it doesn't make you angry," I said. "Not even a little."

His hands slowed down, and his face turned thoughtful. "Sometimes," he said quietly. "When they spoil my broccoli."

I blinked. "Broccoli?"

"I love broccoli," Irwin said, looking up at me, his expression serious.

"Kid," I said, smiling, "no one loves broccoli. No one even *likes* broccoli. All the grown-ups just agree to lie about it so that we can make kids eat it, in vengeance for what our parents did to us."

"Well, I love broccoli," Irwin said, his jaw set.

"Hunh," I said. "Guess I've seen something new today." We finished and I said, "Go get some more lunch. I'll take care of this."

"Thank you," he said soberly. "Um, Norm."

I grunted, nodded to him, tossed the dropped food, and returned the tray. Then I sat back down at the corner table with my lunch and watched Irwin and his tormentors from the corner of my eye. The two bullies never took their eyes off Irwin, even while talking and joking with their group.

I recognized that behavior, though I'd never seen it in a child before; only in hunting cats, vampires, and sundry monsters.

The two kids were predators.

Young and inexperienced, maybe. But predators.

For the first time, I thought that Bigfoot Irwin might be in real trouble.

I went back to my own tray and wolfed down the "food" on it. I wanted to keep a closer eye on Irwin.

Being a wizard is all about being prepared. Well, that and magic, obviously. While I could do a few things in a hurry, most magic takes long moments or hours to arrange, and that means you have to know what's coming. I'd brought a few things with me, but I needed more information before I could act decisively on the kid's behalf.

I kept track of Irwin after he left the cafeteria. It wasn't hard. His face was down, his eyes on his book, and even though he was one of the younger kids in the school, he stood out, tall and gangly. I contrived to go past his classroom several times in the next hour. It was trig, which I knew, except I'd been doing it in high school.

Irwin was the youngest kid in the class. He was also evidently the smartest. He never looked up from his book. Several times the teacher tried to catch him out, asking him questions. Irwin put his finger on the place in his book, glanced up at the blackboard, and answered them with barely a pause. I found myself grinning.

Next I tracked down Irwin's tormentors. They weren't hard to find, either, since they both sat in the chairs closest to the exit, as though they couldn't wait to go off and be delinquent the instant school was out. They sat in class with impatient, sullen expressions. They looked like they were in the grip of agonizing boredom, but they didn't seem to be preparing to murder a teacher or anything.

I had a hunch that something about Irwin was drawing a predatory reaction from those two kids. And Coach Vogon had arrived on the scene pretty damned quickly—too much so for coincidence, maybe.

"Maybe Bigfoot Irwin isn't the only scion at this school," I muttered to myself.

And maybe I wasn't the only one looking out for the interests of a child born with one foot in this world and one in another.

I was standing outside the gymnasium as the last class of the day let out, leaning against the wall on my elbows, my feet crossed at the heels, my head hanging down, my wheeled bucket and mop standing unused a good seven feet away—pretty much the picture of an industrious janitor. The kids went hurrying by in a rowdy herd, with Irwin's tormentors being the last to leave the gym. I felt their eyes on me as they went past, but I didn't react to them.

Coach Vogon came out last, flicking out the banks of fluorescent lights as he went, his footsteps brisk and heavy. He came to a dead stop as he came out of the door and found me waiting for him.

There was a long moment of silence while he sized me up. I let him. I wasn't looking for a fight, and I had taken the deliberately relaxed and nonconfrontational stance I was in to convey that concept to him. I figured he was connected to the supernatural world, but I didn't know *how* connected he might be. Hell, I didn't even know if he was human.

Yet.

"Don't you have work to do?" he demanded.

"Doing it," I said. "I mean, obviously."

I couldn't actually hear his eyes narrow, but I was pretty sure they did. "You got a lot of nerve, buddy, talking to an instructor like that."

"If there weren't all these kids around, I might have said another syllable or two," I drawled. "Coach Vogon."

"You're about to lose your job, buddy. Get to work or I'll report you for malingering."

"Malingering," I said. "Four whole syllables. You're good."

He rolled another step toward me and jabbed a finger into my chest. "Buddy, you're about to buy a lot of trouble. Who do you think you are?"

"Harry Dresden," I said. "Wizard."

And I looked at him as I opened my Sight.

A wizard's Sight is an extra sense, one that allows him to perceive the patterns of energy and magic that suffuse the universe—energy that includes every conceivable form of magic. It doesn't actually open a third eye in your forehead or anything, but the brain translates the perceptions into the visual spectrum. In the circles I run in, the Sight shows you things as they truly are, cutting through every known form of veiling magic, illusion, and other mystic chicanery.

In this case, it showed me that the thing standing in front of me wasn't human.

Beneath its illusion, the spindly humanoid creature stood a little more than five feet high, and it might have weighed a hundred pounds soaking wet. It was naked, and anatomically it resembled a Ken doll. Its skin was a dark gray, its eyes absolutely huge, bulbous, and midnight black. It had a rounded, high-crowned head and long, delicately pointed ears. I could still see the illusion of Coach Pete around the creature, a vague and hazy outline.

It lowered the lids of its bulbous eyes, the gesture somehow exceptionally lazy, and then nodded slowly. It inclined its head the smallest measurable amount possible and murmured, in a melodious and surprisingly deep voice, "Wizard."

I blinked a few times and waved my Sight away, so that I was facing Coach Pete again. "We should talk," I said.

The apparent man stared at me unblinkingly, his expression as blank as a discarded puppet's. It was probably my imagination that made his eyes look suddenly darker. "Regarding?"

"Irwin Pounder," I said. "I would prefer to avoid a conflict with Svartalfheim."

He inhaled and exhaled slowly through his nose. "You recognized me."

In fact, I'd been making an educated guess, but the svartalf didn't need to know that. I knew precious little about the creatures. They were extremely gifted craftsmen, and were responsible for creating most of the really cool artifacts of Norse myth. They weren't wicked, exactly, but they were ruthless, proud, stubborn, and greedy, which often added up to similar results. They were known to be sticklers for keeping their word, and God help you if you broke yours to them. Most important, they were a small supernatural nation unto themselves: one that protected its citizens with maniacal zeal.

"I had a good teacher," I said. "I want your boys to lay off Irwin Pounder."

"Point of order," he said. "They are not mine. I am not their progenitor. I am a guardian only."

"Be that as it may," I said, "my concern is for Irwin, not the brothers."

"He is a whetstone," he said. "They sharpen their instincts upon him. He is good for them."

"They aren't good for him," I said. "Fix it."

"It is not my place to interfere with them," Coach Pete said. "Only to offer indirect guidance and to protect them from anyone who would interfere with their growth."

The last phrase was as emotionless as the first, but it somehow carried an ugly ring of a threat—a polite threat, but a threat nonetheless.

Sometimes I react badly to being threatened. I might have glared a little.

"Hypothetically," I said, "let's suppose that I saw those boys giving Irwin a hard time again, and I made it my business to stop them. What would you do?"

"Slay you," Coach Pete said. His tone was utterly absent of any doubt.

"Awfully sure of yourself, aren't you."

He spoke as if reciting a single-digit arithmetic problem. "You are young. I am not."

I felt my jaw clench, and forced myself to take a slow breath, to stay calm. "They're hurting him."

"Be that as it may," he said calmly, "my concern is for the brothers, not for Irwin Pounder."

I ground my teeth and wished I could pick my words out

of them before continuing the conversation. "We've both stated our positions," I said. "How do we resolve the conflict?"

"That also is not my concern," he said. "I will not dissuade the brothers. I will slay you should you attempt to do so yourself. There is nothing else to discuss."

He shivered a little, and suddenly the illusion of Coach Pete seemed to gain a measure of life, of definition, like an empty glove abruptly filled by the flesh of a hand.

"If you will excuse me," he said, in Coach Pete's annoying tone of voice, walking past me, "I have a detention over which to preside."

"To preside over," I said, and snorted at his back. "Over which to preside. No one actually talks like that."

He turned his head and gave me a flat-eyed look. Then he rounded a corner and was gone.

I rubbed at the spot on my forehead between my eyebrows and tried to think.

I had a bad feeling that fighting this guy was going to be a losing proposition. In my experience, when someone gets their kids a supernatural supernanny, they don't pick pushovers. Among wizards, I'm pretty buff—but the world is full of bigger fish than me. More to the point, even if I fought the svartalf and won, it might drag the White Council of Wizards into a violent clash with Svartalfheim. I wouldn't want to have something like that on my conscience.

I wanted to protect the Pounder kid, and I wasn't going to back away from that. But how was I supposed to protect him from the Bully Brothers if they had a heavyweight on deck, ready to charge in swinging? That kind of brawl could spill over onto any nearby kids, and fast. I didn't want this to turn into a slugfest. That wouldn't help Irwin Pounder.

But what could I do? What options did I have? How could I act without dragging the svartalf into a confrontation?

I couldn't.

"Ah," I said to no one, lifting a finger in the air. "Aha!"

I grabbed my mop bucket and hurried toward the cafeteria.

The school emptied out fast, making the same transition every school does every day, changing from a place full of life and energy, of movement and noise, into a series of echoing chambers and empty halls. Teachers and staff seemed as eager to be gone as the students. Good. It was still possible that things would get ugly, and if they did, the fewer people around, the better.

By the time I went by the janitor's closet to pick up the few tools I'd brought with me and went to the cafeteria, my bucket's squeaking wheels were the loudest sound I could hear. I turned the corner at almost exactly the same time as the Bully Brothers appeared from the opposite end of the hall. They drew up short, and I could feel the weight of their eyes as they assessed me. I ignored them and went on inside.

Bigfoot Irwin was already inside the cafeteria, seated at a table, writing on a piece of paper. I recognized the kid's rigid, resigned posture, and it made my wrist ache just to see it: Coach Pete had him writing a sentence repetitively, probably something about being more careful with his lunch tray. The monster.

Coach Pete stood leaning against a wall, reading a sports magazine of some sort. Or at least, that was what he appeared to be doing. I had to wonder how much genuine interest a svartalf might have in the NBA. His eyes flicked up as I entered; I saw them go flat.

I set my mop and bucket aside and started sweeping the floors with a large dust broom. My janitorial form was perfect. I saw Coach Pete's jaw clench a couple of times, and then he walked over to me.

"What are you doing?" he asked.

"Sweeping the floor," I replied, guileless as a newborn.

"This is not a matter for levity," he said. "No amount of it will save your life."

"You grossly underestimate the power of laughter," I said. "But if there's some kind of violent altercation between students, any janitor in the world would find it his honor-bound duty to report it to the administration."

Coach Pete made a growling sound.

"Go ahead," I said. "Let your kids loose on him. I saw how they behaved in their classrooms. They're problem cases. Irwin's obviously a brilliant student and a good kid. When the administration finds out the three of them were involved in a fight, what do you think happens to the Troublemaker Twins? This is a private school. Out they go. Irwin is protected—and I won't have to lift a finger to interfere."

Coach Pete rolled up the magazine and tapped it against his leg a couple of times. Then he relaxed, and a small smile appeared upon his lips. "You are correct, of course, except for one thing."

"Yeah? What's that?"

"They will not be exiled. Their parents donate more funds to the school than any ten other families—and a great deal more than Irwin's mother could ever afford." He gave me a very small, very Gallic shrug. "This is a private school. The boys' parents paid for the cafeteria within which we stand."

I found myself gritting my teeth. "First of all, you have got to get over this fetish for grammatically correct prepositions. It makes you sound like a prissy twit. And second of all, money isn't everything."

"Money is power," he replied.

"Power isn't everything."

"No," he said, and his smile became smug. "It is the only thing."

I looked back out into the hallway through the open glass wall separating it from the cafeteria. The Bully Brothers were standing in the hall, staring at Irwin the way hungry lions stare at gazelles.

Coach Pete nodded pleasantly to me and returned to his original place by the wall, unrolling his magazine and opening it again.

"Dammit," I whispered. The svartalf might well be right. At an upper-class institution such as this, money and politics would have a ridiculous amount of influence. Whether aristocracies were hereditary or economic, they'd been successfully buying their children out of trouble for centuries. The Bully Brothers might well come out of this squeaky clean, and they'd be able to continue to persecute Bigfoot Irwin.

Maybe this would turn out to be a slugfest after all.

I swept my way over to Irwin's table and came to a stop. Then I sat down across from him.

He looked up from his page of scrawled sentences, and his face was pale. He wouldn't meet my eyes.

"How you doing, kid?" I asked him. When I spoke, he actually flinched a little.

"Fine," he mumbled.

Hell's bells. He was afraid of me. "Irwin," I said, keeping my voice gentle, "relax. I'm not going to hurt you."

"Okay," he said, without relaxing a bit.

"They've been doing this for a while now, haven't they?" I asked him.

"Um," he said.

"The Bully Brothers. The ones staring at you right now."

Irwin shivered and glanced aside without actually turning his head toward the window. "It's not a big deal."

"It kind of is," I said. "They've been giving you grief for a long time, haven't they? Only lately it's been getting worse. They've been scarier. More violent. Bothering you more and more often."

He said nothing, but something in his lack of reaction told me that I'd hit the nail on the head.

I sighed. "Irwin, my name is Harry Dresden. Your father sent me to help you."

That made his eyes snap up to me, and his mouth opened. "M-my . . . my dad?"

"Yeah," I said. "He can't be here to help you. So he asked me to do it for him."

"My dad," Irwin said, and I heard the ache in his voice, so poignant that my own chest tightened in empathy. I'd never known my mother, and my father died before I started going to school. I knew what it was like to have holes in my life in the shape of people who should have been there.

His eyes flicked toward the Bully Brothers again, though he didn't turn his head. "Sometimes," he said quietly, "if I ignore them, they go away." He stared down at his paper. "My dad . . . I mean, I never . . . you met him?"

"Yeah."

His voice was very small. "Is . . . is he nice?"

"Seems to be," I said gently.

"And . . . and he knows about me?"

"Yeah," I said. "He wants to be here for you. But he can't."

"Why not?" Irwin asked.

"It's complicated."

Irwin nodded and looked down. "Every Christmas there's a present from him. But I think maybe Mom is just writing his name on the tag."

"Maybe not," I said quietly. "He sent me. And I'm way more expensive than a present."

Irwin frowned at that and said, "What are you going to do?"

"That isn't the question you should be asking," I said.

"What is, then?"

I put my elbows on the table and leaned toward him. "The question, Irwin, is what are *you* going to do?"

"Get beat up, probably," he said.

"You can't keep hoping they'll just go away, kid," I said. "There are people out there who enjoy hurting and scaring others. They're going to keep doing it until you make them stop."

"I'm not going to fight anyone," Irwin all but whispered.

"I'm not going to hurt anyone. I . . . I can't. And besides, if they're picking on me, they're not picking on anyone else."

I leaned back and took a deep breath, studying his hunched shoulders, his bowed head. The kid was frightened, the kind of fear that is planted and nurtured and which grows over the course of months and years. But there was also a kind of gentle, immovable resolve in the boy's skinny body. He wasn't afraid of facing the Bully Brothers. He just dreaded going through the pain that the encounter would bring.

Courage, like fear, comes in multiple varieties.

"Damn," I said quietly. "You got some heart, kiddo."

"Can you stay with me?" he asked. "If . . . if you're here, maybe they'll leave me alone."

"Today," I said quietly. "What about tomorrow?"

"I don't know," he said. "Are you going away?"

"Can't stay here forever," I replied. "Sooner or later you're going to be on your own."

"I won't fight," he said. A droplet of water fell from his bowed head to smear part of a sentence on his paper. "I won't be like them."

"Irwin," I said. "Look at me."

He lifted his eyes. They were full. He was blinking to keep more tears from falling.

"Fighting isn't always a bad thing."

"That's not what the school says."

I smiled briefly. "The school has liability to worry about. I only have to worry about you."

He frowned, his expression intent, pensive. "When isn't it a bad thing?"

"When you're protecting yourself, or someone else, from harm," I said. "When someone wants to hurt you or someone who can't defend themselves—and when the rightful authority can't or won't protect you."

"But you have to hurt people to win a fight. And that isn't right."

"No," I said. "It isn't. But sometimes it is necessary."

"It isn't necessary right now," he said. "I'll be fine. It'll hurt, but I'll be fine."

"Maybe you will," I said. "But what about when they're done with you? What happens when they decide that it was so much fun to hurt you, they go pick on someone else, too?"

"Do you think they'll do that?"

"Yes," I said. "That's how bullies work. They keep hurting people until someone makes them stop."

He fiddled with the pencil in his fingers. "I don't like fighting. I don't even like playing Street Fighter."

"This isn't really about fighting," I said. "It's about communication."

He frowned. "Huh?"

"They're doing something wrong," I said. "You need to communicate with them. Tell them that what they're doing isn't acceptable, and that they need to stop doing it."

"I've said that," he said. "I tried that a long time ago. It didn't work."

"You talked to them," I said. "It didn't get through. You need to find another way to get your message through. You have to show them."

"You mean hurt them."

"Not necessarily," I said quietly. "But guys like those two jokers only respect strength. If you show them that you have it, they'll get the idea."

Irwin frowned harder. "No one ever talked to me about it like that before."

"I guess not," I said.

"I'm . . . I'm scared of doing that."

"Who wouldn't be?" I asked him. "But the only way to beat your fears is to face them. If you don't, they're going to keep on doing this to you, and then others, and someday someone is going to get hurt bad. It might even be those two jackasses who get hurt—if someone doesn't make them realize that they can't go through life acting like that."

"They aren't really bad guys," Irwin said slowly. "I mean . . . to anyone but me. They're okay to other people."

"Then I'd say that you'd be helping them as well as yourself, Irwin."

He nodded slowly and took a deep breath. "I'll . . . I'll think about it."

"Good," I said. "Thinking for yourself is the most valuable skill you'll ever learn."

"Thank you, Harry," he said.

I rose and picked up my broom. "You bet."

I went back to sweeping one end of the cafeteria. Coach Pete stood at the other end. Irwin returned to his writing—and the Bully Brothers came in.

They approached as before, moving between the tables, splitting up to come at Irwin from two sides. They ignored me and Coach Pete, closing in on Irwin with impatient eagerness.

Irwin's pencil stopped scratching when they both were about five feet away from him, and without looking up he said in a sharp, firm voice, "Stop."

They did. I could see the face of only one of them, but the bully was blinking in surprise.

"This is not cool," Irwin said. "And I'm not going to let you do it anymore."

The brothers eyed him, traded rather feral smiles, and then each of them lunged at Irwin and grabbed an arm. They hauled him back with surprising speed and power, slamming his back onto the floor. One of them started slapping at his eyes and face while the other produced a short length of heavy rubber tubing, jerked Irwin's shirt up, and started hitting him on the stomach with the hose.

I gritted my teeth and reached for the handle of my mop— except it wasn't a mop that was poking up out of the bucket. It was my staff, a six-foot length of oak as thick as my circled thumb and forefinger. If this was how the Bully Brothers started the beating, I didn't even want to think about what they'd do for a finale. Svartalf or not, I couldn't allow things to go any further before I stepped in.

Coach Pete's dark eyes glittered at me from behind his sports magazine, and he crooked a couple of fingers on one hand in a way that no human being could have. I don't know what kind of magical energy the svartalf was using, but he was good with it. There was a sharp crackling sound, and the water in the mop bucket froze solid in an instant, trapping my staff in place.

My heart sped up. That kind of magical control was a bad, bad sign. It meant that the svartalf was better than me—

probably a lot better. He hadn't used a focus of any kind to help him out, the way my staff would help me focus and control my own power. If we'd been fighting with swords, that move would have been the same as him clipping off the tips of my eyelashes without drawing blood. This guy would kill me if I fought him.

I set my jaw, grabbed the staff in both hands, and sent a surge of my will and power rushing down its rune-carved length into the entrapping ice. I muttered *"Forzare"* as I twisted the staff, and pure energy lashed out into the ice, pulverizing it into chunks the size of gravel.

Coach Pete leaned forward slightly, eager, and I saw his eyes gleam. Svartalves were old-school, and their culture had been born in the time of the Vikings. They thought mortal combat was at least as fun as it was scary, and their idea of mercy only embraced killing you quickly as opposed to killing you slowly. If I started up with this svartalf, it wouldn't be over until one of us was dead. Probably me. I was afraid.

The sound of the rubber hose hitting Irwin's stomach and the harsh breathing of the struggling children echoed in the large room.

I took a deep breath, grabbed my staff in two hands, and began drawing in my will once more.

And then Bigfoot Irwin roared, *"I said no!"*

The kid twisted his shoulders in an abrupt motion and tossed one of the brothers away as if he weighed no more than a soccer ball. The bully flew ten feet before his butt hit the ground. The second brother was still staring in shock when Bigfoot Irwin sat up, grabbed him by the front of his shirt, and rose. He lifted the second brother's feet off the floor and simply held him there, scowling furiously up at him.

The Bully Brothers had inherited their predatory instinct from their supernatural parent.

Bigfoot Irwin had gotten something else.

The second brother stared down at the younger boy and struggled to wriggle free, his face pale and frantic. Irwin didn't let him go.

"Hey, look at me," Irwin snarled. "This is not okay. You were mean to me. You kept hurting me. For no reason. That's over. Now. I'm not going to let you do it anymore. Okay?"

The first brother sat up shakily from the floor and stared agog at his former victim, now holding his brother effortlessly off the floor.

"Did you hear me?" Irwin asked, giving the kid a little shake. I heard his teeth clack together.

"Y-yeah," stammered the dangling brother, nodding emphatically. "I hear you. I hear you. We hear you."

Irwin scowled for a moment. Then he gave the second brother a push before releasing him. The bully fell to the floor three feet away and scrambled quickly back from Irwin. The pair of them started a slow retreat.

"I mean it," Irwin said. "What you've been doing isn't cool. We'll figure out something else for you to do for fun. Okay?"

The Bully Brothers mumbled something vaguely affirmative and then hurried out of the cafeteria.

Bigfoot Irwin watched them go. Then he looked down at his hands, turning them over and back as if he'd never seen them before.

I kept my grip on my staff and looked down the length of the cafeteria at Coach Pete. I arched an eyebrow at him. "It seems like the boys sorted this out on their own."

Coach Pete lowered his magazine slowly. The air was thick with tension, and the silence was its hard surface.

Then the svartalf said, "Your sentences, Mr. Pounder."

"Yessir, Coach Pete," Irwin said. He turned back to the table and sat down, and his pencil started scratching at the paper again.

Coach Pete nodded at him, then came over to me. He stood facing me for a moment, his expression blank.

"I didn't intervene," I said. "I didn't try to dissuade your boys from following their natures. Irwin did that."

The svartalf pursed his lips thoughtfully and then nodded slowly. "Technically accurate. And yet you still had a hand in what just happened. Why should I not exact retribution for your interference?"

"Because I just helped your boys."

"In what way?"

"Irwin and I taught them caution—that some prey is too much for them to handle. And we didn't even hurt them to make it happen."

Coach Pete considered that for a moment and then gave me a faint smile. "A lesson best learned early rather than late." He turned and started to walk away.

"Hey," I said in a sharp, firm voice.

He paused.

"You took the kid's book today," I said. "Please return it."

Irwin's pencil scratched along the page, suddenly loud.

Coach Pete turned. Then he pulled the paperback in question out of his pocket and flicked it through the air. I caught it in one hand, which probably made me look a lot more cool and collected than I felt at the time.

Coach Pete inclined his head to me, a little more deeply than before. "Wizard."

I mirrored the gesture. "Svartalf."

He left the cafeteria, shaking his head. What sounded suspiciously like a chuckle bubbled in his wake.

I waited until Irwin was done with his sentences, and then I walked him to the front of the building, where his maternal grandmother was waiting to pick him up.

"Was that okay?" he asked me. "I mean, did I do right?"

"Asking me if I thought you did right isn't the question," I said.

Irwin suddenly smiled at me. "Do I think I did right?" He nodded slowly. "I think . . . I think I do."

"How's it feel?" I asked him.

"It feels good. I feel . . . not happy. Satisfied. Whole."

"That's how it's supposed to feel," I said. "Whenever you've got a choice, do good, kiddo. It isn't always fun or easy, but in the long run it makes your life better."

He nodded, frowning thoughtfully. "I'll remember."

"Cool," I said.

He offered me his hand very seriously, and I shook it. He had a strong grip for a kid. "Thank you, Harry. Could . . . could I ask you a favor?"

"Sure."

"If you see my dad again . . . could you tell him . . . could you tell him I did good?"

"Of course," I said. "I think what you did will make him very proud."

That all but made the kid glow. "And . . . and tell him that . . . that I'd like to meet him. You know. Someday."

"Will do," I said quietly.

Bigfoot Irwin nodded at me. Then he turned and made his gangly way over to the waiting car and slid into it. I stood and watched until the car was out of sight. Then I rolled my bucket of ice back into the school so that I could go home.

GREAT-GRANDMOTHER IN THE CELLAR

PETER S. BEAGLE

I THOUGHT HE had killed her.

Old people forget things, I know that—my father can't ever remember where he set down his pen a minute ago—but if I forget, at the end of *my* life, every other thing that ever happened to me, I will still be clutched by the moment when I gazed down at my beautiful, beautiful, sweet-natured idiot sister and heard the whining laughter of Borbos, the witch-boy she loved, pattering in my head. I *knew* he had killed her.

Then I saw her breast rising and falling—so slowly!—and I saw her nostrils fluttering slightly with each breath, and I knew that he had only thrown her into the witch-sleep that mimics the last sleep closely enough to deceive Death Herself.

Borbos stepped from the shadows and laughed at me.

"*Now* tell your father," he said. "Go to him and tell him that Jashani will lie so until the sight of my face—and only my face—awakens her. And that face she will never see until he agrees that we two may wed. Is this message clear enough for your stone skull, Da'mas? Shall I repeat it, just to be sure?"

I rushed at him, but he put up a hand and the floor of my sister's chamber seemed to turn to oiled water under my feet. I went over on my back, flailing foolishly at the innocent air, and Borbos laughed again. If *shukris* could laugh, they would sound like Borbos.

He was gone then, in that way he had of coming and going, which Jashani thought was so dashing and mysterious, but which seemed to me fit only for sneak thieves and housebreakers. I knelt there alone, staring helplessly at the person I loved most in the world, and whom I fully intended to strangle when—oh, it had to be *when!*—she woke up. With no words, no explanations, no apologies. She'd know.

In the ordinary way of things, she's far brighter and wiser and simply *better* than I, Jashani. My tutors all disapproved and despaired of me early on, with good reason; but before she could walk, they seemed almost to expect my sister to perform her own *branlewei* coming-of-age ceremony, and prepare both the ritual sacrifice *and* the meal afterward. It would drive me wild with jealousy—especially when Father would demand to know, one more time, why I couldn't be as studious and accomplished as Jashani—if she weren't so ridiculously decent and kind that there's not a thing you can do except love her. I sometimes go out into the barn and scream with frustration, to tell you the truth . . . and then she comes running to see if I'm hurt or ill. At twenty-one, she's two and a half years older than I, and she has never once let Father beat me, even when the punishment was so richly deserved that *I'd* have beaten me if I were in his place.

And right then I'd have beaten *her,* if it weren't breaking my heart to see her prisoned in sleep unless we let the witch-boy have her.

It is the one thing we ever quarrel about, Jashani's taste in men. Let me but mention that this or that current suitor has a cruel mouth, and all Chun will hear her shouting at me that the poor boy can't be blamed for a silly feature—and should I bring a friend by, just for the evening, who happens to describe the poor boy's method of breaking horses . . . well, that will only make things worse. If I tell her that the whole town knows that the fellow serenading her in the grape arbor is the father of two children by a barmaid, and another baby by a farm girl, Jashani will fly at me, claiming that he was a naive victim of their seductive beguilements. Put her in a room with ninety-nine perfect choices and one heartless scoundrel, and she will choose the villain every time. This prediction may very well be the one thing Father and I ever agree on, come to consider.

But *Borbos* . . .

Unlike most of the boys and men Jashani ever brought home to try out at dinner, I had known Borbos all my life, and Father had known the family since his own youth. Borbos came from a long line of witches of one sort and another, most of them quite respectable, as witches go, and likely as embarrassed by Borbos as Father was by me. He'd grown up easily the handsomest young buck in Chun, straight and sleek, with long, angled eyes the color of river water, skin and hair the envy of every girl I knew, and an air about him to entwine hearts much less foolish than my sister's. I could name names.

And with all that came a soul as perfectly pitiless as when we were all little and he was setting cats afire with a twiddle of two fingers, or withering someone's fields or haystacks with a look, just for the fun of it. He took great care that none of our parents ever caught him at his play, so that it didn't matter what I told them—and in the same way, even then, he made sure never to let Jashani see the truth of him. He knew what he wanted, even then, just as she never wanted to believe evil of anyone.

And here was the end of it: me standing by my poor, silly sister's bed, begging her to wake up, over and over, though I knew she never would—not until Father and I . . .

No.

Not ever.

If neither of us could stop it, I knew someone who would.

Father was away from home, making arrangements with vintners almost as far north as the Durli Hills and as far south as Kalagira, where the enchantresses live, to buy our grapes for their wine. He would be back when he was back, and meanwhile there was no way to reach him, nor any time to spare. The decision was mine to make, whatever he might think of it afterward. Of our two servants, Catuzan, the housekeeper, had finished her work and gone home, and Nanda, the cook, was at market. Apart from Jashani, I was alone in our big old house.

Except for Great-Grandmother.

I never knew her; neither had Jashani. Father had, in his youth, but he spoke of her very little, and that little only with the windows shuttered and the curtains drawn. When I asked hopefully whether Great-Grandmother had been a witch, his answer was a headshake and a definite *no*—but when Jashani said, "Was she a demon?" Father was silent for some while. Finally he said, "No, not really. Not exactly." And that was all we ever got out of him about Great-Grandmother.

But I knew something Jashani didn't know. Once, when I was small, I had overheard Father speaking with his brother Uskameldry, who was also in the wine grape trade, about a particular merchant in Coraic who had so successfully cornered the market in that area that no vintner would even look at our family's grapes, whether red or black or blue. Uncle Uska had joked, loudly enough for me to hear at my play, that maybe they ought to go down to the cellar and wake up Great-Grandmother again. Father didn't laugh, but hushed him so fast that the silence caught my ear as much as the talk before it.

Our cellar is deep and dark, and the great wine casks cast bulky shadows when you light a candle. Jashani and I and our friends used to try to scare each other when we played together there, but she and I knew the place too well ever to be really frightened. Now I stood on the stair, thinking crazily that Jashani and Great-Grandmother were both asleep, maybe if you woke one, you might rouse the other . . . something like that, anyway. So after a while, I lit one of the wrist-thick candles Father kept under the hinged top step, and I started down.

Our house is the oldest and largest on this side of the village. There have been alterations over the years—most of them while Mother was alive—but the cellar never changes. Why should it? There are always the casks, and the tables and racks along the walls, for Father's filters and preservatives and other tools to test the grapes for perfect ripeness; and always the same comfortable smell of damp earth, the same boards stacked to one side, to walk on should the cellar flood, and the same shadows, familiar as bedtime toys. But there was no sign of anyone's ancestor, and no place where one could possibly be hiding, not once you were standing on the earthen floor, peering into the shadows.

Then I saw the place that wasn't a shadow, in the far right corner of the cellar, near the drainpipe. I don't remember any of us noticing it as children—it would have been easy to miss, being only slightly darker than the rest of the floor—but when I walked warily over to it and tapped it with my foot, it felt denser and finer-packed than any other area. There were a couple of spades leaning against the wall further along. I took one and, feeling strangely hypnotized, started to dig.

The deeper I probed, the harder the digging got, and the more convinced I became that the earth had been deliberately pounded hard and tight, as though to hold something down. Not hard enough: whatever was here, it was coming up now. A kind of fever took hold of me, and I flung spadeful after spadeful aside, going at it like a rock-*targ* ripping out a poor badger's den. I broke my nails, and I flung my sweated shirt away, and I dug.

I didn't hear my father the first time, although he was shouting at me from the stair. "What are you doing?" I went on digging, and he bellowed loud enough to make the racks rattle, *"Da'mas, what are you doing?"*

I did not turn. I was braced for the jar of the spade on wood, or possibly metal—a coffin either way—but the sound that came up when I finally did hit something had me instantly throwing the instrument away and dropping down to half sit, half kneel on the edge of the oblong hole I'd worried out of the earth. Reaching, groping, my hand came up gripping a splintered bone.

Great-Grandmother! I flung myself face down, clawing with both hands now, frantic, hysterical, not knowing what I was doing. Fingerbones . . . something that might have been a knee, an elbow . . . *a skull*—no, just the top of a skull . . . I don't think I was quite sane when I heard the voice.

"Grandson, stop . . . stop, before you really do addle my poor old bones. Stop!" It was a slow voice, with a cold, cold rustle in it: it sounded like the wind over loose stones.

I stopped. I sat up, and so did she.

Then Father—home early, due to some small war blocking his road—was beside me, as silent as I, but with an unfriendly hand gripping the back of my neck. Great-Grandmother wasn't missing any bones, thank Dran and Tani, our household gods, who are twins. The skull wasn't hers, nor the fingers, nor any of the other loose bones; she was definitely whole, sitting with her fleshless legs bent under her, from the knees, and her own skull clearing the top of my pit to study me out of yellowish-white empty eye sockets. She said, "The others are your Great-Aunt Keshwara. I was lonely."

I looked at Father for the first time. He was sweating himself, pale and swaying. I realized that his hand on my neck was largely to keep me from trembling, and to hold himself upright. "You should not have done this," he said. He was almost whispering. "Oh, you should never have done this." Then, louder, as he let go of me, "Great-Grandmother."

"Do not scold the boy, Rushak," the stone rustle rebuked

him. "It has been long and long since I saw anything but dirt, smelled anything but mold. The scent of fear tells me that I am back with my family. Sit up straight, young Da'mas. Look at me."

I sat as properly as I could on the edge of a grave. Great-Grandmother peered closely at me, her own skull weaving slightly from side to side, like a snake's head. She said, "Why have you awakened me?"

"He's a fool," Father said. "He made a mistake, he didn't know. . . ." Great-Grandmother looked at him, and he stopped talking. She repeated the question to me.

How I faced those eyeless, browless voids and spoke to those cold, slabby chaps, I can't tell you—or myself—today. But I said my sister's name—"Jashani"—and after that it got easier. I said, "Borbos, the witch-boy—he's made her sleep, and she won't wake up until we give in and say he can marry her. And she'd be better off dead."

"What?" Father said. "How—"

Great-Grandmother interrupted, "Does she know that?"

"No," I said. "But she will. She thinks he loves her, but he doesn't love anybody."

"He loves my money, right enough," Father said bitterly. "He loves my house. He loves my business."

The eye sockets never turned from me. I said, "She doesn't know about these things . . . about men. She's just *good*."

"Witch-boy . . ." The rusty murmur was all but inaudible in the skeletal throat. "Ah . . . the Tresard family. The youngest."

Father and I gaped at her, momentarily united by astonishment. Father asked, "How did you . . . ?" Then he said, "You were already . . ." I thanked him silently for being the one to look a fool.

Great-Grandmother said simply—and, it might have been, a little smugly—"I listen. What else have I to do in that hole?" Then she said, "Well, I must see the girl. Show me."

So my great-grandmother stepped out of her grave and followed my father and me upstairs, clattering with each step like an armload of dishes, yet held firmly together somehow by the recollection of muscles, the stark memory of tendons and sinews. Neither of us liked to get too close to her, which she seemed to understand, for she stayed well to the rear of our uncanny procession. Which was ridiculous, and I knew it then, and I was ashamed of it then as well. She was family, after all.

In Jashani's chamber, Great-Grandmother stood looking down at the bed for a long time, without speaking. Finally she said softly, almost to herself, "Skilled . . . I never knew a Tresard with such . . ." She did not finish.

"Can you heal her?" The words burst out of me as though I hadn't spoken in years, which was how I felt. "She's never hurt a soul, she wouldn't know how—she's foolish and sweet, except she's *very* smart, it's just that she can't imagine that anyone would ever wish her harm. *Please*, Great-Grandmother, make her wake up! I'll do anything!"

I will be grateful to my dying day that Jashani couldn't hear a word of all that nonsense.

Great-Grandmother didn't take her empty eyes from my sister as I babbled on; nor did she seem to hear a word of the babble. I'm not sure how long she stood there by the bed, though I do recall that she reached out once to stroke Jashani's hair very lightly, as though those cold, fleshless fingers were seeing, tasting . . .

Then she stepped back, so abruptly that some bones clicked against other bones, and she said, "I must have a body."

Again Father and I stared stupidly at her. Great-Grandmother said impatiently, "Do you imagine that I can face your witch-boy like this? One of you—either one—must allow me the use of his body. Otherwise, don't waste my time." She glowered into each of our pale faces in turn, never losing or altering the dreadful grin of the long-dead.

Father took a long breath and opened his mouth to volunteer, but I beat him to it, actually stepping a bit forward to nudge him aside. I said, "What must I do?"

Great-Grandmother bent her head close, and I stared right into that eternal smile. "Nothing, boy. You need do nothing but stand so . . . just so . . ."

I cannot tell you what it was like. And if I could, I wouldn't. You might ask Father, who's a much better witness to the whole affair than I, for all that, in a way, I *was* the whole affair. I do know from him that Great-Grandmother's bones did not clatter untidily to the floor when her spirit—soul, essence, life-force, *tyak* (as people say in the south)—passed into me. According to Father, they simply vanished into the silver mist that poured and poured into me, as I stood there with my arms out, dumb as a dressmaker's dummy. The one reasonably reliable report I can relay is that it wasn't cold, as you might expect, but warm on my skin, and—of all things—almost *sweet* on my lips, though I kept my mouth tightly shut. Being invaded—no, let's use the honest word, *possessed*—by your great-grandmother is bad enough, but to *swallow* her? And have it taste like apples, like *fasteen*, like cake? I didn't think about it then, and I'm not thinking about it now. Then, all that mattered was my feeling of being crowded to the farthest side of my head, and *hearing* Great-Grandmother inside me saying, dryly but soothingly, "Well done, Da'mas—well done, indeed. Slowly, now . . . move slowly until you grow accustomed to my presence. I will not hurt you, I promise, and I will not stay long. Slowly . . ."

Sooner or later, when he judged our anguish greatest, Borbos would return to repeat his demand. Father and Great-Grandmother-in-me took it in turns to guard Jashani's chamber through the rest of that day, the night, and all of the following day. When it was Father's turn, Great-Grandmother would march my body out of the room and the house, down the carriageway, into our orchards and arbors; then back to scout the margins again, before finally allowing me to replace Father at that bedside where no quilt was ever rumpled, no pillow on the floor. In all of this I never lost myself in her. I always knew who I was, even when she was manipulating my mouth and the words that came out of it; even when she was lifting my hands or snapping my head too forcefully from side to side, apparently thrilled by the strength of the motion.

"He will be expecting resistance," she pointed out to us, in my voice. "Nothing he cannot wipe away with a snap of his fingers, but enough to make you feel that you did the best you could for Jashani before you yielded her to him. Now put that thing *down!*" she lectured Father, who was carrying a sword that he knew would be useless against Borbos, but had clung to anyway, for pure comfort.

Father bristled. "How are we to fight him at all, even with you guiding Da'mas's hand? Borbos could appear right now, that way he does, and what would you do? I'll put this old sword away if you give me a spell, a charm, to replace it." He was tired and sulky, and terribly, terribly frightened.

I heard my throat answer him calmly and remotely, "When your witch-boy turns up, all you will be required to do is to stand out of my way." After that Great-Grandmother did not allow another word out of me for some considerable while.

Father had not done well from his first sight of Jashani apparently lifeless in her bed. The fact that she was breathing steadily, that her skin remained warm to the touch, and that she looked as innocently beautiful as ever, despite not having eaten or drunk for several days, cheered him not at all. He himself, on the other hand, seemed to be withering before my eyes: unsleeping, hardly speaking, hardly comprehending what was said to him. Now he put down his sword as commanded and sat motionless by Jashani's bed, slumped forward with his hands clasped between his knees. A dog could not have been more constant, or more silent.

And still Borbos did not come to claim his triumph . . . did not come, and did not come, letting our grief and fear build to heights of nearly unbearable tension. Even Great-Grandmother seemed to feel it, pacing the house in my body, which she treated like her own tireless bones that needed no relief, though I urgently did. Surrounded by her ancient mind, nevertheless I could never truly read it, not as she could pick through my thoughts when she chose, at times amusing herself by embarrassing me. Yet she moved me strangely once when she said aloud, as we were crouched one night in the apple orchard, studying the carriageway, white in the moon, "I envy even your discomfiture. Bones cannot blush."

"They never need to," I said, after realizing that she was waiting for my response. "Sometimes I think I spend my whole life being mortified about one thing or another. Wake up, start apologizing for everything to everybody, just on the chance I've offended them." Emboldened, I ventured further. "You might not think so, but I have had moments of wishing I were dead. I really have."

Great-Grandmother was silent in my head for so long that I was afraid that I might have affronted her for a second time. Then she said, slowly and tonelessly, "You would not like it. I will find it hard to go back." And there was something in the way she said those last words that made pins lick along my forearms.

"What *will* you do when Borbos comes?" I asked her. "Father says you're not a witch, but he never would say exactly *what* you were. I don't understand how you can deal with someone like Borbos if you're not a witch."

The reply came so swiftly and fiercely that I actually cringed away from it in my own skull. "I am your great-grandmother, boy. If that is not all you need to know, then you must make do as you can." So saying, she rose and stalked us out of the orchard, back toward the house, with me dragged along disconsolately, half certain that she might never bother talking to me again.

My favorite location in the house has—naturally enough—always been a place where I wasn't ever supposed to be: astride a gable just narrow enough for me to pretend that I was riding a great black stallion to glory, or a sea-green *mordroi* dragon to adventure. I cannot count the number of times I was beaten, even by Mother, for risking my life up there, and I know very well how foolish it is to continue doing it whenever I get the chance. But this time it was Great-Grandmother taking the risk, not me, so it plainly wasn't my fault; and, in any case, what could I have done about it?

So there you are, and there you have us in the night, Great-Grandmother and I, with the moon our only light, except for the window of Jashani's chamber below and to my left, where Father kept his lonely vigil. I was certainly not about to speak until Great-Grandmother did; and for some while she sat in silence, seemingly content to scan the white road for a slim, swaggering figure who would almost surely not come for my sister that way. I ground my teeth at the thought.

Presently Great-Grandmother said quietly, almost dreamily, "I was not a good woman in my life. I was born with a certain gift for . . . mischief, let us say . . . and I sharpened it and honed it, until what I did with it became, if not as totally evil as Borbos Tresard's deeds from his birth, still cruel and malicious enough that many have never forgiven me to this day. Do you know how I died, young Da'mas?"

"I don't even know how you lived," I answered her. "I don't know anything about you."

Great-Grandmother said, "Your mother killed me. She stabbed me, and I died. And she was right to do it."

I could not take in what she had said. I felt the words as she spoke them, but they meant nothing. Great-Grandmother went on. "Like your sister, your mother had poor taste in men. She was young, I was old, why should she listen to me? If I am no witch, whatever it is that I am had grown strong with the years. I drove each of her suitors away, by one means or another. It was not hard—a little pointed misfortune and they cleared off quickly, all but the serious ones. I killed two of those, one in a storm, one in a cow pen." A grainy chuckle. "Your mother was not at all pleased with me."

"She knew what you were doing? She knew it was you?"

"Oh, yes, how not?" The chuckle again. "I was not trying to cover my tracks—I was much given to showing off in those days. But then your father came along, and I did what I could to indicate to your mother that she must choose this one. There was a man in her life already, you understand—most unsuitable, she would have regretted it in a month. The cow pen one, that was." A sigh, somehow turning into a childish giggle, and ending in a grunt. "You would have thought she might be a little pleased this time."

"Was that why she . . . ?" I could not actually say it. I felt Great-Grandmother's smile in my spine.

"Your mother was not a killer—merely mindless with anger for perhaps five seconds. A twitch to the left or right, and she would have missed . . . ah, well, it was a fate long overdue. I have never blamed her."

It was becoming increasingly difficult to distinguish my thoughts—even my memories—from hers. Now I remembered hearing Uncle Uska talking to Father about waking Great-Grandmother again, and being silenced immediately. I knew that she had heard them as well, listening underground in the dark, no soil dense enough to stop her ears.

I asked, "Have you ever come back before? To help the family, like now?"

The slow sigh echoed through our shared body. Great-Grandmother replied only, "I was always a fitful sleeper." Abruptly she rose, balancing more easily on the gable than I ever did when I was captaining my body, and we went on with our patrol, watching for Borbos. And that was another night on which Borbos did not come.

When he did appear at last, he caught us—even Great-Grandmother, I *think*—completely by surprise. In the first place, he came by day, after all our wearying midnight rounds; in the second, he turned up not in Jashani's chamber, nor in the yard or any of the fields where we had kept guard, but in the great kitchen, where old Nanda had reigned as long as I could remember. He was seated comfortably at her worn worktable, silky and dashing, charming her with tales of his journeys and exploits, while she toasted her special *chamshi* sandwiches for him. She usually needs a day's notice and a good deal of begging before she'll make *chamshi* for anybody.

He looked up when Great-Grandmother walked my body into the kitchen, greeting us first with, "Well, if it isn't Thunder-wit, my brother-to-be. How are those frozen brains keeping?" Then he stopped, peered closely at me, and began to smile in a different way. "I didn't realize you had . . . company. Do we know each other, old lady?"

I could feel Great-Grandmother studying him out of my eyes, and it frightened me more than he did. She said, "I know your family. Even in the dirt I knew you when you were very young, and just as evil as you are now. Give me back my great-granddaughter and go your way."

Borbos laughed. It was one of his best features, that warm, delightful chuckle. "And if I don't? You will destroy me? Enchant me? Forgive me if I don't find that likely. Try, and your Jashani slumbers decoratively for all eternity." The laugh had broken glass in it the second time.

I ached to get my hands on him—useless as it would have been—but Great-Grandmother remained in control. All she said, quite quietly, was, "I want it understood that I did warn you."

Whatever Borbos heard in her voice, he was up and out of his seat on the instant. No fiery whiplash, no crash of cold, magical thunder—only a scream from Nanda as the chair fell silently to ashes. She rushed out of the kitchen, calling for Father, while Borbos regarded us thoughtfully from where he leaned against the cookstove. He said, "Well, my goodness," and twisted his fingers against each other in seeming anxiety. Then he said a word I didn't catch, and every knife, fork, maul, spit, slicer, corer, scissors and bone saw in Nanda's kitchen rose up out of her utensil drawers and came flying off the wall, straight for Great-Grandmother . . . straight for me . . . for us.

But Great-Grandmother put up my hand—exactly as Borbos himself had done when I charged him on first seeing Jashani spellbound—and everything flashing toward us halted in the air, hanging there like edged and pointed currants in a fruit-cake. Then Great-Grandmother spoke—the words had edges, too; I could feel them cutting my mouth—and all Nanda's implements backed politely into their accustomed places. Great-Grandmother said chidingly, "Really."

But Borbos was gone, vanished as I had seen him do in Jashani's chamber, his laughter still audible. I took the stairs two and three at a time, Great-Grandmother not wanting to chance my inexperienced body coming and going magically. Besides, we knew where he was going, and that he would be waiting for us there.

He was playing with Father. I don't like thinking about that:

Father lunging and swinging clumsily with his sword, crying hopelessly, desperate to come to grips with this taunting shadow that kept dissolving out of his reach, then instantly reappearing, almost close enough to touch and punish. And Jashani . . . Jashani so still, so still . . .

Borbos turned as we burst in, and a piece of the chamber ceiling fell straight down, bruising my left shoulder as Great-Grandmother sprang me out of the way. In her turn, she made my tongue say *this*, and my two hands do *that*, and Borbos was strangling in air, on the other side of the chamber, while my hands clenched on nothing and gripped and twisted, tighter and tighter . . . but he got a word out, in spite of me, and broke free to crouch by Jashani's bed, panting like an animal.

There was no jauntiness about him now, no mocking gaiety. "You are no witch. I would know. What *are* you?"

I wanted to go over and comfort Father, hold him and make certain that he was unhurt, but Great-Grandmother had her own plans. She said, "I am a member of this family, and I have come to get my great-granddaughter back from you. Release her and I have no quarrel with you, no further interest at all. Do it now, Borbos Tresard."

For answer, Borbos looked shyly down at the floor, shuffled his feet like an embarrassed schoolboy, and muttered something that might indeed have been an apology for bad behavior in the classroom. But at the first sound of it, Great-Grandmother leaped forward and dragged Father away from the bed, as the floor began to crack open down the middle and the bed to slide steadily toward the widening crevasse. Father cried out in horror. I wanted to scream; but Great-Grandmother pointed with the forefingers and ring fingers of both my hands at the opening, and what she shouted hurt my mouth. Took out a back tooth, too, though I didn't notice at the time. I was too busy watching Borbos's spell reverse itself, as the flying kitchenware had done. The hole in the floor closed up as quickly as it had opened, and Jashani's bed slid back to where it had been, more or less, with her never once stirring. Father limped dazedly over to her and began to straighten her coverlet.

For a second time Borbos Tresard said, "Well, my goodness." He shook his head slightly, whether in admiration or because he was trying to clear it, I can't say. He said, "I do believe you are my master. Or mistress, as you will. But it won't help, you know. She still will not wake to any spell, except to see my face, and my terms are what they always were—a welcome into the heart of this truly remarkable family. Nothing more, and nothing less." He beamed joyously at us, and if I had never understood why so many women fell so helplessly in love with him, I surely came to understand it then. "How much longer can you stay in the poor ox, anyway, before you raddle him through like the death fever you are? Another day? A week? So much as a month? My face can wait, mother—but somehow I don't believe you can. I really don't believe so."

The bedchamber was so quiet that I thought I heard not only my own heart beating but also Jashani's, strong but so slow, and a skittery, too-rapid pulse that I first thought must be Father's, before I understood that it belonged to Borbos. Great-Grandmother said musingly, "Patience is an overrated virtue."

And then I also understood why so many people fear the dead.

I felt her leaving me. I can't describe it any better than I've been able to say what it was like to have her in me. All I'm going to say about her departure is that it left me suddenly stumbling forward, as though a prop I was leaning on had been pulled away. But it wasn't my body that felt abandoned, I know that. I think it was my spirit, but I can't be sure.

Great-Grandmother stood there as I had first seen her. Lightning was flashing in her empty eye sockets, and the pitiless grin of her naked skull branded itself across my sight. With one great heron-stride of her naked shanks she was on Borbos, reaching out—reaching out . . .

I don't want to tell about this.

She took his face. She reached out with her bones, and she took his face, and he screamed. There was no blood, nothing like that, but suddenly there was a shifting smudge, almost like smoke, where his face had been . . . and there it was, somehow *pasted* on her, merged with the bone, so that it looked *real*, not like a mask, even on the skull of a skeleton. Even with the lightning behind her borrowed eyes.

Borbos went on screaming, floundering blindly in the bedchamber, stumbling into walls and falling down, meowing and snuffling hideously; but Great-Grandmother clacked and clattered to Jashani's bedside, and peered down at her for a long moment before she spoke. "Love," she said softly. "Jashani. My heart, awaken. Awaken for me." The voice was Borbos's voice.

And Jashani opened her eyes and said his name.

Father was instantly there, holding her hands, stroking her face, crying with joy. I didn't know what those easy words meant until then. Great-Grandmother turned away and walked across the room to Borbos. He must have sensed her standing before him, because he stopped making that terrible snuffling sound. She said, "Here. I only used it for a little," and she gave him back his face.

I didn't really see it happen. I was with my father and my sister, listening to her say my name.

When I felt Great-Grandmother's fleshless hand on my shoulder, I kissed Jashani's forehead and stood up. I looked over at Borbos, still crouched in a corner, his hands pressed tightly against his face, as though he were holding it on. Great-Grandmother touched Father's shoulder with her other hand and said, impassively, "Take him home. Afterward."

After you bury me again, she meant. She held onto my shoulder as we walked downstairs together, and I felt a strange tension in the cold clasp that made me more nervous than I already was. Would she simply lie down in her cellar grave waiting for me to spade the earth back over her and pat it down with the blade? I thought of those other bones I'd first seen in the grave, and I shivered, and her grip tightened just a bit.

We faced each other over the empty grave. I couldn't read her expression any more than I ever could, but the lightning was no longer playing in her eye sockets. She said, "You are a good boy. Your company pleases me."

I started to say, "If my company is the price of Jashani . . . I am ready." I *think* my voice was not trembling very much, but I don't know, because I never got the chance to finish. Both of our heads turned at a sudden scurry of footsteps, and we saw Borbos Tresard charging at us across the cellar. Head down, eyes white, flailing hands empty of weapons, nevertheless his entire outline was crackling with the fire-magic of utter, insane fury. He was howling as he came.

I automatically stepped into his way—too numb with fear to be afraid, if you can understand that—but Great-Grandmother put me aside and stood waiting, short but terrible, holding out her stick-thin arms. Like a child rushing to greet his mother coming home, Borbos Tresard leaped into those arms, and they closed around him. The impact caught Great-Grandmother off-balance; the two of them tumbled into the grave together, struggling as they fell. I heard bones go, but would not gamble they were hers.

I picked up a spade, uncertain what I meant to do with it, staring down at the tumult in the earth as though it were something happening a long way off, and long ago. Then Father was beside me with the other spade, frantically shoving *everything*—dirt and odd scraps of wood and twigs and even old wine corks from the cellar floor—into the grave, shoveling and kicking and pushing with his arms almost at the same time. By and by I recovered enough to assist him, and when the hole was filled we both jumped up and down on the pile, packing it all down as tightly as it would go. The risen surface wasn't quite level with the floor when we were done, but it would settle in time.

I had to say it. I said, "He's down there under our feet, still alive, choking on dirt, with her holding him fast forever. Keeping her company." Father did not answer, but only leaned on his spade, with dirty sweat running out of his hair and down his cheek. I think that was the first time I noticed that he was an inch or so shorter than I. "I feel sorry for him. A little."

"Not I," Father said flatly. "I'd bury him deeper, if we had more earth."

"Then you would be burying Great-Grandmother deeper, too," I said.

"Yes." Father's face was paper-white, the skin looking thin with every kind of exhaustion. "Help me move these barrels."

CROW AND CAPER, CAPER AND CROW

MARGO LANAGAN

PEN WALKED A long time back and forth, clacking the shells in her pocket. The light was harsh and yellowish, the clouds were like smoke off some disaster, and the sea had a nasty impatience about it, waves crossing one another and throwing their hands up. But now was the moment. All day its imminence had hummed in her skull; she had scratched at her head, stirring her hair up wilder than ever. The whole world had gone soft today and started shifting—it was time for Pen to do the little she could to nail it back into shape.

Four walnut-shell halves she had, all perfect, saved from Christmas. She herself was full to the brim. She had taken no strong drink in the year since the wedding. She had been eating well, was plump as a Christmas pig, in fact, for the voyage. And she had stretched and run and swum in the sea and climbed the hills; she was fitter than she'd ever been. She wouldn't have done this just for herself, but for a child, for a grandchild, she could turn herself into that machine, well oiled, well tuned, and with its battery charged to the full. She must, in fact, for there was no one else of her blood who could do this thing, who could make this journey, and bless the child as it should be blessed.

She readied her powers, admiring the powerful sea, the gathering darkness, the last yellow light leaking and sulking in the clouds. She felt ahead for the moment. It *eased* toward her, but she was too far gone into her plan to feel excited about it; she must be practical now and bring to bear all her eye and instinct and old, old skill.

She had stopped pacing without even noticing, had stood back from the water. Foamy wavelets raced up and reached for her toes. Now she took a shell and, bending down, laid it on a ripple. She uttered a Word and pulled from the shell an improbable boat—still walnut shell and no mistake, but with a mast to stand and cling to, and a seat athwart it to sit and croon upon when standing grew wearisome. There was a little flag from the top of the mast, a pennant, yellow, with a golden star; this would give her courage. The whole construction bobbed lightly as bubble-weed on the wavelets. It looked fragile and unbalanced, but it was made entirely of her own devotion and willfulness, and both those things, she knew, were strong and steady.

She stepped aboard, or the boatlet took her on—it was hard to tell and it did not matter, for the boat was part of her, after all. And she set out, first lifting and dropping and calculating a way through the waves, remembering how to balance, then moving faster and more smoothly across the less broken water, as much like flying as floating. Her boat had no sail, and the wind did not blow her; she was her own prevailing wind, and always the pennant flapped behind, pointing the way she had come. She had looped her mind around the arriving grandchild and now she was reeling herself in. The water had only the merest shading of green now, and the light was fading further. Soon there would be just these small scrolls and rolls of foam on the blackness. Then, if the clouds persisted, the foam would vanish, too, and she would only feel the tap and punch of wave tops against the shell-boat's breast in her feet and hands if she stood at the mast, in her spine if she sat against it—and the clamp and release of her magic, automatic as a sleeper's breathing, hurrying her through the night.

What did I do? she had asked Rowan. *Whatever did I do that you would go so far away?*

Nothing, Ma! He'd laughed and hugged her. *It's the job; it's the opportunity. And Sophie—*

And Sophie, she had said heavily.

No, all I meant was, Sophie says it's a great chance and we ought to go after it. She's going from her mum, too, you know, her mum and dad and her sisters and all her family. It's not all about you.

But some of it is. She dislikes me.

She's only frightened. Lots of people are; you know that.

Pen had looked up into his kind face. She was about to hurt him, but she must speak anyway. *I had hoped you would find a woman who wasn't one of the fearful.*

They must be very rare, he'd said. *Because I looked, Ma; you know I did. But I couldn't look forever.*

You are still so *young—*

Mum, I love Sophie for what she is. I can only care so much about what she's not.

She had admired him; he had seemed rather noble. But she had mocked him to herself, too: *He only doesn't mind because he's young,* she'd thought. *Give him time, and years catering to Sophie's limitations, and he will understand me, understand the mistake he is making.*

Morning climbed up behind her into the stars, and the streaky clouds grew gaudy with it. An albatross glided in angled flight low to the waves; some dolphins rose and fell past her as if they were fixed to some huge invisible merry-go-round. Tired, cold to the bone, Pen could no longer think; she had been pummeled all night by wind and water, and felt bruised from head to toe.

She came to land. The boat tipped her onto the beach, and she stamped about on the hard sand, waking herself, getting her land legs, watching the boat shrink back to walnut size and be overwhelmed by the next wavelet. Then she walked up the softer beach and followed a path through the dunes. On the far side lay a road, and a man was just opening the shop opposite. A line of houses stretched out either side of it, beach shacks, their lawns neatened for the summer.

Pen plucked a leaf from a hedge and used it to pay for a drink, for a packet of biscuits. She sat on the dew-damp iron seat outside the shop, and chewed three biscuits, and drank the drink; it was like eating mouthfuls of sand and washing them down with sweetened bilge water.

When she had eaten, she did her stretches. People came to the shop to buy their milk, their bread, their newspapers, and looked sidelong at her mad sea-blown hair, her dark, odd clothes, the strange postures she was taking up against the seat, against the shop wall. Families with small children, carrying bright towels and gaily colored floating toys, came walking along the road and turned down the path to the beach. "Good morning," said these mums and dads determinedly, and the children stared and reached for their parents' hands. Pen had no wish to frighten children, but if their parents raised them to be fearful there was not much she could do about it.

She chose a quiet moment and slipped in among the dunes. When she was all alone with the wind in the whistle-grass, she took out a walnut shell and with a Word and a sweeping gesture threw it into the careless sky. There it blossomed into a craft somewhere between a hawk and a microlight, but still keeping something of the woodenness and knobbliness of a walnut about it. She laughed with fondness for it and reached up her arms, and the thing swooped down and picked her up in its claws or its clamps or its breast, whatever it had, and carried her off over the country.

Pen looked ahead. The knowledge opened like a fat flower toward her from the middle of the continent. "She is born! She is born!" she cried, and already she was too high for people to hear her or to think her more than a distant bird. She felt a great joy, very pure—perhaps the purest she had ever felt. It was purer even than when she had carried Rowan inside her and brought him forth, for that joy had always been shadowed by fear, fear that she would fail him somehow, fear that he would hurt her by coming to harm himself. This granddaughter was at a safe remove from her; Pen could never do wrong by her. Nothing was required of Pen, not even love if she did not want to give it—but she did, of course; it flowed up and out of her like springwater, refreshing as it went.

There was still a good distance to be covered. Exulting, she flew on, over the land of her granddaughter's birthing. Oh, it was a beautiful thing, a country from above, like a masterpiece painting. You could see how it had come to be, piled and pushed up, and then blown and washed down, worn to plains and then through to gorges. It was subtly colorful and delicately patterned; everything that was so ugly when you were down among it seemed from this distance nicely worked, and human effort seemed rather dear and hopeless, even though it had cleared and scarred and excavated such great tracts of land, ruined them every which way. Dammed and channeled waters winked, traffic beetled along the many roads, cities hung in their shawls of smog. In between the clumps and blotches of smaller towns, crops lay golden and green, and dark plantations flowed over the hills. Only a few areas had been left raw, allowed to stay irregular in their forms and growths, and these gave up a thin power, which Pen drew on instead of her own store, much reduced from her night's paying out aboard the boat.

She was warm in the breast feathers of the walnut-hawk; they were like very thin roof shingles, and they rattled musically about her ears and stung her hands and arms with their flapping. If she pushed her face forward to crane after something she had just passed below, the cold went into her forehead like an ax blow, and pained right down her face to her teeth.

It was a very long day, because she traveled west. Midafternoon she began to seek out on the ground the features she had marked in her memory to tell her the way: the dogleg in the river, the three towns making a triangle, the cloverleaf where the highways crossed. When they came, she ticked them off one by one. She had not traveled a distance like this for a good while, not since she was in love as a girl—why not, when it was such a pleasure, the sensations and the sights, when it was so simple, really, if she prepared herself?

She dropped into an orchard of some kind; the fruits were hard and green, some kind of citrus. Her feet set down in sunny grass—that was nice, being in touch with the earth again. The walnut shell fell through the fruit-tree leaves behind her and patted to earth, too.

The hospital was not far away. She walked out to the highway, picking money from a tree as she went. She sat awhile at a bus stop, and then a bus came and took her to the edge of a car park, and on the other side the hospital loomed, enormous, white, and glassy, with somewhere inside it her granddaughter, and beside the girl, her mother.

The bus drove away and quiet fell, warm afternoon quiet in which things moved slowly, if at all. Half her strength, half the weight she had put on was gone now, merely from traveling here, with still the blessing to be done, and the traveling home. She walked slowly and kept a careful eye out for vehicles, for she felt a little dazed. She was also too warm in her dark clothing, now that she had thawed out from the flying; she would love a hot shower, or better, a bath with scented oils in it, and a candle and a glass of wine glowing on the rim.

In the hospital doors her sunlit reflection took fright, and tried to straighten her travel rags and tame her hair. It was no good; she was clearly a wild woman. Look at the claws in that hair, the bags under those red eyes! She hadn't calculated for this, but she pulled on a glamour of shining permed-and-set hair, neat jacket and skirt, stockings and well-kept shoes and handbag—all dark, as if she were in mourning, so that people would think twice about stopping her and asking what she was about. She was hungry; she pulled a few leaves from the plane tree nearest her, found a purse within the handbag, and slipped the leaves inside.

The glass doors slid open. She proceeded into the corridors and up the stairs toward the baby, not hurrying, not lingering where people might ask her her business. Reaching ahead for the little one, she was, and examining all around her, to see what would be necessary, how much delay, how much disguise.

The afternoon was drawing on; some patients had visitors, some lay alone and wakeful, some were asleep. Nurses conferred or chatted at their stations. An orderly with a drinks-and-snacks trolley trundled about; Pen immediately liked his manner, both hearty and gentle. The warm light through the sunlit blinds gave everything a sleepy-sickroom feel, only with more equipment—fire extinguishers, signage and warnings, phones and filing systems and computers. The floors that bore it all up shone and shone, polished right to the edges and into every corner.

Sophie shared a ward with three other women, each with a plastic cradle beside her high, narrow bed. Two of the women slept; one of these was Sophie—by the window there, on the right, behind that curtain. Of the two awake, one lay reading a gossip magazine; the other had visitors murmuring around her, taking turns with her baby. All heads turned to Pen in the doorway.

She put a finger to her lips and stepped in. Her sensible shoes made no noise on the gleaming floor. She crossed to the foot of Sophie's bed. Sophie lay on her back, her lovely lips a little parted in sleep, her hands folded on her still slightly rounded belly. Only now did Pen realize that the girl had been cut open to bring the baby out, as had two of the other mothers in this room—she looked around at them. What a pity. What they had missed out on. She had birthed Rowan in a crouch, catching him with her own hands. The whole earth had backed her up in doing that, the whole sky, the whole ungodly wonderful mess of the universe; she had laughed, surrendering to something else's power for a change.

The baby girl lay expertly wrapped, a saintly maggot, one hand at her chin to assist her in her sage thoughts. Pen leaned over and looked and laughed through her nose. To all other eyes this face would have seemed utterly still; to Pen, its tiny movements flashed out at her baby Rowan's face, her own face, her father's, her ex-husband Arsenio's in turn, as well as Sophie's, and others that must be Sophie's family's. This baby belonged to them all; she *was* them all in the future; she was Pen and the rest of them, carried forward.

Delicate pale reddish hair crowned the baby's head. Someone had tried to part it already, but it had sprung back over to the place it had been used to lying in, in the womb. Pen ventured to help it there. The hair itself was warm, and the skin with the skull beneath it was that miraculous combination of firm and soft that she remembered from her baby son.

Under cover of the visitors chatting, Pen whispered a welcome and a well-wishing. She planted a little seed so that the girl would recognize and accept her when they met again; she tweaked the fabric of things just slightly, so that circumstances would be kind to this girl and favorable. It was utter pleasure to make these murmurings; there was not the least trace of fear in what she did. She stroked the fine hair again, took hold of a tuft of it, and spoke it gently away from the child's head. From her handbag she brought a tiny ziplock bag, and she sealed the pale hairs into it. You never knew what work might be required for the girl in the future, from across the water.

The handbag closed with a *clop*. Pen's gaze leaped to Sophie's face, and she couldn't tell if the sound or the stab of her own fear fluttered the eyelids open. Sophie locked eyes with her mother-in-law, let out a little scream and started to sit up, but subsided under the pain of her wound. "You! What are you do—"

Pen put out a hand to subdue the girl, to erase this memory, to send her back to sleep.

But the hand flung back, as if she'd touched a hot stove. Sophie had resisted, thrown her off. Sophie *had known how to* throw her off—the gesture had been fast, smooth, practiced, quite invisible.

Pen took a step back. They stared at each other.

"I knew you'd come," said Sophie.

"You knew a whole lot more than you ever let on." Confused, a little stung, Pen decided to opt for being pleased. "At the wedding, even. At our little chat. That was a nice bit of concealment."

The girl began to blush. She checked her arm for a watch that wasn't there, consulted it on the side table. "Rowan will be here in half an hour. You don't want him to know you've visited." Maneuvering herself more upright in the bed, she spared a hand to wave Pen closer to the baby. "I need you to see, though," she said. "No one else will understand. Wake her up."

"Wake her? Are you mad?"

"Look in her eyes. Just for a second, but *properly*, you know." She reached over and gave the baby bundle a little shake. "Come on, Chrissy. Show Grandma." She looked sharply up at Pen. "Do you want to be Grandma, or Nan, or what? Now's the time to imprint it."

Pen balked. "She's as sensitive as *that*?" She met Sophie's level gaze. "I want to be Pen," she said breathlessly.

"Come on, Chris. Here we go. Just a glimpse is all Pen needs. Look right in," she said to Pen.

Baby Chrissy's face flitted through several expressions: Churchillesque stolidity, haughty surprise, crumpled on the point of crying. Her tiny bud-mouth tore itself open, her eyelids parted, and her slate-blue eyes swam nearly blind within. Pen bent to look in.

She did not show herself, the little one, so much as *throw* herself outward, not at Pen particularly, but furiously blasting in all directions, at all things and beings. It was not an event, a detonation, so much as a glimpse of a constant outpouring, outroaring state of being, snatched in a millisecond before the fragile eyelids closed again.

"Ah!" Pen clanged back against the foot of the far bed. The woman there woke with a cry; all the visitors turned, aghast, and saw Pen without her disguise. "What on *earth*?" came through the curtain from the next bed. A nurse appeared at the door as if Pen had magicked her up from the worst that could happen.

"What's going on here?" The nurse stared at the madwoman intruder, her rags, her wide eyes, her wild hair.

"Nothing," said Pen, putting out hands to calm them all.

But it was Sophie who stroked down the air, turned the visitors' faces away, glued the woman opposite back down into sleep, threw a fuzz of forgetment through the curtain, snuffed out the nurse's alarm into boredom and sent her on her way. There was nothing left for Pen to do but to resume her mourning glamour.

Legs shaking, she crossed back to Sophie, took the chair against the wall beside the bedside cupboard, breathed.

Sophie was making the wryest mouth at her, beyond the watch and the water glass. Pen's own face had fallen open, cleansed of any expression by surprise.

"So you see," said Sophie.

A three-note run of cold laughter loosed itself from Pen's throat.

"I will need you," said the girl, eyeing the crib. "I was worried about letting you see what I was. I thought someone so powerful would scorn me, not think I was good enough for her son. But now?" She gave a helpless laugh. "Look what we've got on our hands. None of that matters—liking, not liking, who's greater than whom. Guarding this . . . *creature,* keeping her safe from herself—oh my God, Pen, I've hardly the first idea."

"Nor me," said Pen. "I only raised an ordinary boy, after all."

"There's nothing ordinary about Rowan."

Their gazes went from the crib to each other. Sophie was lit up from the inside; Pen allowed herself to glow somewhat with pride and love. "Does he know?"

"He begins to know, about me. He hasn't a clue about Chris.

All he knows is that she's the most amazing baby that's ever lived—because she's his, not because of all that you and I see in her, not from anything in herself. Perhaps he'll never know more, if I bring her up right. She might only look like a genius of this world; he might not realize she has dominion in the other."

Dominion. The crib was misty with tiny scratches from nurses' use and cleaning, from countless previous babies being laid to sleep, being lifted out. Baby Chrissy lay motionless, her strengthless round fists beneath her sleeping chin. Pen stood and laid a hand on the tight-wrapped bundle, admiring the outer tininess, the harmless parcel containing the bomb flash, the shock, the star's worth of power she had seen in the beyond. Pen herself was pinhead-sized in that place, bright and hot and well-made but *small,* and her inflowings and her outgoings were like roots and tree branches either side of that pinhead, slow, established, spread wide, doggedly shunting the forces along themselves. This girl—oh, this girl!—she was a boiling-surfaced sun. She had put out few tendrils, and none of any great reach yet, but those few flickered their messages in, flashed them out, seethed, raced with light. Pen didn't know of anyone this powerful—now, or in history, or foretold. She didn't know what this meant for the world, whether it presaged disaster or glory. She only knew that she herself, with her nutshell work and her feeble blessings, she and Sophie here with whatever small talent Sophie had, had been laid down like paving stones in this time and place for this queen to tread as she walked forth into her fullness.

"I will give her my gift, still." So doubtfully did she say it, she was almost asking permission of the mother.

Sophie nodded. She looked immensely tired, shadows in her

young face. Pen saw, as women do, ordinary women with no special talents, that Sophie would not age as well as she herself had, that she had no residual handsomeness that would allow her to go about wild-haired and pleasing herself. She would have harder work of it when her prettier days were done.

Pen stood over the crib, put her hands to the wrapped baby, closed her eyes, and cautiously entered the other world. Sideways she went this time, for her own protection, and she felt for one of the smaller outthrowings of her granddaughter's forceful self. She found no more than a thread. It petered out on the darkness yet pulled all of Pen askew with the force inside it, the baby's hunger, huge, unfocused, endless, its sucking of everything toward its light.

I have very little, she apologized. *I know hardly anything of what you'll need. But take it all, and use it as you wish.* She held on to her core and let the rest be taken. It was less a giving than a surrendering, but it pleased her immensely to be so emptied, to contribute as she could to whatever great things this granddaughter, this grand granddaughter, would accomplish.

She stayed a moment in that place, averted from the heat and light yet basking in it, a cautious small reveling and astonishment. Then she withdrew into the ward, the accidental here, the arbitrary now, where all was flat and quiet and stayed in its place. She bent and kissed Chrissy's round cheek, then wiped away with her thumb the trace of crimson lipstick her disguise had left on the baby.

Sophie had a cowed look about her that Pen recognized: face tipped down, eyes turned up. Pen sensed how cruel she might let herself be toward this lesser witch, either directly or by many acts of benevolence, many offerings of advice, many withhold-ings and stagy ponderings of her own wisdom. She must not use Sophie to salve her own old wounds. She must try to keep her dealings with her straight and plain.

She laid her hand on the waffle-weave blanket over the girl's knee. "I'll go," she said. "You know where I am. Call me if you need me."

"Thank you for coming." Sophie strengthened, uttering the formality.

Pen patted her knee and left. Her son passed her on the stairs; he smiled at her, alight with father-love; he was bring-ing bright flowers in an ornamental box, fruit in a basket. How happy he was in this world, unconcerned with the workings moiling away behind the surface of things! The neat middle-aged woman, somebody's grandmother, smiled back at him. She had not much energy left. She would need food—ah, she was so hungry! She would need hours curled up in the sunny grass under the fruit trees before she could fly again.

Home's coast rose out of the kicking sea. Home's cove, home's beach rose out of the coast, headlands like arms, the sand bless-edly still, blessedly soft-looking. The boat bottom skidded up the shelving sand. Pen took off her shoes, stepped out into the shallows, and waded to the beach. The boat shrank and sank behind her.

She walked up the path through the rocks and hardy wild plants, emptying her pockets of loose change, of spare leaves. The baby hair in its packet? She hadn't known what she was taking. She had thought to do favors for an earthly, ordinary child, using these pieces of her; instead she had an offcutting of a great power. How might she use it? Bind it into a ring, perhaps, and wield it, have her own way awhile as the new queen grew into her talents? She herself was one of the people Sophie sought to protect Chrissy from, the people who might take advantage. Pen dropped the packet, with the coins, into the toe of a shoe.

A paper flapped on the kitchen door of her little gray house, pressing out against the screen. "Ha." This would be from the people up at the store, who used phone and computer on her behalf.

It's a girl! their daughter had written in crimson and pink pencil, and she'd attached a sticker of a pink-wrapped baby, outlined in gold, and another sticker of three balloons, red, purple, blue, on golden strings. Pinned behind this paper was the email from Rowan, the general announcement, with a list at the top of all the people they had sent it to—that was showy, and possibly unwise, when she thought of it. The baby's name was Kristina Opal. (With a *K*! But she approved of the Opal.) And there was her weight, laughable next to her actual significance. Baby and mother, Rowan had typed, were "doing well"—she remembered the baby's pure clean skin, the mother's shadowed face, pained as she tried to move a body wounded, repaired, and only just beginning to knit itself back together.

Pen took down both papers and stuck the pin back in the door for whatever note might come next, whatever news—a death, new spring stock of clothes or garden tools, another baby, the newsletter she always read about people she didn't know and hoped never to meet. In the hall, she laid the papers on the shallow table, weighted them there with the shoes. The little bag

with the tuft of hair she took from the shoe's toe. All through the
house she went, opening everything she had shut before she left
against possible wind and rain. Sea sound washed in, very gentle
now that she was not on top of it taking the water's thumps and
battings; the thin hiss of wind in the bent trees passed through
and around the house. She loved these four rooms, their clut-
ter and haphazardness, their comforts, the fact that everything
was in easy reach, fitted to her own size and habits. She laid the
witch-queen's hair on her night table and switched on the lamp
above it like a ward-candle. There would be no binding, no
wielding—she was beyond being tempted by such things. She
would only keep the talisman here by her head, to see first thing
when she woke in the morning, and last of all before she slept,
every night.

ACKNOWLEDGMENTS

THIS BOOK HAS been a pleasure to work on, but it is the product of a lot of hard work by a lot of people. First and foremost, I'd like to thank Jim Thomas and everyone at Random House, who have been wonderful to work with and who have made sure the book is terrific. I'd also like to thank my agent, the dapper and ever-reliable Howard Morhaim. Special thanks to Jilli Roberts for her invaluable help with information on witches' hats, and to Tansy Rayner Roberts for her kindness, support, and enthusiasm for this book. I'd also like to acknowledge my coeditors on this project, my wife, Marianne, and my daughter Sophie, both of whom read and discussed stories with me during the preparation of the book. Finally, as always, my deepest thanks to Marianne, Jessica, and Sophie, from whom each and every moment spent working on this book was stolen.

ABOUT THE AUTHORS

PETER S. BEAGLE was born and raised in the Bronx, where he grew up surrounded by the arts and education. His parents were teachers, three of his uncles were gallery painters, and his immigrant grandfather was a respected writer, in Hebrew, of Jewish fiction and folktales. As a child Peter used to sit by himself in the stairwell of his apartment building, making up stories. He is the author of such fantasy classics as *The Last Unicorn, A Fine and Private Place,* and "Two Hearts." His story here, "Great-Grandmother in the Cellar," is the latest in his Innkeeper's World series (after *The Innkeeper's Song,* the novel that first introduced it).

Peter has written teleplays and screenplays for the animated versions of *The Lord of the Rings* and *The Last Unicorn,* as well as the fan-favorite "Sarek" episode of *Star Trek: The Next Generation.* His nonfiction book *I See by My Outfit* is considered a classic of American travel writing, and he is also a gifted poet, lyricist, and singer-songwriter. He makes his home in Oakland, California.

HOLLY BLACK is the author of bestselling contemporary fantasy books for kids and teens. Her titles include the Spiderwick Chronicles (with Tony DiTerlizzi), the Modern Faerie Tale series, the Good Neighbors graphic novel trilogy (with Ted Naifeh), and her Curse Workers series, which began with *White Cat* and continues with *Red Glove* and *Black Heart.* Holly has been a finalist for the Mythopoeic Award, a finalist for an Eisner Award, and the recipient of the Andre Norton Award. She lives in New England with her husband, Theo, in a house with a secret door.

JIM BUTCHER was born in Missouri in 1971. An avid martial artist and horse rider, Jim began writing as a child. He wrote *Storm Front*, the first volume in the *New York Times* bestselling Harry Dresden series, as an exercise for a writing course when he was twenty-five. He spent two years trying to find a publisher for the book, and it appeared to great acclaim in 2000. It was followed by twelve more novels and a short-story collection, and was adapted for television by the Sci Fi Channel in 2007. A graphic novel based on the series was nominated for the Hugo Award in 2009. Jim is also the author of the Codex Alera series of fantasy novels.

ISOBELLE CARMODY wrote her first book, *Obernewtyn*, when she was fourteen, so she knows very well how powerful someone can be regardless of their age. She learned everything she knows about writing from telling stories to her seven brothers and sisters and still feels the pleasure of binding an audience to her tale. She is best known for her highly acclaimed eight-volume Obernewtyn Chronicles series, *Scatterlings*, and the CBC Book of the Year Award winner *The Gathering*. She has received awards for her short stories and books, including the Golden Aurealis Award for *Alyzon Whitestarr*. Isobelle also edited the anthology *The Wilful Eye* (with Nan McNab). She divides her time between her home on the Great Ocean Road in Australia and an apartment in Prague with her partner, who is a poet and jazz musician, and her daughter, who, when asked what she wants to be when she grows up, says, dazzlingly, "Everything."

CHARLES DE LINT is a full-time writer and musician who lives in Ottawa, Canada. Having published thirty-six novels and thirty-five books of short fiction, he is a pioneer and master of the contemporary fantasy genre. Other books include his young adult novel, *The Painted Boy*; a short-story collection, *The Very Best of Charles de Lint*; and *The Mystery of Grace*, an adult novel. Charles is currently at work on a new young adult series, and has released *Old Blue Truck*, a CD of his original Americana story songs.

NEIL GAIMAN was born in England and worked as a freelance journalist before coediting *Ghastly Beyond Belief* (with Kim Newman) and writing *Don't Panic: The Official* Hitchhiker's Guide to the Galaxy *Companion*. He started writing graphic novels and comics with *Violent Cases* in 1987; with the seventy-five installments of the award-winning series *The Sandman*, he established himself as one of the most important comics writers of his generation. His first novel, *Good Omens* (with Terry Pratchett), appeared in 1991, and was followed by *Neverwhere*, *Stardust*, *American Gods*, *Coraline*, and *Anansi Boys*. His most recent novel is *The Graveyard Book*. Neil's work has won the Caldecott, Newbery, Hugo, World Fantasy, Bram Stoker, Locus, Geffen, International Horror Guild, Mythopoeic, and Will Eisner Comic Industry awards. He lives near Minneapolis.

FRANCES HARDINGE was brought up in a sequence of small, sinister English villages, and spent a number of formative years living in a Gothic-looking, mouse-infested hilltop house in Kent. She studied English language and literature at Oxford, fell in love with the city's crazed archaic beauty, and never found a good enough reason to leave.

While working full-time as a technical author for a software company, she started writing her first children's novel, *Fly by Night*, and was with difficulty persuaded to submit the manuscript to a publisher. *Fly by Night* went on to win the Branford Boase Award, and was shortlisted for the *Guardian* Children's Fiction Award. Her subsequent books, *Verdigris Deep* (*Well Witched* in the United States), *Gullstruck Island* (*The Lost Conspiracy* in the United States), and *Twilight Robbery* (*Fly Trap* in the United States), are also aimed at children and young adults.

Frances is seldom seen without her hat and is addicted to volcanoes.

ELLEN KLAGES is the author of two acclaimed novels for young adults: *The Green Glass Sea,* which won the Scott O'Dell Award, the New Mexico Book Award, and the Lopez Award; and *White Sands, Red Menace,* which won the California and New Mexico Book Awards. Her short stories have been published in eight countries and have been nominated for the Nebula, Hugo, World Fantasy, and Campbell awards; some appear in her collection, *Portable Childhoods.* Her story "Basement Magic" won a Nebula Award in 2005. She lives in San Francisco, in a small house full of strange and wondrous things, including a puppet or two.

ELLEN KUSHNER grew up in Cleveland, but spent second grade in France, which marked her for life, mostly in good ways. Her first novel, *Swordspoint: A Melodrama of Manners,* introduced the world to her imaginary city (with its notorious Riverside district), to which she has returned in *The Fall of the Kings* (with Delia Sherman), *The Privilege of the Sword,* and a growing collection of short stories. Her second novel, *Thomas the Rhymer,* won the Mythopoeic Award and the World Fantasy Award. Ellen edited *Welcome to Bordertown* with Holly Black. She has taught writing at the Clarion and Odyssey workshops, and at Hollins University. Ellen used to live in Boston, where she was a host on WGBH public radio, and created the national series *Sound & Spirit.* She now lives in Manhattan, on Riverside Drive, with her partner, the author and editor Delia Sherman. She loves to travel, and hates to sort through piles of paper, which is a shame, as she has so many of them.

Ellen wishes to thank all the wonderful Finns she now calls friends, who first lured her to their shores with an invitation to FinnCon, then squired her around their amazingly beautiful country with unbounded, gracious hospitality, and whose answers to her many questions—from "What would a country tailor keep in his pack?" to "What are Finnish witches, anyway?"—made this story possible. She hopes they and their compatriots do not mind too much the considerable liberties she took with known facts about Elias Lönnrot and the Kalevala.

MARGO LANAGAN lives in Sydney. Her four collections of short stories (*White Time*, *Black Juice*, *Red Spikes*, and *Yellowcake*) have won and been shortlisted for many awards, as has her novel *Tender Morsels*. She has won four World Fantasy Awards (for short story, novella, collection, and novel) and has been on the Tiptree Honor List twice. She is not actually a witch.

TANITH LEE was born in North London and didn't learn to read—she is dyslexic—until she was almost eight (and then only because her father taught her). This opened up the world of books, and by age nine she was writing. Tanith worked in various jobs—shop assistant, waitress, librarian, clerk—and spent a year at art college. In 1974, DAW Books, under the leadership of Donald A. Wollheim, bought and published her first novel, *The Birthgrave*, and thereafter twenty-six of her novels and collections.

Since then Tanith has written ninety books and almost three hundred short stories. Four of her radio plays have been broadcast by the BBC; she also wrote two episodes for the TV series *Blake's 7*. Some of her stories regularly get read on radio.

In 1992 she married the writer-artist-photographer John Kaiine, her companion since 1987. They live on the Sussex Weald, near the sea, in a house full of books and plants, with two black-and-white overlords called cats.

PATRICIA A. McKILLIP was born in Salem, Oregon, received an MA in English literature from San Jose State University, and has been writing ever since. She has published fantasy novels for adults and young adults, among them the World Fantasy Award winner *The Forgotten Beasts of Eld*. Her other works include *Ombria in Shadow* and *Solstice Wood*, both of which won the Mythopoeic Award, and the short-story collection *Harrowing the Dragon*. She won the World Fantasy Award for Life Achievement in 2008. She and her husband, poet David Lunde, live on the Oregon coast.

GARTH NIX grew up in Canberra, Australia. When he turned nineteen, he left to drive around the United Kingdom in a beat-up Austin with a boot full of books and a Silver Reed typewriter. Despite a wheel's literally falling off the car, he survived to return to Australia and study at the University of Canberra. He has since worked as a bookshop publicist, a publisher's sales representative, an editor, a literary agent, and a public relations and marketing consultant. His first story was published in 1984 and was followed by the novels *The Ragwitch, Sabriel, Shade's Children, Lirael,* and *Abhorsen;* the six-book young adult fantasy series The Seventh Tower; the seven-book series The Keys to the Kingdom; and *Troubletwisters* (cowritten with Sean Williams). He lives in Sydney with his wife and their two children.

DIANA PETERFREUND is the author of eight novels for adults and teens, including the Secret Society Girl series, the fantasy novels *Rampant* and *Ascendant,* and the postapocalyptic *For Darkness Shows the Stars,* as well as several short stories and critical essays on popular children's fiction. Her work has been translated into twelve languages, and her short stories have been on the *Locus* Recommended Reading lists and anthologized in *The Best Science Fiction and Fantasy of the Year.* She lives in Washington, DC, with her husband, her daughter, and her dog, Rio. Like Malou in "Stray Magic," Diana loves animals and volunteers with rescue organizations that foster shelter dogs.

TIM PRATT's short fiction has appeared in *The Best American Short Stories, The Year's Best Fantasy,* and other nice places. His short stories are collected in *Little Gods* and *Hart and Boot and Other Stories.* His work has won a Hugo Award and has been nominated for World Fantasy, Sturgeon, Stoker, Mythopoeic, and Nebula awards. He blogs intermittently at timpratt.org, where you can also find links to many of his stories. Tim is also a senior editor at *Locus: The Magazine of the Science Fiction and Fantasy Field.* He lives in Berkeley, California, with his wife, writer Heather Shaw, and their son, River.

M. RICKERT grew up in Fredonia, Wisconsin. When she was eighteen, she moved to California, where she worked at Disneyland. She still has fond memories of selling balloons there. After many years (and through the sort of "odd series of events" that describe much of her life), she got a job as a kindergarten teacher in a small private school for gifted children. She worked there for almost a decade, then left to pursue her life as a writer. Her short fiction, which has been awarded World Fantasy and Crawford awards, has been collected in *Map of Dreams* and *Holiday.*

DELIA SHERMAN was born in Tokyo and brought up in New York City. She has spent a lot of time in schools of one kind or another. Her first novel, *Through a Brazen Mirror,* led to a nomination for the Campbell Award for Best New Science Fiction Writer. Her second novel, *The Porcelain Dove,* was a *New York Times* Notable Book and won the Mythopoeic Award. Her short stories for younger readers have appeared in numerous anthologies. "CATNYP," a story of a magical New York Between, inspired her first novel for children, *Changeling,* and its sequel, *The Magic Mirror of the Mermaid Queen.* Her novel *The Freedom Maze,* a time-travel fantasy set in Louisiana, was published in 2011.

Delia lives with fellow author and fantasist Ellen Kushner in a rambling apartment on the Upper West Side of New York City. She is a social rather than solitary writer and can work anywhere, which is a good thing because she loves to travel, and if she couldn't write on airplanes and in noisy cafés, she'd never get anything done.

JANE YOLEN, often called the Hans Christian Andersen of America, is the author of over three hundred books, including *Owl Moon, The Devil's Arithmetic,* and *How Do Dinosaurs Say Good Night?* Jane's books range from rhymed picture books and baby board books through middle-grade fiction, poetry collections, nonfiction, and novels and story collections for young adults and adults. She has won the Nebula Award twice, has won the World Fantasy Grand Master Award, and has been named a Grand Master of science fiction/fantasy poetry by the Science Fiction Poetry Association. Six colleges and universities have given her honorary doctorates, and her Skylark Award, given by the New England Science Fiction Association, set her good coat on fire.